victims of

of bold dece...
and unfulfilled desires . . .

One book—
offers all the passion and intrigue from two of the
best authors Signet Regency has to offer . . .

His Lordship's Mistress
JOAN WOLF

"Joan Wolf writes with an absolute emotional
mastery that goes straight to the heart."
—Mary Jo Putney

Married by Mistake
MELINDA MCRAE

"Ms. McRae dares to paint a complete portrait
of a wastrel lord who finally finds the inspiration to
rise above his indolent lifestyle to search his own heart,
and reach out for the love that is his to claim."
—*Romantic Times*

His Lordship's Mistress

Joan Wolf

Married by Mistake

Melinda McRae

A SIGNET BOOK

SIGNET
Published by New American Library, a division of
Penguin Putnam Inc., 375 Hudson Street, New York, New York 10014, U.S.A.
Penguin Books Ltd, 27 Wrights Lane, London W8 5TZ, England
Penguin Books Australia Ltd, Ringwood, Victoria, Australia
Penguin Books Canada Ltd, 10 Alcorn Avenue, Toronto, Ontario, Canada M4V 3B2
Penguin Books (N.Z.) Ltd, 182–190 Wairau Road, Auckland 10, New Zealand

Penguin Books Ltd, Registered Offices: Harmondsworth, Middlesex, England

Published by Signet, an imprint of New American Library, a division of
Penguin Putnam Inc. *His Lordship's Mistress* was first published in April 1982,
copyright © Joan Wolf, 1982. *Married by Mistake* was first published in
May 1992, copyright © Melinda McRae, 1992.

First Printing, December 2000
10 9 8 7 6 5 4 3 2 1

PUBLISHER'S NOTE
This is a work of fiction. Names, characters, places, and incidents are either the
product of the author's imagination or are used fictitiously, and any resemblance to
actual persons, living or dead, business establishments, events, or locales is entirely coincidental.

His Lordship's
Mistress

Chapter One

But keep the wolf far thence ...
—JOHN WEBSTER

Two weeks after her stepfather was buried, Jessica Andover sat in the mellow, panelled library of Winchcombe listening to her lawyer detail the state of her affairs. They were not good. In fact, they were disastrous.

"It is in the highest degree unfortunate that your father did not secure the estate directly to you, Jessica my dear," Mr. Samuel Grassington said sadly. "However, he was a young and vigorous man when he died. He could not be made to see the importance of settling his affairs, and without the proper safeguards your property was at the free disposal of your mother's second husband."

Jessica's lips tightened. "I know that all too well, Mr. Grassington."

Mr. Grassington cleared his throat. He had been an uncomfortable spectator at one of Jessica's confrontations with Sir Thomas Lissett. "Ah, yes," he said.

"How much did my stepfather squeeze the estate for, Mr. Grassington? The horses, the card games, and the women must have cost a pretty penny I should imagine."

The old lawyer looked unhappy. "I wish they were the whole of it, my dear."

Her gray eyes darkened. "What do you mean?"

"It has become regrettably clear that Sir Thomas Lissett made a great number of unwise investments."

"With my money?"

"With your money."

Jessica fixed the lawyer with somber eyes. "What is the total debt?"

"Considering that Sir Thomas has not been dead three weeks and that all the creditors have not yet applied to me . . ."

"How much?" Jessica repeated steadily.

He told her.

There was a stunned silence. "It is worse than I thought," she finally said quietly.

"It is not good, my dear. I am so very sorry."

Jessica sat for a minute with bent head; then she looked up. "What about the boys?" she asked stiffly.

"I had more success with your stepfather about making a will than I had with your father. He could not name you as guardian of your half brothers as you are not yet twenty-one, so I persuaded Sir Thomas to name me the legal guardian of all three of you."

Warm color flushed into Jessica Andover's cheeks. "Thank you, Mr. Grassington. I could not have borne it if . . ." She stopped and bit her lip, emotion for the moment overcoming the cool composure she usually presented to the world.

"Needless to say, I have no intention of interfering with how you rear Geoffrey and Adrian. You have had them in charge since the death of your mother and you seem to be succeeding admirably." The elderly man reached across the table, and in an uncharacteristic gesture of affection covered her hand. "I only wish I could have done more, my dear. But there was no way I could stop him from running through your property."

"I know." She raised her chin in a gesture only too familiar to Mr. Grassington. "My situation then is this. I have myself and my two brothers to support. Adrian is to start Eton this year and the money must be found to send him. Money must also be found to pay Geoffrey's tuition for his remaining five years at Eton. I don't think Geoffrey is at all interested in going to the university, but Adrian must certainly go to Cambridge. You tell me the farms are all heavily mortgaged and I cannot afford to redeem them. They must be sold, then. The money will help to pay off some of the debt. The loss of the farms leaves me bereft of regular income, however."

"Tuition is very expensive," murmured Mr. Grassington.

"I know." Jessica's voice was very firm. "I shall have to make money out of the horses."

"The horses? Of course you will have to sell the horses, Jessica."

"I have no intention of selling the horses," she returned. "Didn't I just say I needed a regular income?"

"I don't understand what you mean. How are you going to get a regular income out of the horses?"

"My stepfather spent a great deal of money on those horses, Mr. Grassington, and whatever his faults, he knew horseflesh. I have the makings of a

3

very impressive little stud at Winchcombe. A very profitable little stud, I might add, if it is handled properly."

"But my dear . . ." the old lawyer protested faintly.

Jessica's gray eyes were burning with intensity. "You live in Cheltenham, Mr. Grassington. You can't be unaware of the amount of money that a wealthy owner will pay for a good race horse. I plan to breed good race horses and collect some of that money. I have the initial investment sitting right in my own stableyard, eating their heads off. I'd be a fool not to take advantage of it."

"Are you serious, Jessica?"

"Deadly serious, sir. I have very few talents, but I do know horses. And I'm not afraid of work."

Mr. Grassington looked very uneasy. "Jessica, my dear, there is no need for you to turn yourself into a stableboy. There are certainly other ways of dealing with this problem."

"I should be very happy if you would tell me what they are."

Mr. Grassington cleared his throat. "You are an extremely attractive young woman," he said finally, "You come from one of the best families in the county. There are many men, men of substance, who would be pleased to marry you if only you would give them a chance."

She stared for a minute at the kind, concerned face of the old lawyer who had known her since her birth, then abruptly turned away toward the window. "No," said Jessica, directly, firmly, and finally.

"Why not?" he persisted.

The girl gazed steadily out the window, her profile aloof and withdrawn. "That was my mother's solution, if you remember," she said evenly. "The burden of running an estate was too much for her, so she married again to have someone to take the burden off her shoulders." She turned now to face the lawyer, and passion burned in her clear gray eyes. "Do you really think, having just gotten out from under the yoke of my stepfather's greed, that I am going to turn my property and my person over to some *other* man?"

"Jessica! All men are not like your stepfather."

"I know that," she replied steadily. "But I have no intention of marrying, Mr. Grassington. I am perfectly capable of taking care of myself and of my brothers."

"Selling off the farms will cover only a part of Sir Thomas's debt," he reminded her gently.

"So I see. I had hoped I wouldn't have to do this," said Jessica, "but I shall have to mortgage Winchcombe."

Mr. Grassington sat frowning at the table for almost a full minute; then he spoke slowly. "I think perhaps Sir Edmund Belton would help you. He was a friend of your father's. I should feel comfortable knowing that he was the one who held the mortgage on Winchcombe."

Jessica nodded thoughtfully. "Yes, that is a good idea. I'll go to see him tomorrow."

The lawyer began putting his papers away. He looked up at last and said, "Are you sure this is what you want to do?"

"Yes."

A rueful smile crossed the old man's face as he

looked at the determined face of the girl he had been trying to advise. "You are just like your grandfather," he said.

She gave him her rare smile. "I take that as a compliment."

He picked up her hand and kissed it with old-fashioned courtesy. "It is, my dear. It is."

Sir Edmund Belton was more than pleased to be able to help Jessica. He was a man of fifty or so, but since the death of his only son in the Peninsula he had aged twenty years. He assured her he would be happy to advance her whatever sum she needed. He did not even want to hold a mortgage in return, but Jessica insisted. After they had decided to put the whole transaction into the hands of their respective lawyers, they sat drinking tea and chatting comfortably in Sir Edmund's old-fashioned drawing room. One of the pleasures Sir Edmund found in talking to Jessica was that he never had to ask her to repeat herself. He was rather hard of hearing, a defect he hated to admit to. He often had to strain to hear a speaker, but as he became intensely annoyed if someone shouted at him, his conversational partners often found themselves in a quandary. Not Jessica. She had a superbly deep, clear voice which she could pitch effortlessly to Sir Edmund's hearing level without seeming to shout at all.

She was rising to take her leave when the door opened and a tall, dark man came into the room. "Oh, there you are, Harry," said Sir Edmund. "I want you to meet my nephew, Jessica. Captain Henry Belton.

6

This is Miss Jessica Andover of Winchcombe, Harry."

Jessica gazed steadily at the dark, rather hard face of Harry Belton. He was, she knew, heir to Melford Hall now that Sir Edmund's son John was dead. "How do you do," she said, and held out her hand.

Captain Belton took it slowly, his own eyes intent on Jessica. He saw a tall, slim girl of striking appearance. Her face was thin, with beautiful, translucent skin and long, finely drawn features. Her brows and lashes were dark, but the large eyes were pale gray and very clear, like water. Her thick hair, which was braided in a coronet on top of her head, was brown, but there was a shade of tawny autumn leaf in it, a color indescribable and one he had never seen before. "I am very pleased to meet you, Miss Andover," he said, and held her hand for a moment too long.

"Are you making a long stay, Captain?" Jessica asked, recovering her hand.

"I am afraid not," he said regretfully. "My regiment is going to Ireland, unfortunately. I shall be here only a week or so."

"Well, perhaps we shall see more of you at some future time," she said, dismissing him from her thoughts. "I must be going now, Sir Edmund. I cannot thank you sufficiently. I think you know what it means to me."

"My dear girl, I am happy to be able to help. You know how fond of you I am. Come again and see me soon."

Jessica leaned forward and kissed him lightly on the cheek. "I will," she said. She directed a brief smile at Captain Belton and was gone.

The captain stood looking after her before he turned to his uncle. "What was that all about?" he asked in tones that had been trained on the parade ground.

"There's no need to shout, Harry," Sir Edmund replied crossly. "The poor girl has found herself in the devil of a fix, that's all. That scoundrel Sir Thomas Lissett has gone and gotten himself killed and left her with two young boys and a mountain of debt. I just told her I'd hold a mortgage on Winchcombe."

There was a very intent look in Captain Belton's brown eyes. "I thought Winchcombe belonged to the Andovers. Surely Lissett couldn't touch the estate."

"He could and he did," Sir Edmund replied shortly. "Pity he didn't get killed sooner."

"How did he die?"

"Hunting accident."

"I see. And you are going to hold a mortgage on Winchcombe so Miss Andover can pay her stepfather's debts?"

"Yes."

"How very interesting," said Captain Henry Belton softly.

Chapter Two

Trust not therefore the outward show;
                    —THOMAS RICHARDSON

It was a beautiful early August day almost a year later when Sir Henry Belton, owner for two months now of Melton Hall, drove his grays up the drive of Jessica Andover's home. His dark eyes rested appreciatively on the mellow pink brick of Winchcombe, which was looking at its best against the dark green foliage of the surrounding park. It was not a great mansion; it had been built by a seventeenth-century Andover as a comfortable, easy-going gentleman's house, and it still retained that look. When Sir Henry inquired for Miss Andover at the door he was informed that she was down at the stables, so he turned his horses into a wide, shaded, avenue at the side of the house.

The first person he saw when he pulled into the stableyard was Adrian Lissett, Jessica's youngest brother. "How do you do, Sir Henry," he said, politely coming over to the phaeton. "Are you looking for my sister?"

As Adrian was holding his horses for him, Sir Henry got down from the phaeton. "Jem!" the boy called, and a stableboy came running. "Take Sir

Henry's horses, will you?" Adrian asked, and then turned to look inquiringly at the man standing next to him. The younger Lissett was a slim boy of ten with brown eyes, shining brown hair, and a tan that showed he had spent his summer vacation for the most part out of doors. He was dressed in well-worn riding breeches and his shirt sleeves were rolled up.

"Yes," Sir Henry replied in his clipped, military voice. "They told me at the house that Miss Andover was down here."

"She's working Northern Light down in the paddock." Adrian fell into step beside him as he walked past the stable block and headed toward the paddock area. Geoffrey, two years older than Adrian and more broadly built, was sitting on top of the paddock gate. Standing next to him was a towheaded stableboy. Both boys turned at the sound of Adrian's voice.

"Jess has got him going like a lamb," Geoffrey informed his brother. "He's a beauty!" he added with enthusiasm. Then, a definite afterthought, "How do you do, sir."

Sir Henry nodded, and all four of them turned to look at the horse and rider in the paddock. But Jessica had seen them and called "Geoff, that's enough for today, I think. Take him back to the stable for me."

The boy jumped with alacrity to do her bidding, and Jessica dismounted and came over to Sir Henry Belton. "He's going to be a marvel," she said easily. "Riding him is like sitting on a keg of dynamite." Like her brothers she was dressed in boots and breeches and her hair fell in a thick braid down between her shoulders.

"I hate to see you working yourself like that," Sir Henry said in his abrupt way.

A faint frown appeared between Jessica's dark brows. She didn't consider that he had any right at all to comment upon her welfare, but it had become her policy to be as pleasant to him as possible, and she returned a noncommittal answer.

"I am leaving tomorrow for Lancashire," he said, "and before I go I should like an opportunity to speak to you privately."

Her narrow nostrils quivered slightly, but she replied calmly enough. "Certainly. We'll go up to the house if you like."

"Thank you," he said crisply, and the two of them turned up the path he had driven down only a short time earlier.

Jessica was very quiet at dinner that evening. Dining at Winchcombe was a highly informal affair. Gathered around the table in the faded blue dining room were Jessica, Geoffrey, Adrian, and Miss Sarah Burnley, Jessica's onetime governess, who now spent her time running the house, as Jessica was fully occupied by the stables.

Miss Burnley had been engaged by Mr. Christopher Andover seventeen years ago to instruct his daughter and had been at Winchcombe ever since. Her credentials as governess were somewhat limited, for she did not know Italian, painted very poorly, and had extremely strange ideas about geography. She had once solemnly assured Jessica that Tripoli was in the Southern Hemisphere. What she did have, however, was a beautiful speaking voice, and Mr. Andover, who prized good speech above all else, had engaged her on the strength of that. She had been successful in training Jessica's voice to reach her own high standards. She had also imparted to her young charge her profound enthusiasm for the plays of William Shakespeare. Many long winter afternoons had been spent in the schoolroom of Winchcombe reading aloud—"with *feeling*, Jessica dear"—from the plays of the great bard.

Now she looked at Jessica's abstracted face and asked gently, "I hope Sir Henry did not bring bad news this afternoon, Jessica?"

"Not precisely," said Jessica in the cool voice that told them all she did not want to discuss it.

"Perhaps he wants to buy Northern Light," Adrian said around a mouthful of beef pie.

"Don't talk with your mouth full, Adrian," his sister said automatically. "He is not interested in Northern Light and even if he were it would do him no good. Northern Light is not for sale."

"Of course he isn't!" Geoffrey put in indignantly. "Northern Light is the best two-year-old in the country. He is sure to win all the major races next year. Why, there isn't enough money in the world to buy Northern Light!"

Jessica smiled at Geoffrey, then turned to Miss Burnley, who was saying, a pucker between her thin brows. "But Jessica, I didn't know you were going to *race* horses. I thought you were just going to sell them."

"One must demonstrate the value of one's horses, Burnie, before one can sell them," Jessica replied, helping herself to some more beef pie. The physically active life she was leading always left her ravenously hungry by dinner time. "If Northern Light does as well as we hope," she explained to the puzzled face of her governess, "he will command enormous fees when we retire him to stud. And the stud fees are what are going to pay our bills in the future."

Miss Burnley put down her fork. "'A horse, a horse, my kingdom for a horse!'" she quoted thrillingly, and Geoffrey and Adrian exchanged long-suffering looks. It was a quotation they were overfamiliar with.

"Now, Burnie, don't get started on that fellow Kean again," Geoffrey said hastily. "Ever since you and Jess saw him in Cheltenham last week you have been talking about nothing else."

"And *your* conversation, my dear Geoffrey," said Miss Burnley with gentle dignity, "is somewhat limited as well."

Adrian grinned. "Burnie's right, Geoff. All you ever talk about is horses."

"If you boys had accompanied us to the performance of *Richard III* you would have found yourselves as much in awe as Jessica and I. Such power. Such feeling."

Geoffrey opened his mouth to reply, then met his

sister's eyes. Resolutely he shut his lips and applied himself to his plate. Serenely, Miss Burnley continued. "I understand from my cousin in London that Covent Garden stood half empty all last season. Mr. Kemble is, of course, a well-known actor, but if Covent Garden is to compete with Drury Lane the management will have to find an actor to rival Mr. Kean. And that," she sighed nostalgically, "will be very difficult."

Jessica was staring at her, an arrested look in her gray eyes. "How much money do you think Mr. Kean makes, Burnie?" she asked.

"I don't know what his salary is, my dear, but I'm sure he gets bonuses. He received several hundred pounds for that one performance in Cheltenham. I know that from Mr. Francis, the manager of the Cheltenham Theatre."

"Oh," said Jessica, frowning thoughtfully.

"Are you going to see that mare of Redgate's tomorrow?" Geoffrey asked his sister after a suitable pause had assured him that the topic of Edmund Kean was concluded.

"No," she returned. "I am going into Cheltenham to see Mr. Grassington."

"May I come with you?" asked Adrian, who never missed an opportunity to visit Dr. Morrow, their physician. Adrian was fascinated by medicine.

"Of course," his sister assured him. Adrian, she knew, would be closeted with his idol for the morning and she would be free to consult privately with Mr. Grassington.

Geoffrey and Miss Burnley exchanged glances, but neither said anything further. They knew that look on Jessica's face and knew that further questions would be pointless. If something were up they would have to wait until she chose to tell them.

Mr. Grassington knew that look also. He asked her to sit down and gazed worriedly at the remote, austere face of the girl he held in such affection. "How can I help you, my dear?" he asked quietly.

She came directly to the point. "What are the terms of the mortgage on Winchcombe? Does it run for a specified period of time or can it be called in at any time?"

Mr. Grassington looked appalled. "You don't mean Sir Henry has asked you for the money?"

Her mouth, which was peculiarly expressive, looked very firm. "What are the terms of the mortgage?" she asked again.

"Mr. Canning, Sir Edmund's lawyer, drew it up," he said. "He naturally wrote it in favor of the holder."

"Do you mean he can call it in any time he chooses?"

"He must give you two months' notice," he replied, his mouth very dry. "Jessica, my dear, what has happened?"

There was no flicker of expression on her face. What she thought, what she felt, she had long since learned to keep to herself. Ever since her mother had died ten years ago she had stood on her own feet. She was aware of the sympathy on the old man's face but instinctively she shied away from it. She could not afford it. It would weaken her. So she said now in a calm, self-possessed voice, "Sir Henry wants to marry me. If I do not agree to his extremely distasteful proposal, he intimates that he will foreclose on my mortgage."

"He could not mean that, Jessica! Why, such behavior is, well, blackmail."

Jessica's lips twisted contemptuously. "He meant it. It is just the sort of thing a man of his stamp would resort to."

Mr. Grassington nervously shuffled some papers on his desk. "I did not know that Sir Henry had ever been over to Winchcombe," he said tentatively.

"He has been coming regularly this past month," she replied. "I thought he was interested in the horses. It now appears he was interested in the whole property."

"*Or* the property's owner," put in Mr. Grassington meaningfully.

Jessica looked scornful. "Oh, he made me a ridiculous speech about how he had decided to marry me a year ago when first he met me at Melford Hall. It's more likely that he decided then to acquire Winchcombe. It would set fewer people's backs up if he did it by marrying me, but I am not going to oblige him."

"Is it so difficult for you to believe that a man might want you for yourself?" the old lawyer asked gently.

Her dark brows rose. "He has gone about demonstrating that in rather an odd fashion."

"Yes. Sir Henry is a crude man, I fear. But, Jessica, I do not think his interest is Winchcombe." He paused. "Do you possibly think you might consider marrying him?"

"No."

"But to lose Winchcombe—and after you have worked so hard, my dear!" He looked in distress at her thin face—too thin, he thought. She was wearing herself out. The beautiful white and rose of her skin had turned a pale golden brown from the sun. He shook his head mournfully. "What else can you do?" he asked.

"If I marry Sir Henry I lose Winchcombe anyway," said Jessica. "A married woman has little say over her own property. No, as I told you once before, I have no intention of making the same mistake my mother did. I will manage by myself."

"But how?"

"I will pay Sir Henry the mortgage money."

"I do not see how you can get it. If I had it I would give it to you, you must know that. But I do not have it."

She smiled at him. "You are very kind, Mr. Grassington, and I thank you." She rose, and the smile died away, to be replaced by a look so intense it seemed to burn through him. "I will get that money if it kills me," she said in a taut, determined voice. "No one is going to take Winchcombe away from me."

"Oh my dear," he said helplessly.

"No one," she repeated fiercely, and her eyes looked almost silver in her suddenly pale face. She turned on her heel and left the room with swift grace.

The old lawyer stared after her with worried eyes. When Jessica was angry she was capable of anything. And from the look on her face he knew that she was very angry indeed.

Chapter Three

Give money me; take friendship whoso list!
—BARNABY GOOGE

Three days later Jessica set out for London, accompanied by Miss Burnley. She paid a visit to Clarges Street, where she arranged to borrow money at a depressingly high interest rate from Mr. King, a well-known moneylender. The money from Mr. King she would use to pay off Sir Henry Belton. Unfortunately, the only collateral she had to offer Mr. King was a mortgage on Winchcombe. Jessica then spent a week at Stevens' Hotel; during that time, unknown to Miss Burnley, she paid another visit, this one to Mr. Harris, the manager of the Covent Garden Theatre.

Jessica had six months to pay back Mr. King, and she had every intention of doing so. After many hours of deep thought she had determined a course of action for herself. It was not an easy decision for her to make, but she did not have many options. Marry for money she would not do. The thought of putting herself into the power of some man for the rest of her life filled her with horror. She might as well sell herself, she thought.

Which had brought her to her second option. She knew the amount of money her stepfather had spent on women. It appeared, she thought grimly to herself, that there was a good chance of making money by selling oneself temporarily. If anyone two years ago had told her she would consider becoming some rich man's mistress she would have stared incredulously. But in her present situation she didn't see any other way out. The world would condemn such a course of action, she knew. But then she had no intention of letting her world know what she had done. And Jessica, who had highly ethical but unusual standards, found the idea less distasteful than swearing to love, honor, and obey someone she hated and despised.

Simply stated, she had two boys who had to be put through school, and a mortgage on her only means of income. If she lost Winchcombe there would be no Eton, no Cambridge, no future for her brothers. Or for Miss Burnley. Or for her either if she steadfastly refused to marry. She was not even qualified to be a governess. The only solution was to clear Winchcombe of debt and go back to raising horses. Before she and Miss Burnley left for London Jessica had made up her mind, and when her mind was made up an earthquake would not move her.

In September Adrian and Geoffrey left for school. After they had left, Jessica received an urgent message from a distant cousin in Scotland. The cousin was very ill and wanted to see Jessica.

"I never heard of this Jean Cameron!" protested Miss Burnley.

"I have," Jessica replied ressuringly. "My mother was Scottish, you know, even if she was born and raised in France. My grandfather fought at Culloden and consequently had to flee the country. He joined the French army and married another Scottish exile. My mother was their only child. This Jean Cameron is the daughter of my grandfather's first cousin. She is quite elderly now and apparently rather wealthy. She says something about making 'restitution' to my grandfather's only grandchild for all he suffered for the 'cause.' " Jessica looked up from the letter she was holding. She knew it by heart, since she had written it herself. "It sounds as though she is thinking of leaving me some money, Burnie. God knows we could use it. I'd better go."

Miss Burnley had finally agreed and Jessica had packed her bags. She told Miss Burnley that Cousin Jean had arranged for a boat to take her from Dover to Perth, and she persuaded her old governess that she did not need any escort. "A friend of Cousin Jean's will be waiting for me when I arrive in London," she said glibly. "I shall be well taken care of, Burnie. You are needed here." After overcoming Miss Burnley's objections Jessica wrote a letter to her brothers giving them the same information she had imparted to the governess. She also wrote to Mr. Grassington. On September 16 she set out for London.

The place she went first after settling into the inexpensive lodging she had found during her week's sojourn in London with Miss Burnley was Covent Garden Theatre. Men looked for mistresses who were actresses or opera dancers, so Jessica's limited worldly wisdom told her. She couldn't be an opera dancer to save her soul, but she had, thanks to Miss Burnley, a well-trained speaking voice. She thought she could act. Apparently Mr. Harris had thought so too, for he had engaged to hire her a month ago.

Covent Garden was in trouble and none knew it better than Thomas Harris. The famous classical actor John Kemble and his equally talented sister Mrs. Siddons had been the mainstays of the theatre for years. But Mrs. Siddons was retired now and Kemble had given up most of his roles to Charles Mayne Young. Young was a tall, good-looking man with a melodious voice he used to good effect, but he could not vie with Edmund Kean. All of last season Kean had packed Drury Lane with his magnetic, naturalistic acting. Clearly the classical style of acting so nobly embodied in Kemble and Young was on the wane. Thomas Harris realized quite well that Kemble now was not an adequate draw and that it would be madness to allow Covent Garden to remain exclusively the home of classical acting. He needed someone who could compete with Kean. And then a young girl who called herself Jessica O'Neill arrived. She told him she was an actress who had previously only worked in small playhouses in the west of Ireland, and he gave her an audition.

He had been immediately taken by her marvelous voice. There was also a distinction about her that he thought would go over well with a London audience. He liked the way she held her head, so erect and beautifully balanced. He was struck by the cool, shining look of her large eyes. She looked as if she had the habit, founded on experience, of not being afraid of anything. She had read the trial scene from *The Merchant of Venice* for him and her rendering of Portia had power and authority, yet was at the same time unmistakably feminine.

Harris had no intention of mounting a production of *The Merchant of Venice*. Kean's Shylock was justly famous, and however good a Portia he presented, Harris knew he could not avoid unfavorable comparisons to Drury Lane. What he wanted was to present an actor—or actress—who embodied the same style of acting as Kean, romantic and naturalistic, in a new role, and preferably one unsuited to the talents of the Drury Lane star. The day Jessica presented herself at Covent Garden to begin work Harris had her read Juliet. The next day he put her on the stage and had her do the balcony scene with Charles Mayne Young. The result was even better than he had dreamed; he had his new star.

Jessica was somewhat bewildered at finding herself taken so seriously by the Covent Garden management. She had hoped merely for a small part, one that would give her the kind of exposure she needed to accomplish her purpose. She was not sure she wanted to be a star on the scale Mr. Harris was envisioning, but as the weeks went by and rehearsals intensified she found herself caught up in the production and, most of all, in the role.

She had enormous sympathy for Juliet. Romantic love was something Jessica was unfamiliar with, but the intensity of Juliet's feeling was something she could understand. Wasn't she herself prepared to venture into a strange and alien world for the sake of two young brothers whom she loved? And Juliet's terrible isolation as the play moved toward its conclusion was frighteningly familiar to Jessica. When she stood before the friar, deserted by father, mother, and nurse, Juliet's words seemed to come from within her own deepest self:

O' bid me leap, rather than marry Paris,
From off the battlements of yonder tower,
Or walk in thievish ways, or bid me lurk
Where serpents are; chain me with roaring bears,
Or shut me nightly in a charnel house,
O'ercovered quite with dead men's rattling bones,
With reeky shanks and yellow chapless skulls;
Or bid me go into a new-made grave
And hide me with a dead man in his shroud—
Things that, to hear them told, have made me tremble—
And I will do it without fear or doubt . . .

They were Jessica's exact feelings about marriage with Sir Henry Belton.

The Covent Garden management was delighted with Jessica and raised her salary to twenty pounds a week. All during the weeks of rehearsals rumors of her beauty and genius were skillfully spread throughout London. *Romeo and Juliet* was to open on October 6, and by early that afternoon the various entrances to Covent Garden Theatre were surrounded by crowds eager to obtain admission. When the doors opened at half-past five an immense throng poured into the house and rushed into the pit and galleries. Before long the boxes and circles were filled with the most famous men and women of the age, all eager to see Jessica O'Neill, the "new Siddons."

Jessica stood in the Green Room frozen into immobility. When she was called to the stage she stood in the wings certain she would not be able to utter a word. She heard Mrs. Brereton, who was playing the nurse say, "Where's this girl? What, Juliet!" and, taking a deep breath, she walked on stage.

Chapter Four

He was . . . to each well-thinking mind
A spotless friend, a matchless man,
whose virtue ever shined.
—FULKE GREVILLE

London could talk of nothing but Jessica O'Neill. When the curtain had fallen on her first performance the audience had burst into a wild tumult of applause. The management had announced a new play for the following evening, but hundreds of voices had shouted back, demanding another performance of *Romeo and Juliet*. The manager had yielded, and *Romeo and Juliet* ran the next night as well.

The critics were universally enthusiastic. The *Morning Chronicle* wrote, "It was not altogether the matchless beauty of form and face, but the spirit of perfect innocence and purity that seemed to glisten in her speaking eyes, and breathe from her chiselled lips." The *Morning Post* raved, "A sense of innate delicacy, of rare sensibility glowing through the fervour of her words, and the presence of passion and growing strength, rendered her performance a delight to behold." And William Hazlitt, writing for the *Champion*, thought "she perfectly conceived what would be generally felt by the female mind in the extraordinary

and overpowering situations in which she was placed."
Crowds were turned away from the theatre each night
she played. Jessica, to her own astonishment, was famous.

Philip Romney, Earl of Linton, came to London
near the middle of October to find the town still in an
uproar over Jessica O'Neill. The Romneys belonged
to that select group of families who had virtually ruled
England during much of the seventeenth and
eighteenth centuries. Together with the great Whig
houses of Cavendish, Russell, Grenville, and Spenser,
they owned vast numbers of acres and were born to
an almost automatic right to a voice in the government and a seat in the cabinet. And of all the great
landowning Whig aristocrats none looked more the
part than did the present Earl of Linton. He was at
this time twenty-seven years of age and possessed a
personal presence that instantly suggested a prince in
very truth, a ruler, warrior, and patron. Ironically, he
was not involved with government, the Whigs having
been out of power for many years, but he was interested in certain areas of social reform and made it a
point to be in the House whenever one of his causes
came up for a vote. He spent the greater part of the
year in Kent on his principal estate of Staplehurst.

He had come up to town because his elder sister
and her children had arrived at Staplehurst for a prolonged visit with his mother and he had long ago decided that a little of Maria's company was more than
sufficient. She was ten years his senior and tended to
dwell at great length on the fact that as the only son

of the family it was his duty to get married. He knew very well that it was his duty and he had every intention of fulfilling it—some day. In the meanwhile he did not relish Maria's strictures and he did not want to upset his mother by quarrelling with his determined sister, so he decided that it would be a good idea for him to pay a visit to London.

His many friends were delighted to see him, and it wasn't long before Lord George Litcham invited him to share Lord George's sister's box at Covent Garden. "You really must see Miss O'Neill, Philip," he said. "She has quite stolen Kean's thunder, you know."

"Well, if she is half as good as Kean she is worth seeing," Linton replied good-naturedly. "I saw him as Shylock last year and I still haven't forgotten the impression he produced. Like a chapter of Genesis, I thought."

"She is every bit as good. And infinitely more beautiful."

"Oh?" Linton raised an inquiring eyebrow.

Lord George smiled briefly. "After her performances the Green Room is so filled with her admirers that one is fortunate to get two words with her."

Linton looked amused. "Then certainly I must see her, George. Thank Lady Wetherby for me and say I shall be happy to make one of her party tomorrow evening."

Lady Wetherby's box was very near the stage, and Linton had an excellent view of Jessica's performance. He had rather thought he had outgrown *Romeo and*

Juliet and was surprised and then deeply moved by the swift and tragic beauty of the story as it unfolded before him. Jessica's beautiful voice, clearly audible in the farthest reaches of the gallery, gave such an intensity of feeling to the poetry that lines that had hitherto seemed outrageous now appeared glorious expressions of the truth and ardor of young love. And she was indeed striking, with that magnificent skin, that mouth with the curve that could be so tender yet so resolute, the arch of those dark eyebrows with the wonderful gray eyes beneath them.

"I'd like to meet Miss O'Neill," he said to Lord George after the performance was over.

"Oh Lord, Philip, I hope *you* aren't going to enter the sweepstake for her favors," said Lord George.

"Is there a sweepstake?"

"Assuredly. The betting at the clubs is in favor of Ashford at the moment. He is the richest one of the lot."

"A high flyer, I see."

"Oh, definitely."

They had entered the Green Room by now, and it was indeed thronged with the great and the famous. Jessica was standing with her back to the full-length mirror talking to Lord Debenham. "Can you introduce me, George?" Linton asked softly.

"Come along," replied his friend, and prepared to shoulder his way through the crowd. But it was not necessary. People naturally stepped aside for Philip Romney; it was his fine unconscious way, his friend thought ruefully, of outshining, overlooking, and overtopping the swarming multitudes. He was smiling now, throwing a brief word or two to those he knew, but not halting in his determined progress toward the tall girl at the far end of the room.

Jessica looked up and saw him coming. The light from the Green Room lamps gilded his hair, the color of ripe corn and as thick and gleaming as ten-year-old Adrian's. He was tall and broad-shouldered and the eyes that met hers across the space of twelve feet were blue as the sea. His face was still lightly tanned from the sun, and the thought flashed through Jessica's mind that he looked just like a Viking. But the deep voice was surprisingly soft as he murmured an acknowledgement of Lord George's introduction and reached out to take her offered hand in his own large, strong grasp.

"I admired your performance enormously, Miss O'Neill," he was saying.

"Thank you, my lord," she replied, looking straight at him with that beautiful fearless gaze of hers. Gray eyes met blue with a sudden shock of what could have been recognition. Jessica's face was very still.

"I wonder if you would care to drive out with me tomorrow, Miss O'Neill?" said Linton in his grave, soft voice.

There was a brief pause while Jessica continued to look at him. Then she said, "Yes, I should like that very much."

"Damn!" said Mr. Melton to Sir Lawrence Lewis. "If Linton is interested in Miss O'Neill the rest of us may as well retire from the field."

"Unfortunately, you are right, Melton," replied Sir

Lawrence. "What he wants Linton usually gets. And he don't mind paying a high price."

"He's had no one under his protection since the Riviera. And that was at least six months ago."

"Damn!" Sir Lawrence said to Mr. Melton, as he watched Linton smile at Jessica. "I'm very much afraid he *is* interested. I wonder how long he plans to remain in London this time?"

Lord George asked his friend the same thing. "For how long do you mean to remain away from your pigs and your cows, Philip?" he queried Linton humorously as they made their way toward Brooks' later that evening. As Staplehurst was one of the most famous and beautiful estates in the country the references to livestock were seemingly facetious. But Lord George was not as fanciful as it might appear; Philip Romney was in fact one of the most advanced farmers and enlightened landlords in England. He administered all his own estates, and the grinding rural poverty that was affecting so much of England due to the postwar economy and the Corn Laws was not in evidence anywhere on Romney land.

Linton belonged to that diminishing number of wealthy, powerful, landed gentry who were genuinely attached to the land they owned and the people who worked it for them. He was known to every farmer and laborer on his vast estates, and had been since his childhood. The land, to the Earl of Linton, was more than the rents it brought in; it was also the people who cultivated it. Staplehurst, that great golden stone house surrounded by ponds, waterfalls, and Capability Brown's famous park, was also the center of some of

31

the most efficient and profitable agriculture in England.

Linton laughed at Lord George's question. "My sister Maria and her children are planning to remain at Staplehurst through Christmas. Her husband, most unfortunately, is going to Vienna for the Peace Conference and, as Maria is expecting another child in February, she has decided to remain in England." He sighed. "With five children of her own and one more on the way you would think she'd have enough to occupy her mind."

"After you to get married?" said Lord George sympathetically.

Linton's blue eyes looked rueful. "Incessantly. My mother tries to divert her attention, but Maria. . . . Well, suffice it to say that I am in London for a few months at least."

"Until Christmas?" said Lord George with a poker face.

Linton grinned. "Until Christmas," he agreed.

"It is not a very lively time of year for London."

"No." There was a humorous look around Linton's firm mouth. "I shall have to find something to divert myself, won't I?"

Lord George looked at the profile of the man walking beside him. "You already have, Philip."

"Yes, I rather think I may have," replied Linton with enviable tranquility.

Chapter Five

Have you seen but a bright lily grow
Before rude hands have touched it?
—BEN JONSON

Jessica walked slowly around the house in Montpelier Square, looking at everything but in actuality seeing very little. Somehow it didn't seem quite real—the small but elegant house, the matched pair of bays in the stable together with the handsome carriage. Most of all, the money that now reposed in her bank account.

She had gone driving with Philip Rodney and had had supper with him twice. She had found herself liking him very much, much more than any of the other men who had been throwing out lures to her. There was a look of smiling tenderness in his eyes and about his mouth when he looked at her that got immediately under her guard and caused her to relax in his company. The thought crossed her mind that more than one woman had probably been undone by that lazy, sweet smile and those glinting blue eyes.

He had broached the topic that had brought her here with infinite delicacy. He had taken her back to her lodgings after a late after-theatre supper and had sat for a minute beside her in the carriage, his eyes on

33

the narrow, shabby front door of her temporary home. "I have a house in Montpelier Square that is standing empty at the moment," he had said thoughtfully. "It would make me very happy if you would move into it and let me take care of you."

Even in the dim light of the carriage she had been able to see the blue of his eyes. "I cannot afford to run a large establishment," she had answered in a voice that was not quite her own.

"It is not a large establishment," he had returned gently, "and of course I should make you a monthly allowance to enable you to cover all expenses." He then had named a sum that had caused her to blink, and, after a breathless moment she had accepted his offer.

He had sent the carriage to her lodgings this morning and it had brought her and all her belongings to this charming little house. He had bought it, Jessica realized somewhat blankly, solely for the use of his mistresses. There were flowers and a note waiting for her. He would escort her home from the theatre that evening, he wrote. She was to tell the cook to have a supper prepared for them.

For perhaps the first time Jessica realized the enormity of what she had done. She sat down in a delicate chair in her bedroom and stared at the large, silk-hung bed. He was coming this evening. "My God," Jessica said out loud. "I don't have the faintest idea what I'm supposed to *do*." She looked around the room again. "What am I supposed to wear?" she asked the green silk walls. "Or am I supposed to wear anything?" She cast her mind over her collection of nightgowns and, involuntarily, grinned. But it was not a laughing matter and she soon sobered. Jessica was an intensely private person, but she was intelligent enough to realize that at this particular moment she needed advice. With sudden decision she put on her pelisse and went downstairs to order the carriage. She was going to pay a visit to Mrs. Brereton.

Eliza Brereton, one of Covent Garden's staple character actresses, was well equipped to advise Jessica. In her youth she had enjoyed the favors of some of the town's most notable men and she now resided in a comfortable, well-furnished house that was the fruit of her labors. She acted because the theatre was in her blood, not because she needed the money.

Jessica had been frank with her, and Mrs. Brereton had been impressed. "Linton is quite a catch, my dear," she had told Jessica admiringly, and, when the terms of the agreement had been disclosed, her eyes had widened. "He is being extremely generous." She had looked thoughtfully at Jessica. "You are not at all the usual thing, though, my dear. You have Quality."

"I am not the usual thing, Mrs. Brereton," Jessica had replied honestly. "That is why I am here." She met the other woman's gaze directly. "I haven't got the vaguest idea of how I should behave and I hoped you would not be offended if I asked you to advise me."

The old actress looked from the proud, intense face of the girl sitting across from her to the subdued, conservative cut of her merino walking dress. "I see," she said quietly. "Well, you have come to the right person,

Jessica. First, let us have some tea. Then we have some shopping to do."

When Jessica returned to Montpelier Square later that afternoon she had a collection of boxes in the carriage. Much as she had hated spending the money, she realized the necessity. Her own wardrobe was certainly not adequate for her present role. She also had an herbal concoction that Mrs. Brereton had pressed on her. "Take some every morning," the old actress had warned her. "It is not an infallible prevention of pregnancy, but it has a decided efficacy." Jessica had accepted it gratefully. Pregnancy was the one aspect of this whole venture that truly terrified her.

Jessica was performing that evening in a new role, one she had played only twice before, Rosalind in *As You Like It*. Thomas Harris was still adhering to his original plan of offering productions that would be unsuitable to the talents of Edmund Kean, and so far his program had been successful. Jessica's Rosalind had won wide acclaim and Kean, faced with this kind of competition, was preparing yet another part. He would open in *Macbeth* the following night.

Linton had not seen *As You Like It*, yet, and for this performance he had taken a box, which he was sharing with two friends, Lord George Litcham and Mr. Henry Farnsworth. He spoke to them amiably enough at the intermissions, but his attention was clearly centered on the stage, and more particularly on the play's star. Jessica's Rosalind was a joy. She brought to the role all her own qualities of independence, decision, and intelligence. He watched her attentively, enjoying the bell-like tones of her voice and the glint of happiness in her eyes as, dressed in boy's clothes, she teased the unsuspecting Orlando: "There is a man haunts the forest that abuses our young plants with carving 'Rosalind' on their barks; hangs odes upon hawthorns, and elegies on brambles; all, forsooth, deifying the name of Rosalind. If I could meet that fancy-monger, I would give him some good counsel, for he seems to have the quotidian of love upon him."

Orlando, unaware that the disguised boy was in truth his love, protested, and Rosalind shook her head, put her foot up on a fallen log, and replied mockingly. Linton leaned a little more forward in his chair as he watched her. The boy's clothes only served to emphasize the beauty of her flexible young body, the long slim legs, the extraordinary fineness of her narrow waist. The play was delightful, but he found himself impatient for it to end.

Jessica did not share his impatience, but end the play finally did, and shortly she found herself beside Linton in the carriage that was taking them inexorably toward Montpelier Square. He made no attempt to touch her after handing her in and chatted easily during the drive about her performance and the theatre in general. When Jessica confessed to curiosity about Kean's Macbeth he instantly volunteered to take her to see it. They arrived at Montpelier Square more swiftly than she had thought possible and sat down to the champagne supper the servants had ready. Jessica did not usually drink champagne but decided that tonight she might need it, so she allowed him to fill her glass twice. When they had finished he smiled at her, his eyes like sapphires in the candlelight. "I am going to smoke a cigar," he said serenely. "Why don't you wait for me upstairs?"

"All right," she replied as coolly as she could, and rose from the table. A maid was waiting to unhook her dress and brush out her hair. She put on the creamy lace negligée Mrs. Brereton had chosen for her that afternoon, dismissed the maid, and stood waiting. She was nervous, because the whole situation was so strange, but she was not afraid. She knew what the mechanics of sex were; she had not bred horses for nothing. And her instincts told her that this tall, straight, strong, golden-haired man got his pleasure in a perfectly normal fashion. She was not looking forward to the coming encounter, but, she told herself sternly, it was certainly preferable to marriage to Harry Belton.

The door opened and Linton came in. He stood for a moment looking at her, then said quietly, "You are very beautiful, Jessica."

Quite suddenly she smiled. "So are you, my lord," she answered truthfully.

A flicker of surprise showed in his eyes and then he smiled back. He came across to her and lightly touched her hair, unbound and loose on her shoulders. "It is the color of the autumn leaves at Staplehurst," he said, and bent to kiss her.

For a moment Jessica was quite still; then she raised her arms to put them around his neck. His hands were strong behind her back and she closed her eyes. They opened again almost immediately as he lifted his head, moved his hands to her shoulders, and held her away from him. She looked up and found his blue gaze full upon her, narrowed now and puzzled. "This is the first time for you, isn't it?" he asked with dawning astonishment.

Jessica hesitated. "Would it make a difference?" she asked cautiously.

"Certainly it would."

"But why?"

He made a small gesture. "I am not accustomed to seducing virgins."

Jessica stared at him, her mind racing. This was a contingency she had not thought of. She opened her mouth to answer him, and he said pleasantly, "I'll find out soon enough if you lie to me, and I won't be pleased."

Jessica looked at him harder a moment. Her expressive mouth compressed a little. "Yes," she said then. "It is the first time."

"My dear girl," he said in exasperated bewilderment. "I had no idea."

"Well, there must be a first time for everyone, my lord," she said reasonably. "I can't see that it makes all that much difference." An idea struck her. "Oh, do you mean I won't be—adequate?"

"No. That was not what I meant."

"Oh." Her gray eyes were steady on his face. "Then what is the difficulty? Are you saying it would be all right if I were experienced but that you don't want to be the one to 'corrupt' me?"

He was frowning now, his golden brows drawn together. "Something like that."

"It sounds an odd sort of morality to me," she said a trifle tartly.

"I suppose it is." He stared at her intently. "What are you doing this for? Do you really understand the consequences of all this?" and he gestured, comprehensively, to the room and to the bed.

She drew herself up to her full height. "Yes," she said uncompromisingly. "I do."

He smiled a little. "I doubt it. How old are you?"

"Twenty-one." She walked away from him to the fire, and he watched her in silence, observing the grace of her arms and neck and head, the straight beauty of her legs, visible through the thin folds of her negligée. She turned to face him and the firelight lit her hair to copper. "I did not make this decision lightly, I assure you of that, my lord. I need quite a large sum of money and this is the only way I can get it." She paused, then said slowly, "If it isn't you it will be someone else." He did not answer. She made a small movement of her hand and said tentatively, "I would rather it was you. I am a quick learner. I will try to please you."

He thought suddenly that it was wretched of him to make her beg him. He *was* making her, and this for him wouldn't do at all. She was very beautiful as she stood there, facing him in all her desire to persuade, to please. She meant it, he thought. If it wasn't him, it *would* be someone else. He saw her brace herself slightly to meet his refusal. He smiled at her, his blue eyes suddenly full of the familiar lazy sunshine she had found so attractive. "You've convinced me," he said in his soft, slow voice, and held out a hand to her.

Color flushed into her cheeks and her mouth relaxed slightly. She crossed the floor and stood before him once again. "You'll have to show me what to do," she said a trifle unsteadily.

"There's no hurry," he replied, and gathered her lightly into his arms and kissed her again. It was a kiss that was thorough, leisurely, and surprisingly effective. When he finally raised his head she stood for a moment in the circle of his arms, blinking up at him. "Good heavens," she said faintly.

"Good heavens, indeed," he returned in a voice that was huskier than usual. Without further comment he picked her up and carried her over to the bed.

When he departed a few hours later he left a stunned Jessica behind him. She had had no idea her body could react the way it had. After he had dressed and was ready to go he had bent and kissed her lightly on the temple. "It will be better next time," he had promised. The thing that frightened her most was that she believed him.

Chapter Six

Come live with me and be my love,
And we will all the pleasures prove.
—CHRISTOPHER MARLOWE

If Jessica was unsettled by what had occurred that surprising night Linton was scarcely less so. He had known as soon as he had seen Jessica that he wanted her. Her cool assurance had misled him; he had never dreamed but that she was experienced in the ways of love. He should have remembered that she was an actress, he thought. But she could not disguise her inexperience when he had kissed her. Philip Romney knew women and he recognized the innocence of that tentative kiss. He recognized too that it had only made her more desirable to him. It shouldn't have. He had spoken the truth when he said that virgins did not interest him. But Jessica did, and more than ever after what had happened between them last evening. It had been intense and tender, sweet and lingering. He had been very gentle, aware of her innocence and careful not to offend it. It had been, he thought with a wry smile as he sat over a solitary breakfast the next morning, rather like a wedding night.

He went to considerable trouble to make arrangements to take her to *Macbeth* for Kean's opening performance. The boxes had been sold out for over a week but he managed to procure one from Mr. Martin Wellingford at Brooks' in the afternoon. Mr. Wellingford, a rather nondescript young man who was anxious to make his way in society, was very pleased to do a favor for the Earl of Linton. Linton made a mental note to include the young man in some upcoming scheme of his own, thanked him warmly, and sent off a note to Montpelier Square, telling Jessica he would call for her that evening in order to take her to Drury Lane.

The theatre was packed when Jessica and Linton arrived. There was an electric feeling about the crowd, as if it knew it was present at a momentous occasion. Jessica's appearance in the box with Linton helped to raise the excitement to fever pitch. There was scarcely a person present who had not seen her Juliet and all were well aware that the resounding hit she had made in that part was one of the stimuli for Kean's tackling Macbeth at this particular moment.

"How does it feel to be on the other side of the curtain?" Linton asked, his mouth close to her ear.

She smiled faintly. "A lot less nerve-wracking. But I have seen Kean before. In fact it was he who gave me the idea of acting."

"Really?" He sounded interested. "Where did you see him? He only made his mark in London last spring."

Too late Jessica realized her mistake. She continued

to look at the stage and shrugged a little. "Oh, I scarcely remember; it was a while ago."

He didn't pursue the subject, but his eyes rested speculatively upon her averted head, so beautifully and proudly set on its long neck. She had acted in Ireland, or so the Covent Garden management had given out. Linton didn't think Kean had played in Ireland before the previous summer. Jessica was aware of his scrutiny and felt herself beginning to tense up. She was grateful when the lights began to dim.

The crowd sat in breathless silence through the opening scenes, but when Edmund Kean made his entrance the pit rose and cheered and the women in the boxes waved their handkerchiefs. It was some moments before his harsh voice could be heard above the thunder of appreciation.

At the intermission Linton turned to Jessica. "He dominates the play," he said to her.

There was a faintly ironic look in her eyes. "He certainly does. Lady Macbeth is cast quite into the shade."

He grinned. "I believe you'd like to do Lady Macbeth yourself!"

The corners of her mouth curled. "I?" she said demurely. Before he could answer the door to their box opened and Lord George Litcham and Mr. John Mowbray entered.

"Philip, you dog, do you know what an uproar you have caused by bringing Miss O'Neill? The whole house is agog at the spectacle of two great actors confronting each other across the curtain, as it were."

Lord George turned to Jessica. "How do you do, Miss O'Neill, and how do you like Kean this evening?"

Jessica hesitated, her eyes going to Linton. He met her gaze and realized she was looking to him for guidance. He cut in and said easily, "Miss O'Neill was telling me how much she admired Mr. Kean's performance before you burst in so enthusiastically, George. And that, I should say, was the general consensus of opinion in the house. He is very powerful."

"Yes, he is," said Jessica composedly. "Are you enjoying the play, Mr. Mowbray?"

"Very much, Miss O'Neill," responded that gentleman courteously, but before he could continue the conversation the door opened to admit two more gentlemen. Both Jessica and Linton were quietly friendly, but all the visitors were aware of a distance that surprised them a trifle.

Linton's purpose was to protect Jessica from the overfamiliarity that her now public relationship with him would invite. She herself did not know how to behave. She would see what he would do—so their briefly locking eyes had told him—and she would act accordingly. And he had been swift to set a tone of impeccable courtesy and respect. After a slightly stilted beginning Jessica's own breeding asserted itself. She had been born and reared a lady; she simply behaved in the way that was natural to her. After his friends had departed Linton looked at her with approval. She was dressed in a new gown of wine-dark Italian crape that set off her brilliant coloring. Its neckline was more deeply cut than any she had worn before, but many great ladies in the audience wore gowns even more revealing. She had her mother's diamonds in her ears, but her throat was bare. He smiled at her faintly, his lids half hiding his very blue eyes. It was a smile whose intimacy rather took her breath away. She didn't know whether to be glad or sorry when the curtain rose for the next act.

They went to the Piazza for supper after the play. When they were seated in one of the charming booths and were each sipping a glass of wine Jessica said curiously, "Tell me what you do at Staplehurst, my lord. I gather from Lord George that you spend most of the year in the country."

"What do I do to amuse myself?" he asked smilingly.

She looked a little startled. That was not what she had meant. Jessica, who had worked very hard at Winchcombe all her life, was not a person who thought very much about amusement. "I suppose so," she replied a little uncertainly.

His eyes narrowed a little as he watched her face, then he said truthfully, "I farm."

She looked interested. "Do you? Do you have an experimental farm like Lord Cochrane?"

He put down his glass of wine and regarded her thoughtfully. He had not expected her to know the name of Lord Cochrane. "No, although I find Lord Cochrane's work extremely interesting. My work is more administrative, I'm afraid."

"Do you own a great deal of land?"

"I do. And I am happy to say that the people who work for me now are the people who have farmed Staplehurst land for hundreds of years. Not one family has been forced off my land."

She was surprised by the note of suppressed passion in his voice. "What do you mean?"

He sighed. "I mean that a great change is coming in this country, Jessica. It has already begun, in fact. Today most Englishmen still work on the land or in trades connected to agriculture. That will not be true twenty years from now. Country populations are already moving into the cities to work in industrial factories. The whole face of agriculture is changing. It has become more efficient, more scientific, more centralized. That can be very beneficial, but it also has its drawbacks."

"Drawbacks? How can greater efficiency be a drawback?"

"Because the small independent farmer is no longer efficient. He can't compete. In many cases his farm has been bought by a larger, wealthier landowner. Many of the old smallholders have become landless agricultural laborers. The commons have been enclosed and so cottagers have nowhere to graze a cow or find fuel. We are in a state of transition from an agricultural to an industrial economy and at Staplehurst I am fighting what could be called a holding action."

She was listening to him intently. "At least you are employing a large number of people."

"I am," he replied a trifle grimly, "but unless something is done politically to stabilize the economy the efforts of a few well-intentioned landowners like myself will go for naught."

"Most of the big landlords seem to be pressing for another Corn Law," she said neutrally.

His eyes began to get very blue. "What we do *not* need is to hinder the import of cheap foreign corn. There will be famine if we do it. With 250,000 demobilized soldiers and sailors thrown on the labor market there will be disaster. Wages will be down for those who can get jobs. For those who cannot the Poor Relief will be the only answer. And neither those with jobs at below-subsistence wages or those on Poor Relief will be able to afford corn if it is stabilized at 80 shillings a quarter."

"I have never been much in favor of the Poor Relief," Jessica remarked. "Not, at least, when it is used to supplement wages. It may assist the worker temporarily, but in the long run it benefits the employer, who is relieved of the necessity of paying a living wage. And the small parish taxpayer is forced to subsidize, via the poor rate, the payroll of the big farmer and manufacturer."

"Good for you, Jess," he said strongly. "When I think of the number of people I have tried to impress that fact upon I could weep."

The faint bitterness was back in his voice, and Jessica's eyes fixed themselves thoughtfully upon his face. Under Linton's serene, gentle exterior there evidently lurked the soul of a reformer. "You surprise me," she said frankly.

"Not half as much as you surprise me," he returned. "You are really interested in all this aren't you?"

"Yes." She looked very serious. "I can imagine how

it would feel to be thrown upon the world with nothing behind you, no land, no job, no government to help you out." At the bleak look that touched her face he felt a sudden stab of fierce protectiveness.

"You can always come to me," he said.

"Thank you, my lord," she replied with an effort at lightness. "I shall remember that."

Chapter Seven

So every sweet with sour is tempered still,
That maketh it be coveted the more;
For easy things, that may be got at will,
Most sorts of men do set but little store.
            —EDMUND SPENCER

Jessica and Linton had not been unobserved at the Piazza. Lord George Litcham and Mr. John Mowbray were seated at no very great distance, and they had been joined by Bertram Romney, one of Linton's cousins. "I wonder what Philip is being so serious about," Lord George commented as he watched his friend with speculative eyes.

"It don't look like a jolly little coze, does it?" replied Mr. Mowbray. As they watched, Jessica said something and Linton replied, the set of his mouth very determined.

"I know that look of Philip's," Mr. Romney said. "I believe he must be talking about the economy."

"To *Miss O'Neill*?" Mr. Mowbray sounded incredulous.

"She doesn't look bored," returned Lord George. All three men looked surreptitiously at Jessica's absorbed face.

"No, she doesn't," agreed Mr. Mowbray.

Jessica and Linton rose to leave, and on their way out passed by Lord George's table. Linton nodded at them in a friendly if abstracted way as he followed behind Jessica. He didn't pause to chat, but took Jessica's elbow in a firm grasp and steered her past the remaining booths and out the door.

"He was in rather a hurry to leave," said Mr. Romney.

"You would be too if you were going home with Jessica O'Neill," said Lord George. And, upon an instant's reflection, Mr. Romney agreed.

Jessica was performing the following two evenings, and the evening after that Linton took her to a very exclusive gaming club in St. James's Square. "My cousin Bertram is very enthusiastic about it," Linton told Jessica. "To own the truth I'd like to see the lay of the land. Bertram is only twenty-four and not very shrewd. The place may be perfectly honest; in fact Crosly and Abermarch assure me the play is fair, but I'll feel better if I take a look myself. Do you care to accompany me?"

Jessica's large gray eyes looked luminous. "To a gaming hell. I should love to go."

He smiled a little. "I shouldn't exactly call it a hell. And why do you want to go?"

"I'd love to see the place where all that money changes hands; where fortunes are lost and men blow their brains out."

He laughed at her. "No one blows their brains out

51

in the club, Jess. Very bad ton to do that. One waits until one is decently home."

"Too bad," she said cryptically.

"Too bad?"

"Yes. I should love to see some stupid ass who had bankrupted himself and his family blow his brains out right in front of me." The memory of Sir Thomas was still raw in her memory and he winced a little at the note of contempt in her voice.

"Not everyone who gambles bankrupts himself."

"I suppose not. Do *you* gamble, my lord?"

"I have been known to upon occasion," he answered with sonorous gravity.

The corners of her mouth quirked with amusement. "I bet you win, too, you wretch."

"Upon occasion," he repeated serenely, and Jessica laughed.

Mr. Romney had been startled when his cousin had informed him he was bringing Jessica. "But why, Philip?" he had said. "We're going with Litcham and Harry Crosley. She'll be the only woman."

"I have no intention of staying until the small hours, Bertram, and we will meet you there," Linton replied imperturbably. "I am taking Miss O'Neill because she hopes to see someone blow his brains out."

"I beg your pardon?" said Mr. Romney, unsure if he had heard correctly.

"No need to do that," Linton assured him kindly. "We'll see you this evening, Bertram." He began to move away.

"But aren't you dining with us?" Mr. Romney called after him.

"No," came the definite reply.

Bertram was right to be puzzled, Linton thought as he walked down the front steps of Brooks'. Whenever he had joined a party like this in the past they had always commenced with a comfortable dinner and gone on to their destination, a good-humored, high-spirited, all-male group. He was breaking with tradition by taking Jessica. Why?

It was quite simple, really, he thought as he took the reins of his phaeton. He preferred her company to a party of his friends. There was nothing so odd in that, he told himself. After all, she was a very beautiful woman. The fact that no beautiful woman had ever come between him and his bachelor pursuits before was a thought he did not pursue.

Jessica wore the last of her newly purchased gowns, a creamy silk that made her skin seem to glow with a shell-like luster. Linton looked at her bare neck for a moment in silence then said, "Have you no jewelry, Jess?"

The beautiful color in her cheeks deepened. "Very little," she answered shortly. It had all been sold to help pay her stepfather's debts.

"I shall have to remedy that," he said smilingly.

"No!" He looked at her, his blue eyes wide with surprise. "You are very kind," she said with an effort, "but I assure you I do not wish for any jewelry."

"I see," he said equably. He did not see, of course, but there were many things he did not understand about Jessica. After the first few times, however, he had ceased to question her about the things that puzzled him. When she was questioned she became taut and wary and aloof. Philip Romney was one of those large, strong, powerful men who are extraordinarily gentle in all their dealings with those who are smaller and weaker. Jessica was a very independent person who obviously was used to standing alone and asking no quarter of anyone, but he sensed the vulnerability that lurked behind that efficient exterior. He did not want to distress her, so he held his peace and filed away in his formidable memory all of the odd scraps of information she unknowingly let drop.

The gaming house was large and elegant and busy. They were welcomed by Mrs. Farrington, the owner and hostess, who gushed with enthusiasm to see the very rich Lord Linton enter her portals. Lord George, Mr. Romney, and Sir Harry Crosley had already arrived and were playing cards in the blue salon, so Mrs. Farrington informed them. Jessica and Linton then proceeded up the stairs to join them.

It didn't take Jessica long to decide that gambling was an exceedingly tedious pastime. Everyone sat staring, mummylike, at their cards, and even the sight of so much money on the table soon lost its novelty. "Mrs. Farrington said there was a roulette wheel here," she murmured into Linton's ear at last. "I am going to watch that for a while."

"Would you like to wager something for me?" he

asked. She had refused to take any money from him before they came.

She shook her head. "No. I'll just observe." He watched her until she had left the room, then turned back to the table, a slight frown between his brows.

Jessica found the roulette more interesting. At least she could see what was going on. She also met and chatted to several men she knew from the Green Room gatherings at Covent Garden. She had moved away from the roulette game and was standing at the far side of the room looking at a landscape that reminded her a trifle of Winchcombe when she heard a smooth voice say, "I hate to intrude on beauty admiring beauty, but I am really most anxious to meet you, Miss O'Neill." Startled, Jessica looked around to find herself standing next to a tall man of some thirty-five years. He was dramatically good-looking, with coal black hair and strange hazel eyes. "I'm Alden, you know, and I have been longing to tell you how very much I admire you."

Maximilian Chatham, Lord Alden, was a well-known figure in Regency society. He was very rich, very bored, very aristocratic, and very ruthless. He had a bad reputation when it came to women. Jessica had not met him because he had only just returned to London after a stay of several months in France. She looked at him now and did not like him. He reminded her of a horse her stepfather had once owned: very good-looking, but vicious. "Thank you," she said firmly, and turned to move away. He put a hand on her arm.

"Don't run away so quickly," he said softly. "Linton is safely occupied in the card room. Stay and talk to me a little."

She stared silently at his hand and he removed it. "I do not speak to gentlemen to whom I have not been introduced," she said coldly.

A distinctly unpleasant smile curled his thin lips. "But I just introduced myself," he said silkily.

There was a quiet murmur by the door and Jessica turned to see Linton entering the room. He looked around, saw her, and strode purposefully across the polished floor. Jessica's eyes were fixed on him. His hair gleamed like a golden helmet under the bright chandelier, and she met his eyes with a little shock of concussion. "Philip," she said. No one, he thought, had ever made his name sound quite like that. His blue eyes smiled at her.

"There you are, Jess. I've come to take you down to supper." She placed her hand on his arm, and finally he turned to the other man standing next to her. "I didn't know you were back in town, Alden."

"I arrived only a few days ago, Linton, and have been trying to repair some of the ravages of my absence by making Miss O'Neill's acquaintance. She has rather an odd scruple, however, about the propriety of my doing so. Would you be so kind as to present me yourself?"

Linton's blue eyes regarded him inscrutably for a moment. "But if I did that she might feel free to speak to you," he finally said pleasantly. "Good evening, Alden." And turning, with Jessica on his arm, he walked away.

"I don't like him," she said frankly as they went down the stairs. "Who is he?"

"A Bad Man," he replied gravely. "Stay away from him."

"With pleasure," she replied decidedly.

Mr. Romney joined them for supper. Linton sat back and watched with a mixture of amusement and respect as Jessica handled his young cousin. She got Bertram to admit, somewhat to his own surprise, that there were better things to be doing with his life and fortune than gambling. She asked him if he liked horses and listened with grave attention that clearly flattered him as he discussed his favorite pastime at great length. Mr. Romney, whose father had left him a tidy inheritance, had ambitions to race his own horses. Linton thought he could almost see Jessica's attention click as Bertram said that. "I should imagine there are few thrills more exciting than seeing one's own horse cross the finish line first," she said.

Mr. Romney agreed enthusiastically. In fact, he confided, there was going to be a private sale at Sevenoaks on Thursday and he rather thought he might pick up some bargains.

"Hunter selling out?" asked Linton.

"Yes. The whole stable is going," replied his cousin.

"Hunter?" Jessica looked startled. "He's one of the biggest breeders in the country. What happened?"

Two pairs of eyes widened in surprise. "I wouldn't expect you to know Hunter, Miss O'Neill," Romney said naïvely.

"I'm part Irish," Jessica replied glibly. "Of course I know horses. What happened to Hunter?"

Linton folded his hands piously. "The evils of gaming are boundless as the sea. Alas, poor Hunter is the latest victim."

"You're joking me," she said incredulously. "He bankrupted himself gambling?"

"He did."

Jessica's eyes sparkled. "Well, let that be a warning to you, Mr. Romney. I hope in a few years I won't be going to buy *your* horses at a bargain."

"By Jove, I hope not too!" replied Bertram.

"Ah—are you going to the sale of Hunter's horses?" Linton inquired of Jessica.

"Shouldn't think you'd like it," Mr. Romney said frankly. "You do an awful lot of standing about, you know."

"I don't mind standing and I love looking at horses. But you needn't worry about me. I have the bays. I am perfectly capable of going by myself."

"If you want to go I will take you," Linton said firmly. "I had quite forgotten about the Sevenoaks sale. I'd like to go myself."

As they were leaving the club he said to her, "I must thank you for your well-judged words to Bertram. He doesn't really care for gambling that much; he just thinks it is the thing to do. You handled him very well."

She smiled. "He is a nice boy and I've had a lot of practice dealing with boys. In some ways he doesn't seem very much older than my brothers."

"Oh?" He kept his voice carefully neutral. "How old are your brothers?"

"Ten and twelve," Jessica said, her voice suddenly clipped.

Tactfully, he changed the subject.

Chapter Eight

Desire, desire! I have too dearly bought,
With price of mangled mind, thy worthless ware.
—SIR PHILIP SIDNEY

Jessica was furious with herself for telling Linton
about her brothers. The problem was that this was not
the first such slip she had made. There was something
about this man that disarmed her, lulled her into a
state of comfortable security where she revealed things
she had had no intention of revealing. It just seemed so
natural to be with him, to share thoughts and ideas
with him, that she inevitably slipped and said things
that were at variance with her new identity.

She had to guard against him, and in more ways
than one. It frightened her, the depths of passion he
could provoke in her. She was afraid of what he made
her feel. She found herself thinking about him when
he wasn't present and when he was with her he absorbed her. She felt herself turning toward him as a
flower turns and opens to the warmth of the sun. And
she resisted.

She had been relieved to see him coming toward
her in the roulette room. She had known he would
stand between her and the unpleasant, persistent Lord
Alden. And that was another danger. She mustn't get

into the habit of looking to him for protection. All her life she had stood alone. She mustn't lose her toughness now. Linton was handsome, and charming and considerate, but their relationship was only temporary. By March she would have enough money to pay off Mr. King. Winchcombe would be clear and she could go home to her old life. She would be glad, she told herself sternly, when March finally arrived.

She revealed more about herself at the Sevenoaks sale. When Linton called for her he was pleasantly surprised to find her dressed in boots and a warm gray pelisse that was distinctly unfashionable but admirably suited to a horse sale. She asked him about his own stables, something they had never discussed before, and he admitted that he occasionally raced his horses. "I wouldn't mind picking up a likely mare," he said. "We must keep our eyes out for one."

There was quite a large crowd of people present, walking about the stables and examining the horses. It occurred to Jessica as she walked among them that it was going to prove difficult to resume her own identity and take her place in the horse world as a breeder when her face had become one of the most famous in London. Everyone there seemed to know who she was. Resolutely she beat down the thought, telling herself that people were quick to forget.

They met Mr. Romney, who was there with Sir Francis Rustington, a young man as enthusiastic and rich as he was, and the four of them went round the stables together. By the time they finished, Jessica's status had risen from inconvenient female to resident expert. She didn't say much, but what she did say was informative and to the point. After he watched her feel the legs and look into the mouth of a chestnut colt with professional competence, Mr. Romney burst out, "Where did you learn about horses, Miss O'Neill? You don't miss anything."

She looked at him kindly. "Why don't you call me Jessica? I told you I was part Irish. I grew up with horses. Don't buy this one, Mr. Romney."

"Bertram," he put in.

"Bertram," she nodded gravely. "He looks all right, but his breeding is questionable. There's speed there all right, but neither his sire nor his dam had any staying power at all. Much better to go with the dark bay."

"The Tabard colt?" said Linton.

"Yes. If you can get him for a hundred guineas you've got a bargain."

They moved toward the stableyard where the auction was going to take place and Linton asked "Did you see a mare for me?"

She flashed him a look. He had been very quiet on the stable rounds. The two younger men had not noticed, being full of comment themselves, but Jessica had. "The same one you saw, I should imagine," she returned composedly.

The faintest and briefest glimpse of a smile showed in his eyes. "The Dolphin filly?"

"The Dolphin filly."

The filly they were speaking of was a big, deep-chested chestnut. Neither of them had mentioned her when they had observed her in the stall, and she had not attracted the attention of either Bertram Romney or his friend. Jessica said now, "Her dam was Classic Princess."

Linton nodded, his face never changing. "Well, let us see how many others have their eyes on her." The first horse was brought out and the auction was begun.

Jessica had never seen so many beautiful thoroughbreds for sale. There were mostly yearlings and two- and three-year-olds; the stallions and the best of the brood mares had already been sold privately. Bertram got the bay colt Jessica had recommended and another gray that they all agreed looked likely. Sir Francis was restrained from purchasing a flashy looking black yearling when Jessica said quietly, "Look at his legs." They all watched intently as the groom ran before the horse, trotting it around the ring.

"I don't see anything," Sir Francis frowned.

"Watch him as he comes toward you," Jessica said, her eyes still on the colt. "He throws his feet out sideways."

"So he does," said Linton slowly.

"Well, what about it?" asked Sir Francis.

"He'll never be fast," Linton explained kindly. "I shouldn't bid if I were you, Rustington." So Sir Francis had stood quietly and watched another man get the colt for thirty guineas.

"Thirty guineas!" he complained. "I missed a bargain."

"Not with that foot action you didn't," Jessica said positively. "There are two Moorrunner colts coming up that will prove to be much better buys in the long run. I should bid on one of them if I were you." Sir Francis took her advice.

The sale proved to be extremely satisfactory to all parties. The two young men were delighted with their acquisitions, Linton had gotten the filly he wanted at a surprisingly good price, and Jessica had gotten some experience in what was going to be her future trade. As they were all cold and hungry by the end of the afternoon they repaired to the Sevenoaks Inn for supper. By this time Bertram and Sir Francis regarded Jessica as quite one of their oldest friends, and the party that gathered around the fireside table was merry and comfortable.

"I didn't even know you were interested in that filly," Bertram said to Linton reproachfully. "You never said a word and then you jumped in at the end of the bidding with a fifty-guinea raise in price. You surprised everybody."

"I didn't surprise Jess," Linton said, his eyes going to her face. She looked very beautiful to him as she sat in front of the fire in her russet wool dress. The leaping flames brought out the copper in her hair, braided so neatly into a coronet on top of her head. She turned to answer Bertram, and Linton thought that she had the most beautiful movements of any woman he had ever seen.

"Your cousin Philip is an old hand at buying horses, Bertram. He observes scrupulously the first rule of the game: never let anyone know how interested you are, otherwise the price will go up."

"Oh." Bertram looked thoughtful.

"I say, Miss O'Neill," said Sir Francis admiringly, "you are a regular mine of information. If you ever decide to give up the stage you could always take up selling horses." He spoke jokingly and Bertram laughed readily. At this moment the waiter came over with the bottle of wine they had ordered, so neither of them noticed the stricken look that had come over Jessica's face at Sir Francis' words.

Linton noticed, however and, under cover of Bertram's tasting the wine, he asked her quietly, "What has happened to distress you?"

She took refuge behind an expression of mute aloofness. "Nothing," she replied briefly.

His eyes, so deeply and changeably blue, remained fixed on her face for what seemed to her a very long time. Then he said, "Very well," and turned to speak to Bertram.

He tried to get her to talk about her past during the drive home. It was clear to the meannest intelligence that Jessica's knowledge of horses was far more extensive than any ordinary person's, male or female, would be. But all she would repeat was that she had spent some time around horses in her childhood.

He didn't believe her. For one thing he suspected she had never set foot in Ireland. When he had tried to pin down about where "in the west" she had performed she had replied glibly, "Oh, Wexford." He had not said anything, so she did not realize that Miss Burnley's lamentable lapses in geography had caused her to give herself away. Wexford was most certainly not in the west of Ireland, as Linton, who had visited there, had first-hand reason to know.

And the knowledge she had displayed this afternoon could only belong to someone who had worked or owned or bred horses—race horses—seriously. He pressured her a little, gently, but she had closed up against him. He had looked at her as she sat on the seat beside him, bent slightly forward, braced and on edge, and he had wanted to put his arms around her and beg her to trust him. But he had known such an action would only frighten her more—frighten her, perhaps, into running. And that, he realized, was something that frightened *him*. He did not want to lose her. There was something about her that attracted him as no other woman ever had.

When they reached Montpelier Square he set himself to reassure her. On the surface she seemed perfectly composed but the signs of strain were there to his discerning eye: her air of withdrawal and the austerity of the set of her lips revealed clearly the tension she was feeling. He had some brandy brought up to the bedroom, and taking off his coat and loosening his cravat he stretched himself comfortably on the chaise longue. "You must be cold after that drive, Jess," he said in his deep, warm voice. "Let me give you a splash of brandy."

She was standing by the fireplace, her right hand resting on the marble and her left keeping her skirt from the fire while she held out a foot to the warmth. "Only my feet are cold," she replied.

"Then take your boots off," he told her. As she hesitated he put down his glass, went across to the fire, and picked her off her feet as easily as if she were a child. He sat her down, knelt down himself, and pulled the boots in question off her feet. He then handed her a small glass of brandy. "Drink it," he said sternly, fixing on her his very blue, steady, and now somewhat imperious gaze.

Reluctantly she took it; then, as he continued to stare at her, she sipped it cautiously. It brought tears to her eyes but she could feel its warmth coursing through her. She sipped again, more assuredly, and looked up to find his eyes still on her. Her mouth compressed a little and then, irresistibly, she laughed. "How odious in you to always be right," she said.

"Do you think I'm always right?" he asked serenely.

"Well, I am still waiting to catch you out."

He smiled, leaned back on the chaise longue, and held out an arm. "Come and get warm," he invited. She put her glass down and went to sit in the circle of his arm. Humorously and reminiscently he began to tell her about an incident from his boyhood where he had been, regrettably, very wrong indeed. Jessica lay still against him, listening and absorbing warmth from his big body, and slowly he could feel the tension draining out of her. Her head was pillowed comfortably against his shoulder. He felt the relaxed weight of her and she seemed to him very small and fragile and tender as she rested against him. There rose in him, as there had before, an overwhelming desire to protect. Why this self-contained girl who had, he suspected, more courage and toughness than many men he knew, should call forth this feeling from him he did not understand. But there was a quality of gallantry about her that moved him very much. She was in trouble, that much was clear to him. He wished he could help her, aside from the monthly allowance he was making her. But he knew, without asking, that she would not allow him to. He bent his head and gently kissed the top of her head. "You're tired," he said softly. "I'll go."

She stirred a little and rubbed her cheek against his shoulder. "I'm not tired. Don't go unless you want to."

"All right," he replied after a minute, his lips once again against her hair. "In that case I'll stay."

Chapter Nine

No more, my dear, no more these counsels try;
—SIR PHILIP SIDNEY

On December 21 Linton left London to go to Staplehurst for Christmas. It was a tradition for as many Romneys as could physically manage it to gather under the Staplehurst roof at this particular time of year, and the head of the family must naturally be on hand to greet them. Linton, who enjoyed his large and noisy family, usually looked forward to Christmas. This year, he realized with a flicker of dismay, he did not want to leave London. The cause of this strange reluctance was Jessica. She had upset the pattern of his life, and he was beginning to be a trifle alarmed at himself. It would probably be better to get away from her for a time, he decided. A few weeks at Staplehurst would help him put her in perspective.

The initial feeling of homecoming he had as he drove up the winding avenue of Staplehurst seemed to confirm his wisdom. He came out of the woods and there before him, its golden stone brilliant in the December sun, was the house, serene and sumptuous, surrounded by avenues and sheets of water stretching into the far distance. He crossed a graceful bridge and drove down one of the avenues, across another bridge, and into the stableyard. He was detained for twenty minutes by his head groom, who was patently delighted to see him; then he walked back up the avenue to the house, feeling the familiar peacefulness of Staplehurst seeping into him.

Things did not remain peaceful for long. He was greeted in the hall by his butler and three noisy nephews. "Uncle Philip! We thought you were never coming," said Matthew, the eldest, a boy of thirteen. "School let out days ago. Remember you said you would take me shooting the next time I came to visit you?"

"Me too!" clamored Lawrence, the next nephew in size.

"I want to ride a *big* horse," chimed in John, age six.

"One at a time, if you please!" he laughed at them. "And at least let me get my coat off and say hello to your grandmother." He allowed his butler to help him remove his caped driving coat. "Lady Linton is in the morning parlor, my lord," said his retainer with a rare smile. "May I say how please we all are to see you?"

"Thank you, Timms. Run along for a moment, boys. I'll see you later."

They groaned but obediently began to move away. "It's been *boring* without you, Uncle Philip," John said reproachfully as he went up the stairs. "Why did you stay away so long?"

Linton merely smiled at his small nephew and began to walk in the direction of the west wing. His grandfather had built a magnificent sequence of formal reception rooms around two sides of the old house, but when the family was in residence by itself they used the smaller, more intimate rooms of the old west wing. Lady Linton was sitting alone working on a piece of embroidery when her son came into the room. She recognized his step and looked up instantly, her face lighting with the bright look it always wore whenever she saw him. Her heart swelled with pride as she watched him cross the room toward her, his thick hair gleaming in the winter sunlight. "Hello, mother," he said in his familiar, beloved voice, and she held out a hand to him.

"Philip!" Her dark blue eyes smiled up at him as he bent over her. "It is so good to see you. I missed you. We all did."

"Did you, love?" He sat down next to her on the sofa, an identical smile in his lighter eyes. "I'm sorry, but there was really no bearing Maria another moment."

She sighed. "Dear Maria. She has such a—definite—personality."

He grinned. "She is a boss, you mean. I am very fond of Maria and there is no one I would rather depend upon if I needed help, but she has bullied me ever since I was born. Having five children of her own hasn't altered one iota her determination to mother *me*. I don't know why; I've got a more than adequate mother of my own." He picked up Lady Linton's hand and kissed it lightly.

She smiled at him lovingly. "No one has ever successfully bullied you, my son."

"Not now, perhaps," he retorted, "but when I was a

child I suffered unmercifully from her sisterly interest in my affairs."

Lady Linton moved a little restlessly on the sofa, then stood up to go rearrange some flowers on a side table. She was a woman of sixty or so, with beautifully coiffed white hair and a remarkably flexible figure for her age. "I had better warn you," she said finally. "Maria's friend Lady Eastdean and her daughter Caroline have joined us for the Christmas holidays."

"What!"

"Now, Philip," said Lady Linton pacifically. "Lady Caroline is a beautiful girl. All Maria wants is for you to meet her."

"I do not need Maria to find a wife for me," he said quietly and deliberately, but Lady Linton did not like the set of his jaw. She knew the obstinacy that lay hidden under her son's usually gentle speech and manner.

"You do not have to marry the girl, Philip," she said now, a trifle astringently. "But she is a nice child. There is no need to ignore her just because her mother is one of Maria's friends."

"I hope I have more courtesy than to ignore a guest under my roof," he replied a trifle stiffly. Then, with a glitter in his eyes his mother recognized, he continued, "The fact that it *is* my roof doesn't seem to worry Maria. I don't mind *her* visiting—that is, I do mind but I will put up with it. But it is the outside of enough for her to be inviting half of her acquaintance to join her!"

"Two people are scarcely half her acquaintance," his mother pointed out gently. "And she didn't invite them. I did."

At that he frowned. "You did? But why, mother? Christmas is always a family party."

"I like Lady Caroline," his mother replied. "And it *is* time you were getting married, Philip."

As he went upstairs to his bedroom to change for dinner Linton's brow was furrowed. It did not smooth out when he encountered his sister in the hallway. "Oh, there you are, Philip," she said in her clear, imperious voice. "Come into my room. I want to speak to you before dinner."

Without replying he followed her in, and when she turned to look at him his frown was more pronounced. There was little in Lady Maria Selsey's appearance to produce such an unpleasant look. She was an extremely beautiful woman whose statuesque blonde loveliness had not been impaired by the birth of five children or by her present pregnancy. "Has Mama told you about Lady Caroline?" she demanded immediately.

"Yes," he replied. His clipped voice ought to have given her warning but she plunged on.

"She is the loveliest, sweetest thing Philip. I do not think there is a girl to equal her around today, and as a patroness of Almack's I think I may say I get to see them all. She will be going to London this spring but I wanted you to meet her first."

"Maria," he said in a quiet, dangerous voice, "if you ever do this to me again I swear to you I will humiliate you, mother, and myself by leaving immediately. I will be polite to Lady Caroline this time

73

because mother has asked me to be, but never again. Do you understand me?"

"I understand you," she replied sweetly. "Don't be angry, Philip. I'm only doing this for your own good."

"Maria," he said grimly, "you have told me that ever since I can remember. *Don't help me any more.* What do I have to do to make you understand? I simply cannot keep fleeing from my home."

"Is that why you went to London?" she asked curiously. "Because I mentioned your obligation to get married once or twice?"

"Once or twice?" he almost shouted. "You have nagged me mercilessly for the last three years! There isn't a girl who has crossed the threshold of Almack's that you haven't ruthlessly thrust upon me at one time or another. If you keep it up I won't ever marry, just to spite you."

"You're spoiled rotten, that's the problem," snapped his loving sister. "You've always been the apple of mother's eye. And becoming Earl of Linton at age seventeen was bad for your character."

"Being born ten years before me was bad for *your* character," he answered between his teeth. "It turned you into a bully."

She stared at his set face for a moment and then her lips began to quiver. "What a terrible thing to say to me," she said in a shaking voice. "I am *not* a bully."

Linton could never bear the sight of a woman or a child in tears. "Stop it, Maria," he said irritably and then, as she began to cry in earnest, he went across the room and put his arm around her. "I am sorry," he said resignedly, patting her shoulder. "You are not a bully and I will be nice to Lady Caroline."

"Th-thank you, Philip," she said, wiping her beautiful green eyes. "And I promise not to nag you. I—I miss Matt, you see, and that makes me crabby."

He looked at his sister's bulky figure and real contrition smote him. "I'm a brute," he said. "Invite as many girls as you want if it will amuse you."

"It won't amuse me if you're not around to see them," she sniffed.

He sighed. "Ria, I have every intention of getting married. I know my duty. But give me the freedom to pick my own wife. Please."

Quite suddenly she capitulated. "All right. I promise never to mention the word marriage again—provided you are nice to Lady Caroline."

"I have said I would be," he replied patiently.

"Fair enough." She grinned at him mischievously. "I won't have time for you in a year or so anyway. Annabelle will be making her come out and I shall have to be on the watch for a husband for her."

"Heaven help London's bachelors when you descend on them in earnest," he said comically, and escaped from the room as she picked up a pillow and made as if to throw it at him.

Chapter Ten

Brown is my love, but graceful;
And each renowned whiteness
Matched with thy lovely brown
looseth its brightness.

—ANONYMOUS

Linton met Lady Caroline when he came down for dinner. The company was to assemble in the blue drawing room and Linton was the first one down. He was standing in front of a painting by Angelica Kauffmann when a young girl came in alone. She stopped when she saw him and he smiled reassuringly. "You must be Lady Caroline. I'm Linton, you know. Do come over to the fire where it is warmer."

The girl came toward him, a shy smile on her face. "How do you do, my lord. Mama wasn't ready yet so I came down by myself."

"Quite right," he replied. "I detest waiting around myself. My sister tells me you and Lady Eastdean arrived yesterday. I trust you have been made comfortable?"

She flushed a little and replied eagerly, anxious to reassure him that they were very well taken care of. Caroline was indeed a beauty. She reminded him of a winter rose, so fair and delicate with her golden curls and pink and white face. The eyes she raised to his were the same color as his mother's, dark blue, almost violet. At this moment his sister came into the room, followed by his niece Annabelle. "Uncle Philip!" the girl cried delightedly, and ran across to kiss him.

"Are you indeed grown-up enough to join us, Belle?" he said, smiling down at her.

She raised her chin. "I am sixteen—almost."

He looked struck. "So you are. And getting prettier every day, if I may say so."

She sparkled back at him, a younger more radiant version of her mother. "Of course you may say so," she assured him, and they laughed at each other, the family resemblance between them momentarily remarkable.

They had dinner in the family dining room. When the rest of the party—several aunts and uncles and assorted cousins—arrived tomorrow they would be using the great formal dining room in the north wing, but for tonight Lady Linton had put them in the more intimate room she knew her son preferred. Lady Caroline sat on Linton's right and conversed with him with a sweet seriousness that was peculiarly pleasing. By the time dinner was over Linton had decided that his mother was right—she was a very nice child.

He was true to his word and went out of his way to be kind to Lady Caroline. The assembled Romneys might have overpowered an army, he told her humorously, and if she felt herself overwhelmed she had just to say so.

"Oh, no, my lord," she had replied with her sweet smile. "I can't ever remember having such a good time. Your family is such fun. And Lady Maria has always been so kind to me."

He looked at her, his eyes full of blue lit-up laughter. "Maria enjoys helping people," he said, the gravity of his voice in vivid contrast to his eyes.

"I think she does," replied Lady Caroline. "She might rather overwhelm one at first, but I can never forget what a good friend she was to mama and me when my father died."

He looked a little rueful. "That is the problem with my sister," he said frankly. "Just when you are ready to murder her for her overbearing ways she turns around and does something so damn *good* that you're left with nothing to say."

She twinkled up at him. "I like her. And I like Annabelle and the boys."

"Yes. Well I have to admit I like them too. Do you and Annabelle care to ride with me to the Harley farm tomorrow?"

"I should love to," answered Lady Caroline delightedly.

Maria was true to her word as well and made no attempt to hector her brother, although she watched him shrewdly. She had been very pleased with herself for thinking of Caroline Shere for Linton. The girl was totally unspoiled, beautiful with a touch of gentle seriousness about her that Maria thought would appeal to her brother very much. At first she watched with satisfaction as he went out of his way to be a gracious host to the young girl, but as the week went by a cloud began to darken her magnificent green eyes whenever they lighted on her brother's disgracefully good-looking face.

"I don't understand Philip," she complained to her mother. "He can't hope to find another girl as sweet and as beautiful as Caroline, yet he is letting her slip through his fingers."

"I thought he was being very attentive to the child, Maria," responded Lady Linton. The two women were in Lady Linton's private sitting room where Maria had run her mother to earth in order to air her grievances.

"Oh, he is being charming!" Maria replied bitterly. "He treats her as if she were Annabelle's age—and his niece to boot. Really, mother, I could shake him."

Lady Linton put down her embroidery. "Leave Philip alone, Maria," she said, and there was a ring of authority in her voice. "He will marry when he is ready to."

"And when will that be?"

"When he has fallen in love, I expect," came the firm answer.

Maria's eyes fell. "They have been after him for years, all the mamas with their pretty little daughters. He could marry anyone—and it is not only the earldom. He is just so damn handsome, and *nice*, that girls fall in love with him constantly. But he has never shown any serious interest in anyone."

"He has not found the right girl," replied Lady Linton.

Maria sighed. "I suppose you're right, mother. You needn't worry about me nagging him, at any rate. From now on I plan to leave him strictly alone. If he doesn't like Caroline Shere he will have to find another paragon by himself."

Lady Linton raised her eyebrows. "Do you mean that, Maria?"

"I do." Lady Maria's eyes flickered a little before her mother's shrewd look. "I know how far I can go with Philip, mother," she said in a low voice.

"And you have reached your limit?"

"Yes." A rueful smile flitted across Maria's face. "He almost lost his temper with me. I had to resort to tears. The last time Philip lost his temper with me he was nine years old and I was nineteen. It was an occasion I still remember vividly."

"So do I," her mother said drily.

Maria smiled at her tone. "Philip's tempers are much less frequent and much less noisy than mine. However, they are far more unnerving. When he starts talking through his teeth I know it is time to capitulate."

"He is so like your father," Lady Linton said softly.

"Well, perhaps there's hope yet," Maria answered with an attempt at humor. "After all, Papa got married."

"Philip will get married too. It is just a question of his finding the right girl."

"I suppose so. But I am beginning to wonder what kind of girl *will* make an impression on such a hardened case."

"That must be for Philip to decide," said Lady Linton. Then, with a pensive look in her eyes. she admitted, "Shall I tell you the truth, my dear? I had hopes of Lady Caroline too."

Linton was asking himself many of the same questions his mother and sister were posing about him. He even tried to drum up a little enthusiasm for the sweet tempting morsel that was Caroline Shere, but he failed dismally. She was a lovely, charming, delightful child but she did not interest him. He found himself spending more time than was comfortable thinking of a reserved and sensitive face with crystal gray eyes set off by extraordinary black lashes and brows. He worried about her. In the middle of the joyous festivities of Christmas Day his thoughts went winging back to London. Was she lonely? Did she miss him? The longer he was away from her the clearer it became that he was missing her.

He held out for two more weeks after Christmas. He was to drive his two eldest nephews back to Eton, and he told his mother he would not be returning to Staplehurst.

"But why, Philip?" she had asked, a faint line between her delicate brows. "Maria has been very good lately. And she is leaving for Selsey Place in a few days anyway."

"It isn't Maria, mother," he replied. "And I think she should stay here, by the way. I don't like the idea of her by herself at Selsey. Why doesn't she wait until after the baby is born?"

"I agree with you but there is no moving Maria. All her children were born at Selsey, she says, and this one will be too."

"As if Matt cared."

"Maria does, unfortunately. I shall go to Selsey myself in a few weeks' time. Certainly she can't be left alone with just the children and the servants."

He frowned a little. "That will leave nobody here at Staplehurst."

"Not if you are in London," his mother agreed gently.

"Well, I shall probably be back before you leave," he said. "And everything is in order here. Should something come up a message can always be sent to Grosvenor Square. I can be back here in a few hours."

"I am sure we shall manage, Philip," his mother told him, and gave him an unshadowed smile. Something was drawing him back to London, and his refusal to confide in her made her think it was a woman. If that was so it explained somewhat his lack of interest in Lady Caroline Shere. Lady Linton was far too wise to question her son. She determined to get her information elsewhere.

Matthew and Lawrence were pleased to be going back to school. They chattered unceasingly during the whole drive, thrilled that they were being returned in a smart phaeton driven by their magnificent uncle. "I'll bet everyone else is sent in a stuffy coach!" Lawrence said scornfully.

"Yes," agreed Matthew. "I hope Geoff is around so he can see your horses, Uncle Philip."

"Who is Geoff?" Linton asked his eldest nephew.

"Geoffrey Lissett, my best friend. His family raises race horses and Geoff helps to train them. Isn't he lucky? He said I might come and visit them this summer if it is all right with mamma. I asked her this

Christmas and she said I might." He gave a little wiggle of anticipation. "Geoff will love your grays. He is even more horse-mad than I am," he confided.

But the Lissetts had not yet arrived at Eton to Matthew's disappointment, and Linton deposited them, gave them both a guinea, put up in town for the night, and left the next morning for London.

Chapter Eleven

O make in me these civil wars to cease;
I will good tribute pay, if thou do so.
——SIR PHILIP SIDNEY

The weeks of Linton's absence had seemed very long
to Jessica. She had written to Miss Burnley and the
boys telling them she would not be home for Christmas and giving them an imaginative description of the
slow decline of the mythical Cousin Jean. She had
written four pages of instructions to Geoffrey telling
him what to do about the horses during his weeks at
Winchcombe. Geoffrey was only twelve years of age,
but he was extremely reliable and competent. Jessica
had depended on him heavily all during last summer
and he had not failed her.

It was her first Christmas away from Winchcombe,
her first Christmas away from her brothers. She knew
they would be missing her, and her heart ached when
she thought of them but, to her consternation, it was
not her brothers whose absence preoccupied her most.
It was impossible to deny to herself that she missed
Linton. Jessica was not a person who shrank from facing the truth, but she found herself seeking excuses for
her inexplicable feelings. He was the only person she
really knew in London, she told herself. Of course she

felt lonely and displaced when he was gone. If she had been at Winchcombe with her family, Philip Romney would be very far from her thoughts. When she went home in March she would forget him.

Linton arrived in London at midday. He spent some time that afternoon at Rundell and Bridge's, a fashionable jewelers, and then stopped by Brooks'. He found Lord George Litcham there.

"Philip!" His friend looked extremely surprised to see him.

"How are you, George?" Linton replied easily.

"Surprised to see you here," Lord George said frankly. "I thought you'd be at Staplehurst until the start of the season.

"I felt the need for a respite from my family," Linton replied somewhat mendaciously.

Lord George rolled his eyes sympathetically. "Lady Maria still visiting, eh?"

"Yes," replied Linton, ruthlessly sacrificing his sister's reputation. "I am exceedingly fond of Maria, but . . ." He paused eloquently.

"I know," replied Lord George. "Sisters!" He had three of his own and knew whereof he spoke. Linton grinned and Lord George continued, "I suppose that means you won't be giving up Miss O'Neill for a while."

"What do you mean?" snapped Linton, a decided edge to his voice. "Of course I am not giving up Miss O'Neill."

"Well there is no need to chop my head off," Lord George said, giving his friend a puzzled look. "I just thought, since you usually stay at Staplehurst until April . . ."

"Well I am not at Staplehurst now," Linton interrupted, his voice clipped with rising temper. A thought struck him, and he fixed glittering blue eyes on Lord George's pleasant, good-natured face. "What has been going on here while I was away?" His voice sounded distinctly dangerous.

"Nothing! Good God, Philip, stop looking at me like that. Nothing has happened. No one has even seen Miss O'Neill except on the stage." He looked at Linton's face for a moment in silence and then said, "She doesn't come into the Green Room and no one is allowed into her dressing room. I know because there are a number of men who have tried to see her. I was not the only one who assumed you may be bowing out."

Linton drew himself up to his impressive height. "Well, you were all wrong," he said grimly. "Good day, George." And he walked away, leaving an extremely puzzled Lord George staring after him.

Jessica was performing that evening, which was why Linton had stayed away. When he finally saw her he wanted her undivided time and attention. And this evening's performance had a special significance, as he had discovered from Mr. Mowbray whom he had met in Bond Street. On January 2 Edmund Kean, at the strong but misguided insistence of the Drury Lane committee, had appeared as Romeo. It was not at all the sort of role suited to him. It was impossible for him to look like a boy, and the ardor of young love was an emotion he found difficult to project. For the first time he invited direct comparison to Jessica, whose Juliet was considered a masterpiece. She was playing Juliet tonight for the first time since the end of December, and the public, with Kean's performance in mind, had come to test hers against it.

Linton waited until the play had begun before he slipped into his seat. He did not want Jessica to know he was there until he could face her directly. When she came on stage he was almost immobile, his eyes closely following her, knowing by heart her special beauty of movement and line, her springing, intense vitality that reached out and captured every man in the audience as surely as the enraptured Romeo.

When the play was finally over the audience rose, cheering and shouting, giving notice, in case anyone had doubted, that Jessica O'Neill owned *Romeo and Juliet*. They quieted only long enough for Thomas Harris to make an announcement: "Ladies and gentlemen, two weeks from tonight I am happy to tell you that Jessica O'Neill will perform in William Shakespeare's *Macbeth*." As the theatre went wild, Linton thought with a wry smile, so she is carrying the war into *his* territory now.

Jessica had taken her costume and her makeup off and was sitting in front of the dressing table mirror brushing her hair when there came a knock on the door. "I am not seeing anyone, Jenny," she said to the girl who was hanging up her costume, and the girl nodded and went to the door.

When she saw who was there her eyes widened, but

he shook his head gently at her and motioned her out. Obediently she slipped past him and he entered the room, closing the door behind him. He stood for a minute, watching Jessica at the dressing table. Her back was to him and, unaware of his presence, she went on serenely with what she was doing. Her head was tipped a little to one side as she brushed, and her hair fell over her bare shoulders, a shining rippling mass of autumnal silk glinting with threads of copper as she stopped and swung it back from her face. "Who was it, Jenny?" she asked, and turned her head, beautiful as a flower on its stem. Her eyes met his, and he heard the sudden sharp intake of her breath. "Philip!"

"Did you miss me?" he asked, and crossed to the dressing table to raise her up. His hands on her bare shoulders, he looked for a minute into her large gray eyes, his own narrow and brilliant in his intent, concentrated face. Then his mouth came down on hers.

The hardness of his kiss surprised her. It was different from the way he had kissed her before. More demanding. Hungry. She remained passive within his arms at first, still surprised by his sudden appearance. Her head lay back against his shoulder, the mantle of her hair streaming over his arm. She felt his body, strong and hard against hers, and slowly her mouth answered to the urgency of his, her response gathering force and passion, her body arched up against his, her arms holding him closely. After a long time he raised his head. His blue eyes were blazing. "Jess," he said.

She laughed unsteadily. "Where did you come from?" His eyes were on the sofa, and he didn't answer. They could lock the door, he was thinking. But no, that wasn't what he wanted, what he had waited all day for. He wanted time with her. Time to bury himself in the inexhaustible depths of her.

"Let's go home," he said, his voice harsh in his own ears.

"All right." She looked around, then, bewildered. "Where is Jenny? I need my dress."

"I sent her out." He looked once more at her bare arms and throat, luminous against the white of her fine camisole. "I'll get her and wait for you outside."

Her eyes, gray as the dawn, met his. "All right," she said again, very softly this time.

When she joined him in the carriage he didn't speak, and she sat beside him, careful not to touch him. The drive to Montpelier Square seemed interminable, and by the time they arrived they were both nearly frantic. They walked together in the front door and, still not speaking, went directly upstairs to the bedroom. Jessica was quivering all over, conscious only of the man beside her, aching for him to touch her.

Her maid appeared, and he sent her away. He turned Jessica around and, still in silence, began to undo the hooks on her dress. She stepped out of it, leaving it lying on the floor, and with trembling hands sat down to take off her stockings. When she looked up he had his shirt off and she stared in fascinated wonder at his broad chest and shoulders, so astonishingly strong and muscular under that well-cut, elegant coat. "I missed you," she told him huskily, answering

89

the question he had asked back in her dressing room an hour ago.

He held out his hands and she came to him, melting against him, her eyes closing. He bent over and his mouth found hers.

It was the first time she had let her barriers down. His unexpected arrival had thrown her off balance, and then the irresistible demands of her body, which had recognized him the first time their eyes had met, had taken control. A curious sense of fatalism settled over her now as she lay beneath him, relaxed and at peace, cherishing the feel of his weight as it pressed her down into the bed. She ran her hand caressingly through his hair and it sprang, sparkling like new-minted gold, from her fingers. His breathing had finally slowed. Whatever happens, she thought, I shall always have the memory of this.

Half an hour later she was closed up against him, watching him with open, remote eyes that filled his soul with bitter anger. He had given her a ruby-and-diamond necklace.

Chapter Twelve

They love indeed who quake to say they love.
—SIR PHILIP SIDNEY

It was a Christmas present, he told her. He had commissioned it before he left for Staplehurst. "I meant to give it to you earlier this evening," he said as he put it into her hands, "but I forgot."

It was exquisite: delicate and glowing and obviously very expensive. She didn't want it, but she knew, looking from the spill of gems in her hand to his face, that she would have to accept it.

"Thank you," she said in a voice she strove to keep even. "It is very lovely."

There was a long pause as he took in the deadness of her tone. She was sitting up in the center of the bed, her back straight, her hair spilling over her white shoulders, the bedside lamp lighting her thick lashes and clear profile. He stood looking at that shuttered, remote face and felt the bitterness begin to rise in his heart. "You don't want it," he said.

"I did not say that."

"You didn't have to. It is written all over your face." He moved away from her and began to dress. "Well, it is yours," he said after a moment. "Do with it as you like. You can always sell it; it is worth a significant amount of money."

Jessica flinched as if he had struck her across the face, but he didn't seem to notice. A lock of bright hair had fallen over his forehead, and impatiently he pushed it back, away from the ice blue of his eyes.

She couldn't speak. She felt frozen, numbed to the heart by what she saw in his eyes. I have never seen him like this, she thought. "Do you want me to leave?" she asked, and in spite of herself her voice quivered.

He stood looking at her for a minute, and his mouth set like a vice. "No. I believe you said you wished to go to the opera tomorrow evening. I'll call for you then." He nodded to her curtly. "Good night, Jess," he said, and left.

Jessica slept very little and arose the next morning with a heavy head. She tried to study her lines but they seemed to slip from her mind as soon as she said them, and the character of Lady Macbeth eluded her completely. She ate very little and didn't notice the worried way the servants looked at her. They had seen many women come and go in that house on Montpelier Square, and everyone was in agreement that they wanted to see Jessica stay. Peter, the footman, had seen Lord Linton leaving last night and it was clear, he reported to the kitchen contingent the next day, that my lord had been very angry. As no one had ever remembered seeing Linton angry before this report cast a pall over the house which was not alleviated by Jessica's obvious depression.

She took a long time getting dressed that evening. She wore the cream silk dress that was her favorite and noticed, with a detached part of her brain, that her skin looked more luminous than usual and her breasts fuller. The maid picked up the ruby necklace from where it lay on top of the dressing table. "It's beautiful, miss," she breathed, and started to put it on Jessica.

It looked magnificent against the white column of her throat. The maid was fastening the catch when Jessica said in a harsh voice, "Take it off. I am not going to wear it."

"But miss," the maid said, shocked into speech, "didn't Lord Linton give it to you?"

"Yes." Her throat felt tight. Part of her wanted to wear it, wanted to please him and placate him, but the other part of her thought in horror of all the people in the theatre who would stare at it and know it for what it was: a payment. She couldn't bear it. "Take it off," she said again.

She was ready and waiting for him downstairs when he arrived. His gaze flickered over her briefly, noting her bare throat, then he said drily, "If you are ready let's go. I don't like to keep the horses standing."

It was a long and painful evening for Jessica. She loved music but scarcely heard a note of the opera. Every nerve end in her body was conscious of him, sitting so close beside her, keeping himself to himself. Her overtures of peace were met with a perfectly courteous, solid resistance. Jessica was discovering what Linton's family had known for years: he was not easily angered, but when he was he was not easily pacified. She thought, as she stole a glance at him from under her lashes, that she had been right when she had first likened him to a Viking. His subsequent gentleness had seemed to negate the comparison, but looking now at his beautiful, clean profile, his firm, merciless mouth, it did not seem so farfetched. When the lights came up for the intermission he turned to her, and it seemed as if the cold, blue North Sea glittered in his eyes.

She gave up trying to reach him and retreated herself behind the cool, aloof expression that had been her camouflage for so many years. Their box was crowded with Linton's friends during the intermissions, and Jessica responded to all questions and comments with a distant politeness that was like a shield between her and them. At one point she looked absently out over the opera house and her eyes came to rest, inadvertently, on the box opposite to Linton's. There was a single man in it, standing watching her with an expression on his face that made her shiver. Lord Alden bowed to her, a slight smile lifting the corners of his thin mouth. Jessica stared right through him and, instinctively, took a step closer to Linton. Alden saw it and laughed.

They went to the Piazza for supper, and they might have been two strangers with nothing between them but a common experience at the opera. Jessica's face was utterly remote, her voice cool and impersonal as she discussed the opera of which she had heard not a note. He accompanied her back to Montpelier Square but did not come in. "I promised Crosley I would meet him at Watiers," he said easily. "Good night, Jess. Sleep well." He kissed her hand lightly and went back out through the door to the waiting carriage.

She did not see him again for five days. She fought against missing him, fought to maintain her defenses and protections. She sought refuge in her work. The production of *Macbeth* had not been Jessica's idea. Thomas Harris, exultant at Kean's failure as Romeo, had conceived the idea of challenging him with material he had made his own. Not only did Harris have Jessica for Lady Macbeth, but a new actor had appeared on the Covent Garden horizon. Lewis Garreg, a young Welshman, had been recommended to him by an acquaintance who had seen him perform in Shrewsbury, and Harris had given the young man a contract. He was also giving him the part of Macbeth.

Garreg knew that it was the chance of his lifetime, and he was both eager and apprehensive. He was twenty-six years of age, of medium height with dark brown hair and clear hazel eyes. He was broadly built and had a voice like an organ, a deep, rolling baritone. He had been very nervous with Jessica at first, but her friendly, calm, professional demeanor soon began to put him at ease. They spent several hours discussing the play and the characters and came up with an interpretation they both felt comfortable with.

"It will be different from the usual portrayal," Jessica had said, "but it has to be, I think. We are both of us much younger than the actors who usually do *Macbeth*. Not that Kean is old, but somehow he never manages to look very young, does he?"

Garreg thought of Kean's Romeo and chuckled. "No."

"Well, I certainly can't play Lady Macbeth as the fiendish devil that Mrs. Siddons made so famous. It wouldn't look right. I shall play her as a young woman who loves her husband and who wants, desperately, to see him king. Her weakness is that she does not understand the consequences of the murder she pushes him to commit."

"You don't think she dominates him, then?" he had asked carefully.

"I think there is a balance to the play, Lewis," she answered. "I do not want to dominate it. Macbeth must be a strong man or her love for him makes no sense—she, certainly, is a strong woman. She is able to influence him due to the fact that he loves her also. I see them as two ambitious, proud people who, tragically, destroy each other."

His hazel eyes had blazed. "Let us get started then."

But rehearsals had proved frustrating. Jessica liked to have all of her movements worked out before she went on stage, and her actions, for this play, depended on another actor as they never had before. It was the relationship between Macbeth and his wife that interested her, and she felt as if she were working in a vacuum. She and Lewis Garreg finally sat down together to decide on their movements, but the carpenters were working in the theatre and it was noisy, so Jessica suggested they go to Montpelier Square where they could work without interruption.

They worked all of Wednesday afternoon and made excellent progress. By Thursday they were ready to rehearse the first three acts. They had not gotten through Act One when, unnoticed, Linton walked in. He watched in silence as a burly young man put his arms around Jessica. "My dearest love," a deep, rich voice intoned. The young man looked down into her face. "Duncan comes here tonight," he said, and Jessica's eyes, looking past him, widened.

"Philip!" she said in astonishment, and the burly young man jumped.

Linton looked steadily back at their two startled faces. "I appear to have come at an inopportune moment."

"Well, you did, rather," Jessica replied candidly. "We were rehearsing. May I present Lewis Garreg, Philip, who is to play *Macbeth* with me next week. Lord Linton, Lewis."

Lewis Garreg was extremely uncomfortable. He knew, of course, about Jessica's relationship with Linton, and he did not at all care for the expression in Linton's very blue eyes. "We have been working on the play, my lord." he hastened to second Jessica. "I hope you do not mind?"

"Did you want me for some reason, my lord?" said Jessica in a deceptively gentle voice. She did not care for Linton's look either, and she felt her temper rising.

"I came to see if you cared to go driving with me." There was an audible note of anger in the usually soft tones of his voice.

Their eyes met and locked, and Lewis Garreg instinctively dropped his own gaze. When he looked up again he saw two people whose faces were calm, assured and devoid of passion, but he had seen the anger in those two pairs of eyes now so veiled and cool, and he closed his book with an audible thump. "I'll be going, Jess," he said to her. "I'll see you at the theatre tomorrow. Good day, my lord." With considerable dignity considering its haste Lewis Garreg made his departure, leaving Jessica and Linton alone together.

Chapter Thirteen

Love is a great and mighty lord
——GEORGE PEELE

There was silence in the room until they heard the front door close behind him. Then Linton said, "Your *Macbeth* will be a sensation if that was a sample."

"Would you care to explain what you mean by that remark, my lord?" she asked in a brittle voice.

"I mean that you and that actor looked very cozy," he said, a grim look about his mouth.

A deep, familiar coldness came over Jessica as she looked bleakly back at him. Just so had she stood many times before, alone and in bitter opposition to her stepfather. As she stiffened her back against Linton he took two steps closer to her and halted. A shaft of pale sunlight from the window fell on his thick blond hair and illuminated his grim, white face and blue eyes. Her own eyes widened for a moment, arrested, and it suddenly was though the veil that had blurred her vision for so long had ripped away and she was standing, naked and defenseless, before the frightening truth. She took a deep, shuddering breath. Her throat ached. All her anger died away, to be replaced by a despair so absolute that it withered her soul. It was pain to look at him. Her eyes fell. "I'll pack and be gone by morning," she said tonelessly.

He had seen her eyes before the lids came down. "What is it, Jess?" he asked, his voice gentler than it had been. "What is the matter?"

She shook her head hopelessly. She could not tell him. She could not even blame him for thinking of her and Lewis Garreg as he did. "Do you understand the consequences?" he had asked her on their first night together. She had not, she thought now, with pain a hard knot inside her. Never in a million years had she dreamed that she would fall in love with him. She made a small gesture that was like the cry of a lost child. "I'll go," she repeated doggedly.

He came closer. "Where will you go?"

Her mind went blank at the question. Where? Home? But she still did not have the money for the mortgage. To another man? Blindly she shook her head and wrapped her arms protectively around herself. She could not answer him.

He put his hand under her chin and tilted her face up. Her eyes, wide and distraught with unhappiness, met his. The cool composure that had been her shell for so long was destroyed. "Do you love this Garreg fellow?" he asked painfully.

"No!" She stepped back, away from him, away from the temptation to throw herself into his arms, to tell him it was he she loved. It was no good, she thought. Love was not in the bargain they two had made.

Linton was silent, his blue eyes strangely impersonal, looking into her eyes as if he were trying to find the truth that was hidden there. She stared back as if hypnotized by that steady and intent gaze. "Jess," he finally said quietly, "why won't you wear my necklace?"

She tore her eyes from his and turned to walk to the window. She rested her forehead against the cold glass and closed her eyes. "Because it makes me feel like a whore," she said wearily. "Which is a very stupid reason, I know, since that is exactly what I am."

There was a stunned silence, then he said in a voice that was barely audible, "Oh my God." She didn't move and he came across to where she stood at the window. "Do you think that is how I regard you?" There was a note in his voice that pierced the fog of despair that was engulfing her, and she turned slowly to face him.

"How do you regard me?" she asked simply, all defenses shattered.

"I regard you as the woman I love," he answered, and reached out to pull her into his arms. The relief she felt was so intense that her knees buckled. He held her close and she pressed against him. She was shaking.

"Philip," she said. "Philip."

"I gave you that necklace because I love you," he was saying. "I'd spin the moon out of the sky to give you if I thought you wanted it."

"I just want you." Her voice was muffled by his shoulder.

She felt so slim and light in his arms. "I'm sorry, Jess. I'm sorry, darling." His lips were against her temple. Then, suddenly, his hands were hard on her

101

shoulders, holding her away from him. She looked up to meet his eyes. They were bluer than the sea on a summer day, and deeper. "Don't ever say that about yourself again. Do you hear me?"

Mutely she nodded.

He smiled a little, and her own eyes, clear as the sea but not of its color, smiled back. "Do you still want to go driving?" she asked huskily.

"No," he replied, his hand lightly touching her mouth. "I have another idea."

They went upstairs to the bedroom and stayed there until noon the next day.

For Jessica the world had changed. When she had embarked on this enterprise her intentions had been solely monetary. It had never once crossed her mind that she might fall in love. But she had never imagined that a man like Philip Romney existed in the world.

He was a man she could trust. She had known that, instinctively, from the moment they first had met. With everyone else she had ever known she had had to play a role; she had had to be strong and resolute, fearless and independent. For some reason only he had the power to force her outside her defenses. He had caused her to strip away all her protections, layer by layer, until she was left vulnerable and defenseless before him.

And she was happy as she had never been before. She let go her hold on herself, she relinquished herself to him. All her doors at last were open. "I love you," she whispered to him deep in the night. "You own me, body and soul, do you know that?"

His mouth was on her, feeling her silken smoothness as she lay there, open to him as a flower lies open to the sun. His voice, when it came, was husky and unsteady. "The things a man owns, my darling, hold him far more securely than he holds them."

She smiled. "Then we own each other."

He did not answer her in words.

When they woke for the last time the sun was slanting into the room through the drawn blind. She stirred in his arms. Her eyes focused dreamily on the bedpost, and she lay still, listening absorbedly to some inner voice. "I'm hungry," she said finally in a surprised tone. Then, more strongly, "I'm starving. What time is it?"

"I don't know," he said calmly, as if it was not of the slightest importance, and she sighed and rested her head on his shoulder. The minutes ticked by.

"If I don't get some food soon I am going to expire," she said at last in a sepulchral tone, and he chuckled.

"We'll get up." They didn't move. She listened to the beating of his heart, so steady and reassuring. She yawned a little, and he kissed her lightly and sat up. "I'll ring for one of the servants." He went across to the wardrobe and pulled out a green velvet robe which he tossed to her. "You'd better put that on," he advised, sliding his arms into his own dressing gown.

They had breakfast brought up to the bedroom. Jessica ate hugely. It seemed to her she had never been this hungry before. By the time they had finished Linton's valet had arrived from Linton House in Grosvenor Square. Linton had sent for him to bring a change of clothes. He used the dressing room off Jessica's room while she dressed in the bedroom. When he was attired in biscuit pantaloons, well-polished Hessian boots, and a blue coat of Weston's superb tailoring, he went into her room. She was seated in front of the dressing table having her hair done.

"I have to go down to Holland House this afternoon," he told her. "Would you like to go to dinner at Grillon's this evening?"

"I would like that very much," she assured him as her maid put the last pin in her hair. "I'm going to the theatre this afternoon. *Macbeth* opens next week and Mr. Harris is probably having apoplexy about now."

He grinned. "I hope that Garreg fellow hasn't reported that I've murdered you."

"I'm sure Miss Favel is hoping," she replied, referring to her understudy.

"I'll drive you there if you're ready," he offered, and she rose promptly and accompanied him downstairs.

He was driving his grays. The winter day was cold and clear, making driving in the open phaeton a pleasure. She sat close beside him and neither of them spoke. He watched the road through the ears of the horses, driving with steady attention through the busy London streets. Only now and then did she turn to look at him, at his profile clean as a chiselled thing as he studied the road with grave intent. One of her hands was in her muff, the other, gloved in soft kid, lay relaxed on her lap. Without looking at her he put his own upon it and covered it. She gave a faint smile but said nothing. When they reached Covent Garden she disappeared quickly inside the theatre, and he drove on toward Kensington.

Chapter Fourteen

What's done is done.
— WILLIAM SHAKESPEARE

Jessica worked as hard as she ever had in her life during the following week. Her own happiness with Linton distracted her and she found herself having a very difficult time getting a grasp on Lady Macbeth. She had built the character, as she always did, from the outside in. She knew what gestures she would make, how she would hold her head, where she would move on the stage and when. But that inner spark of concentration, which enabled her to project the essence of the character through this outward guise she had created, was missing.

She rehearsed with dogged persistence, spending the whole day in the theatre and then the night with Linton. She was looking very beautiful, with a silvery radiance to her face that drew men's eyes like a magnet. She tried to concentrate on *Macbeth* but her thoughts kept slipping away to rest on lazy, laughing blue eyes, strong, long-fingered hands, a mouth full of determination and of humor, that yet could look so tender . . . "You're on, Jess," said Thomas Harris testily, and she pulled herself from her reverie to hear Garreg repeating, "How now? What news?"

With an apologetic glance at Harris she walked on stage and crossed to Lewis Garreg. "He has almost supped," she said clearly. "Why have you left the chamber?" But ten minutes later her mind had wandered again and she missed another cue.

Linton was surprised by the amount of time Jessica put in preparing for the opening. He himself had spent one whole afternoon giving her her cues so that she could get her lines down. "Somehow one doesn't think of actors having to memorize a part," he said to her.

Jessica smiled, white teeth flashing in the grave intentness of her face. "How did you think we learned the lines, then?"

"I didn't think about it at all. One just assumed that you were born knowing them, I suppose."

"It would be much easier if we were," she replied fervently. Then, a minute later, as she missed a line in the murder scene, "Damn! I can't ever remember having such trouble committing a part to memory. And Lady Macbeth has far fewer lines than Juliet or Rosalind." She closed her eyes, frowning. "Let's do it again."

Obediently he flipped back in his script. "Act II?"

"No. Let's start from the beginning."

"You may not know your lines but I certainly am getting to know Garreg's," he replied humorously. "All right, begin with the letter."

She got up and began to pace around the room.

"They met me in the day of success . . ." she began with energetic determination, and he followed along in the script, stopping her when she made a mistake. By the end of the day she had the lines down letter perfect. But still the character escaped her.

The night of the opening Jessica went to the theatre early and by herself. "You'll only distract me," she had told Linton, the glimmer of a smile in her eyes.

"Will I? Good." Then, as she had shot him a look, half amused, half exasperated, he had given in. "All right. I'll stay away. But afterwards we'll go out to supper."

"All right."

"You are really nervous, aren't you, Jess? I've never seen you like this before."

"You've never seen me before I've opened in a new part!" she retorted. "If you think I'm nervous now you should have seen me before I first went on as Juliet. I didn't think I'd be able to speak at all that night, let alone remember the lines."

"Well, considering that it was your first time on stage, it's understandable," he said.

He had caught her entirely off guard. "I suppose so. At any rate I was petrified." Then, as the magnitude of her admission hit her, her head jerked up and she stared at him warily.

His blue eyes glinted through narrowed lids. "I never did believe that story about the west of Ireland," he said gently.

"Oh." She thought for a minute. "Why?"

"Wexford, my darling, is on the east coast."

Quite suddenly she grinned. "My dreadfully inadequate education comes home to roost. No, I was never in Ireland and yes, the first time I ever set foot on a stage was when I played Juliet at Covent Garden."

"Quite a jumping-off point for a beginner," he commented neutrally.

"It wasn't my idea," she replied vigorously. "I was looking for a small part, a lady of the court or something like that. It was Mr. Harris's brilliant notion to cast me as Juliet. I even tried to talk him out of it, but he was determined." She sighed. "I would infinitely prefer to be more anonymous. I had no intention of becoming famous. It is—rather uncomfortable at times. But, as Lady Macbeth so eloquently says, 'What's done is done.' "

He looked at her in silence, taking in the clear burning brightness of her, then he asked quietly the question that had haunted him. "Who are you, Jess?"

There was a long, shivering pause. He had violated her unwritten rule, not to ask questions about her background. At last she whispered, "I can't tell you that. Someday, perhaps. Not now."

There was another pause while he debated what to do. He loved her. He wanted to hold her. She was not really his, he knew. She might go away. It was the fear that lay deep-buried at the bottom of his happiness, that he might lose her. "Don't you trust me?" he asked at last.

She bent her head, exposing the soft whiteness of her nape. It was a pose that made her seem very vulnerable, very young. "I can't tell you, Philip," she repeated helplessly. "Not yet. Please don't ask me."

There was a white line around his mouth. "For how long do you think you can remain anonymous? The name of Jessica O'Neill must be familiar to every literate person in England by now. I don't know where you come from, but you are English, of that I'm sure. One day someone who knows you is going to walk into that theatre and recognize you." She winced as if he had struck her, but he continued inexorably, "You said you did not want to become famous, but you *are* famous, Jess. Your identity can't remain hidden forever."

"It doesn't need to be hidden forever," she replied quickly. "I don't plan to go on acting forever."

His face was grim. This was what he had feared. "And one day you will just disappear, back to obscurity, and Jessica O'Neill will be no more?"

"That is what I planned to do," she answered him honestly.

"And what of me, Jess? What of me?"

Slowly she raised her bent head until her eyes, wide and gray and fathomless, rested on his face. She felt as though he had a knife to her heart. For these past few days she had allowed herself to be swept along on the tide of his love, refusing to acknowledge where the sea was carrying her. There was no future for her with Philip Romney. She knew that. Once she had the money for the mortgage she would have to leave him, and the thought was terrible to her. She felt as though there were a black, deep ravine separating her from all her previous days. She knew now, now that it was too late, what it was in life that she wanted. And she could not have him. He was not for her. But she must not let him know. She must reassure him so that at least the weeks she had left would be hers. It was little enough happiness for a lifetime, she thought.

"What of you?" she repeated softly. "I said I was going to leave the stage, Philip. Not you. Not ever you. You'll have to throw me out when you want me to go."

She saw his face change at her words, his mouth taking on an expression that made her knees go weak. "I'm far more likely to chain you up," he said roughly.

At that she laughed unsteadily. "I always thought you looked like a Viking," she said, and his blue eyes glittered.

"You are a prize I mean to hold onto, my darling," he told her, and centuries of possessiveness sounded for the moment in the deep tones of his voice. She smiled but did not reply.

Linton arrived at Covent Garden about twenty minutes before the play was scheduled to begin. He paused for a short time in front of the playbill that announced the night's production, his eyes on the names listed and on one name in particular.

PLAYBILL JANUARY 28, 1815
COVENT GARDEN THEATRE

THE TRAGEDY OF
MACBETH

111

Duncan, King of Scotland, *Mr. Powell*
Macbeth, *Mr. Garreg*
Banquo, *Mr. Holland*
Macduff, *Mr. Walleck*
Malcolm, *Mr. Dawson,* Donalbain, *Mr. Palmer,*
Lennox, *Mr. Crooke,* Ross, *Mr. Fisher,* Menteith,
Mr. Miller, Angus, *Mr. Ray,* Caithness, *Mr. Evans,*
Fleance, *Mr. Carr,* Siward, *Mr. Maddocks,*
Young Siward, *Mr. Hughes*

Lady Macbeth, *Miss O'Neill*
Lady Macduff, *Miss Favell,*
Gentlewoman, *Mrs. Brereton*

With an inscrutable face he entered the theatre and made his way to his box. He had not wanted to ask anyone to join him but he knew his solitary presence would occasion the kind of remark he most disliked, so he had invited his cousin Bertram, Bertram's friend Sir Francis Rustington, and Lord George Litcham. The three other men were already in the box when he arrived. The theatre was filled to overflowing. "By Jove, Philip, they've all turned out to see Jessica tonight!" Bertram said enthusiastically.

Sir Francis shook his head sadly. "I don't understand it. Nice girl. Marvelous girl, really. Dash it all, how's she going to play Lady Macbeth? Woman's a horror. We had to read the play at Harrow." He shook his head again in bewilderment, and Linton smiled.

"I don't think you'll see a nice girl on the stage

tonight, Francis," he said, a flicker of irony in his voice.

"I don't know how she can do it," Bertram said with a shudder. "Imagine having to stand in front of all these people."

Jessica was feeling the tension, but not nearly as much as Lewis Garreg. No matter how the production went, Jessica O'Neill would still be Jessica O'Neill, the first actress of the London theatre. But if Lewis Garreg failed it was back to the provinces for him, back to poverty and oblivion. He wanted very much to succeed—much more than Jessica did. She stood next to him in the Green Room and when his name was called she squeezed his hand slightly. "You'll be wonderful," she said firmly. He smiled at her gratefully, took a deep breath, and headed for the stage.

Twenty minutes later her own call came. The curtain was down as the scenery was being changed and she took her place on center stage, a letter in her hands. She wore a black velvet gown of medieval cut. Her hair was loosely pulled off her face and coiled on her neck. She stood perfectly still, no expression on her face, and the curtain slowly began to rise. At the sight of her, standing solitary in the middle of the wide stage, the theatre erupted.

Her eyes looked out into the auditorium toward the cheering throng. They passed over the professional men jammed uncomfortably together on benches in the pit, over the aristocrats in the boxes, up to the vast reaches of the gallery where sat the people. Gradually the noise died away and she bent her eyes to the paper she was holding. "They met me in the day of success," she began, her deep clear, resonant voice perfectly audible throughout the theatre.

She went through the speech faultlessly, as Linton, who was mentally reciting it with her, was aware. She finished and the messenger came on with news of the king's arrival. With the entrance of the messenger something clicked in Jessica's mind and she had it at last, that total and undistracted concentration on the character she was portraying that she had sought so vainly this last week. The theatre, the audience, Linton . . . everything fell away from her but the words she was to say. The messenger exited and she lifted her face, beautiful and bright and pitiless, and slowly, with terrible intensity, she began Lady Macbeth's powerful invocation to the evil spirits. When she had finished the atmosphere in the theatre was electric and Lewis Garreg, coming on stage, met, not the Jessica he had been rehearsing with all week, but a bright angel who fixed on him eyes of possession and passion and desire.

"My dearest love," his rich, beautifully flexible voice matched hers in power. He held her close for a moment, then looked down unflinchingly into her face. "Duncan comes here tonight."

As the act progressed Linton looked around the theatre. It was deathly silent, not a cough, not a rustle of paper or of silk was to be heard. The full attention of the hundreds of spectators was trained on the stage, on the duel that was being fought between Macbeth's better nature and his wife, between Lewis Garreg, who was turning in a magnificent performance, and Jessica.

He looked back to the stage. Garreg had turned away from her, his jaw set stubbornly.

> Prithee peace!
> I dare do all that may become a man.
> Who dares do more is none.

He walked to a bench on stage left and sat down, his eyes brooding upon the ground. There was a long silence as Jessica regarded him, and then she exploded into passion and anger.

> What beast was't then
> That made you break this enterprise to me?

Slowly she walked across the stage until she stood before him. She put her hands on his shoulders. He raised his head, and her gray eyes, burning and intent in her proud, determined face, held his relentlessly.

> I have given suck, and know
> How tender 'tis to love the babe that milks me

She paused and then went on, no anger in her voice now. It was clear and cold and truthful.

I would, while it was smiling in my face,
Have plucked my nipple from his boneless gums
And dashed the brains out, had I so sworn
as you
Have done to this.

Beside him Linton could hear the shocked intake of Bertram's breath. Lord George's knuckles were white as he gripped the front of the box. On the stage Garreg began to waver.

If we should fail?

An enchanting smile lit Jessica's face.

We fail?
But screw your courage to the sticking place,
And we'll not fail.

The tension in the theatre was thick and palpable. On stage the last of Macbeth's objections fell and his own ambition answered forth to his wife's. They stood together, two passionate, proud people in the intensity of their fixed purpose, their two young, formidable faces looking for the moment strangely alike. When the curtain came down on Act I there was at least one full minute of stunned silence before the applause began.

The remainder of the play was of the same caliber. There wasn't a person present at that performance who didn't remember it vividly for the rest of his life: the first and only time Jessica O'Neill played Lady

Macbeth. Lewis Garreg would play Macbeth many more times, and he always gave a powerful, moving performance, but never again would there be that electricity in the air, that knowledge that one was watching what the *Morning Post* would call the next day "one of the finest pieces of acting we have ever beheld, or perhaps that the stage has ever known."

Chapter Fifteen

... and all things keep
Time with the season; only she doth carry
June in her eyes, in her heart January.
            —THOMAS CAREW

After the performance Linton found Jessica in the Green Room. She was standing with Lewis Garreg, introducing him to the famous and the great who were thronging to congratulate her. Linton watched her in silence for a moment from the doorway. It was Garreg's night as well as hers; her demeanor made that clear. The young man was obviously both exhilarated and nervous. He had never met so many members of the nobility in his life. With some amusement Linton thought that he was clinging to Jessica as if she were a lifeline.

Her head turned, and across the room their eyes met. Lord George, standing next to Linton, intercepted that look and, startled, turned to his friend. What he saw for a brief unguarded moment on Linton's face made his heart begin to pound. It couldn't be, he thought involuntarily. *What* couldn't be, another part of his mind asked objectively as he followed Linton across the floor. Lord George did not answer himself. He only knew he was conscious of a wish that Lady

Maria Selsey was not indisposed at the moment. He had a horrible sinking feeling that Linton was in deeper than was safe and might very well have to be rescued.

Jessica, unaware that she had alarmed Lord George, greeted him with friendliness. And she laughed at Bertram when he said, "You scared me to death, Jessica!"

"Indeed you did," a smooth voice said next to her elbow, and she turned to find Lord Alden looking at her with a mixture of speculation and desire that she found peculiarly repulsive.

"Did I, my lord?" she asked stiffly.

He smiled and her eyes narrowed. Bertram's attention had been momentarily distracted, and for a brief minute she and Lord Alden might have been alone. "Linton can't possibly appreciate a woman like you," he said softly.

"And you think you can?" Her voice expressed nothing but a kind of wary contempt.

"I am sure of it." His voice hardened. "Whatever he is giving you, I'll double it."

Slowly she shook her head. "No, you won't," she said, and now her voice was under its familiar control, aloof and contained. Linton put a hand on her shoulder and she turned back to him with relief.

"I've asked Mr. Garreg to accompany us to a champagne supper at the Grillon. Some of the rest of the cast are coming and a few of my own friends."

She smiled with genuine pleasure. "Thank you, Philip. This is really Lewis's triumph, you know."

"No, it is not," he replied soberly. "Garreg was

119

marvelous, that I agree. But you were more than that. And you know it."

Her lips curved a little, but she made no reply. In fact she said nothing about the performance until the large company was seated around a table in the Grillon's private dining room and toasts were being made. "To many more performances like the one we saw tonight," said Thomas Harris, raising his champagne glass to Jessica and Lewis Garreg. After the toast was drunk Jessica got to her feet.

"I thank you very much, all of you, for your kind words. I have an announcement to make that I am afraid will make some of you unhappy. Tonight was my last performance. I am retiring from the theatre."

Cries of protest and of incredulity rose from every pair of lips. Of all the table only Jessica and Linton remained silent. She sat down, impervious to the noise and the pleas around her, aware only of the man who sat so quietly at the opposite end of the long table. He was looking at the tablecloth in front of him as if it contained the answer to a secret he had long wanted to unlock. Finally, aware of her gaze, he looked up, and the sudden lift and turn of his head was as direct as a touch. Her face relaxed a little and he raised a reassuring eyebrow.

"I will not change my mind," she said then.

"But *why?*" Thomas Harris almost wailed. "For God's sake, Jessica, *why?*"

"I am tired of acting," she said simply. "I don't want to do it any more."

He stared at her with first exasperation, then incredulity, then astonishment. She meant it. Jessica

O'Neill, who had all of London at her feet, was leaving the theatre. And he thought he knew why. He directed his gaze, filled with reproach, at the Earl of Linton.

Linton's face was inscrutable. With seemingly little effort he got the upset dinner party back on its proper path again, although it was distinctly more subdued than it had been before Jessica's announcement.

It had been raining steadily all evening, and while they had been at supper the rain had turned to sleet. Jessica and Linton made a dash for the carriage. She had the hood of her velvet cloak pulled over her head. His head was bare and once they were safely inside the carriage she cast a reproachful look toward it, unmistakably bright in the darkness next to her. "You are going to contract pneumonia one day the way you go around bareheaded in all sorts of weather. It isn't even fashionable."

"A little damp isn't going to hurt me," he said with slow amusement.

She raised her hand to his hair. "That is not a little damp," she said severely.

"If I contract pneumonia you will have the pleasure of saying, 'I told you so,' " he replied serenely.

She leaned back and looked at him, but he was only a shadow in the darkness of the coach. "When I first met you I thought you were the most gentle, patient, good-natured man I had ever known. You are also, I have since discovered, obstinate as a pig."

"What an odd simile," he mused thoughtfully.

"Why, I wonder, should pigs be more obstinate than other animals?"

Reluctantly she laughed. "You are impossible."

"My sister tells me I am spoiled rotten," he said in a detached, objective tone.

"You are," she agreed cordially. "And I have no doubt your sister is partly to blame."

He reached out and took her hand. "No. She blames it all on my mother." He pulled her toward him, then slid an arm around her shoulders. Her hood slipped back and his lips found the warm spot just below her ear where he knew she liked to be kissed. "Will you spoil me, Jess?" he murmured.

"Why not?" she whispered in reply. "The damage is already done."

They got back to Montpelier Square at about two in the morning. Jessica had told her maid not to wait up for her, so Linton undid the hooks of her dress. She stepped out of it, smoothed its silk folds, and went to hang it in the wardrobe. He took his own coat off and laid it on a chair. "You gave the finest performance I have ever seen tonight," he said as he slowly undid his shirt. "Are you quite sure you won't miss the stage?"

She took the pins out of her hair. "Quite sure."

There was silence in the room; the only sounds were the crackling of her brush as she pulled it through her loosened hair and the sleet pelting against the window. "Why, Jess?" he said at last. "Why did you do it?"

She thought for a minute, her head bent a little, her

brow grave. "I have been thinking of what you said earlier, about the likelihood of someone recognizing me. And the reasons I gave to Mr. Harris are also true. I enjoyed doing *Macbeth* tonight. I'm glad I did it well. But I don't want to do it again."

"You won't miss it?" he asked again.

She turned on the dressing table chair until she was facing him. His hair was ruffled from her hand, his eyes the intense blue emotion always turned them. "What are you worried about, Philip?" she asked, real puzzlement in her voice. "Do you think I'm going to pine away once I'm removed from the excitement and the applause?"

"Something like that," he replied evenly.

She smiled a litle wryly. "All my life I have been a rather solitary person. I grew up in the country. I am not accustomed to being surrounded by a great number of people. I won't miss it."

"Would you like to live in the country again, Jess?" he asked, and his voice was deadly serious.

She looked at him and her heart ached. He would give her whatever she wanted. She knew that. If she said she wanted to race horses he would buy her a stud. If she wanted to live in the country he would buy her an estate. He would give her anything, except what she wanted most of all. He could not give her that. Any chance she ever had of sharing a normal life with him was gone, irrevocably. She was Jessica O'Neill. An actress. His mistress. There was no way in the world she could ever become his wife. So she smiled around the pain and said, "For now I am happy as I am."

He came and knelt before her. "You will stay here with me?"

She cupped his face between her hands. "Yes."

"I have an idea for the future. Will you trust me to work it out for us?"

"Yes," she said again. She looked into his face, held so lightly between her two hands. "I plan to keep myself very busy," she said softly.

"What are you going to do?"

"Spoil you," she returned, her mouth curving tenderly.

His face took on a look she recognized and her heart began to race. "Are you now?" he said. His hands came up to cover hers and move them to his mouth.

"Yes," Her eyes were held, drowning, in his.

He kissed the palms of her hands. "Good." He rose and pulled her unresisting body up, effortlessly, into his arms. "Then let's go to bed," he said, and once again, with eyes closed this time, she said,

"Yes."

Chapter Sixteen

Yet therein now doth lodge a noble Peer,
Great England's glory, and the world's wide
wonder,
—EDMUND SPENSER

Three weeks later Linton took Jessica with him to dinner at Holland House. Lord Holland had long been one of his favorite friends and whenever Linton was in London he invariably spent a good deal of time at the stately red brick Jacobean mansion in Kensington. The most remarkable men of the time were often to be found crowded around the dinner table at Holland House. There one could find statesmen, writers, artists, and distinguished foreigners. Holland House was the intellectual center of the Whig culture that was Linton's heritage. He enjoyed evenings in the long library, where flourished vigorous and cultivated discussions that could pass from politics to history, from history to literature, with a freedom and intellectual depth to be found nowhere else in England.

Holland House was the only one of the houses he usually visited to which Linton felt he could bring Jessica. Many of the ladies in the highest of London society were notably promiscuous, but there was a subtle line between what society condoned and what it condemned. Jessica had crossed that line when she went on the stage.

Lady Holland, however, was another person who had violated society's rules of decorum. She was a divorced woman. She had run away from her first husband, Sir Godfrey Webster, and had lived with Lord Holland openly before her divorce became final. Although she was hostess to some of the most brilliant gatherings in Europe, she was still not received by the most rigid ladies who ruled the ton. So the rule for an invitation to Holland House was talent, genius, and wit, not social status.

When Linton had asked her if he might bring Jessica she had looked surprised at first but then she readily agreed. The high-handed bossy manner she adopted with most people was noticeably softened whenever Lady Holland spoke to Linton. "By all means, Linton," she had said cordially. "Lord Holland and I shall be happy to have such a brilliant addition to our company."

Lady Holland's surprise was slight compared to Jessica's when Linton told her of the invitation. "You can't be serious," she said incredulously. "I can't go there."

"Why not? You are invited."

"But I'm an *actress,* Philip. I can't be received by society."

"You are not an actress any longer," he replied. "I want you to meet Lord Holland. He is one of my dearest friends. And he wants to meet you. So where is the difficulty?"

"I can't go," she repeated.

"You are going," he said flatly. His jaw was set in a way she had seen only once or twice before. There was a tense pause.

"All right," she capitulated faintly, a trifle bewildered to find herself so helpless and pliant before his determination.

He smiled, his eyes warm with approval. "Good. You'll surprise yourself and have a good time. I promise you."

He was right. Jessica had never experienced anything quite like Holland House. The dining room table was jammed and she ate as best she could, her arms glued to her sides. At one point Lady Holland loudly demanded that Mr. Parkinson change places with Mr. Rogers and both gentlemen complied with much good-natured grumbling. Jessica sat at Lord Holland's right, and her initial nervousness disappeared quite soon under the influence of his infectious good humor.

They spoke about Linton, who was jammed in halfway down the table from them. "It is a pity Philip is so uninterested in politics," Lord Holland said to her. "Lord Grey and I have been trying for years to get him to take a hand, with little success I might add."

"Do you and Philip agree on politics, my lord?" Jessica asked cautiously. She did not think Linton was uninterested in the subject. She did know that Lord Holland headed the Foxite faction of the Whig party. He and Lord Grey had dedicated themselves to the preservation of the ideas and policies of Charles James Fox, who also happened to be Lord Holland's uncle. Charles Fox, however, had been dead for six

127

years, and the world had changed considerably since his demise. Linton might love Lord Holland as a friend but Jessica did not think he loved his friend's politics.

"We have a few minor disagreements," Lord Holland assured her cheerfully. "Philip's concern for his agricultural workers sometimes overbalances his native good sense. But then Lord Grey and I certainly are in favor of reform. There can be little disagreement on that issue."

"I should think not," Jessica murmured quietly.

He raised his black, bushy eyebrows. "Are you a reformer too, Miss O'Neill?"

"I grew up in the country, my lord, so I am aware of the hardships country people are facing these days. The Corn Laws benefit the landowner and large farmer at the expense of everybody else. Farm laborers who are fortunate enough to have an employer like Philip have cottages and gardens where they can grow their own vegetables and keep a pig and some chickens. Those who are not so fortunate live marginal existences on bread, butter, and half-rotten potatoes."

Lord Holland was nodding in agreement. "It is disgraceful, certainly, and all too often the result of cits and commercials buying estates and trying to set themselves up as landed gentry. The country is filled with nabobs, contractors, commissioners, loan-jobbers, retired generals and admirals. They have no care for their own people, as we do. Take Philip for example. He is a nobleman who lives up to his title. He has a great sense of responsibility toward those beneath him or in his charge and he wholeheartedly protects the people who work for him. He is just, charitable, and generous. To want to hand the government of the country from *him* to the likes of a manufacturer from Yorkshire is what I have no patience with."

Jessica gently pointed out that the country was not governed by Philip and his like but by diehard Tories, led by Lord Liverpool, who were adamantly opposed to change of any sort.

"Quite right," replied Lord Holland instantly. "That is why we need Philip to take an active hand in unseating the Tories."

"Why Philip?" she asked.

"Everybody likes him so much," replied Lord Holland promptly. "I hardly know anyone of whom everyone entertains so favorable an opinion."

She smiled at Lord Holland, a flicker of irony in her gray eyes. "Are you asking me to be your recruiter, Lord Holland?"

He smiled easily back, full of the charm and bonhomie that made him so lovable. "Why not, Miss O'Neill? Why not?"

Jessica and Linton drove home late that evening. He was very pleased. He had had ulterior motives for wishing Jessica to venture out to Holland House, and the evening had been a resounding success. Before they left Lady Holland had called him over to her and said in a low voice, "How serious is this, Linton?"

He had laughed, the firelight calling forth sparks of blue from his narrowed eyes. "Very serious," he had said.

"So. She is an unusual girl." There was a little

silence as she continued to look at him. Then she said, "She will always be welcome here."

He took her hand. "Thank you, ma'am." He was very grave now. "We may have need of a friend."

She nodded decisively. "You have one in me. And in Lord Holland as well."

He was thinking of this exchange now as he said to Jessica, "You and Lord Holland seemed to get along like a house on fire."

"What a nice man he is!" she replied warmly.

"He is. What did you talk about?"

"You." Laughter hovered in the corners of her mouth. "He wants me to convince you to go in for politics."

"Oh Lord," he groaned.

"He said lovely things about you."

"He wouldn't say them if he knew my true thoughts about his politics."

"And what are your true thoughts?"

"The Whigs are hopeless at the moment," he said brutally. "There are factions within factions. First there are the Grenvillites, who are just like the Tories only they think Lord Grenville should be prime minister and not old Liverpool. Then there are the Foxites. Did Holland tell you he was in favor of reform?"

She nodded.

"Of course. Just don't ever ask him to put theory into practice. Besides, the Foxites have no use for economics and economics is, of course, the whole point of reform. Then there are the reformers, people like Whitbread and young Grey and Brougham. But they all disagree with each other as well as with the Grenvillites and the Foxites."

"Heavens. It seems as though the opposition party is in opposition to itself."

"The problem is they can discover nothing on which they can agree to unite in opposition."

"Have you spoken to Lord Holland about this?"

He shrugged. "What's the point, Jess? If there were a party for me to join, I'd join it; but it's either the Whigs or the Tories, and I certainly can't become a Tory!"

"But perhaps Lord Holland and the others could agree to compromise?"

He snorted. "Holland and Grey make it a point of honor not to work with anyone they disagree with about anything."

"Oh."

"Precisely. So I keep my mouth pretty well shut. All these people happen to be my friends, you see, and I do like them enormously."

"The world is changing despite them, Philip," she said. "As you once told me, England is turning from an agricultural to a manufacturing country. The economic power is no longer solely in the hands of the landowners. The new holders of the country's wealth, those manufacturers and nabobs Lord Holland spoke so scornfully about, are going to demand their share of the political power as well."

"Of course. And they will get it, eventually. In the meantime I'll just continue to farm."

She reached out and took his hand. "You are one of a rare breed, my lord, do you know that?"

"What breed?" he asked.

"You are a genuinely independent man," she answered. "And I love you."

Linton had bought Jessica a horse, and they had formed the habit of rising early and riding in Hyde Park. There was no one around to frown at them as they galloped hard through the cold February mornings, their breaths hanging white on the chill air. They would return to Montpelier Square, cheeks glowing, to consume an enormous breakfast and to plan their day.

The morning after the dinner at Holland House was no exception to their usual routine, a routine that had all the sanctity of three weeks of practice. They were sitting in the dining room over breakfast when a decided break in that routine occurred. Peter entered the room and said woodenly, "Sir Matthew Selsey to see you, my lord."

Surprise flickered in Linton's eyes. "Show him in here."

"Very good, my lord."

Linton turned to Jessica. "My brother-in-law," he said briefly.

"I'll go." She rose from her seat, but he reached out and his fingers clamped hard on her wrist. "No. I want you to stay." She couldn't pull away from him without a struggle, and there was the sound of steps in the hallway. There was a spark of anger in her clear gray eyes but she sat down. He released her wrist as his brother-in-law came into the room.

"Matt!" He rose and held out his hand. "I didn't even know you were in the country. How is Maria?"

Sir Matthew Selsey was a pleasant-looking man in his middle forties, with brown hair and surprisingly vivid hazel eyes. He took Linton's hand. "I am happy to tell you you have a new niece," he said, his face breaking into a grin.

"Congratulations!" Linton sounded delighted. "Another girl after all those boys. And how is Maria?"

"Fine. I only arrived home a week ago, and she had the baby the next day. It was all the excitement of my unexpected arrival, she said."

Linton laughed, then he turned to Jessica. "I beg your pardon, Jess, but good news often makes me forget my manners. May I present my brother-in-law, Sir Matthew Selsey. Miss Jessica O'Neill, Matt."

Jessica's face wore its aloof, guarded expression, but Sir Matthew smiled at her warmly. "How do you do, Miss O'Neill. Forgive me for breaking in upon you so rudely."

"It is quite all right," she replied. "Will you sit down, Sir Matthew, and have some breakfast?"

"I'll have a cup of coffee, gladly."

He sat down across from her, and Linton said, "I didn't know you were coming back to England."

"I wasn't, originally," Sir Matthew replied, stirring his coffee, "but I found myself getting more and more worried about Maria. This may be our sixth child but after all she *is* thirty-eight even if she doesn't look it. And it has been six years since John." His eyes suddenly twinkled. "Don't ever tell her I said that, Philip."

"I wouldn't dare." They both laughed. "What are you doing in London, Matt?"

"I had to see Castlereagh. I've been in London two days and I'm going back to Selsey this afternoon. Unfortunately I must leave for Vienna next week. Maria and the children will join me in April."

"Have you been staying in Grosvenor Square?"

"Yes."

"Ah." Linton's eyes, full of blue light, rested thoughtfully on his brother-in-law's face.

Sir Matthew's expression remained placid; he was, after all, a diplomat. He turned to Jessica. "Linton's man gave me your direction. I shouldn't have come barging in if I hadn't been so short of time." He gave her his warm smile. "I did want to break the good news myself."

Jessica looked back and then her thin, grave face lit with an answering smile. "Of course you did. It is not every day one has a new daughter. What are you calling her?"

Matt grinned. "The boys wanted to name her Hortense."

Jessica's rich, deep laugh rippled. "Aren't boys wretched?"

"Jess should know," Linton said, amusement in his own voice. "She has two brothers about Matthew's and Lawrence's ages. What name *did* you decide on, Matt?"

"Elizabeth Maria Deborah."

"That's lovely," Jessica said.

"It is my mother's name," Linton told her with a pleased smile.

Sir Matthew stayed for perhaps twenty more minutes, and when he left Linton saw him to the door.

"I can see why you aren't spending your time in Grosvenor Square, Philip," his brother-in-law said. "She is lovely. And—unusual."

"Unusual. That was Lady Holland's word also."

Sir Matthew looked startled. "Lady Holland! Have you taken her to Holland House then?"

"Yes."

Sir Matthew looked at Linton's face and said no more. They shook hands and parted the good friends they had always been. Linton walked back to the dining room where Jessica still sat. "Maria will have it all out of him in half an hour," he said. "Come into the drawing room. I have to talk to you."

Chapter Seventeen

What is love? 'Tis not hereafter,
Present mirth hath present laughter,
What's to come is still unsure.
—WILLIAM SHAKESPEARE

Linton's absence from Grosvenor Square had been noticed by people other than Sir Matthew Selsey. A number of friends, missing him at the club, had called at Linton House to be informed by a wooden-faced butler that "Lord Linton is not in." Nor, it appeared, was he expected.

Lord George Litcham was one of the first to take serious alarm. He had spent as much time as anyone in the company of Linton and Jessica, and he was not insensitive. After a great deal of thought he broached the matter to Bertram Romney.

"Worried about Philip?" said that young man. "I don't understand you, Litcham. Dash it all, Jessica isn't one of those avaricious harpies who take a man for all he's worth. And even if she were it wouldn't matter. Linton is too rich to be fleeced like that."

"I know she isn't one of that breed, Romney," replied Lord George. "That is precisely what worries me. She is different. *They* are different." He hesitated. "I am very much afraid Linton is serious about her."

"Serious?"

Lord George said patiently, like a man talking to a very small child, "I am afraid he means to marry her."

Bertram's eyes widened. "He couldn't."

"I don't know," Lord George said slowly.

There was a very long silence. "We need my cousin, Maria Selsey," Bertram finally said. "She scares me half to death, but she'll know what to do."

"I thought Lady Maria was expecting a child any day now."

"Burn it, so she is! Isn't that just like a woman? As soon as she has a chance to make herself useful she's indisposed."

"What about Lady Linton?" Lord George asked, ignoring Bertram's strictures on the opposite sex.

Bertram looked unhappy. "Dash it all, my Aunt Elizabeth thinks the sun rises and sets on Linton's head. What am I to do? Write and tell her he is in danger of marrying his mistress? Which I'm not at all sure he is, by the way." There was a little silence as Bertram looked at the paper lying on his table. "Besides, she's a first-rate girl, Jess. I like her."

"I know," said Lord George. "So do I. And that, Romney, is the problem."

In the end they decided that Bertram would write a letter to his own mother asking her to come up to town for a week or two. "Very sensible woman, my mother," Bertram had assured Lord George. "She likes Philip. If he needs rescuing she'll be glad to lend her assistance. I'm sure of it."

* * *

137

Others were not so considerate of the delicate state of Lady Maria or the fond motherly heart of Lady Linton. Both of these ladies received missives from various friends who were staying in London at present and who found Linton's behavior sufficiently odd to inspire a report to his womenfolk. At first they had shrugged off the letters as gossip, then they had been angry, finally they became alarmed.

"Look at this, mother," Maria said two mornings before her baby was born. "A letter from Emily Cowper."

"About Philip?" asked Lady Linton, anxiety in her voice.

"Not *about* Philip. Emily is too polite for that. She merely *mentions* Philip, but her comments are very much to the point."

They were sitting in the morning parlor at Selsey Place, and now Lady Linton laid down her pen and put aside the letter she had been writing. "What does she say?"

"I saw Linton yesterday," Maria read. "It was a wretched, rainy day but I had to go to Worth's for a fitting and as I was on my way home I passed him and Miss O'Neill as they were coming out of the park. They had evidently been riding in the rain, something I wouldn't do if my life depended upon it. But they were both laughing—even with water streaming down their faces! He is as handsome as ever, Maria, even waterlogged. I don't see him at all socially, so perhaps you can write to ascertain if he has caught pneumonia or not." Maria looked up. "Then she goes on to something else." She closed the letter. "I don't like it, mother. Emily would not have written to me if she hadn't thought I should know what is going on."

"But what *is* going on, Maria?" asked Lady Linton. "Philip has a mistress. He has had mistresses before and no one got upset like this."

"He is living with her," Maria said slowly. "Evidently he is never at Grosvenor Square. And you heard what Emily Cowper wrote. He isn't going out socially. From what I can gather he spends all his time with this actress."

"But what can we do?" asked Lady Linton.

"I think you should go up to London, mother," Lady Maria said decisively.

But Lady Linton refused to leave her daughter at such a critical time, and the next day Sir Matthew Selsey came home. In the end he was the one charged with "finding out what Philip is up to."

Sir Matthew had not been overly pleased about his commission. He had a great deal of liking and an equally great deal of respect for his brother-in-law and was quite positive that jealous gossip was at the root of all the reports that had been reaching Selsey Place. But he had to go up to London anyway, so he placated his wife by assuring her that he would look into the matter.

After two days at Grosvenor Square he had not been so sanguine. Then he had a conversation with Bertram's mother, a woman whose good sense he had always respected. The fact that Bertram, a careless young scamp if ever he saw one, had seen fit to call in his mother sounded an alarm to Sir Matthew immediately. An alarm Mrs. Romney herself did little to soften.

."He is getting himself talked about," Mrs. Romney said frankly. "And that is something Linton never did before. You can see them frequently at the opera and at the theatre. Of course he can't take her into good company, but neither does he take her into the sort of company she *could* frequent." She raised her eyes and looked at Sir Matthew very soberly. They were seated in the drawing room of the house of Lady Marchmain, Mrs. Romney's sister with whom Mrs. Romney was staying during this brief visit to London. She had written asking Sir Matthew to visit her as soon as she had heard he was in town. "I've met her," she said to him now.

He said nothing, but his brows rose a trifle.

"At the opera," she replied to his silent query. "I made Bertram take me to their box."

"My dear ma'am!" protested Sir Matthew.

"Oh, we were very discreet," Mrs. Romney assured him. "We all stood at the back of the box, almost in the corridor."

"What did Philip do when you appeared?"

"I think he was glad to see me. He introduced Miss O'Neill immediately."

"Did he?" said Sir Matthew slowly. "And what did you think of her, ma'am?"

"She's striking. And well-bred. And proud. And there is something very serious between her and Linton."

He frowned. "How can you say that?"

"It's hard to explain, Matthew, but I am not mistaken." She frowned a little herself in the effort to explain what she meant. "Linton was charming—you know how he can be when he exerts himself. And she was pleasant, if a little reserved. But I felt almost as if I were intruding. Not because they didn't want to see me. I told you earlier I think Linton was glad of an opportunity to introduce her. But it is as if the bond between them is so strong that it keeps everyone else at a distance, even though they don't mean it to."

Sir Matthew had come away from Lady Marchmain's considerably perturbed. It was his conversation with Mrs. Romney that had precipitated his descent on Montpelier Square. It was a visit that left him, if possible, even more concerned.

It took, in fact, forty-five minutes for Lady Maria to elicit the main reasons for Sir Matthew's concern.

"He took her to Holland House?" she asked incredulously.

"I've already told you that, Maria."

"And introduced her to Catherine Romney?"

"Yes."

Maria was reclining on a chaise longue in her bedroom, and she had moved her legs aside to make room for her husband to sit. Her pale hair was tied loosely back from her face and she wore a foamy sea green negligee. She most emphatically did not look thirty-eight years old. "What do you think, Matt?" she asked now directly.

"I think Philip is in love with this girl," he answered gravely.

There was a pause. "Damn!" said Lady Maria.

"Yes."

Her green eyes narrowed. "You don't think he is planning anything foolish?"

He shook his head. "I don't know. She is an extraordinary girl, Maria. A person to be reckoned with."

"How does she feel about him?"

He smiled a little crookedly. "Can you imagine any woman, however extraordinary, who could resist your brother when he sets out to charm?"

"Oh dear," she said in a suddenly small voice.

"And of course it is much more than that," he went on. "He made it very clear how he expected her to be treated. He was completely pleasant but he was there, like a rock, between her and any possible familiarity or insult." He sighed a little wearily. "I had no idea what the diplomatic corps was missing in Philip."

"He can't possibly mean to marry her?" said Maria in a horrified voice.

"I don't know what he means, my love," replied her husband. "But I certainly wouldn't rule it out."

Chapter Eighteen

But ah, to kiss and then to part!—
How deep it struck, speak, gods, you know
Kisses make men loath to go.
—THOMAS CAMPION

Jessica was unaware of the furor her relationship with Linton was causing in the breasts of his family and friends. She had too many other things on her mind.

At first, after her final appearance in *Macbeth,* she had just relaxed and given herself up to the joy of being with him. It was too constant a pain to be continually dwelling on the inevitable future, so she shut it out and lost herself in the richness of her union with him. It was so sweet and satisfying to be with him, to love and to know herself loved in return. There had never been anyone to whom she could talk as she talked to him. And when they were silent it was the comfortable, sustaining silence of deep intimacy, a silence that was sometimes more communicative than words.

But this cocoonlike state of mind could not last. On February 4 she got a statement from her bank saying her monthly allowance had been paid into her account. She sat in front of the desk where she kept her accounts and looked at her figures. With a bitter, searing pain in her heart she realized that she had the mortgage money. The next month's allowance would pay the interest. Winchcombe would be clear and she could go home. She would have to go home.

For a short time she sat at the desk, eyes closed, wishing uselessly, hopelessly, achingly, that she had not. But she could not stay on here indefinitely as Linton's mistress. She had the boys to consider. And herself. She had felt morally justified to do what she was doing because of her dire necessity. Once that necessity was removed her actions would have to be viewed in quite another light and she wasn't sure if she could face up to the picture that would be presented to her then.

There was also a final and overriding fact that made her leaving him an absolute necessity. She was sure she was with child.

When she had missed her menses at the end of December she had not been greatly concerned. She had missed occasionally before and had always assumed it was because of the hard, active life she led. She was working hard in the theatre as well. She had not been overly disturbed. She had had faith in Mrs. Brereton's herbs.

Then she missed in January as well. She had never gone two months before. And her breasts were larger and very tender. With a tightness of fear in her chest she realized what the probable cause of these symptoms was.

Her first reaction had been panic. She had heard talk among the actresses she worked with. There was probably something she could do about getting rid of it.

But the more she thought about it the more impossible such a course of action became. What am I going to do with it? one part of her mind asked. How am I going to explain? But—a child, the other part answered. Philip's child. And her hand went, unconsciously, to her stomach. I may lose Philip, but I will have his child, she thought. And suddenly, fiercely, she knew she wanted this child, would fight to keep it. I can tell them at home that I was married, she thought. I'll think of some story. They still won't need to know the truth.

Nor could she tell the truth to Linton. She didn't know what he would do but she was quite sure he would do something. She didn't want the status quo upset. She wanted her last month with him. She wanted her memories that would have to last her for a very long time. For the rest of her life, in fact.

And then he took her to Holland House. And the next morning Sir Matthew Selsey came to Montpelier Square. And Linton said, "Come into the drawing room. I have to talk to you."

She went with him, a puzzled look in her eyes. But she obediently sat down on the sofa he indicated, folded her hands in her lap, and gazed up at him as he stood before the mantel.

He looked tense. A muscle flickered once in the angle of his jaw, and she frowned. "What is it, Philip?"

"Jess." His voice was deeper than usual. "How much do you love me?"

She looked at him in silence for a moment, her large eyes steady on the cleanly sculptured face she knew better than her own. "If you don't know the answer to that question by now you never will," she answered quietly at last.

"I want you to marry me," he said.

There was a moment of stunned silence before she answered. "What did you say?" She sounded as if the breath had been knocked out of her.

He crossed the room to kneel before her, taking her cold hand in his two large, warm ones and looking compellingly into her eyes. "I want you to marry me," he repeated.

She closed her eyes so he should not see the longing she knew must be there. "It is not possible," she breathed.

"Why not?" She did not answer, and he held her hand more tightly. "Look at me, Jess!" he said strongly. "Why not?"

Her eyes opened. She ran her tongue over lips that were suddenly dry. She looked into the face she loved and her heart began to slam in slow painful strokes. His eyes were intensely blue, brimming with a fierce purpose that frightened her. "We can live at Staplehurst," he said. "You won't have to come to London if you don't want to. You'll like Staplehurst. And we shall be together."

Weakly, she shook her head. "You would be disgraced if you married me. What of your mother? Your sister? They would be horrified. They must be wondering already. That is why they sent Sir Matthew, isn't it?" He didn't answer, and she went on. "You don't even know who I am."

"I don't care who you are." His voice was quiet but there was a note in it Jessica recognized. She shivered, feeling herself bending to his will, vulnerable and disarmed as only he could leave her. She needed time to think. She knew what she wanted to do. She had to decide what it was she ought to do. She made a small negative movement with her head and he said, "I love you."

"Philip." She leaned forward and pressed her face against the hardness of his shoulder. He locked his arms tightly around her body and held her to him.

"Marry me, Jess," he said softly.

"I need to think about it," she said, her voice muffled.

His jaw tightened, but his voice remained quiet. "Don't think for too long, will you?"

She stayed where she was, her body pressed tightly against his. "No," she said. "I love you."

"I know you do," he answered. "The thing to keep in mind is that I feel the same way about you."

At Selsey Place Lady Maria held a council of war with her husband and her mother. "You say Philip took her to Holland House?" Lady Linton asked her son-in-law.

"Yes."

"And Catherine Romney says she is worried." put in Lady Maria. "Mother, you must go up to London! It simply isn't like Philip to behave like this."

"No. It is not like him at all," replied Lady Linton. There was a faint line between her delicate brows. "I have made it a rule never to interfere in Philip's affairs, but I think this time is different. I will go up to London."

"When?" asked her daughter.

"Tomorrow morning," said Lady Linton. "If you will excuse me I'll tell Weber to pack."

At about the same time that Lady Maria was speaking to her husband and mother, Mrs. Romney received a note that surprised her greatly. "Could you possibly meet me in one hour's time at the British Museum?" it read. "There is something of great importance that I must discuss with you. I shall be looking at the Townley collection. Jessica O'Neill."

An hour and fifteen minutes later Mrs. Romney came up to Jessica as she stood gazing intently at a Greek statue. "Miss O'Neill?" she said in her quiet, cultured voice.

Jessica's head turned quickly. Her cheeks flushed, then went very pale. 'Thank you for coming." The room was empty, and Jessica gestured to a bench along one of the walls. "If you will be seated for a few moments I will tell you why I asked you to come."

Mrs. Romney moved obediently to the proffered seat and Jessica sat down next to her. "I need some advice," she said, her eyes fixed straight ahead of her. "Lord Linton has asked me to marry him." She spoke in a low, steady voice; her hands were clasped tightly together in her lap.

Mrs. Romney felt as though a bolt of lightning had

just shot through her. It was one thing to entertain certain fears and quite another to have them so baldly confirmed. Catherine Romney had a deep affection for Lord Linton's mother and a great deal of respect for Linton himself. She resolved to do what she could to save him from this disastrously unwise marriage he had evidently set himself on. She looked at Jessica. "And what have you answered him?" she asked cautiously.

"I told him I needed time to think about it." Jessica's gray eyes were dark as they turned to regard Mrs. Romney gravely. "He has told me that a marriage between us is possible. I have come to you to ask if that is so."

There was a moment's silence as Mrs. Romney looked consideringly at Jessica. Her first thought had been that the girl wanted money, but now she was not so sure. It was entirely possible that what she had said was true, that her answer to Linton would depend on what Mrs. Romney told her. "If you love him," she said flatly, her eyes holding the gray ones of the girl, "you will not marry him."

Jessica's eyes fell. "I see," she said quietly.

"I wonder if you do. If you marry him it will bring inexpressible dismay to all those who are bound to him by ties of blood. You will rob him of all his friends and degrade him in the eyes of his peers. If you love him you will not subject him to such a sorrow."

It was a full minute before Jessica replied and when she did her voice was perfectly normal. "You may put your mind at rest, Mrs. Romney. I will not marry him to have him disgraced and rejected by his own people." She turned her proud head toward the woman seated next to her. "Thank you for coming and for your advice. It was not unexpected."

Catherine Romney looked back at the carefully shuttered face of the girl Linton loved. "I am sorry, my dear." She spoke quite gently, now that she had won.

"So am I," replied Jessica, politely, distantly.

"I shall say nothing of this interview to Linton."

"No."

Mrs. Romney rose to leave. She hesitated. "How will you tell him?" she asked.

"I won't have the courage to tell him," said Jessica, her voice very even and quiet and almost concealing the underlying note of bitterness. "I shall simply go away and leave him a letter."

Catherine Romney's face looked relieved. "That will be best," she agreed. She hesitated for another moment, then turned and walked quickly out of the room. Jessica remained seated for perhaps ten more minutes, and then she, too, rose and walked steadily out the door and down to the carriage that was to take her back to Montpelier Square.

Chapter Nineteen

Love is a law, a discord of such force
   That twixt our sense and reason makes divorce.
                —ANONYMOUS

They had dinner at home that evening. Linton had been out when Jessica returned to Montpelier Square and she had spent an hour lying quietly on her bed conducting a private and unpleasant inventory. Her conversation with Mrs. Romney had merely confirmed what she had known all along. She could not marry Linton. There was no path that pride, regard, convention, self-respect, and conscience did not block. Nor could she remain with him until March as she had originally planned. He would not wait that long for her answer. And she was afraid to lie and tell him she would marry him. She no longer trusted her ability to deceive him.

She would have to sell the necklace, she decided ruthlessly. That would more than pay for the interest she owed Mr. King. She would do it tomorrow, she thought, despair like dust in her throat. There was no point in prolonging this agony any longer.

Linton was in a carefree mood that evening. He had spent a few hours that afternoon discussing a Reform Bill with Mr. Grey and he was delighted at the thought of returning soon to Staplehurst. He told Jessica all about his home during dinner and she smiled and listened and encouraged him, all the while knowing in her heart she would never see it.

They went into the drawing room after dinner and she asked him a few more questions, the questions of someone curious about a place she is soon to visit. He was sitting in his favorite chair in front of the fire and she sat across from him, her eyes hungry on his strong, cleanly planed face, her ears drinking in the sound of his deep yet curiously soft voice. She watched the brilliant blue of his eyes, the laughter at the corner of his mouth. Philip, she said silently to herself, over and over. Philip.

The tea tray came in, and as she made the tea and handed him a cup the thought came to her that she would ask nothing more out of life than this, that she should sit just so every night and make him his tea. If she could only stop time and hold this moment forever, she thought. Silence had fallen, but it was the rich silence of deep, inarticulate companionship. He put down his cup and smiled at her, long and lazily. "Let's go to bed," he said.

She slept very little that night. She lay quietly against his hard body, and the pain within her was almost unendurable. One more day, she told herself. I will pay off the mortgage tomorrow and buy a ticket on the mail. The day after tomorrow I shall go.

Toward morning she fell asleep and so did not hear him when he got up. She woke as he came back, fully dressed, into the bedroom. "What time is it?" she asked.

He laughed at her. "Eight-thirty, sleepy one. I have an engagement to talk to a man about buying apples and I probably won't see you until after lunch."

"Why do you want to buy apples?" she asked, puzzlement and sleep clogging her voice.

He grinned. "I don't want to buy apples, I want to sell them. My agent has written me about this fellow, so I think I had better see him while I'm here in London." He crossed to the bed and leaned over, kissing her hard and fierce and quick. "I'll see you later," he murmured, his mouth still lightly touching hers. "And I'll want an answer."

"Yes." She watched as he walked away from her and out of the room, and lay back against her pillows once more, her eyes closed.

She transacted her business without difficulty. Mr. King was not happy to see his loan repaid so promptly. He would have liked to have gotten his hands on Winchcombe, but the interest he had made was ample and he was quite pleasant to Jessica.

Her encounter with Mr. King had been far more comfortable than an encounter she had had with Lord Alden earlier in the day. She had been coming out of Hoare's Bank just as Lord Alden was alighting from his phaeton.

"Miss O'Neill. What an unexpected pleasure." His strange greenish eyes had glinted between half-closed lids, and Jessica found herself repressing a slight shudder. There was something about this man that gave her a physical and moral chill.

"Lord Alden," she said, nodded curtly, and made to walk past him. He stepped in front of her.

"The theatre has sorely missed your presence," he said in his silky voice, and looked at her with eyes that undressed her.

Jessica felt her temper rising. "Indeed?" she replied coldly. "If you will excuse me, my lord, I must be going."

"Have you thought of my offer at all?" he asked.

"No."

His eyes narrowed even more until they were barely slits in his masklike face. "I see I have in Linton a formidable rival."

Jessica's eyes were gray ice. "There is not even a contest," she said, and pushed past him to walk to her waiting carriage.

She had arrived home in time for lunch. Linton came in about three o'clock and they decided to go for a ride in the park. When Jessica came downstairs dressed in her riding habit she found him in the hall holding a piece of notepaper in his hand. There was a slight frown between his golden brows, but his forehead smoothed as he looked up and saw her. "I'm afraid I'm going to have to bow out of our ride, Jess. I've just gotten a note from my mother. She is in town. I'll have to go and see her."

"Of course," she answered quietly.

He stood absorbed in thought for a moment and the frown crept back between his brows. "I'll be back tomorrow before lunch," he said then, decisively. "Don't look for me tonight."

"All right." Her voice gave no hint of the desolation that had just swept through her. She would not see him again.

He bent over and lightly kissed her cheek. "Chin up, darling," he murmured, then he left.

"Will you still be wanting your horse, Miss O'Neill?" the butler asked her.

"No. I mean, yes," she answered. After all, she had to do something to fill in the hours until tomorrow morning.

She did not sleep at all that night. The mail coach to Cheltenham was not leaving until eleven in the morning, and at six-thirty she rose, put on her riding habit, and walked around to the stables. She felt she had to get out of the house for a while. The hours of the night had been interminable.

Jerry, the groom who usually looked after her horse, was not around, so Jessica saddled the black mare herself. As she was leading Windswept out of the stable Francis, the young boy who assisted in the stable work, appeared with a bucket of water. Jessica smiled at him. "I am taking Windswept for a ride in the park. I shan't be gone more than an hour."

"Yes, ma'am," the boy said, and watched as she walked the horse out of the yard.

Twenty minutes later Jerry appeared. "Where's the mare?" he asked.

"The lady took him out," returned his subordinate.

Jerry swore with picturesque amplitude. "That

mare has a loose shoe," he explained as he saddled Linton's horse. "She came in with it yesterday. I'd better go after her or she's going to have to walk home." He finished saddling Linton's bay stallion, vaulted into the saddle, and clattered out of the stableyard. He was a block from Hyde Park when he saw Jessica coming out through the gate leading Windswept. "I knew it," he muttered to himself and prepared to urge the bay into a canter when he saw a carriage stop in front of Jessica. He pulled up for a minute, and as he watched a dark-haired man in evening dress got out. He turned to say something to the groom who rode beside the driver on the box, and the man jumped down and went to take the horse from Jessica. She appeared to be arguing with the man and Jerry again began to walk the bay down the street toward her. Then, with a suddenness that stunned him, the tall man opened the coach door, grabbed Jessica ruthlessly, and thrust her inside. She screamed once; then the coach door closed and drove briskly off.

Jerry pulled the bay stallion up once more. The groom holding Jessica's horse began to walk it slowly away, and Jerry looked carefully at his livery, memorizing the colors and markings. Then he turned the bay and rode as fast as he could through the London streets to Grosvenor Square.

Linton's meeting with his mother had not been comfortable for Lady Linton. She had spoken the truth when she had told Maria that she never interfered in her son's affairs. But there were times, she had thought to herself as she waited in the Grosvenor

Square house for Linton to present himself, when one was justified in interfering. If the circumstances were such that a loved one's actions were sure to be ruinous, then coercion from the outside was needed. And she was here to apply that coercion.

They had passed the afternoon pleasantly enough. It was after dinner, as they sat in the drawing room before a warm fire, that Lady Linton introduced the subject that had brought her to London. "When are you coming home to Staplehurst, Philip?" she asked.

His long fingers were laced together, and he regarded her over them thoughtfully. "Very soon now, mother. And I shall be bringing my wife home with me."

"So it is true," his mother said slowly. "You are serious about this Jessica O'Neill."

"Yes."

Lady Linton looked at the shining blond head of her beloved son and then into the brilliant blue of his eyes. She recognized the look his face wore. Under so much that was gentle, patient, and civilized Linton had passions that were fiercely strong and tenacious. When he gave his love and his loyalty he did not change. If he really loved this girl . . . "What do you know about this Jessica O'Neill, Philip?" she asked quietly. "What is her family? I did not think I would ever have to remind you of this but you have a duty to your own family, to your name and to the ancient rank you carry. An Earl of Linton may not do as he pleases, as may another man."

A gleam had come into those very blue eyes of his. "No, mother, you do not have to remind me of who I am." His voice was kept, with perceptible effort, quiet and ordinary. "Miss O'Neill is a woman that even an Earl of Linton would be proud to call his wife."

"So you think, my son. There are others who will think differently."

"If you are one of those others I shall be sorry, mother," he replied steadily.

She leaned forward, pleadingly, in her chair. "Philip, think about what you are doing. Please."

"I have thought about it," he returned. "My mind is made up."

They had separated for the night not long after that. Linton had not slept well in his solitary bed, and when a footman came into him at a little after seven-thirty he was wide awake. "My lord," the servant said hesitatingly, relieved at least not to be waking him. "There is a groom here from Montpelier Square. He insists he must see you immediately. He says it is an emergency."

Linton threw back his covers. "Show him up." When Jerry entered the vast bedroom a few minutes later he found the Earl of Linton with his hair tousled and wearing a dressing gown. "What has happened?" Linton asked curtly.

Jerry told him what he had seen. He described the servant's livery. Linton swore. "Alden!" he said grimly. "He lives in Mount Street. I'll go at once." His eyes, filled with a cold blue light, briefly rested on his groom's face. "Thank you. You were right to come to me." He nodded, and Jerry backed hastily out of the room. He was glad he wasn't the one who was going to have to face the Earl when he had that look in his eyes.

It took Linton fifteen minutes to get to Mount Street. He left his groom holding the reins of his phaeton and ran up the steps of Alden's house. He tried the door and, surprisingly, found it open. He entered and made a swift search of the downstairs rooms. There was no one around. He took the steps two at a time, and at the sound of a man's voice he halted outside an upstairs door. Then Jessica spoke.

Linton tried the door, and this one was locked. "Open up, Alden," he said clearly, "or I'll shoot the lock off."

He heard Jessica cry, "Philip!" and then the door opened. She was standing at the far side of the room. Her hair had loosened and was falling on her shoulders. Her lip was cut; he could see blood on it. And she held a poker in her hand. A slow white rage took possession of Linton.

"Are you all right?" he asked her.

"Yes." She put down the poker and ran across the room to him. "Thank God you came, though."

"One of the grooms saw the incident." He turned from her to look at the man standing midway across the room. Alden took two steps back as he met that gaze.

"I didn't touch her, Linton," he said. "There's no need to look so grim."

"Go downstairs and wait for me," Linton said to Jessica.

She hesitated, looked at his face, and went. She walked halfway down the stairs then stopped. She had never seen Linton look like that. Suddenly she was afraid, even more afraid than she had been earlier. What was Philip going to do? She began to run back up the stairs. When she was nearly at the top her foot caught in the carelessly held-up length of her riding skirt. She felt herself losing her balance and grabbed for the rail. She missed and cried out as she toppled slowly, helplessly, down the long, elegant staircase.

The next thing she knew was Linton's face, bent over hers. From a long distance away she could hear his voice. He was calling her name. She made a great effort. "Yes?"

"Are you all right, Jess?" His face had come into focus for her now. He looked frightened. "Can you move?"

Slowly she tried to sit up. "Yes," she said again. She moved her legs. Her body was aching all over and her head hurt, but she could move. He bent and lifted her in strong arms and, gratefully, she rested her face against his shoulder. "My friends will call on yours, Alden," she heard him say, and then he strode out the front door, still holding her tightly in his arms.

Chapter Twenty

If I could shut the gate against my thoughts
   And keep out sorrow from this room within
Or memory could cancel all the notes
   Of my misdeeds, and I unthink my sin.
                                        —ANONYMOUS

As soon as they reached Montpelier Square Linton
sent for the doctor. Dr. Bayer's diagnosis was that
Jessica was painfully bruised and might have a slight
concussion, but he didn't think any permanent damage had been done. He prescribed some medicine
which caused Jessica to fall asleep almost immediately. She slept all through the day and did not
awaken until eleven the following morning.

By then Linton had put a bullet through the Mar-
quis of Alden's shoulder.

Lord George Litcham had tried to dissuade Linton
from calling Alden out, but his words had fallen on
deaf ears. "If you won't act for me, I'll get someone
who will," said Linton relentlessly.

So Lord George had made the arrangements, and
at six o'clock in the morning Linton and Alden had
met out at Paddington and Linton had relieved his

feelings by shooting Alden neatly through his right shoulder. Lord George had been enormously relieved. He had been afraid Linton had meant to kill Alden.

At two o'clock in the afternoon, as Linton was sitting on Jessica's bed watching her try to eat some soup, Lord George was presenting himself in Grosvenor Square. Lady Linton had heard about the duel.

Lord George started by pleading ignorance, but the look in Lady Linton's sapient blue eyes soon put him to rout. It wasn't long before he was telling her the whole story. It took a stronger man than Lord George to hold out against the combined charm and concern of Linton's mother.

"Evidently Alden was coming home after a night on the town," Lord George told her. "I doubt if he was sober. Well, stands to reason—how could he have been? Well, as he was driving by the park out came Miss O'Neill leading her horse. Alden stopped the carriage and got out. I imagine it looked like a perfect opportunity to him. From what he said I gather she had refused several offers from him; and not in a manner calculated to flatter him. He was after a little revenge it seems." Here Lord George recruited himself with a sip of sherry. Lady Linton said nothing. She just sat still and waited.

"So he pushed her into his carriage and forced her into his house. She evidently delayed him for some time by pretending to reconsider his offer. Then, when matters got serious, she grabbed the poker. That was when Linton arrived."

"I see."

"I have never seen Philip that angry. Never. There was no talking to him. I'm only glad he settled for Alden's shoulder."

"I'm glad it wasn't Philip who got shot," said Lady Linton tartly.

"Oh, there was never any fear of that," returned Lord George. "Linton is deadly with the pistols. You should have seen Alden's face. He was sick as a horse at having to face Philip. Of course there was nothing else he could do."

"Men!" said Lady Linton with scornful contempt. "As if a duel could ever solve anything. What does Miss O'Neill think of all this?"

"I doubt if she knows. You see she fell down the stairs at Alden's house and knocked herself out. The doctor gave her a sleeping draught and she was still sleeping this morning. Philip went right back to Montpelier Square after the meeting but I doubt if he'll tell her about it. I'm quite sure she wouldn't like it."

"She fell down the stairs? Is she hurt?"

"Not badly, thank God. If she had been seriously injured I really think Linton would have killed Alden."

"Well, I suppose we must be grateful for small blessings," snapped Lady Linton and dismissed the uncomfortable Lord George.

When Jessica awoke the next morning she felt achy and heavyheaded, which she put down to the aftereffects of Dr. Bayer's sleeping draught. The doctor came to see her again at about noon and recommended that she spend the rest of the day in bed. She alarmed Linton by submitting to the doctor's edict with scarcely a murmur.

By late afternoon she felt hot and ill, and when Linton felt her forehead it was cold with sweat. Once more he sent for the doctor. He was deathly afraid she had seriously injured her head in the fall, and when the doctor came slowly into the downstairs salon after seeing Jessica, Linton asked him sharply, "Is it brain fever?"

Dr. Bayer looked surprised. "No, my lord. It has nothing to do with her head. Indeed, if I had known about Miss O'Neill's condition I would have warned you this might happen. That was a very nasty fall she took."

"Her condition?" said Linton.

The doctor glanced at his face and then quickly looked away. "Miss O'Neill is three months pregnant. She is having a miscarriage."

"Will she be all right?" the Earl asked at last, his voice unusually harsh.

"Yes. It should be over soon, my lord. I'll stay with her."

"Is there anything you can do?"

"To save the child? No, my lord," the doctor's voice was firm but gentle. "She asked me the same thing. There is nothing to be done now, I'm afraid."

"I see."

The doctor returned upstairs, and about an hour

and a half later one of the servants came to tell Linton he could come upstairs if he wanted to.

The initial shock of the doctor's revelation to Linton had given way to a deep, quiet fury. He bitterly regretted his duel of that morning. He wished passionately that he had known then what he knew now. "I would have killed the bastard," he grated between clenched teeth. As he walked up the stairs to Jessica's room he felt that his limbs and movements were rigid with the anger that possessed him. He stopped outside her door for a minute to school his features; then he went in.

Jessica was lying quietly in bed; the doctor was standing by the window. The room was immaculate; there was no sign of what had just happened. Her head turned at the sound of the door opening. She saw him and her eyes suddenly came to life in the tired gray mask of her face. He stood still in the doorway for a long moment, his eyes on that face. He felt a wrench at his heart, so painful he could swear it was physical. Then everything inside him broke up, broke down and gave way, and he was sitting on the side of the bed holding her in his arms, his face buried in her hair. She began to cry, deep, hard sobs, and he held her closer, giving her the only comfort he could, the knowledge of his own grief and love.

Dr. Bayer ordered Jessica to stay in bed for four days, and she obeyed. She felt drained and empty, incapable of a thought that projected beyond the next hour. She had lost her baby. She could not bear to contemplate yet the loss of her love.

Linton was infinitely gentle with her. The blind fury that he had lived with since first he heard of her kidnapping had left him. He could not help Jessica by his anger. He had realized that as soon as he had seen her face. And she needed him. The fierce protectiveness that she had always aroused in him was his main emotion at present. It was why he asked her no questions, talked only of trivial, unemotional topics, and most of all gave her the steady comfort of his undemanding physical presence.

Lady Linton had not seen her son since he had left the house to rescue Jessica. He had written her a brief note telling her about Jessica's miscarriage. She had known he would have been happy had she come to Montpelier Square, but, holding fast to the news she had had from Mrs. Romney, the Countess had kept herself aloof. It seemed as if Linton's family did not need to save him from Jessica O'Neill, as the girl was prepared to do that herself. Lady Romney felt a pang of pity for Jessica, who obviously did love her son, but she did not want to do anything that might cause the actress to change her mind. If she thought Linton's mother would countenance such a marriage she might very well change her mind. So Lady Linton stayed away.

Her absence was not unnoticed by either Jessica or Linton, although it was unremarked upon. Linton was sorry. He did not want to cause a breach with his mother, but if she would not accept Jessica then a breach there would be.

Lady Linton's absence was far more bitter to Jessica. The Countess's judgment had been correct. Had she appeared in Montpelier Square Jessica would have weakened and allowed Linton to persuade her to agree to what her heart so sorely wanted. But his mother's absence said loudly that she was not prepared to accept such a marriage, and Jessica, as the days went by, was forced to realize that nothing had changed.

She had left home six months ago, and in that half-year's time her whole life had altered. She thought back now to the arrogant, innocent girl she had been. Not for her the sitting back and allowing destiny to take its course. Not for her a convenient marriage to some unknown, boorish, rich man. It was all right for other, less proud, less determined women. Not for her. Not for Jessica Andover.

She would take her fate into her own hands. She would dare to do what few women of her class would do. She would dare to stand alone.

She thought now she would have been wiser to marry Sir Henry Belton. He, at least, would never have been able to touch her. It might not have been a happy life, but there would not have been the soul-deep loneliness she knew was in her future now. It would be so hard to go on without him.

A week after the miscarriage she told Linton she wanted the carriage to go shopping. He was delighted. It was the first sign she had shown of coming out of the fog of depression that had gripped her all week. "Buy yourself some wedding clothes," he told her.

"We'll be married next week and go down to Staplehurst after."

She didn't go shopping at all. She bought a ticket for the next day's mail to Cheltenham.

Chapter Twenty-One

Philip, the cause of all this woe, my life's content,
farewell!
— FULKE GREVILLE

It was just one more sleepless night out of a host of others, this, the last night she would lie beside him in the dark. She listened to his quiet, even breathing and thought how his nearness only made the pain the sharper. She was lying perfectly still, but quite suddenly she heard his voice. "Are you awake, Jess?" She moved her head a little, unable to speak, and then she was in his arms. "Don't grieve so, my darling," he said softly. "We must begin to think of the future now."

It was precisely the thought of the future that was causing her grief, but she couldn't tell him that. She clung to him. "Hold me, Philip. Love me."

His lips were against her temple. "I'm afraid I'll hurt you."

"I need you," she said in a strangled whisper.

"Jess . . ." His mouth came down over hers and his hands were gentle upon her and for the moment the loneliness receded as she gave herself to his growing passion. "Am I hurting you?" he asked.

She shook her head, and her voice was deep and

husky when she answered, "I love it when you come into me like this."

"God . . ." The careful restrictions he had been imposing on himself fell at her words, and they moved together with the urgency and hunger of a desperate need. When at last they lay quietly, satisfied and peaceful, she raised her hand and ran it lightly through his hair.

"I wanted a little boy with corn-colored hair and bright blue eyes," she said.

His body was still half covering hers and he smiled now and rubbed his rough cheek against her smooth one. "You'll have him," he promised. "And I'll have my red-headed little girl. We have years ahead of us to make a whole army of children."

She answered the only part of his speech that she could. "I don't have red hair."

He laughed. "Go to sleep, Jess." He turned her on her side and pulled her into the curve of his own body and she slept.

He wasn't there when she awoke, for which she was profoundly grateful. She had a cup of coffee, got dressed, and sat down to write him a letter. Then she ordered the carriage and had it take her to Madame Elliott's on Bond Street. She told the coachman to come back for her in two hours; as soon as he had driven off, she got into a hackney cab. Forty minutes later she was in the mail coach on her way to Cheltenham.

*   *   *

Linton arrived back in Montpelier Square at about three in the afternoon. He had a special marriage license in his pocket and was eager to show it to Jessica. "My lord," Peter said to him as he let him into the house, "Miss O'Neill went out at ten this morning to drive to Bond Street. She has not yet returned."

Linton frowned at the man's grave face. "Well, she must have decided to go somewhere else afterward."

"No, my lord. Or at least she didn't go in the carriage. She told Jerry to return for her in two hours and when he did she wasn't there. What's more, they said at the dressmaker's that she had only stayed five minutes. She said she had a headache, and they got a hackney for her. But she didn't come back here."

Linton's eyes had begun to burn with a cold blue light as Peter told his story, but when he got to the part about the hackney Linton frowned. It couldn't have been Alden again, not if Jess had gone off voluntarily in a hackney. Besides, Alden was laid up with an injured shoulder. At this point Jessica's maid appeared in the hall.

"Miss O'Neill left a letter for you, my lord," she said somewhat breathlessly. "She asked me to give it to you when you came in."

Linton looked for a minute at the white envelope in the girl's hand, and a dreadful foreboding began to fill him. Very slowly he put up his hand, and when he had the envelope he walked into the drawing room and shut the door. He went to the window and stood there in the harsh light, his face white and strained.

171

With sudden decision he ripped open the envelope and took out the letter. Jessica's small, neat writing filled the page. With a taut line between his eyes he bent his head and read.

Montpelier Square, Wednesday
Dear Philip,

It is difficult, now that I have sat down to write this letter, to find the words to tell you all that is in my heart.

I love you. I shall never love anyone but you. And that is why I have left.

I find, after all, that I can write what I could not say to you. I cannot be your wife. I am not fit to be the wife of the Earl of Linton. I should injure you and disgrace you and that I cannot bear to do.

I could not say this to you because I know you would not allow me to. You would say you think me fit to be the wife of the best man in the world. But, my darling, others would think differently. And those others are ones so closely concerned with you, and would be so closely concerned with me, as to trouble the very foundation of our life together. I will not subject you to the sorrow of choosing between your wife and your family and friends.

You are not to worry about me. I have gone home to my family, where I am loved and needed. I shall be in no want. Except, of course, the want of you.

Forgive me. I wish I could say forget me, but I am not after all as selfless as that.

Jess

Linton finished reading the letter. He stared, unseeing, for a few moments longer at the neat lines of black script. He remembered last night. Then he closed his eyes. This was the thing he had feared the most, and it had happened. And he didn't even know where to begin to look for her. His eyes were a dark, bitter blue as he went upstairs and prepared to take apart all of her belongings in hopes of finding a clue to her real identity.

Jessica received a royal welcome home from Miss Burnley. The little governess had been frantic with worry over Jessica's sojourn in Scotland and when Jessica walked in the door of Winchcombe looking thin and tired but demonstrably alive Miss Burnley had wept with relief.

"I'm so glad to see you, my dear," she said for perhaps the fifteenth time as they sat in the morning parlor having tea. "It was such an anxious time. I always wondered if the letters we sent to that postal address you gave us in London ever reached you."

"Now Burnie, you know they did," Jessica said placatingly. "I always wrote back. But it was a very strange experience and not one I would care to repeat." Jessica's eyes closed briefly.

"I don't blame you," Miss Burnley said warmly, and bent forward to pat Jessica's hand. "It must have been dreadful, taking care of an old and dying woman."

"I think, if you don't mind Burnie, I'd rather not talk about it. Ever."

"All right, my dear. I understand." There was a pause; then the governess said tentatively, "Were you able to pay back Mr. King?"

"Yes." For the first time since she had come home Jessica smiled. "We're in the clear, Burnie. Winchcombe belongs to no one but me. We all of us, you and I and Geoff and Adrian, have a home that no one can take away from us."

"Thank God," said Miss Burnley devoutly.

"Thank Cousin Jean," Jessica said with pious hypocrisy.

She made the same comment two days later to Mr. Grassington. The lawyer had been strongly opposed to her borrowing money from a London moneylender but, as she had pointed out gently, she was of age and there was nothing he could do about it. He had acted as Jessica's intermediary and redeemed the Winchcombe mortgage from Sir Henry Belton. And he had always been skeptical about the sudden call from Cousin Jean Cameron.

"I don't believe a word of this story, Jessica," he told her now with a melancholy sigh. "I have no idea where you got that money, but it did not come from this mythical cousin. You may fool Miss Burnley and your brothers with that story but you cannot fool me."

Jessica shrugged, a small gesture that emphasized the thinness of her shoulders. "I am sorry you feel that way, Mr. Grassington."

"I have been worried to death about you," the old man said dispassionately.

"There was no need to worry. I am perfectly fine, as you can see for yourself. And Winchcombe is clear."

"You don't mean to tell me how you got that money?"

"You have heard the only explanation I am prepared to give."

He looked at her in silence for a tense moment. Then he nodded. "I think perhaps I do not want to know," he said a trifle grimly. He folded his hands on his desk. "The rest of your affairs are in order. If there is anything I can do for you please let me know."

Jessica's gray eyes softened. "You are always so good to me." She bent and kissed him on the cheek. "Come and dine with us next week."

"Thank you, my dear," he replied as he carefully polished his glasses. "I should like that very much."

Chapter Twenty-Two

But I, who daily craving
Cannot have to content me,
Have more cause to lament me,
  Since wanting is more woe than too much
    having.
                              —SIR PHILIP SIDNEY

News reached England at the beginning of March that
Napoleon Bonaparte had escaped from Elba and
landed in France. This great event effectively drew all
the ton's interest from the affair of Philip Romney and
Jessica O'Neill. Linton's duel with Lord Alden,
Jessica's disappearance, and Linton's subsequently icy
demeanor had all been a source of endless comment,
but now the affairs of the world once again took prece-
dence. London waited to hear that France had risen
to halt Napoleon's march toward Paris. It learned instead that the Seventh Regiment had gone over to the
Emperor at Grenoble and shortly after that the King's
troops spontaneously changed sides, deserting the
Bourbon King Louis XVIII. On March 20 Napoleon
triumphantly entered the Tuileries.

Linton returned to Staplehurst at the end of March,
and Lady Maria drove over from Selsey Place one af-

ternoon to see him. "It will be war, Maria," he told her. "Have you heard from Matt?"

"He wrote to say that the Congress has declared Napoleon an outlaw. He says there will be war over Belgium if over nothing else. He thinks the alliance against Napoleon will reform."

"It already has. Wellington has been appointed commander-in-chief. You cannot possibly think of going to Vienna at this point."

"So Matt says too," replied Lady Maria reluctantly. "What a detestable little man Napoleon is. One had so hoped this dreadful war was over with for good."

"I know. Now there will be more bloodshed. And Castlereagh has pledged five million pounds sterling to the Allied army. That is bad news for the economy. Unfortunately there is nothing else to do but fight. Matt is right. Napoleon will never be satisfied until Belgium is part of France, and Britain can't and won't stand for that."

Lady Linton had come into the morning parlor shortly after that and Linton had excused himself to go and look at his new plantations. "I don't like the way Philip looks at all," his sister said immediately after he had gone.

"He has been like this for almost a month now," Lady Linton replied. "I am hoping that being here at Staplehurst will help. London was too hectic, too filled with memories. Now he is home he can busy himself with the things he loves. In time he will forget."

"She just walked out, mother?" Lady Maria asked. "Has he tried to find her? You wrote that she disappeared. It seems odd for a person of such celebrity to be able to do that."

"Evidently her name was not really O'Neill and the history she gave to the Covent Garden management was fictitious. No one knows who she really is. I will say that I am convinced she loved Philip." There was a pause, and Lady Linton raised sober eyes to her daughter's. "I saw the letter she left him."

"Oh?" Maria's brows were raised.

"Yes. Catherine Romney had talked to her; I wrote you that. Evidently Catherine made a very strong impression on the girl. She wrote Philip that she was not fit to be the wife of the Earl of Linton."

Maria sighed. "It is a thousand pities that this had to happen. But she is right. Such a marriage would be impossible."

"I know, my dear. But it is breaking my heart to look at Philip."

The days went by. Linton resumed his old schedule of work at Staplehurst and followed the war news in the newspapers. On the surface, to his tenants and to his workmen, he seemed the same. But his mother saw the shadow of strain in his eyes, the grim, painful set of his mouth. All the lazy sunshine was gone from him. He was always pleasant, always courteous. But he was too often silent, and it was a silence whose quality made Lady Linton very uneasy.

May came, and June, and the armies of the coalition were assembling in Belgium. Sir Matthew Selsey was still in Vienna. He had written to his wife that she was to remain in England until he was able to join her sometime during the summer. Consequently Matthew and Lawrence Selsey, who were to have stayed at Staplehurst for the summer vacation if their mother was in Vienna, would be going instead to Selsey Place. Lady Linton didn't know whether to be glad or sorry. She thought perhaps his young nephews would have livened Linton up, if they didn't drive him distracted, which was the other possibility.

On June 19 word came to Staplehurst that Wellington had engaged Napoleon at Quatre Bras. Linton prepared to go up to London to await further news. His mother came into the library as he was writing out some instructions, and she stopped for a moment just inside the door and looked at his intent face. The sunlight from the window fell on the still, golden wing of his hair, the same thick silky gold that had clung to her fingers when she had brushed it in childhood. The clean angle of cheek and jawbone had long since lost all traces of childish softness, but she longed now to press her own cheek against his and comfort him as she had done so often long ago. He looked up. "Oh, there you are, mother. I am leaving to go up to London immediately. As soon as I know what has happened I'll return to tell you."

"All right, Philip," she answered steadily. "I think I shall ask Maria to come over. She will want to know the news as soon as possible, I'm sure."

"Very well." He had risen at her entrance, and he came across the room now to stand next to her. He was so tall, Lady Linton thought. "It seems a long time ago that I had to bend over to kiss you," she murmured as his lips brushed her cheek. He smiled but did not reply, and in a moment he was gone.

Late in the afternoon of June 22 the Earl of Linton stood in the window of Brooks'. Behind him young Lord Melville was telling a spellbound group of men that he knew for a fact that the Prussians had been wiped out, that the Anglo-Allied army had been destroyed and Wellington himself killed. In the middle of Melville's discourse Linton turned, touched him on the arm, and said, "Look there." Everyone immediately came to the window and, looking out, saw a chaise and four horses driving down the street followed by a running, cheering mob.

"What is that sticking out the windows?" asked Lord George Litcham.

Linton's eyes were very blue. "Those, George," he answered quietly, "are three French Imperial Eagles."

Shortly after that the tower guns began to fire a 101-gun salute, and church bells pealed out all over London. Once more Napoleon Bonaparte had been defeated.

"Well, I thank God we won but my heart goes out to the families of those who were slain," Lady Linton said as she, Maria, and Maria's two eldest sons sat listening to Linton's report on the morning of June 23.

"I know." Lady Maria's face was unusually serious as she replied to her mother's comment.

"I wish *I* had been there!" said Matthew Selsey enthusiastically.

"Well, I am very glad you were not," snapped his

mother instantly. "And let me tell you, young man, you have a great deal of growing up to do before you can even contemplate assuming such an adult role in the world. You've been sulking like a baby ever since you came home from school."

"I have not been sulking," said Matthew, a definite pout on his handsome, fair-skinned face.

"What has happened, Matthew, to cause you to be unhappy?" his grandmother asked gently.

"He thought he was going on a visit to Geoffrey Lissett," said Lawrence helpfully. "But it's been cancelled and Matt is mad as a hornet."

"If I had wanted you to answer my question, Lawrence, I would have asked you," Lady Linton said austerely.

Linton looked at his eldest nephew's flushed cheeks and said sympathetically, "Oh yes, I remember you mentioned the visit to me when I drove you back to Eton after Christmas. What happened, Matthew?"

"I don't know, Uncle Philip," the boy answered unhappily. "We had it all fixed up, Geoff and I. They have a stud and I was going to help with the horses. Mama said I might. She said it would keep me out of your hair for the summer."

Linton looked slightly amused. "Oh, did she?"

"I said you might go, Matthew, provided I heard from Geoffrey's sister that it was all right with her."

"And it wasn't all right, I gather?" Lady Linton inquired.

"No." Matthew's lip was definitely drooping. "I can't understand why she doesn't want me. I'd be a *help,* not a bother."

"Well, I can understand," his mother said briskly. "The poor girl is probably at her wit's end. I knew Geoffrey's father. Sir Thomas Lissett was a charming man who hadn't a notion of what the word self-discipline meant. There were rumors all over London that he was badly dipped. All of his debts probably landed in the lap of Geoffrey's sister. I have no doubt that that is why she is starting a stud."

"I know they need money. Geoff says he is *determined* to help put Winchcombe on its feet again. I know they could use extra help, and I'm good around horses, aren't I, Uncle Philip?"

Linton was looking at his nephew with a strange light in his eyes. "Tell me about the Lissetts, Matthew. How many of them are there? How old is Geoffrey's sister?"

"Oh, Philip," Lady Linton murmured despairingly, but he shook his head at her impatiently.

"Well, actually, Jess is only Geoffrey's half-sister," Matthew responded. He continued readily, unaware of the electric shock that his casual use of Jessica's name had produced in his elders. "She is the real owner of Winchcombe; it belonged to her father, not to Geoffrey's. There are just the two of them and Adrian, Geoff's younger brother. He's at Eton, too. What was the other thing you wanted to know, Uncle Philip?"

"What did you say Geoffrey's sister's name was?" Linton's voice, even to himself, was unrecognizable.

"Jessica. Her last name is Andover." There was a puzzled look in Matthew's eyes as he stared at his uncle.

"And where is this Winchcombe?"

"Just outside of Cheltenham."

Linton's eyes were brilliant. "Have you ever met Jessica, Matthew?"

"No, Uncle Philip."

"About how old is she?"

"Twenty-one or two, I think."

"Good heavens, Philip, surely you don't think. . . ?" It was his sister's voice, and he turned to look at her.

"I don't know what to think, Maria. I do know that I am leaving immediately for Cheltenham."

"Where is Uncle Philip going, mother?" Geoffrey asked as the door closed behind Linton. "To Winchcombe? Why? I don't understand."

His mother ignored him. Her magnificent green eyes were fixed on Lady Linton. "Is it possible?" she asked.

"I don't know, Maria," her mother answered. "But I find myself hoping very much that it is."

Chapter Twenty-Three

Alas, my love! ye do me wrong,
    To cast me off discourteously;
And I have loved you so long,
    Delighting in your company.
                    —ANONYMOUS

Ever since Jessica had returned to Winchcombe she had buried herself in work. Miss Burnley expostulated with her often but Jessica would not listen. The best way to manage the pain, she found, was to work herself to the point of exhaustion. Then, at least, she could sleep at night.

It was better when the boys came home from school, although she had had a moment of panic when she realized that Geoffrey wanted to invite Linton's nephew to spend the summer at Winchcombe. She had been tarter and more abrupt with Geoffrey than she had ever been before, and he had written to Matthew Selsey to cancel the invitation with very little protest. Both Geoffrey and Adrian were aware of a change in Jessica. She didn't seem to hear half of what was said to her, and she seldom laughed. Miss Burnley told them that Jessica was having a reaction to her experience in Scotland and that they must all be considerate and sensitive to her feelings. The boys tried, but they sorely missed their vibrant, intensely alive sister. This Jessica acted like a sleepwalker. The boys found themselves trying to keep as much out of her way as possible.

Geoffrey and Adrian were coming down the front steps of Winchcombe after lunch on the afternoon of June 24 when a smart phaeton drawn by a pair of matched grays came trotting up the driveway. Both boys stayed at the bottom of the steps, their eyes fixed admiringly on the horses. The phaeton was drawn up before them and a man asked in a deep, quiet voice if this was Winchcombe.

"Yes, it is," replied Adrian.

"I say, sir, that is a bang-up pair of grays!" said Geoffrey enthusiastically.

"Thank you," Linton responded courteously. "You must be Geoffrey Lissett. I should like very much to see your sister if she is at home."

"She went into Cheltenham this morning to see Mr. Grassington, our lawyer. But she should be back soon. Should you like to wait for her, sir?"

"Yes," said Linton decisively. "I should."

"If you like I'll drive your phaeton down to the stables and you can wait in the drawing room," Geoffrey said eagerly.

Linton had heard enough about Geoffrey Lissett's horsemanship to allow him to agree. A delighted Geoffrey, with Adrian beside him, climbed up into the driver's seat, and Linton ascended the front steps of Jessica's home.

Stover, the butler who had been at Winchcombe

since before Jessica was born, answered the door and showed him into the drawing room. He was looking around him at the peaceful harmony of faded ivory, crimson, pink, and blue that was Winchcombe's drawing room when the door opened and a small, brown-haired woman who was dressed simply but tastefully in a dress of French blue cambric entered. "Lord Linton?" she asked in a beautiful, clear voice.

He came toward her. "Yes, I am Linton. Your butler said I might wait here for Miss Andover to return."

"Of course," the small woman replied. "Please do sit down. I am Miss Burnley, Miss Andover's former governess. May I offer you some refreshment, Lord Linton?"

He was on the point of refusing when he changed his mind. "A glass of sherry, thank you."

The sherry was brought and served and Miss Burnley, who was obviously dying to know what his business was with Jessica, maintained a gallant flow of light conversation. "Did you meet Miss Andover while she was in Scotland?" she finally ventured.

He looked surprised. "No. I didn't realize she had been in Scotland."

"Yes. She was there for most of the winter. A cousin of her mother's was ill and Miss Andover went to look after her."

He looked thoughtful for a moment, and then he smiled at Miss Burnley. It was a smile Jessica knew well, the warm, lazy, genuinely sweet smile that undid almost everyone he turned it on. Miss Burnley melted in its radiance. "Did this cousin by any chance leave Jess some money?"

The smile, his title, his blond good looks, his use of Jessica's first name, all somehow reassured Miss Burnley that it was perfectly all right for her to confide in him. Afterwards, when she was reflecting soberly on the interview, she did not understand how she had been so forthcoming, but forthcoming she certainly was. "Yes," she said now in answer to his question. "Miss Cameron left her quite a lot of money. Enough, thank God, to pay off the mortgage on Winchcombe."

"I see. That was certainly fortunate."

"Yes. I must say I was very worried when Jessica borrowed the money from Mr. King to pay off Sir Henry. And I still cannot quite see why she found it so impossible to marry him. But, thank God, it all turned out for the best in the end."

Linton didn't answer right away, he was occupied with what Miss Burnley had told him. The little governess, looking at him, thought she had never in her life seen anyone with eyes so blue. "How is the stud going?" he asked then.

"Jessica seems to be pleased with it," returned Miss Burnley. "It is a tremendous amount of work, however. I have been begging her to take on more help but she says we can't afford it. Geoffrey is very helpful, of course, but he is in school for most of the year."

He started to answer her when there came through the opened window the sound of horses' hooves on the gravel. Clear as a bell on the summer air Jessica's voice floated to Linton's ears. "Take the horses down to the stables, Jem. I'll be down shortly myself. Tell Geoffrey to saddle up Northern Light."

Linton's heart was hammering. Until he had heard her voice he had not been sure. "Miss Burnley," he said urgently, "go out and ask Jess to come in here. Don't tell her who I am. Just say there is someone to see her. Please."

Miss Burnley hesitated, looked at his face, nodded, and left the room. Linton heard her voice in the hall saying, "There is someone to see you, my dear, in the drawing room. I think it is about one of the horses."

"Oh?" There was the sound of Jessica's swift, long steps as she came across the hall. She opened the door of the drawing room and stopped as abruptly as if she had walked into glass. Miss Burnley, behind her, almost bumped into her.

"Hello, Jess," he said steadily. "How are you?"

"What are you doing here? How did you find me?" Her voice sounded thin and strained. There was absolutely no color in her face.

"My nephew was very disappointed at not being allowed to come to Winchcombe. When he told me a little about your family I began to suspect. I came to find out for sure." There was a pause, then he said, the bitterness just audible under his deep, even tone, "You have put me through hell, do you know that?"

Her eyes, open and dark, were on his face. At his last words the color came flooding back to her cheeks. "I know. I'm sorry. You shouldn't have come."

"Well I have come," he replied crisply, "and you are damn well going to listen to me. Come in here and sit down."

"Jessica . . ." said Miss Burnley nervously, and they both jumped a little and turned to look at her. So absorbed had they been in each other that they had forgotten the governess's existence.

"It's all right, Burnie," Jessica said then. "This is Lord Linton. I know him." She turned once more to look at the man behind her. Their eyes held for a full three seconds. Then Jessica turned back to Miss Burnley. "Leave us alone, Burnie. I am perfectly safe with Lord Linton."

Miss Burnley looked doubtfully at Linton, then at Jessica. She sighed a little but dutifully turned and left the room quietly, closing the door behind her. Jessica then crossed to a pale pink sofa and sat down abruptly, as if her legs wouldn't hold her any longer. "Why did you come?" she asked him. "You had my letter. Surely you must see the truth of what I wrote. Why stir up the pain again?"

He stood where he was, next to a polished rosewood table. "You look too thin," he said. "Miss Burnley says you are working too hard." He paused, debating how to begin, his eyes on her averted face. "Why wouldn't you marry Sir Henry, Jess?" he asked at last very softly.

Her head jerked around at his words. "What do you know about Sir Henry?"

"Very little. Just that you refused to marry him. I know also that you needed money. But then I always knew that."

She rubbed her forehead a little as if it were aching. "True. There was never much secret about that."

"No."

She smiled a little at his monosyllabic reply. "It's very simple, really," she told him. "Sir Henry Belton is a neighbor and the owner of Melford Hall. When my stepfather died he left a load of debt, and Sir Edmund Belton, who was Henry's uncle and a friend of my father's, agreed to hold a mortgage on Winchcombe. When Sir Edmund died his nephew Henry took over both Melford Hall and my mortgage. He told me if I didn't agree to marry him he would foreclose on Winchcombe." Her eyes were dark and enormous in her thin, narrow-boned face. "I would have lost it, Philip. I could not have allowed that to happen."

"So you decided to become a mistress rather than a wife."

Her lids dropped. "I don't expect you to understand."

"Every other woman in the world would have given in and married that bully," he said slowly. "But not you."

"I couldn't. I couldn't marry him. I knew what that meant, you see. I wouldn't have been myself, ever again. I couldn't do it. I didn't have the courage. I would have slept with him, but not marriage."

Her eyes had been on her hands, lying closed tightly together in her lap. She heard him say clearly, "Do you feel that way about marriage to me?"

She raised her eyes to his face and her mouth curled into something that was not quite a smile. "You know that I don't," she said softly.

"Then marry me."

"We have been through this, Philip. I cannot. There

are things which, if a woman does them, can never be forgotten."

"You are Jessica Andover. What you have done is of no moment."

"That is not true," she replied steadily.

"Are you afraid of exposure then?"

"I should not relish it, but that is not what is holding me back."

He tried another tack. "And am I to be punished, then, because of what you have done? Is that your sense of justice? If you tell me now that you do not love me I will go away and trouble you no more. But if you love me, after what has passed between us, I have a right to demand that you marry me. I do demand it." He came closer to where she sat on the sofa. "Tell me, Jess," he said imperiously, "tell me you don't love me."

The strain this interview was putting on her was evident in her too intense stillness. "It is not that I do not love you," she said at last. "Quite the contrary. It is just that you are out of my reach."

He ran his hand through his hair in frustration. He had never before come up against a force in her that he could not move. The day was very warm, and threads of gold, dislodged by his impatient fingers, spangled the dampness on his forehead. "Go away," she said, the line of her mouth thin and taut with pain. "Go away and forget me."

"I am no good hand at forgetting," he replied.

"Philip," she said. "Please."

His nostrils were pinched and there was a white line around his mouth. "If there is one thing in this world that I abhor," he said bitterly, "it is unnecessary sacrifice."

Her hands, still clasped in her lap, were white with pressure. "I did not think you could be so cruel." Her voice sounded as if she had lost her breath.

He made an involuntary gesture toward her, then checked himself. "I'll go, Jess. But I'll be back." He walked steadily to the door, opened it, and without a backward look exited from her presence. She watched him go in silence and the thought crossed her mind that his erect blond head had the look of a war helm. She had no doubt that he would be back.

Chapter Twenty-Four

What fools are they that have not known
That love likes no laws but his own?
—FULKE GREVILLE

Linton drove straight through to Staplehurst. He arrived in the early morning hours when the house was asleep and went to his room to lie on his bed, sleepless until morning broke and he could see his mother.

Lady Linton always dressed and came downstairs to breakfast, and this morning she was extremely surprised to find her son waiting for her. "Philip! I had not expected you back so soon," she said. Then, looking at his tired, somber face, she asked hesitantly, "Was it she?"

"Yes."

Relief flooded through Lady Linton, but her emotion was not reflected in the stern face of her son. She seated herself across from him at the table. "Then what is the matter?" she asked gently.

He sat down again himself and his eyes, almost black with fatigue and unhappiness, fixed themselves on his mother's sympathetic face. "She won't have me, mother."

"Because of what Catherine Romney said to her? she said after a pause.

He frowned, his attention suddenly focused. "What is this about Catherine Romney?"

Too late Lady Linton realized her mistake. "Tell me, mother," he was saying, a very grim note in his voice, and Lady Linton sighed a little.

"Very well. After you asked her to marry you, your Jessica sought out Catherine. She wanted to know what your family and friends would think of such a match." Lady Linton shrugged a little. "Well, Philip, what was poor Catherine to say?"

"I gather then it was she who told Jess that I should be disgraced and dishonored if she married me."

"Yes."

Linton swore. Then he looked levelly into his mother's eyes. "And do you feel the same way, mother?"

"I did, Philip," she answered honestly. "I do not feel that way any longer."

His eyes began to get bluer. "Really, mother? Would you accept Jess if we married? Welcome her to Staplehurst?"

"Yes."

He drank some coffee, frowning a little in abstraction, his mind racing. "It seems to me," he heard his mother's voice saying calmly, "that if you are really going to marry this girl we had better make plans to assure that she will be received by society."

"I don't even know if she'll marry me, mother," he said tautly. "I am just hoping that your acceptance will make a difference to her."

"What will make a difference to her is the knowledge that marriage to her has not injured your

194

position with either your family or your friends. If you want her to agree to be your wife, you must reassure her on both those matters."

He was paying very close attention to her. "She is of good birth, mother. The Andovers have been at Winchcombe for centuries."

"I remember her father as a young man." Lady Linton folded her hands in her lap. "Philip, how did a girl like that ever decide to go on the stage and how did she ever agree to become your mistress?"

He told her. When he had finished, all she said slowly was, "I see."

"Under those circumstances, mother, can she be accepted by society? It doesn't matter a damn to me what anybody else thinks, but you are right in saying it does matter to Jess."

"The person you need to help you, my son, is Maria," Lady Linton said with decision.

"Maria?"

"Certainly. She is one of the patronesses of Almack's. There are very few women more powerful in the closed world of London society than your sister, my dear. If Maria agrees to sponsor Jessica, I think you may say that any objections society might have will crumble."

He was silent for a minute, assessing what she had said. "But will Maria agree to sponsor Jess? It is hardly the kind of marriage she has been trying to promote for me for years."

"I remember you once told me that if you were in trouble there is no one you would rather go to than

Maria." She raised her brows at him. "I think you are in trouble now, my son."

"I am," he replied soberly. "The worst trouble of my life."

"Well then?"

"I'll ride over to Selsey Place," he replied. He rose from the table and bent to kiss her before he left the room.

Maria was in the drawing room arranging in a vase the flowers she had just cut when her brother walked in. "Philip!" She pushed the last rose haphazardly into the middle of her careful arrangement and turned to him expectantly. "What happened? Is she your Jessica?"

He noted with a flicker of pleasure that both his mother and his sister had referred to Jess as "your Jessica." "Yes," he said. "She is."

"I can't believe it," Maria said, fixing wide eyes on him. "Jessica O'Neill is really Jessica Andover of Winchcombe. Imagine."

"Maria, sit down. I have to talk to you. I need your help."

She moved to a striped silk armchair and sat down. "Oh?" she said. "What is it I can do for you, Philip?"

He remained standing but leaned an arm on the mantelpiece. He took a deep breath and spoke in a carefully controlled voice. "I want to tell you first about Jess, about why she did what she did." Maria's green eyes brightened, and she nodded. Linton went on. "Part of it you know already. You said you knew Jess's stepfather, Lissett, and that you suspected he had left her saddled with a mountain of debt." She nodded again. "You were right. To pay off the creditors she mortgaged Winchcombe. The friend of her father's who held the mortgage died and his nephew succeeded. The nephew told Jess that if she didn't marry him he would foreclose on her. Winchcombe was all she had left to support herself and her brothers. She couldn't lose it."

He paused and Maria said in a neutral tone, "Why wouldn't she marry this man, then?"

"It is hard to understand if you don't know Jess," he replied. "She is so proud, Maria, so independent. She said to me, 'I would never be myself again if I married him.'"

Maria's full lips compressed a little. "She also had first-hand knowledge of just how helpless a woman can be. Thomas Lissett probably milked Winchcombe for everything he could get out of it. It didn't belong to him; it belonged to Jessica, but because she was a minor he could do it. A married woman's property, unless careful steps are taken, is legally as under the control of her husband as a minor's property is under the control of a guardian."

"Yes. She knew that as well."

"And so she decided to get the money for the mortgage in the only way that is open to a woman other than marriage?"

"Yes."

"I don't think I would have had the courage," Maria said candidly.

He took his arm off the mantel and turned to face her fully. "Jess has more courage in her little finger than most men I know have in their entire bodies. And I am not speaking just of physical courage but of a lonely, cold-blooded moral courage that very few possess." He spoke with a rough force that impressed Maria almost as much as his words did.

"What do you want me to do, Philip?" she asked.

He pulled up a chair and sat close beside her. "She won't marry me, Maria. Catherine Romney told her some nonsense about my being disgraced and dishonored by such a marriage and now she refuses to listen to reason. The only chance I have of changing her mind is to convince her that both my family and the society I move in will accept her as my wife. That is where I need your assistance."

"What did mother say?"

"Mother suggested that I ask you to sponsor Jess into society." There was a pause. "Will you, Maria?"

Maria was frowning thoughtfully, the thin arched lines of her brows drawn together, her forehead charmingly puckered. "If she had been a nobody from the backwaters of Ireland it would have been impossible. But she is an Andover . . ." Maria paused and Linton sat silent. "Her mother was a Frenchwoman if I remember correctly," Maria continued after a moment. "I vaguely remember meeting her many years ago. Nothing wrong with the family on that side either."

"There is nothing wrong with *her*," Linton said then, forcefully.

Maria's green eyes rested inscrutably on her brother's face, then she smiled. "I once told mother I wondered what kind of a girl it would take to make an impression on you. I must say I never envisioned this."

He responded more to her smile than to her words. "You'll do it?"

"I will."

He leaned over to kiss her cheek. "You are a paragon of sisters, Maria, and I hereby eat every word I may have said to the contrary." She laughed, and he continued, a note of anxiety creeping into his voice. "It can be done, you think?"

Maria drew herself up regally. "My dear Philip, if I choose to present a person as acceptable you may be sure she will be regarded as such by anyone at all who matters in London."

He grinned. "You are a trump, Maria. Now I have just got to convince Jess."

"That might not be so easy," Maria murmured. "I could convince her far more easily than you. She may think you are being overly optimistic."

"Maria." His hand closed over hers and the blue of his eyes was almost blinding. "Come with me to Winchcombe."

Her own eyes began to sparkle, then clouded with disappointment. "How can I? There's the baby. She's not weaned yet, Philip. I can't leave her."

He sat back. "Of course. How stupid of me. Well, perhaps you would send Jess a letter?"

Her eyes narrowed a little. "Would you mind travelling with a baby?" she asked.

"Of course I wouldn't mind! Do you think you might come?"

"If I do, I shall have to bring Elizabeth."

"Fine. Marvelous. Wonderful. Anything I can do for either of you, you have only to ask."

A very self-satisfied look descended on Maria's beautiful features. "I seem to recall you once told me not to help you any more," she said blandly.

"I must have been mad," he replied promptly.

"Philip, in order to see you in this state of grateful submission I would do anything," she declared with enormous pleasure. "When do we start?"

Chapter Twenty-Five

Greensleeves, now farewell! adieu!
God I pray to prosper thee;
For I am still thy lover true
Come once again and love me.
—ANONYMOUS

For the second time in a week Miss Burnley was surprised to find the Earl of Linton calling at Winchcombe. And this time he had his sister with him. Stover had shown Linton and Maria into the drawing room before he went to inform Miss Burnley of the visitors' arrival. For the moment Maria had left the baby in the carriage with her nurse. As she entered the room Miss Burnley was conscious of a feeling of distinct trepidation. She had gotten little out of Jessica about the Earl of Linton but it had been very clear that his visit had upset her badly. Miss Burnley was afraid that money trouble had risen to plague them once again.

"Miss Andover is down at the stables, my lord," she told Linton as she came into the room. "I have sent someone to inform her of your arrival."

Linton smiled at the small, obviously troubled woman. "Thank you, Miss Burnley. Allow me to introduce to you my sister, Lady Maria Selsey."

Maria smiled at Miss Burnley as well. "You are Miss Andover's old governess, are you not?" she asked.

"Yes, my lady."

Maria looked thoughtfully at Miss Burnley's anxious face. "I think we should take Miss Burnley into our confidence, Philip."

"If she doesn't already know my errand," Linton put in drily.

"No, my lord, I do not," replied Miss Burnley more crisply than usual.

"It is very simple, really," he said with a charming, rueful smile. "I want Miss Andover to marry me. She, although she says she loves me, refuses to do so. She insists she would not be accepted by my family. To prove to her that she is wrong I have brought my sister all the way from Kent to see her."

"I see," said Miss Burnley faintly. She did not see at all, of course. Where had Jessica met this man? And why should she feel unacceptable to his family? Miss Burnley looked with wide eyes at Lady Maria Selsey, whose fame had penetrated even to the Assembly Rooms of Cheltenham. That elegant lady said now, with crisp decision, "Philip, I think I should see Miss Andover by myself, so you will please go and wait in some other room until I send for you. Miss Burnley, I have my four-month-old daughter in the carriage. Would you mind showing my nurse to a spare bedroom where she can care for the baby until I am ready to leave?"

"Certainly, my lady," said a startled Miss Burnley.

She turned to Linton. "Should you care to wait in the library, Lord Linton?"

"That sounds fine, Miss Burnley," he replied, and the two of them moved to the door. Linton cast one more quick glance at his sister, then followed Miss Burnley out.

When Jessica was informed that the Earl of Linton had called, her first impulse was to refuse to see him. Further reflection had changed her mind. If she wouldn't go to him he was perfectly capable of seeking her out, and she did not want to meet him in the full view of her brothers. Obviously the only thing for her to do was to see him and to convince him that she had meant every word she said to him the other day.

"Where is he, Burnie?" she said tensely to a waiting Miss Burnley at the door of the house.

"Your visitor is in the drawing room, my dear," replied that lady with a scrupulous regard for accuracy.

Jessica said nothing else but walked swiftly across the hall, opened the door of the mentioned room, and once again stopped dead on the threshold. Inside was a very beautiful fair-haired woman who was dressed in a fashionable walking dress of almond green. The woman was looking at her appraisingly, and Jessica was suddenly conscious of her ancient riding skirt, open-necked shirt, and rolled-up sleeves. Brilliant color stained her cheeks and her chin elevated a quarter of an inch. "Yes?" she said in a cool voice. "May I help you?"

Maria heard the edge in that voice and realized she had offended. It was not, in fact, Jessica's clothes at which she had been staring but at Jessica herself. She had not known what to expect, but this tall, slender girl with her thin, proud face, direct gray eyes, and thick braid of brown hair falling almost to her waist satisfied Maria's imagination. She had not expected a conventional beauty. She smiled now, a more brilliant, less warm smile than her brother's, but still a smile calculated to disarm. "I beg your pardon for staring," she said, "but I have been most anxious to meet you. I am Maria Selsey, Philip's sister. He asked me to come to see you."

The high color drained from Jessica's face, leaving the pearly curve of the skin over her cheekbones looking thin and white. She said nothing. Maria regarded her with suddenly serious eyes. This interview was not going to be easy; the girl's face looked guarded and faintly hostile. Plainly Maria's smile had not made its proper impression. "May we sit down?" Maria said slowly. "I have travelled quite a long way and I have several things of importance to say to you."

Still in silence Jessica crossed the floor and sat, straight-backed, in a faded armchair six feet from Maria. Maria seated herself gracefully in the chair that stood behind her and regarded the young face across from her thoughtfully. "I have not come on Catherine Romney's errand, Jessica," she said at last, quite gently. Jessica's eyelids flickered but otherwise her expression did not change.

"Oh?" she said unencouragingly.

"No," Maria continued, speaking now with quiet emphasis. "I came to tell you that should you decide to marry Philip my mother will welcome you into the family and I will undertake to see to it that you are received by society as the Countess of Linton should be."

The sudden widening of Jessica's eyes betrayed her surprise. "I don't think I understand you," she said faintly.

"I did not think you would, which was why I came," Maria returned soberly. "You were told the opposite story rather brutally by Catherine Romney, I understand."

"Mrs. Romney was frank," replied Jessica a little stiffly. "I had no communication from any other member of your family."

Maria smiled a trifle ruefully. "I know. And I would not be truthful if I did not say that my mother and I did not regard with favor the idea of a marriage between you and my brother." Her smile became warmer, infectiously charming. "We have since changed our minds."

Jessica's head was in a whirl. She found it hard to comprehend that this was actually Philip's sister who was sitting here, smiling at her, speaking of welcoming her into the family! "And what was it that caused such a change?" she managed to say at last.

"Two things, actually. The first and the less important was our discovery of who you are. You must realize yourself that Jessica Andover of Winchcombe is a very different matter from Jessica O'Neill, Irish actress of unknown origin."

Jessica's eyes, wide and dark and unreadable, were fixed on Maria's face. "And the second?" she asked steadily.

"The second was Philip." Maria looked straight back into Jessica's eyes, her own sober and worried and earnest. "I love my brother," she said clearly. "I did not realize what losing you would do to him." For the first time Maria saw a change in the self-contained face of the girl she was addressing. "And it won't get any better," she continued. "Philip is not the kind who forgets."

Jessica made a small, involuntary gesture with her hand, which was quickly stilled. The pallor of her cheeks had flushed to warm ivory. Maria leaned forward. "He loves you, Jessica. It didn't matter to him who you were. If you love him in return I think you owe it to him to marry him." She paused, then asked deliberately, "*Do* you love him?"

There was something in Jessica's face that caused Maria to avert her eyes for a moment. "I love him," the girl replied simply. "That is precisely why I would *not* marry him."

"Well, it was very noble of you," Maria said briskly, steering away from the shoals of emotion looming at her feet. "Our intentions were noble as well. In fact, we have all been so busy saving Philip from you that we have neglected a very important point. We have, among us, made the poor boy perfectly miserable. The time has come to put matters right."

"Can we?" asked Jessica, a faint gleam of hope glimmering deep within her eyes.

"Certainly. Your birth is excellent. Your conduct, once it is seen in the proper light, will be understandable."

"Will it?" The clear gray eyes were steady on Maria's face. "Do *you* understand it? Does Philip?"

"Philip's exact words to me were that you had more courage in your little finger than most men he knew had in their entire bodies." The gray eyes began to glow a little, and Maria continued, "I find I agree with him, Jessica." She folded her hands in her lap. "There will be a great deal of talk, of course. But if you are married in the presence of both our families and are introduced to society by my mother at a ball given by me, there is no one who will refuse to accept you."

The glow in Jessica's eyes was more pronounced. "Can that possibly be true?" she breathed.

Maria raised a haughty eyebrow. "Scandals worse than yours have been forgiven. Look at the Stanfords. Two years ago no one could talk of anything else. Today they are entrenched at the top of the ton. It all depends on how you carry it off."

Jessica looked for a long minute at the imperious, splendid beauty of Lady Maria Selsey. For the first time in this interview she smiled. "I am quite sure you could carry off anything," she said. "Even me."

The haughtiness vanished from Maria's face, and she grinned. "I don't like to boast, Jessica, but I do wield a great deal of influence. Set your mind at rest. If I say you will be accepted, you will be." She rose to her feet. "Philip is waiting in the library and I'm sure he has paced a hole in the carpet by now. Shall I go and send him to you?"

Wild roses flew in Jessica's cheeks. "Please," she said breathlessly.

Maria left and after what seemed an eternity the

door opened again and he was there. "Jess?" he said, and with a small cry she ran across the room and into his arms.

Half an hour later Maria returned, knocking discreetly on the door before she entered. Jessica and Linton were seated side by side on the sofa. Jessica's eyes looked like stars and Linton's hair was disordered. He grinned at Maria. "You are a pearl among sisters, my dear," he said, rising and setting a chair for her.

She looked into the blue of his eyes and heaved a little sigh of relief. It was all right. She smiled mischievously. "I am having a marvelous time," she declared. "And did you remember to give Jessica mother's letter?"

"He did," Jessica replied softly. "It was very kind. She wants us to be married at Staplehurst."

"I don't care where we are married so long as it is soon," said Linton decidedly.

The stars in Jessica's eyes dimmed. "Philip," she said in a low, muted voice, "what am I going to to tell the boys?"

"I have been thinking about that," he replied, turning to look down into her anxious face. "I assume they will make their home with us at Staplehurst?"

Jessica bit her lip. "They'll have to."

"Yes, they will. For a few years at least. Jess," he picked up her hand and looked down at it intently. "What do you want to do about Winchcombe?"

There was silence as she sat thinking, then he felt

her hand stiffen in his. "Philip," she said excitedly, "I'll give Winchcombe to Geoffrey!"

He kept his eyes on her hand. "Are you sure?"

"Yes. He loves it. It's part of him. And it will enable him to have a financially secure future. Adrian will be a doctor. He's wanted nothing else ever since he was a small boy. But for Geoffrey it's Winchcombe—and horses."

"He sounds exactly like my Matthew," said Maria resignedly. "I suppose that's why they're such great friends."

"Well, that's settled, then," Linton said briskly. "You tell the boys that you are going to marry me and move the family to Staplehurst but that we will continue the stud here at Winchcombe. We can plan to spend a part of their holidays here each year and I'll hire someone to be here at the stables full time, supervising. In fact I have someone in mind. By the time Geoffrey is ready to take over in a few years the place should be established."

Jessica had been watching him steadily all through this speech, and now she said, a hint of accusation in her voice, "You had all this planned out already."

A smile glinted in the blue of his eyes. "It does seem the practical solution."

The corners of her mouth deepened, and she went on looking at him. "You tell the boys you are going to marry me, my darling," he said gently. "Tell them about your plans for Winchcombe. Let me tell them the rest."

Jessica's throat was dry. "I suppose they have to know?"

209

"They have to know something," he said reasonably. "Leave it to me to handle."

"All right," said Jessica, deeply thankful that that was a task she did not have to tackle. It would be bad enough telling Miss Burnley.

They had a celebration dinner at Winchcombe that evening. Whatever Linton had told the boys had left them a trifle awed and respectful of Jessica, a state of affairs that had lasted all of forty-five minutes. By the time they sat down to dinner their usual youthful spirits had been restored. The security of their young lives had been threatened by financial problems ever since the death of their father. They had also been upset by the prolonged absence of their sister and then by her preoccupation when she finally returned. It felt comfortable sitting at the table with this big, fair-haired man who looked at them with interest and who was obviously competent to deal with any problems that might arise to plague them in the future. Geoffrey was happy because he was to have Winchcombe and because he would be living near his greatest friend, whose mother had already invited him on a visit. Adrian, more of a child, was content because his sister looked happy and now he was sure she would not go away again.

Miss Burnley, too, was relieved to know that she would be staying at Winchcombe, although she still had not gotten over the shock of Jessica's revelation that afternoon. That Jessica should become an actress was bad enough, but the other. . . . Even now Miss Burnley's mind shied away from the awful truth. Her eyes went once again to the Earl of Linton who, miraculously to Miss Burnley, wanted to marry Jessica, even after . . .

Linton had been listening to Adrian and, as Miss Burnley watched, his eyes, warm with laughter, turned to Jessica. She was talking to Lady Maria and for a moment Miss Burnley, too, watched that unconscious, serious face.

It had always been a serious face, Miss Burnley reflected. Too serious for so young a girl. But then Jessica had had burdens foreign to most young girls of her age and class. They had been responsibilities she had uncomplainingly taken on her slender shoulders, but if she had not protested, that did not mean they were any the less heavy. She had run Winchcombe for years, watching helplessly as her inheritance was steadily milked of everything that had once made it prosperous. She had virtually reared two small boys by herself. And then, after working like a laborer for over a year, she had faced the prospect of losing everything to a man she distrusted and despised.

Jessica's head turned, and her eyes met Linton's. They looked at each other for a minute, then he turned away to answer something Geoffrey had said to him and Jessica went back to her conversation with Lady Maria. Miss Burnley bent her head and stared at her plate.

It had sounded sordid, Jessica's revelation to Miss Burnley this afternoon. But who was she to judge Jessica, Miss Burnley thought now humbly, as she gazed fixedly at her peas. The very food on her plate, the roof over her head, were there because of Jessica.

She had never had to make the kind of decision Jessica had. She had always been protected by the very girl whose conduct she had been silently condemning.

She had been shocked at Jessica's revelation, but she had been almost equally shocked to find that, instead of being punished, Jessica was actually going to benefit from her misdeed. The wages of Jessica's sin was marriage with one of the richest nobles in the country.

Instead of her peas Miss Burnley saw once again the too thin face of her former pupil. She remembered the withdrawn, sleepwalker's expression that face had worn during these past months. If Jessica had sinned she had suffered as well. And if her future looked bright now—well, no one deserved it more, Miss Burnley thought fiercely.

"Burnie!" It was Jessica's voice, lightly teasing. "Have you gone off into a trance?"

"No, my dear." Miss Burnley looked at the glowing face on her right. "I have been thinking about you."

"About me. Oh." Jessica's voice was ever so slightly defensive.

"Yes," said Miss Burnley clearly. "I have been wondering if Lord Linton realizes how very fortunate he is."

There was a moment of surprised silence; then Jessica smiled, a radiant, youthful smile. "Thank you, Burnie," she said.

"Why is Philip fortunate?" asked Adrian, his inquisitive eyes on his sister and governess.

"Because your sister has done me the honor of accepting my offer of marriage," Linton replied promptly.

"Oh, that," said Adrian. He helped himself to more peas and then, apparently feeling that more of a response was called for, he added kindly, "It's true, you know. There's no one like Jess."

For the second time during the meal Linton's eyes found hers. "I know that, Adrian," he said softly.

"Jess!" said Geoffrey urgently. "If we brought Northern Light to Staplehurst, do you think you could go on working him?"

"No, Geoffrey," Linton said with great firmness. "We will engage adequate staff to fulfill all your instructions. Your sister is going out of the horse-training business. Permanently."

"Goodness," Jessica said to Lady Maria, laughter in her eyes. "Is he always so autocratic?"

"Yes," Maria said decisively. "He may have a smile that melts stones but in his heart of hearts, Philip is a despot."

They all looked from Lady Maria to the blue-eyed man sitting at the head of the table. "But I'm very kind to women and children," he said serenely. He smiled. "May I have some more peas?"

Jessica smiled back. "Certainly you may. Pass Philip the peas, Adrian."

Adrian hastened to obey, and Geoffrey said, "If you aren't going to train horses, Jess, what *are* you going to do?"

Jessica tilted her head reflectively. "I am not quite sure, Geoffrey," she said at last with wide-eyed solemnity. "Perhaps Philip will be able to think of something."

"I'll try," he assured her, his eyes glinting between narrowed lids. "I'm sure I can find something to keep you busy."

Lady Maria, who felt the conversation was entering dangerous waters, firmly changed the subject, and Jessica obligingly followed her lead. Linton calmly went on eating his peas.

Married by
Mistake

Married by
Mistake

Melinda McRae

A SIGNET BOOK

For Kendall Elisabeth,
who wanted to have
her name in a book.

Chapter 1

"**Y**ou have the devil's luck, Alford!" Jeremy Trent tossed his cards upon the green baize table in disgust.

A slow smile crept over the face of Thomas Beresford Swinton, Viscount Alford. He cocked one dark brow. "Blasphemy from you, Trent?"

"Picking all the winners at Newmarket, then taking all the hands this night," Trent grumbled. "It's uncanny."

Alford raised his glass in a toast. "To luck," he said with a grin, then drained his glass in one gulp.

"Yours will run out one day," the man on his left, Seb Cole, warned. To punctuate his words, he upended an empty bottle over Alford's glass. "Brandy's gone."

"Then uncork another, you ass," Lewiston Hervey muttered while he gathered up the cards for another hand.

"Gentlemen, allow me." Alford was on his feet with fluid grace. "As your host, it is my duty."

Only a slight hestitation in his gait as he crossed the room hinted at the amount of brandy Alford had already consumed. He grabbed another bottle from the sideboard, grimacing at his reflection in the mirror above. He passed the low settee pushed up against the wall and none too gently lifted the head of the baby-faced man lying there, then let it fall back against the padded cushion.

"Almhurst's still gone," he announced to no one in particular before he stumbled back toward the table with his prize. He presented the bottle to Cole with a flourish before retaking his seat.

"Hardly unexpected," Cole said. "Lad's never had a head for liquor."

"Leastways he quit snoring," Hervey said, dealing the cards around the table.

7

As if on cue, Almhurst began a nasal rumbling.

"Damnation." Alford took his long discarded cravat from the arm of his chair, wadded it into a ball and lobbed it at the settee, where it bounced off the young lord's nose. The men laughed but the snoring continued.

"Maybe we should toss him out on the walk?" Cole asked hopefully.

"With our luck he'd develop an inflammation of the lungs, die, and we'd all hang for it," Trent said, his expression glum as he examined his cards.

Alford slouched further down in his comfortably worn armchair, studying the cards in his hand. His expression remained impassive.

"Has anyone heard more about the new dancer at the opera?" Cole asked while he sloppily refilled everyone's glass.

"She's been deucedly coy, from what I hear," Trent replied. "Either she's already got a protector lined up or she's a foolish chit."

"Perhaps," said Alford, shifting slightly in his chair, "she is looking for a gentleman of refinement and taste."

Trent guffawed. "I suppose you think you would be more successful?"

"I know I would be," Alford replied, an enigmatic smile lighting his face.

"Monkey says you won't."

Alford's smile widened. "So certain are you of my failure?"

"My money's on Alford," Cole said. "Ain't never yet seen a female who's refused him."

"Well, Alford, what do you say?" Trent prompted him. "Think you can storm her castle?"

Alford picked up his glass and gestured in salute to his cronies. "No bets on this one, gentlemen. The lady and I have already enjoyed a very satisfactory interchange."

"As I said, the devil's own luck," Trent mumbled.

With a laugh, Alford slapped Trent on the back. "Perhaps it will rub off one day."

"My lord?" Alford's valet appeared at the door.

"What is it, Rawlings?"

"Some papers from your father, my lord."

"At this hour?" Alford frowned. "They can wait till later."

"They are regarding your brother's wedding," the valet said. "He has been trying to locate you for three days."

"Any fool would know I'd been at Newmarket." Alford shook his head. "Bring them here."

"So Kit's really going to seal his doom, eh?" Hervey joked as play halted.

"More the fool he," said Alford, squinting at the papers in his hand. "Rawlings! Bring the damn candles over here. Can't see a thing in this light. And a pen. And ink."

"Yes, my lord."

"What does he need a wife for?" Cole asked.

Alford turned back his cuffs and meticulously rolled up his sleeves. "Don't ask me what maggot got into his head— although it was most likely my father. Probably convinced the idiot he would not get a decent post unless he had a wife."

"Who's he marrying?" Trent asked.

Alford shuddered at the memory. "Washburn's chit."

"Washburn? Don't remember a Washburn. What's the matter with her? Does she have a squint? Or freckles?"

"Probably," said Alford as he scrawled his signature across one page. "I haven't seen her since she was a pestilential brat of nine or ten. Washburn's kept her hidden on the Continent for years, so something must be amiss."

"Shouldn't someone warn Kit?"

Alford gave a careless wave of his hand. "It's his life to ruin as he will."

"Kit's marrying a girl he hasn't seen in what—ten years?" Seb Cole was aghast.

"Kit's managed to see her here and there, from what I gather," Alford replied blandly as he flipped through the papers.

"How come Kit's seen her and you haven't? Not like you to ignore the ladies."

"Now, Trent, think on it." Alford absently rubbed the bridge of his nose. "How many days have I spent under my

father's roof in the last ten years? Five? Ten? Whereas Kit,
dutiful son that he is, was constantly underfoot at that house.
He would have been around whenever Washburn and the
girl made an appearance.''

Cole and Hervey exchanged dubious glances.

''Couldn't you talk to Kit,'' Cole asked. ''Make him see
reason? There are all kinds of ways to get out of the noose.''

''Ah, but there will be no opportunity to speak with Kit.''
Alford leafed through the remaining papers, halting once to
scrawl his name again. ''That is the beauty of the arrangement. He is unable to get leave to come home for the
wedding. The marriage is to be done by proxy. By the time
he realizes what he's in for, it will be far too late.'' He
collected the papers and handed them to the waiting
Rawlings, who bowed his way out of the room.

''Who's going to stand proxy for him?'' Hervey said.

Trent gave him a withering look. ''Alford, you clunch,''
he said.

''A rum hand to deal your own brother,'' Hervey
muttered.

''You wound me,'' Alford said, placing a hand over his
breast. ''It was my dearest brother's express wish that I stand
in for him. I am honor-bound to accede to his request.''

''Seems to me a real brother would help him get out of
it,'' Hervey continued.

''Kit's a strapping big laddie now,'' Alford said,
mimicking the ancient Scots groom who had taught them both
to ride. ''He can do what he wishes with his life.''

''Maybe we should investigate the chit,'' Hervey offered.
''We ought to be able to catch a glimpse of this Miss
Whatever-her-name-is. Make sure Kit's doing the right
thing.''

''And how do you propose to locate 'Miss What's-her-
name' when you don't even know it?'' Alford demanded.

''You'll tell us where she is.'' Hervey's face brightened.

''I am sorry to disappoint you, my friend, but I have no
idea where the future Mrs. Swinton is residing.'' Alford
grinned wickedly. ''Although there is a good chance it is

in London. It shouldn't take you more than five or six weeks to locate her."

"Your father would know," Cole pointed out.

Alford shrugged carelessly. "More than likely. But what are you going to do when you find her? Inspect her like some piece of horseflesh at Tattersalls? She might allow you to examine her teeth, but I highly doubt she will appreciate a thorough examination of her hindquarters."

Trent's loud snicker rent the air.

Hervey adopted the air of injured innocence. "We was just trying to help your brother. He won't want to get shackled to an antidote."

Cole and Trent nodded in agreement.

"Gentlemen, it is a matter of supreme indifference to me what my brother plans to do with himself. If he wishes to marry at his tender age, who am I to say him no?" There was an edge to Alford's voice.

Cole and the others wisely kept silent.

Alford looked around the table, the sharp look in his icy blue eyes belying his languid pose. "Now, gentlemen, where were we, before this untimely interruption?"

Almhurst's loud snore punctuated the question.

"Drat this pen!" Florence Washburn tossed down her quill with disgust. "That is the fifth point to splinter."

"Perhaps if you wrote with a lighter hand . . ." her Aunt Agatha suggested.

Florrie scowled. "It is only that there is so much to take care of, and so little time to accomplish it. I cannot believe Kit is behaving so abominably."

"Now, Florrie," her aunt cautioned. " 'Tis not his fault he could not get home for the wedding."

"But what a miserable way to get married," Florrie wailed. "First my groom is unable to attend, and now I find I must have his odious brother standing in as proxy. It is enough to make me scream."

"I am certain Lord Alford will play his role admirably."

"You wait," Florrie warned, her hazel eyes flashing. "He

will find some way to ruin the whole day for me. I loathe
the man. I *detest* him. It is the one bad thing about marrying
Kit—I will be connected to that oaf.''

"You have not seen the boy in ages," Agatha reminded
her. "I am certain he has grown into an admirable young
man."

Florrie stared at her aunt as if she had sprouted wings.
"Do you not ever listen to gossip, Auntie? Alford's name
is on everyone's tongue. He is a dissipated gamester who
chases anything in skirts. His ladies are legion. But then,
I hear he has a fondness for older women, so perhaps you
and he will deal well together."

"Florrie!"

She grinned impishly. "Well, perhaps he will behave
himself at such a solemn occasion." Florrie sighed, absently
twining a lock of her dark blond hair around her finger. "It
will be a rather sad affair to be a married lady without a
husband. Even when I arrive in Portugal there is no guarantee
Kit will be able to join me. I wish he would sell out and take
up a Foreign Office position sooner rather than later."

"You are both still young with plenty of time ahead,"
Agatha said. "A year or two in the military will seem as
nothing one day. And you yourself said it was only gaining
Kit more connections."

"I know," Florrie said, turning with resignation back to
the pile of invitations to be addressed. "And I am certain
Portugal will prove interesting. I will be able to learn
Portuguese and Spanish at the same time."

"As if you did not have enough languages," her aunt
groaned.

"A diplomat's wife must be accomplished," Florrie
reminded her. "Just think how dreadfully boring it would
be if I only knew English. I would miss out on all manner
of exciting conversations."

"Which would probably be all the better for you," her
aunt warned. "Your father told me about that incident in
St. Petersburg."

"Oh, pooh," said Florrie. " 'Incident' is far too strong
a word. It was merely a minor misunderstanding. And had

my Polish been up to the mark, it would not have happened at all. I simply thought we were going for a drive in the country, not eloping.''

''All the more reason to see you safely wed, my dear.'' Sir Roger Washburn strode into the room and planted a kiss on his daughter's brow. Despite the fact he had just passed his fiftieth year, his form was as trim as it had been at twenty. Only the hair that was now more gray than brown gave a hint of his years. ''As a married lady, you will be less of a candidate for these foreign intriguers. You will have a husband to protect you.''

''Which will do me an endless amount of good when he is hundreds of miles away,'' she complained with the slightest hint of a pout.

''I am certain that *Mrs. Swinton* will be able to handle herself with aplomb,'' Sir Roger added. ''Have the invitations been addressed yet?''

''Almost,'' Florrie replied. She ticked the list off on her fingers. ''The food order has been placed with the caterers, the flowers are ordered, I go for my final dress fitting tomorrow, and the musicians have been engaged.''

''Good job, my dear. As always. I am having dinner with the earl tonight, to discuss the final settlements. Barstow informs me that Alford has finally signed the proxy papers, so it appears everything is in order.''

Florrie wrinkled her nose at the mention of her future brother-in-law, a gesture not missed by her father.

''Now, Florrie,'' he warned. ''How can you expect to be an effective diplomatic hostess when you make your aversions so well known? Personal opinion has no place in diplomatic circles.''

''Neither does Alford, thank goodness. If Kit and I are very lucky, we will find ourselves posted to all manner of exotic capitals and I will not even have to think about Alford for another ten years.''

''I doubt Barstow will let you get that far from him. Remember, little one, Kit is next in line until Alford marries and produces a son. And if rumor is correct, he shows no intentions of settling down anytime soon. Barstow will want to keep a close eye on Kit until the succession is secured.''

"Perhaps you can arrange a proxy marriage for Alford."
Florrie brightened at the thought. "Find some ignorant thing
who has not heard his name. All he needs is one son and
Kit is free."

"What, you do not relish the idea of being a countess one
day?'' Sir Roger's eyes twinkled with teasing.

"Oh, I hope to be at least that,'' she retorted with a smug
expression. "But Kit will have his own title, thank you, as
reward for services extended to the Crown. Alford is
welcome to become Earl of Barstow.''

"We shall see,'' her father said, rising. "Since you ladies
have everything so well in hand, I'm off to the club. I'll tell
you about the meeting with Barstow tomorrow.''

Florrie airily waved her papa out of the room and turned
her hand back to addressing the remaining invitations.

She really did look forward to this marriage. Oh, not
because she was top-over-tails in love with Kit. She regarded
him much more as a slightly elder brother, for that was the
role he had played during most of their time together. But
Kit would make an amiable companion, and that counted for
much in the diplomatic circles they would find themselves
in. And even if he was just starting out in his career, she
would rather align herself with him than an older, more
experienced hand. For after acting as hostess to her father
since she was fifteen, Florrie rather liked the idea that she
would be much more familiar with diplomatic life than her
husband. Kit would turn to her for advice and information.
The two of them would make an excellent team.

Still, there was this business with Alford to get through.
She shuddered slightly at the thought. Alford had never made
an effort to hide his contempt for her when they were
children. He had always refused to allow "a girl" to play
pirates or soldiers with him and Kit. And when words had
not been enough to discourage her, he had subjected her to
the full force of his creative torments. If she never set eyes
on him again during her lifetime, it would not be long
enough. And now she was not only going to be forced into
the same room with him, but must repeat her marriage vows

to him instead of Kit. For the hundredth time, she wished she could sail to Portugal and marry Kit there. But with her father off to Sweden, there was no one willing to take the responsibility of chaperoning an unmarried young lady for any length of time. Marriage to Kit would give her the respectability and freedom she needed to travel on her own.

And if it took seeing Alford again to achieve that, it was worth it, Florrie thought. She would be as polite as could be to her future brother-in-law—in public, at least. But she could continue to think what she would about him in private.

The rest of the household was fast asleep by the time Sir Roger sat in the library of his hastily rented London townhouse, staring for an inordinate amount of time at the papers he held in his hand. Did he dare act on them?

He shifted in his chair and took a welcome swallow of port from his glass. He considered his options. His main goal was to do what was right for Florrie. As her father, it was his duty to see that she was properly settled. With no wife to guide him, he had to make the decision he thought best. That was why he had brought his daughter back to England now. The Continent was no place for a young, single woman with the Corsican poised to wreak havoc again.

Plus, it was time his daughter had a life of her own. He would miss her skills as a hostess, but it was time she set up her own establishment. He had thought this marriage to Christopher Swinton was an ideal solution to the problem of Florrie. ''Problem'' was too harsh a word—dilemma, perhaps. The chit had an innate knack for the diplomatic life. She was still young, and a bit impulsive, but with a few more years behind her, she would soon be a force to be reckoned with. It was imperative that she wed a man equal to her talents.

Kit Swinton was a logical choice. He had the advantage of having known Florrie since she was a babe in leading strings. They were amiable companions. And Kit would go far, Sir Roger had no doubt. Although young, he was ambitious and talented enough to aim high. After some much needed seasoning as a staff officer, he would be able to step into an assistant ambassadorship without difficulty. And with Florrie at his side . . . they would be an imposing team.

But how much more power could Florrie wield in a similar position here in England? As wife of a sitting Lord, or cabinet minister . . . The possibilities were endless. And Sir Roger held in his hand the route to that end.

Alford's carelessness did give him pause. Sir Roger had investigated the man most carefully, and much of what he learned did not give him pleasure. The truth of Alford's existence more than corroborated his reputation. The lad was well on his way to a life of dissipation and waste. But that chat earlier with Barstow revealed another side to the story. Washburn could not approve of the way Barstow held his heir on such short rein, and it was only logical that Alford chafed at the strain. True, he had not shown any of the ambitions of his younger brother. But with a skilled hand to guide him . . . There was more than one politician whose wife held the true power.

Sir Roger again leafed through the proxy papers in his hands. An honorable man would return them immediately to the earl. An honorable man would not attempt to trick both his daughter and her future in-laws. An honorable man would abhor the action he contemplated.

But honor went only so far. When it came up against opportunity, the lines blurred. And was not diplomacy the art of taking advantage of opportunity?

Still, it was highly possible his plan would not work. All might be uncovered beforetimes, and corrected. And what would happen later, when the deception was revealed? He must plan very carefully. There had to be a way to make certain that the results could not be challenged. It would take careful doing, but he might be able to manage the arrangements. It was a delicate matter, with innumerable potential for error. But Sir Roger had not risen as high as he had in diplomatic circles without acquiring a number of devious methods. He had a few tricks up his sleeve.

Chapter 2

"Of all the rude, intolerable, rag-mannered starts!" Florrie swept past her aunt with a furious swish of her skirts. "I told you he would find some method of ruining this day."

"Now Florrie," Agatha began. "Alford is only a trifle late. He will be arriving at any moment, I am certain."

" 'Twill be an awkward wedding reception if there is no wedding," Florrie said, stomping across her bedroom. "Perhaps this is merely his idea of a novel approach—first the celebration, then the wedding. I am supposed to be greeting guests in half an hour!"

"The ceremony will not take long." Aunt Agatha attempted to soothe her.

Florrie plopped onto the gilt chair by the window. "I should have gone straight to Portugal. I could have wed Kit there without any fuss."

Her aunt gently pulled Florrie to her feet and straightened her lace overskirt. "You will wrinkle your dress, dear."

"As if anyone will notice," Florrie grumbled. "It will be my continued status as *Miss* Washburn that will draw all the attention. How could he do this to me!"

"Florrie?" Sir Roger's voice came from the corridor.

"Come in," Florrie replied wearily, frowning into the pier glass on her dresser. She looked a fright. A dark, angry flush stained her cheeks and all her agitated wanderings had caused half her curls to tumble down about her shoulders. This was all Alford's fault!

"I have been speaking with the vicar," Sir Roger said upon entering. "He states there is no difficulty in substituting another proxy for Alford."

"You mean we do not have to wait for that miserable creature?" Hope dawned on Florrie's face.

"You may wish to adopt a more politic method of describing your future brother-in-law," Sir Roger chided her gently.

Florrie shot him a look of disgust. "After he ruined what there is of my wedding? I can only hope he does not arrive at all, now. Who have you recruited to take his place?"

"Simmons," Sir Roger replied. "He is here already, picking up the last of the papers for the Foreign Office."

Florrie sighed. "He will do as well as anyone, I suppose." At that point, Mad King George could stand in for Kit and she would not care. She only wanted to get this ordeal over with.

"Then let us proceed with haste to the drawing room," Sir Roger said, offering his arm to his daughter. "We shall have this wedding yet before the guests arrive."

"May I offer a toast to the new Lady Alford?" The vicar beamed from behind his glasses upon the completion of the ceremony as the footmen poured glasses of champagne.

Florrie laughed. "I am sorry to have to deflate myself so, vicar, but I am only plain Mrs. Swinton. Alford's my brother-in-law."

The vicar looked confused. "I had thought . . ."

"A toast to the newlyweds," Sir Roger interjected hastily, and the small gathering lifted their glasses.

"My best to you, *Mrs.* Swinton," Simmons teased. "I am certain your father is relieved to have you safely wed at last."

"Along with Wellesley," joked Sir Roger. "He will no longer have to fear an international incident involving Florrie and some enamored European princeling."

Florrie endured their good-hearted teasing. She knew it was a relief for her father to hand her safely into another's hands. With the Continent in such turmoil, a young daughter was not the best companion. Sir Roger had left more than one post earlier than other diplomats, fearing for her safety. Florrie hoped he would not take any unnecessary chances now that he would be alone. With Napoleon's army dominating Europe, anything could happen.

"Another toast to my new daughter-in-law," Lord Barstow said. He kissed Florrie gently on the cheek. "You will be a welcome addition to the family, my dear. Kit is a lucky lad."

"Thank you," Florrie beamed with pleasure.

"No, I was right."

They all turned toward the vicar, who crossed the room with the marriage papers in hand, a perplexed frown on his face.

"It says quite plainly that Florence Amelia Washburn, spinster, has wed Thomas Beresford Swinton, Viscount Alford, with George Simmons standing as proxy."

"What?" Three voices exclaimed at once.

"Let me look at those." Sir Roger grabbed the papers from the vicar. "My God, it is true. Look here." He stepped next to Barstow and pointed out the incriminating signatures. "Looks like your boy missigned the paperwork. I did not even think to examine it beforehand!"

"I don't believe it," Florrie snapped, snatching the papers from her father's hands. A quick perusal only confirmed his words. "This is insane."

"It will only take a few moments to straighten things out," Sir Roger assured her. He took the papers and returned them to the vicar. "Cross out Alford's name and write in Christopher Swinton. Can't have my girl married to the wrong man."

The vicar smiled weakly. "I am afraid I cannot do that, sir."

"What?" Barstow demanded.

The vicar cleared his throat. "I have just conducted a legal wedding, my lord. With Viscount Alford's signature here," he pointed to the line on the page, "and the proxy's signature there, this is a perfectly legal document."

"Then tear it up and start over," Barstow growled.

"I cannot do that," the vicar said, defensively holding the papers close to his chest. "That would make Miss Washburn —I mean Lady Alford—subject to bigamy charges."

A loud crash resounded in the room. The men turned to stare at Florrie, who stood over the shattered remains of a crystal vase.

"Florrie," her father began warningly.

"Under no circumstances will I consent to this farce of a marriage," she announced with a defiant tilt to her chin. She whirled on the vicar. "You will change those papers and you will do it now."

The vicar protectively moved the papers behind his back as Florrie approached him.

"I cannot do that," he said again, blinking rapidly.

"Agatha, perhaps you would take Florrie upstairs so she can compose herself before the guests arrive," Sir Roger said. "Gentlemen, let us repair to the library where we can discuss this matter more thoroughly. I am certain there is a reasonable solution."

"I will not marry Alford," Florrie reiterated as her aunt dragged her out the door.

After Florrie's departure, Sir Roger dismissed Simmons and guided the vicar and Barstow into the library. When they were settled comfortably, he turned to the vicar. "Well," Sir Roger began, "what must we do to straighten this tangle out?"

"I am certain there are ample grounds for an annulment," the vicar replied nervously. "Under the circumstances . . . I would be quite willing to go over to Doctor's Commons right away and look into it."

"A good idea," said Sir Roger, dispatching the vicar with a wave of his hand. When he was gone, Sir Roger turned to the earl. "Is that heir of yours always so careless?"

Barstow shook his head in disgust. "It is a constant trial to me," he said. "I had thought he would outgrow his youthful escapades, but he seems to be hell-bent on proving he is as wild as ever. I knew I should not have relied on him to do this properly."

"You do not think he did this on purpose, as a prank?" Sir Roger's eyes were wide in questioning. "Is that perhaps the reason he is not here?"

"I do not know," Barstow moaned. He drained his glass in one large gulp. "I tell you, Roger, be glad you have only the girl. Sons are a deuced nuisance. Kit's as steady as they come, yet Alford's my heir and I cannot be easy about his manner of living. Every time I try to talk a little sense into him, he ignores my suggestions and goes his own way." He scowled darkly.

Sir Roger studied his glass. "Sounds like the lad could use a strong, steadying influence," he said carefully.

"I've tried to convince him to marry, hoping a wife might settle him down. Now I'd be content to see him wed just to ensure the succession, but he only laughs in my face at the suggestion," Barstow said. "It was one of the reasons I was so pleased to see Kit married. Assuming he and Florence have children, that matter would be taken care of no matter what Alford does."

"Do you think marriage would be enough to settle Alford down?" Sir Roger asked with a deliberately innocent expression.

"Certainly, if he tied the knot with the right chit. One who would not let him have his own way all the time, who would rein him in from his excesses, and encourage him to take up some other pursuit beside gaming and sporting."

Sir Roger looked pensive. "Florrie has a strong personality," he began hesitantly. "It takes a determined fight to thwart her wishes."

Barstow frowned. "Are you saying we should let this marriage stand?"

Sir Roger shrugged. "I must admit, it does not look like the most auspicious match right now. But if Alford and Florrie could be persuaded . . . She certainly has the strength of will to keep him in line."

The earl pondered his friend's words. "But what about Kit?"

Sir Roger waved a dismissive hand. "We both know this was no love match. It was a political union—the future diplomat with the perfect diplomatic hostess. I am certain Florrie thinks of Kit more as a brother than a husband."

The earl slowly nodded his agreement. "But how in the world do you intend to persuade your daughter to comply? She sounded rather adamant in the drawing room."

"You leave Florrie to me," Sir Roger assured him. "Once she sees the benefit of such a match, she will be of a more receptive mind. I am more concerned about Alford."

"No problem there," said Barstow smugly. "I'll just threaten to cut his allowance. His stable alone eats up half of it. He'll think twice about the matter if he's forced to give up his sporting pursuits."

Sir Roger retained his doubtful expression. "At the same time, I cannot be easy about this. I do not want Florrie tied to a man who will not treat her with the respect she deserves. Or who will only be one step ahead of the duns."

"Alford knows how to go on," Barstow growled. "Present him with this as a *fait accompli* and he will knuckle under. Mayhaps I can throw in a few horses or a new carriage to sweeten the deal. He can be made to see reason."

"Still . . ." Sir Roger feigned reluctance. "Florrie has her heart set on becoming a diplomatic hostess. Alford's interests run more to sport and games. . . ."

"Oh, Alford could hold his own in the political arena if he put his mind to it," Barstow assured him. "He's been after me for years to give him one of the parliamentary seats. Didn't think it necessary, before. Who wants to sit in the Commons?"

This revelation surprised Sir Roger. Was it possible that Alford *did* have a political bent? The news could not be better. Florrie could certainly give Alford an extra push in that direction.

"Perhaps, once the initial shock wears off, they both might listen to a reasoned explanation," Sir Roger said. "I will leave you to explain the situation to Alford, and I will deal with Florrie. It will take them a deucedly long time to go through all the legal rigmarole for an annulment in any event. We shall have plenty of time for artful persuasion."

Barstow grinned in a conspiratorial manner. "To the newly wedded couple," he said, raising his glass. "Lord and Lady Alford."

Sir Roger found the brandy particularly satisfying.

Alford sat impatiently in the worn leather chair, his fingers beating a restless tattoo on the arm. How much longer was this going to take? He frowned at the glass of claret he held. This was not the finest vintage he had ever tasted. In fact, it came close to being one of the worst. But there was little else to help pass the time in this tumble-down inn. It boded ill for the remainder of the day.

"You certain we will still make London in time for the wedding?" Lewiston Hervey asked with apprehension.

"They can't hold the wedding without me, can they?" Alford asked, taking a long swallow of the ruby liquid. He stared glumly at the parlor door for the hundredth time. "How long can it take to reshoe a horse?"

"Told you we should have gone up yesterday," Hervey protested. "Would have been in London with plenty of time to spare."

"And missed the mill this morning?" Alford snorted his contempt. "Don't be a fool, Hervey, or I shall be tempted to leave you here when that bloody horse is finally ready to go. You made a tidy sum on the match."

The young man opened his mouth to protest, but then shut it quickly at the grim look Alford directed at him. He refilled his glass instead.

Alford's frown deepened. He had not wanted to have anything to do with this deuced wedding. If Kit was foolish enough to become a tenant-for-life, let him. But why drag his brother into it? Now Alford was forced to race back to town after a perfectly ripping mill in order to stand proxy at this ridiculous ceremony. *Anyone* could have stood proxy.

Alford did not hold with any sentimental twaddle about standing in for his brother. In fact, he suspected the idea was his father's doing. He scowled deeper at the thought. He and Kit were four years and poles apart. Kit was the son who could do no wrong, the one who was free to do what he pleased with his life, while his elder brother was bound to the useless role of heir. Unencumbered by a title and an estate, Kit had the freedom to choose his own path. While

Alford could do nothing. His own life could not start until his father was dead, until the inheritance passed to him—that is, his life could start if the boredom of waiting did not kill him in the intervening years.

"Do you ever wish, Hervey, that you were not an only child?"

Hervey blinked at him uncomprehendingly. "Why should I?"

"Just imagine," Alford suggested. "If you had an older brother, he'd become the new viscount when your father died and you could be anything you wanted."

"What else would I want to be?" Hervey asked.

"A rag peddler in Covent Gardens, you clunch," Alford said with irritation. "You could be with Wellington on the Peninsula, or trapping beaver in North America, or . . ."

"Sounds cold and wet and nasty to me," Hervey shivered. "I like it here."

"Then how about being a sitting Lord or a member of the Commons? Anything. Something."

Hervey shook his head. "They'd probably be in the middle of some crisis or another just when the next season at Newmarket comes. Can't walk out on the Prime Minister to watch a mill. Besides, you'd have to make speeches. Write them. Read them." He grimaced.

Alford shook his head in disgust. He should have known better than to ask Hervey, whose greatest ambition in life was to own a top-of-the-trees wardrobe and the horses to match. He had no concept of the frustration Alford experienced. No one of his acquaintance did. They were all content to waste their lives on frivolous pursuits while waiting to come into their inheritances. They had no lofty ambitions.

But he did. Or at least thought he did. It seemed his interest grew less and less each year as the reality of his situation sank in. It was only now, with Kit's marriage a reminder of how he was in the thick of things on the Peninsula, that the old resentments arose. Even that stupid Washburn chit had done more than he, spending time at nearly every court in Europe. Alford took another long look at the claret, then drained his glass. Damn life.

Alford's groom stepped through the door. "The horse is shod, my lord."

"It is about time," Alford grumbled. He nudged Hervey. "Time to go." He reached across the table and took hold of the half-empty claret bottle. "We'll take this with us. The roads are terribly dusty this spring."

Hervey grinned.

Chapter 3

By the time he stopped at his rooms at Albany and changed into formal clothing, Alford was willing to concede he *was* late for the blasted wedding. But after splitting not one, but three bottles of claret with Hervey during the last miles to London, Alford did not give a damn how late he was. No one had asked him if he wanted to be at this damned ceremony. They could damn well wait until he was ready.

A ruby fob attached to its chain put the finishing touches on his garb. Waving his valet aside, Alford entered the front room. Finding Hervey with a freshly cracked bottle, Alford insisted on a round of toasts before they departed for Washburn's rented residence.

"To the groom," Alford saluted. "Damn fool idiot that he is."

"To the lovely bride," Hervey mumbled.

"How do you know she's lovely?" Alford demanded querulously. "No one's seen the chit yet."

Hervey shrugged. "Just being polite."

Alford shook his head and laid a companionable arm on Hervey's shoulder. "Politeness will only get you into trouble, *laddie*. No one respects politeness. Rudeness is the key." He raised his glass. "To the bride—may she have spots, freckles, and a squint." He downed his drink in one swallow. "Now, let us seal Kit's doom!"

The lurching motion of the carriage as it jounced over the bumpy London streets caused Alford to realize just how much claret he had consumed. Considering the amount of spirits they had downed the previous night, it was doubtful he had ever been quite sober today. But he rapidly realized he was a bit more muzzle-headed than he would have preferred.

Alford could only guess at the look on his father's face when his elder son arrived at the ceremony totally mopped. T'would serve the old man right for dragging him into this.

Hervey nearly tumbled out the carriage door when it was flung open by the overzealous footman in front of Washburn's rented house. Alford descended more sedately, then climbed the steps to the townhouse with the carefully exaggerated tread of a man who was in his cups. Letting the brass door knocker fall with a resounding thud, he waited impatiently for the door to open, his body swaying slightly as he strove to maintain his balance. The transition from lurching carriage to rock-hard steps was disconcerting.

"Where is this deuced wedding supposed to be?" he demanded loudly of the butler who opened the door.

"To the left at the top of the stairs," the butler replied.

Alford turned back to Hervey, who lagged behind. "Come on, lad. Pick up the pace."

"I was not invited," he demurred.

"Of course you were," Alford insisted. "By me. Come along."

The sight that lay beyond the doors was not exactly what Alford had expected. He noted with dismay the numbers of people who stood about the drawing room. He had thought this was to be a small, private affair. It was ridiculous enough that he was being forced to go through with this inane proxy marriage. He did not want to do it in front of a crush of witnesses.

"Alford!" Lord Haverstoke bore down on him. "How like you to be late for your own wedding."

"Not my wedding," Alford grumbled, nervously grabbing a glass of champagne off a passing footman's tray. "Kit's."

Haverstoke smiled smugly and slipped way.

"What the devil?" Alford looked quizzically at Hervey. "Is Haverstoke bosky?"

Hervey shrugged.

A resounding thump across his shoulder blades nearly caused Alford to choke on his champagne.

"Alford, you sly dog," chortled Seb Cole. "Putting out that this was to be Kit's wedding when all along—"

"Kit's not going to have a wedding if I can't find the damn bride," Alford said curtly. "Who are all these people?" he asked with a wild sweep of his arm that threatened to overset several guests.

Seb took him carefully by the arm and drew him to the side of the room. "Have you seen your father since you arrived?"

Alford shook his head, downing the remainder of the champagne in one gulp. He looked about for another.

"Perhaps you should find him," Seb suggested.

"Can't hold the ceremony without me." Alford shrugged.

"Alford, you certainly took everyone by surprise." Another tulip of the *ton* presented himself before Alford's blurred vision. "Suppose this means you'll give up your rooms at Albany. Put my name on the list."

"Mine too," chimed in another.

"I asked first," the tulip insisted.

"I'll throw in a monkey."

"Two."

"Four."

Alford sauntered away. He'd never let either of those idiots have his rooms. But why should he be giving his rooms away? Where else would he stay? Those two were surely in their altitudes to even suggest such a thing. Wearily he scanned the room, looking for his father. One would think more consideration would be shown to a key member of the wedding party. He sipped his champagne slowly, listening to the conversation swirling around him.

"I heard the bride was livid," one matron said in a voice loud enough to be overheard.

"Wouldn't you be?" her companion replied. "A title would be small recompense for life with one such as *him.*"

"Do you think they will be able to annul the marriage?"

Alford shook his head. Some poor girl had obviously found herself married to an unsuitable *parti.* Parental pressure, no doubt.

"Found your father yet?" Seb reappeared at Alford's side.

He shook his head. "Maybe Kit came to his senses and called the thing off."

Alford felt an elbow dig into his ribs.

"Can't blame you for looking so downcast," Lord Exham said with a sly smile. "Cheer up. My uncle's a solicitor and I am certain he would love to take the case."

"What in God's name is everyone talking about?" Alford turned to Seb.

Seb's smile widened. "You really do need to find your father. I am sure he will enlighten you. Try the morning room. Second room on the left across the corridor." He strolled away.

Alford stared at his departing friend with growing bemusement. He knew he had imbibed more than his wont, but it was not nearly enough to account for his confusion. He did not mistake the odd looks and stifled snickers directed his way. No one he had yet spoken with made any sense. That was what came of being so generous with the champagne for the guests. They were all three sheets to the wind. Alford grew convinced he was the soberest man among them.

Where was his father? It was odd no one had come searching for him, late as he had been. A wicked smile crept over his face. Maybe the bride herself had been in the champagne.

Several futile moments of searching led Alford to believe that his father, as well as the bride, had disappeared. If they were in no hurry to find him, Alford was in no hurry to get on with this ridiculous farce. Half of London must be here at what he had been told would be a "private" wedding. He was damned if he was going to stand amid this crush and be gawked at. Alford appropriated another glass of champagne from a passing footman and went in search of some privacy.

The Washburn chit must be more of an antidote than even he thought, that she would hide herself away on her wedding day. His brow wrinkled in concentration as he tried to conjure up some remembrance of her face, but all he could recall was her plaintive, whiny voice as she begged to trail behind him and Kit. Kit had succumbed to her pleas, but Alford had not. In fact, he recalled with a grin, he had rather effectively taken care of her annoying presence. *That* had been worth the punishment that followed. She still had the sense to stay out of his way.

A few false explorations and the back stairs finally led him to the solitude of the library. Alford flopped his tall frame into one of the comfortably worn chairs before the cold fire grate and sipped at his champagne. Time and enough to worry about Kit's intended later.

Florrie peered cautiously around the corner, making certain no one was in the entry hall. Finding it empty, she hurried across the corridor and into the dining room. If she encountered one more person's false congratulations, she would go mad.

She pushed open the door to the library with a hesitant hand. Relief flooded her face when she found the room empty. Slipping quickly inside, she shut the door behind her.

"The devil and damnation," she muttered, plopping down on the sofa. This had to be the most miserable day of her life. And it was all Alford's fault.

"My sentiments exactly," drawled Alford from his chair in the far corner.

Florrie swore again, silently, at having been caught out in such an unlady-like display of temper in front of this stranger. "I beg your pardon," she said. "I had no idea you were there."

Alford saluted her with his glass. "You are more than welcome to stay. The room is large enough for two." His eyes swept over her in an admiring glance. Damn if this chit wasn't a beauty. His gaze took in her flawless cream complexion, the honey-blond hair, and the very enticing display of bosom above her fashionably low-cut gown. Damned nice.

Florrie eyed the stranger warily. He was handsome enough, his dark hair artfully tousled in the current style, his clothes well-tailored in a fashionable mode. But his good looks were not enough to overcome her irritation at finding her haven occupied.

"Who are you?" Florrie demanded.

"Only a man in search of quiet and solitude," Alford

replied with careful enunciation. He rose and walked with studied care across the room to stand before her, wishing he had thought to bring his quizzing glass. This lady bore further inspection.

Flushing at his avid perusal, Florrie sought to rein in her temper. "I would ask, then, sir, that you respect my need for the same."

"I see you, too, have found today's revelries wearying," he said. He sat beside her without invitation, eyeing her with increased interest.

Florrie groaned inwardly. She had been looking for some quiet retreat, away from all the curious eyes and snickering congratulations of their guests. Good God, how could anyone think that marriage to Alford was an enviable state? And now this odious man—who looked to be well on his way to drunkenness—was leering at her like a French sailor.

"I beg you to leave, sir," she ordered in annoyance.

"Leave?" Alford took her hands in his and drew them to his chest. "The most beautiful woman in the house suddenly appears before my eyes and begs me to depart? Alas, fair lady, I cannot bear to be cast so gracelessly from your presence." He brought one hand to his lips.

Florrie tried to pull her hand away, but he only clenched it harder. There was no question, the man was foxed. Trust her to have wandered into his lair. "I must protest, sir. We have not even been introduced."

"There will be time and enough for that later," he said, slipping his other arm about her waist and pulling her nearer.

The first faint twinges of unease spread through Florrie. Surely this drunken lout was not going to attack her in her own house? Why, someone could walk in at any moment. Was he mad as well as drunk?

She planted a false smile upon her face. "I am dreadfully thirsty," she said. "Could you perhaps bring me a glass of something refreshing?"

"And can I ask a favor from you in return, fair lady?"

"Oh, certainly," she replied. She would make her bolt for the door the instant he released her.

"I have some perfectly wonderful champagne just over

there.'' He nodded toward the corner. ''But I should like to claim my reward first.''

He leaned toward her in a most alarming manner. Florrie edged away. ''First the champagne, then the reward,'' she countered.

''All right.''

Florrie misjudged her timing by the merest fraction. When the stranger removed his arm and dropped her hand, she leaped to her feet. But before she could take her first step, she found herself grabbed about the waist and unceremoniously plunked down upon the man's lap.

''Thought to trick me, did you?'' He chuckled as he wrapped his arms tighter about her.

Florrie felt his warm breath against her neck and fought against her rising panic. She doubted that a scream would be heard amidst all the noise from the celebrants upstairs. How frightfully ironic to be in such an awkward situation in her own home!

She jumped when she felt the man's lips nuzzling her neck. ''Let me go,'' she cried, and began to struggle in earnest. This man had rapidly changed from a rather overbearing drunk into an obnoxious lecher.

''I like a lady with a little spirit,'' he said, holding her flailing arms tightly in his.

''Sir, I am a married lady,'' she cried. ''My husband . . .''

He silenced her with his lips, her final words trailing off in a muffled mumble.

Florrie struggled against his arms, unable to free herself from his hold. She could not even yell for help now, with his mouth pressed against hers.

Even in his drunken state, Alford was not too far gone to recognize the lady's real reluctance. He had no intention of hurting her and quickly loosened his hold. But before the lady took advantage of her freedom, the library door creaked open.

''Good Lord!''

''Thomas!''

The shocked tones of Sir Roger and the Earl of Barstow

reached Florrie's ears. Taking advantage of the disgusting lecher's surprise, Florrie twisted away and stared at her father.

"Looks as though they are eager to get things off to a good start," joked the Earl of Barstow, standing next to Sir Roger in the doorway.

Sir Roger laughed. "I own I was worried that he would entertain some concern about the mix-up. But he seems to have the situation well in hand."

Alford suddenly sobered, feeling an overwhelming sense of dread. "Will someone please explain what is going on?" Alford pleaded. He turned to the woman still clasped in his arms. "Who are you?" he demanded.

"Miss Florence Washburn!" she retorted.

A grimace of dismay crossed his face and he hastily pushed her off his lap back onto the couch. Florrie immediately balled up her fingers into a fist and punched him in the nose.

"You disgusting pig!" she shrieked as she clambered off the sofa.

"My nose!" Alford felt, rather than saw, the blood dripping from his nose, and he scrambled frantically in his pocket for a handkerchief to stem the bleeding.

"A bleeding nose is the least of your worries," Florrie sneered. "My father will be more than anxious to deal with you."

Sir Roger cleared his throat. "Florrie, dear, I fear perhaps you have not recognized your old friend. Kit's brother. Viscount Alford."

Florrie stared in amazement at the man on the sofa. His face was obscured by the large, red-stained handkerchief he held to his nose. His pale blue eyes glared at her from over the edge of the linen. Alford? Wrinkling her nose, she tried to picture the obnoxious youth he had been when she last saw him. Florrie turned a puzzled look to her father and the earl.

Barstow grinned from ear to ear. He elbowed Sir Roger in the ribs. "Looks like he was just a bit too eager to claim his husbandly rights."

It was that which made Florrie realize they were telling the truth; this was Alford. "You oaf!" she yelled, striding over and giving him a firm box to the ears.

"Ow!" Alford recoiled in pain. "Call off this hell-cat, Washburn, before she kills me."

"Now, Florrie, this is no way to treat your husband," Sir Roger cautioned, trying to hold back his mirth.

"Husband!" In his surprise, Alford dropped the handkerchief.

"For God's sake, get that linen back on your nose. You're bleeding like a stuck pig," Barstow said. "Didn't anyone tell you?"

"Tell me what?" Alford demanded.

Barstow heaved a sigh of exasperation. "Thanks to your carelessness with the proxy papers, you've managed to get yourself married to your brother's intended."

"What?"

"You signed where Kit's signature was to go," Sir Roger explained. "You became the groom."

"He will be my husband over my dead body!" yelled Florrie.

"It would be a pleasure," Alford mumbled sourly from behind his handkerchief.

Sir Roger and the earl exchanged conspiratorial glances.

"Perhaps we should allow them some time to become re-acquainted," Barstow suggested. "I am certain Alford can be trusted to behave in a more gentlemanly manner with his *wife*."

"Not bloody likely," the viscount muttered.

Ignoring his son, Barstow took Sir Roger by the arm and they left the library, shutting the door behind them.

Alford cast one withering glance Florrie's way, then tilted his head back against the cushions, keeping his nose elevated.

"Is it broken?" Florrie asked at last.

"How the hell should I know?" he said, his voice muffled.

Florrie looked away. "I really did not mean to break it, you know," she said with a hint of apology. "But you certainly deserved it." She looked sideways at him again. "If you pinch the nostrils, the bleeding might stop."

"This is not the first bloodied nose I've had," he snapped. "I know what to do."

"It certainly does not look like it," she returned with a scathing glance. "Dabbing at it like that will only keep it bleeding longer."

"Oh, I suppose you are a trained physician in addition to being a lady of science?" he sneered.

She began laughing and he glared at her again.

"I can't help it," she gasped, her mirth spilling out. "You look so amusing!"

He shifted on the sofa and turned away from her.

"Oh, don't be so peevish, Alford. You have to admit you well deserved it. What were you thinking of, to grab a lady so? You are lucky it was I, or you would be facing an irate father or husband over the end of a pistol in the morning."

"I can think of worse fates," he grumbled.

"Like being married to you?" She snorted. "You have only yourself to blame for that, *my lord*. 'Twas your misplaced signature that did the deed."

"I do not believe it. This is some scheme cooked up by you or your crafty father."

"Hardly," she replied coldly. "No one in their right mind would wish to be married to you."

"You were eager enough to have Kit."

"Kit is my friend," she said. "I would not have you if you were the last man on earth. Leading apes would prove a better fate."

"They probably would not want you either," he said.

"Hah!" she retorted. "I could have wed any number of men these past years. I am marrying Kit by choice, not necessity."

"Damned convenient he is out of the country," Alford said snidely. "If he spent half a fortnight in your company, he'd change his mind quick enough."

"It takes only five minutes in *your* company to be certain I would not even want to be in the same house with you."

"That can be most easily arranged," he said.

They lapsed into angry silence, marred only by Alford's labored breathing.

He truly could not believe this was all happening. Through some fantastic chain of circumstances, he was wed to this odious witch—it had been corroborated by not only his father, but hers as well. But he clung to a glimmer of hope—certainly a person could not be married against their will in this day and age. All he would have to do is explain the situation to someone in authority and the union would be dissolved. He would not stay married to this shrew no matter how lovely she was.

He twisted slightly and watched her through half-closed eyes. If he had seen her across a room at a rout, and been told she was Florence Washburn, he would have called the man a liar. When he had last seen her she was a raggle-taggle hoyden, with hair done up in braids, her dress torn, and her face dirty. She had been, in fact, a pestilential brat who would not give him or Kit a moment's peace. To think that ragamuffin child had grown into *this*.

For one quick moment he envied Kit. Kit, who had seen her during the years she grew up, and probably knew what a beauty he was capturing. Kit never took a wrong step; Alford should have remembered that. He would never have wed anything less than perfection.

Perfection indeed! Hah! She may have the face and form of an angel, but she had the temper and tongue of a Billingsgate fishwife. Kit was welcome to her. Alford would escort her to the damned dock himself if it meant she was off to Portugal the quicker.

He carefully lifted away his stained handkerchief, dabbing at his nose with one unsullied corner to see if the bleeding had at last stopped. Satisfied it had, he turned toward her again.

"Would you be so kind as to bring me my glass of champagne, Miss Washburn?"

"Miss Washburn? Do you always treat every woman you attack with such formality after?"

"What would you prefer?" he asked sarcastically. "Lady Alford?" He winced at the sound and he felt a new trickle of blood start down his lip. "Damn."

Florrie stood in front of him, grabbin the handkerchief

from his hands. "Trust a man not to know how to do this properly." She twisted one corner into a narrow wad and stuffed it up his bleeding nostril. "Now leave it there!"

"I can't breathe," he complained.

"Breathe through your mouth," she ordered. She crossed the room and procured Alford's glass. Walking back to where he sat, she could not help but laugh at the sight.

"Glad I can amuse you," he said, taking the glass.

"You have to admit you look a fright, with your handkerchief hanging out of your nose." She grinned.

Ignoring her, he carefully pushed the cloth away from his mouth and took a long swallow from his glass.

Florrie sat in a chair, watching him with an assessing eye. He had grown from the gawky adolescent she remembered into a tolerably good looking man. Well, perhaps better than tolerable. The lashes that were closed over those icy blue eyes were indecently long. His face was lean without being thin, and for all the rumors she had heard about his dissipated lifestyle, not a trace of it showed in his face. But no manner of good looks could overcome his odious personality. Florrie almost hoped she had broken his nose—it was unfair that such male perfection hid an unconscionable rake.

Alford's eyes flew open, scowling at the sight of her. "Are you still here?" he groaned. "I had hoped you would be gone by now."

"I thought we should discuss our next step."

"What next step?" he asked suspiciously.

"Getting out of this ridiculous marriage, you idiot."

He sighed. "I assume father's solicitor can take care of it."

"Are you so certain that your father will do so? He sounded suspiciously happy when he was here."

Alford sat upright. "There is no way on earth I will remain in this marriage," he said. "And since we seem to think alike on that point, I think we should proceed immediately to getting the matter disentangled. I will hire my own lawyer if I have to."

Florrie breathed a hidden sigh of relief. Despite all of Alford's protestations, it was *he* who had missigned the papers. It must truly have been an accident.

"Fine," she announced, standing up. "I shall leave matters in your capable hands. Inform me when the matter has been taken care of."

"With pleasure," he grumbled before collapsing back against the cushions again.

Chapter 4

Florrie stood with hands on hips amidst the chaos of her bed chamber, glaring at her maid. Clothes lay in disordered piles on every surface, while two yawning trunks took up much of the floor space. Marie stared back at her with defiant black eyes.

"I have no weesh to go to theese sea coast," the maid protested. "The country—bah!"

"The English countryside is a sight more civilized than Portugal and you had no objections to going there," Florrie retorted.

Marie gave a disdainful sniff. "Portugal is at least close to France. I never heard of theese Hartland."

Florrie tossed up her hands in disgust. "Well, you will not get to Portugal with me if you do not accompany me on this journey first," she stormed.

"Fine weeth me," the maid replied. "I weel find myself a new position in London."

"That you will," Florrie said, shaking with rage at the girl's impertinence. "Out of my sight. Now."

She sank down on the bed as the maid shut the door none-too-gently behind her. The situation went from bad to worse. First the botched marriage to Alford, then her father's insistence that she leave town to still the gossip, now this. She was being shipped off to some horridly isolated corner of the island without even her own maid to accompany her. She'd probably end up having to use some bovine farm girl who did not know which end of a needle to thread, let alone how to care for Florrie's clothes. Not that that haughty French creature had been much better. She had far too great an opinion of herself for a maid. Typical French arrogance.

Florrie set her mouth in a stubborn line. She would not

do it, she decided. Either her father sent her to some location
that was at least on the fringes of civilization, or she would
insist on staying in London until she was free to join Kit on
the Peninsula. She would not be stuffed away in some
desolate back corner of the country as if she had done
something wrong. With renewed determination, she marched
out of her room in pursuit of her father.

She cornered Sir Roger in the library.

"It is impossible," she announced, "for me to go to
Hartland."

"Oh?" Setting his pen aside, he looked inquisitively at
his daughter.

"My maid just quit. I shall have to remain in town. I
certainly cannot depart on such a lengthy journey on my
own."

Unless, of course, you wanted to, Sir Roger thought. "That
problem can be easily resolved. We shall find you another
maid. I am certain London has an ample supply."

"But how can I train a new one properly in the *country*?"
Florrie pronounced the word with about as much enthusiasm
as an exiled member of the Bourbons would say
"Napoleon."

"I am certain you will find some way to manage, my
dear." Sir Roger suppressed a chuckle. He had expected his
daughter's protests to start earlier than this. It was an
indication of how unsettling this whole marriage confusion
had been to Florrie that it had taken her so long to come
up with her excuses.

"And, of course, there is the additional difficulty of finding
a maid who will also be willing to travel with me to
Portugal."

"Not an easy task," her father agreed.

"So I think it would be best for me to stay in London,"
Florrie continued. "I can interview for a new maid and
prepare her for the trip to Portugal when this blessed annulment comes through."

"I do not think that is the wisest course," Sir Roger said,
putting on his sternest face. "My first concern has to be for
you, Florrie, and for your reputation. We have been abroad

for too long. The London matrons are not familiar with you, and have no other way to judge you but by hearsay. It behooves you to behave as circumspectly as possible until this little matter is dealt with.''

"But . . ."

"Your removal from the city, as well as Alford's, will dampen even the busiest of tongues. Later, after the annulment is finalized, you will be able to come back and once again take your place as a young, betrothed lady. There will be no question about your situation."

"It is not fair!" Florrie fumed. "It was not *my* fault this happened."

"Of course not," Sir Roger said soothingly. "I would like to take a horsewhip to Alford for being so careless. But the deed is done and we will have to wait until it can be undone. Besides, it will be a treat for you to spend some time in the English countryside."

"Why cannot I go someplace closer to London? Someplace that is not the next thing to the end of the earth?"

"Now, Florrie, it was not easy trying to find a suitable place for you to stay. It would accomplish nothing if you were to stay in a neighborhood with close connections to London. In Hartland, you will remain totally free of any gossip."

"And totally isolated," she moaned.

"It will be over soon." Sir Roger gave her an encouraging smile. "And you will have plenty of time to study your Spanish grammar. Now decide what requirements you want in a maid and we can go about looking for a new one before you leave."

Florrie sighed, knowing she had lost the argument. It was exile for her, after all. "All right, Papa," she said, bending down to kiss his cheek.

"Won't be the same here without you," Hervey mumbled into his brandy glass.

"Quite true," drawled Seb Cole, leaning negligently against the mantel in Alford's front room at Albany.

"London is likely to be a deuced bore for the rest of the Season without you here, Alford."

"Don't I know it," the viscount replied. He stared morosely at the flickering fire. "I feel like some naughty boy being sent to bed without supper. Promise me you will come to visit."

Hervey and Cole exchanged dubious glances.

"Devon's a long distance away . . ." Seb began hesitantly.

"And will take you away from the pursuit of your pleasures for far too long," Alford continued sarcastically. "At least now I know who my true friends are."

"It's not like you're going to be there forever," Hervey said. "We'd come down for certain then. But if it's only to be a month . . . We'd spend most of the time traveling to and fro."

"Easy for you to say it's not forever," Alford retorted, sinking even lower into his chair. "Two days in Devon would be enough for anyone. I am looking at weeks."

"You can always hie down to Plymouth if you get bored," Seb pointed out.

"They don't even have roads where I am going." Alfred scowled. " 'Hieing down to Plymouth' would be the equivalent of returning to London."

"Your father'd never know if you left," Hervey said. "You wouldn't see anyone in Plymouth who'd spill the tale. The whole point of this is to get out of London to stop the tattle. Seems to me that Plymouth would do just as well as any."

"You don't know my father," Alford moaned. "I would not put it past him to send an armed guard to accompany me. Face it, men, I will have about as much freedom as some French prisoner in Dartmoor."

"Gossip will die down soon," Hervey said with an optimistic tone. "I ain't going to talk about it anymore. Everyone will forget in a week. You will be back before you know it. Plenty of time left in the Season."

"But there's Newmarket. And Epsom. The Derby." Alford groaned at the thought of all that he might miss.

"I'll run your bets for you," Hervey offered.

Alford pierced him with a withering glance. "I never let anyone place my bets," he said coldly. "And certainly not if I am unable to check on the horses beforehand."

"Don't be so Friday-faced," said Seb, clapping Alford on the shoulder. "Think of all the feminine sympathy you can evoke upon your return from exile. The ladies will be enticed with your mournful tale."

"They'll probably have forgotten my name by then," Alford said glumly. "They'll pass me in the street and not even recognize my face."

"Well, they'd hardly know you now anyway with that nose," Hervey pointed out.

Alford scowled, then winced as the movement pained him. He gently touched his fingers to his nose. Although it was not broken, the appendage was swollen and still hurt like hell a full two days after Miss Washburn had landed that stupendous right. He could only be thankful his eyes had not blackened in the bargain.

"I was thinking," Hervey began, looking around the chamber with an eager glance. "With you being out of town and all, this place is going to sit empty. I could stay here, keep an eye on things if you like."

"Oh, wonderful," said Alford. "Now I know why you are so willing to shove me out of town. You want my rooms. Can I get anything else for you, Hervey? Would you like my valet as well? The curricle? The dancer at the opera?"

"Well, since you won't be able to do much for her while you're in Devon, I—" Seb's sharp jab in the ribs silenced him.

"Perhaps you will find adventure in Devon," Seb suggested. "Smugglers. Or a ring of French spies. You can capture them with brave feats of derring-do and come back a hero."

Alford brightened. "Perhaps I can find a source of some decent brandy," he mused.

"That's the spirit," Seb said with an encouraging smile. "The whole thing will be over before you know it. You'll be unleg-shackled in no time and can once again walk the streets of London a free man."

"I won't feel safe until I know that wretched Miss Washburn is safely on her way to Portugal," Alford said. "I will live in fear of another attack until then."

"Still sure you don't want to warn Kit about her?" Hervey looked concerned. "Can't see how your brother would wish to marry a girl who made a habit of unprovoked attacks on men."

Alford had not confessed the true tale of the events leading up to Florrie's well-placed punch. "Kit's a military man. He can keep her in line with his sword, if need be."

"Must have caught you by surprise. You're pretty handy with your own sword," Hervey snickered.

Alford silenced him with a withering glare. "My one consolation is that if Kit's diplomatic career flourishes, I may never have to see her again."

"Wouldn't mind seeing her again, myself," Seb said, pouring a generous measure of brandy into everyone's glass. "She is certainly no antidote. I'll give Kit credit for his taste."

"You'll probably have ample opportunity to ogle the witch," Alford said acidly. "She'll probably be all over town, flaunting my folly." He sighed. "Why should I be the one forced to leave?"

"It's your nose," Hervey suggested. "Might lead to all sorts of embarrassing questions. You wouldn't want it to be known that she popped you one."

Alford felt tempted to pop one of his own—at Hervey. "Devon," he groaned again. The end of the world.

Chapter 5

Alford stared blankly at the opposite wall of the coach, his discomfort growing with each revolution of the wheels. Blast the English rain that kept him cooped up inside. His fingers drummed restlessly on the seat beside him. Would this interminable journey never end? The two days spent on the road already seemed like weeks.

The coach lurched as it hit another rut and Alford's stomach lurched with it. He should never have eaten breakfast at the inn this morning. He knew better. But he had ignored his mental warnings and wolfed down the thick slices of ham and the freshly baked bread dripping with butter and marmalade, then washed it all down with the good local ale. Now the whole meal was a roiling mass in his stomach.

He turned his gaze to the window, searching for some distant landmark to focus upon, to gain the illusion that the whole world was not moving along with him. But the lane was bounded with close-growing hedges which slipped past his eyes in a dizzying manner, further serving to emphasize the motion of the coach.

Alford took a deep breath and swallowed heavily. Closing his eyes, he leaned his head back against the padded cushion. It did not help. In the enveloping darkness, the spinning in his head magnified itself until he felt as if his whole body whirled within the close confines of the coach. His eyes snapped open and he lunged for the window. Jerking it down, he stuck his head through the opening, taking in the fresh, outside air in large, tortured gulps. He had an instant to realize that he had delayed for too long and then his breakfast decorated the peaceful Somerset countryside.

The coach lumbered to a halt, but by the time Alford was able to fling the door open and jump to the ground, his stomach had been thoroughly emptied. Ignoring the misting rain, he leaned weakly against the side of the coach, grateful to have solid, unmoving ground under his feet again. He fought against the waves of dizziness that still washed through his head.

"You want to ride up top for a bit?" the old coachman asked with a sympathetic smile.

Alford shook his head. It had been a number of years since he had suffered such a severe bout of motion-sickness, but he knew, now that his stomach was empty, the usual cure would work. He reached back into the coach and pulled out the chased silver flask of brandy from the side compartment. He spit out the first swig to cleanse his mouth, then he took a long, deep swallow. From experience, he knew that if he consumed enough brandy, the movement of the carriage would no longer bother him. The unsteadiness brought on by the spirits seemed to counteract the external motion. As he tipped the flask back a second time, Alford welcomed the scalding burn down his throat. This was what he should have had for breakfast.

With his stomach settled by the brandy and the swirling in his head halted by the stop, he climbed back into the coach and signalled the driver to proceed. Steadily sipping brandy, Alford kept his eyes firmly focused on the interior of the coach, and in a short time, the soothing numbness flowed through his veins and he felt much more the thing.

At least, he did until his thoughts strayed to the person who had brought all this down on his head. It was bad enough to have been forced from town; the indignity of this miserable carriage ride only heightened his irritation. He could easily have ridden out the gossip in London. But his father insisted it was better for . . . Lord, what was he supposed to call her? Miss Washburn? He certainly was not going to call her Lady Alford!

Admittedly, she was an intriguing chit. Most women would have succumbed to a fit of the vapors after what he had done to her in the library. Instead, she punched him in the nose. He gingerly rubbed that abused part of his face. At least it was almost back to its normal size. Thank God she had not broken it. He could not bear the thought of having to recall her handiwork every time he looked at himself in a mirror.

Once the lawyers finished their yammering, she could be quietly packed off to Kit on the Peninsula. And Alford could go back to his normal pursuits. But until then, he would be marooned in the furthest corner of Devon, all for the sake of protecting the reputation of a chit he had loathed from the instant of their first meeting years ago. The unfairness of it all irked him. Why should he be put through such torture on her account? Devon, for God's sake. What on God's green earth had persuaded his eccentric ancestor to build himself a home in such a remote corner of the island?

Alford snickered. Probably as an escape from his wife.

"What do you mean, the girl is ill?" Florrie stared at the landlady of the Hare's Tail in an uncomprehending manner.

"The poor girl is just plum out of sorts," the innkeeper's wife repeated. "My Maisie went to wake her this morning and the poor thing couldn't move. Weak as a kitten and all flushed with fever."

No wonder the new maid had been so quiet on the journey from London, Florrie thought. She'd been so relieved to be rid of her aunt's incessant chatter and that insolent French baggage that she hadn't given the poor girl a thought. Sally had probably been coming down with some dreadful disease the whole time. And Florrie had just spent three days in a closed carriage with her. The very thought made Florrie feel hot and flushed.

"Can you summon a doctor?" Florrie asked. He could tell her if the maid was able to travel. The thought of another night at this poor excuse for an inn did not appeal to Florrie in the slightest.

The lady nodded. "Perhaps you can go up and sit with her before he comes."

"Me?" Florrie said, aghast. Whyever would she want to go sit with a sick servant girl she barely knew? "I do not think that will be necessary. Have someone bring my break-

fast and send the doctor to me after he has seen Sally. And
perhaps you can spare me a few moments of Maisie's time?''

The landlady bowed out of the room, shaking her head
as she went.

Florrie picked up the lumpy and misshapen pillow that had
so disturbed her sleep during the night and flung it at the
chair in the room's corner. This journey was taking long
enough as it was, without another delay. At this rate, it would
be summer before she even reached her destination.

''I never should have taken a maid in London,'' she
moaned in frustration. ''Continental servants know better
than to be sick. Particularly when a body is travelling.'' She
sank down onto the edge of the bed and thought.

She would have to wait and see what the doctor said. If
Sally was able to travel, they could leave without too much
delay and perhaps reach Barnstaple by evening. All depended
upon the doctor. And Sally. And herself. Florrie could very
well find herself in a similar fix by morning, depending upon
what illness had felled the maid. The thought of being sick,
alone, in only a modest posting-inn like this increased her
frustration. If it came to that, she would summon her father
and force him to take her back to London.

That thought cheered her so much that Florrie almost
looked forward to becoming unwell. She would give anything
to return to the city.

Unfortunately, the doctor's words shattered that hope.

''Chicken pox,'' he pronounced.

''Chicken pox?'' Florrie could not hide her astonishment.
''That is a disease for children.''

The doctor shrugged. ''Some miss it early, and it catches
them later. She is not desperately ill, but she cer tainly will
not wish to travel for several days.''

''Several days?'' Florrie wailed. ''That is impossible. I
have to leave today.''

The doctor shook his head. ''I would advise against it.
Chicken pox is not normally a serious illness, but it
sometimes takes a strange turn in adults. You could risk her
becoming seriously ill.''

''I have half a mind to pack her back to London on the

next stage,'' Florrie muttered. She turned back to the doctor. "How many days until she will be fit to travel again?"

"The fever should abate in a day or two," he said. "It then depends on how severe a case of the pox she has. New ones will be popping out for a week. The itching can be fierce, and the movement of the carriage might only make it worse.''

Florrie considered her options—which at this point were reduced to one: she could stay here until Sally was well and ready to travel on. The thought was intolerable. But what else could she do? Travelling alone was impossible.

Or was it? Her father would be aghast if she tried such a thing. But he was not here to stop her. And certainly, she would encounter far fewer difficulties travelling alone than remaining in this stupid inn for days on end. Without a chaperon, Florrie should properly remain in her room during her entire stay. And she knew that was an impossibility, yet it would occasion comment if she tried to inspect the town on her own. But if she traveled onward, she would only have to spend one more night in an inn alone. Perhaps she could even borrow Maisie, or some other local girl, to accompany her as far as Barnstaple. Certainly she would be able to find some sort of girl to help out once she reached Hartland or Hartford or whatever that ridiculous place was named.

"Will you be able to come every day to check on the girl?" Florrie asked the doctor.

"Certainly," he replied.

"My business is pressing, and I cannot afford to be delayed," Florrie explained. "If the innkeeper is willing, I should like to leave Sally here. She can travel on when she is feeling better and you feel it is safe for her to do so." She smiled sweetly. "Of course, I will be willing to pay extra for your close attention . . ."

The doctor nodded.

Florrie rang for the landlady. The landlady frowned at the plan, but Florrie persuaded, cajoled, and then outright bribed her to accept the idea. Florrie settled a generous amount upon the doctor, who promised he would take special care of the patient, and she prepared to embark on the next leg of her journey. Maisie could not be spared, but she had a young cousin who would do equally well. By mid-morning, Florrie's coach was upon the road again. She was determined to bring his journey to a swift end.

Florrie wondered what Kit would say to all this when he heard the tale. He would admire her ingenuity, commend her for taking charge of matters, and laugh at her travails. And, once the whole tale had been told, it would appear amusing. Kit had a way of seeing things that way.

How unlike his brother he was. Kit was steady, ambitious, determined, while Alford was content to drink and game his way through life. Her vexation with him rose again. If it had not been for his drunken carelessness . . . She had no doubt he had been in his cups the day he signed the papers. His behavior in the library was ample proof that he could not handle his liquor. She only regretted she had not broken that oh-so-arrogant nose of his when she had the chance. He might not fare as well the next time he crossed her path.

Alford leaned gratefully against the side of the stone-walled house, struggling to catch his breath. What had ever possessed him to take his lunch in Clovelly? He had seen water before; why had he felt it necessary to walk all the way down to the quay? For after the novelty of seeing a town clinging to the side of a cliff wore off, he was faced with the unpleasant realization that there were definite disadvantages to exploring a town whose main street a mountain goat would disdain to climb. His side ached, his legs trembled, and he was only little more than halfway back to the top. If he did not hurry, the carter who waited for him at his starting point would probably turn back to Bideford and leave him stranded here, still miles from his destination.

This was all Miss Washburn's fault. This whole damnable journey was her fault. She was the one who had spread the tale far and wide of their accidental marriage. If she had kept her mouth shut, no one would have been the wiser and this all could have been dealt with quietly, *in London.* But because she had complained so vociferously in public, he now found himself in some isolated corner of the country, in a town that would have brought a smile to the lips of a medieval torturer.

A few more minutes of rest brought some semblance of normality to his labored breathing, and Alford struck out again for the top of the cliff overlooking Bideford Bay. Next time he travelled to some out-of-the-way corner of the country he'd invest in a good guidebook—the kind that would warn a person not to investigate Clovelly at close range.

"Enjoy your visit?" the waiting carter asked when Alford at last regained the heights.

Alford attributed the cheery tone in the man's voice to malicious glee. "Edifying," Alford replied. He did not add that he had rested for a full ten minutes just below the lip of the cliff, so as not to appear winded when he crested the top. How was it that he was so damnably out of condition?

The man moved aside and Alford took up his seat beside him.

"Couldn't never figure it out, myself," the carter mused as the yoked donkeys lumbered down what passed for a road. "Why'd anyone want to carve a town out the side of a cliff when there's perfectly good flat spots to build?"

"Why, indeed," replied Alford. Unless it was to trap unwary fools like himself.

The only bright spot in the entire day was that it had stopped raining. Alford could only guess at the joys of making a fifteen-mile journey in an open cart in the pouring rain. Some God had taken pity on him at last and spared him *that*, at least.

"What, precisely, do you mean by a 'cart'?" Florrie glared at the innkeeper of the Appledore Inn in Bideford.

"A cart," he repeated. "No fancy carriage is going to make it more than a mile or two out of town afore the road dwindles to a cart track. Why, the mails think even the road from here to Barnstaple is too rough for their precious coaches. Them that's heading further west goes either by horse or cart."

"And where, precisely, am I to find this cart in order to book passage upon it?"

The innkeeper shrugged. "Old Mort is probably out on his rounds. He takes the mail and whatever people have ordered from town and makes his circuit. He should be back shortly after supper."

"And then he can take me to Hartland tomorrow?" Florrie resisted the impatient urge to tap her foot while she talked with this infuriatingly obtuse innkeeper.

"Well, now, that all depends on what Old Mort's schedule is. Normalwise he don't go out toward Hartland every day. Depends on what people's ordered."

"I may have to spend days here?"

The innkeeper nodded. "Could be. I'll leave word to have Mort come by tonight when he gets back. P'raps you can work out some kind of arrangement with him."

"Is 'Old Mort' the only person in this town with a cart? There must be another carter who accepts passengers." Florrie knew how many innkeepers steered their customers only to certain drivers, with the profit split between them.

"This ain't Lunnon. Ain't much demand for carts from them that don't have them. I'll send Mort to you when he returns."

"Fine," snapped Florrie, and retreated up the stairs to her room. She had never before experienced a journey that had been such an unmitigated disaster. One expected difficulties on the Continent and planned for them accordingly. But in England she had expected matters to be more, well, *civilized*. And it was proving to be far less than that.

The thought of spending one more day in an uncomfortable inn was enough to make her contemplate turning tail and racing back to London. Except that the coach that had brought her here had already departed on its return journey. She was stranded at this inn until "Old Mort" was ready to take her to her destination.

Travelling in a cart, indeed. There must be another way to reach the coast. Some form of carriage must exist that could handle the primitive roadways. Through the dirt-begrimed window in her chamber, Florrie could see the ominous black clouds that hovered on the edge of the bay. Rain was in the offing, and there was no way she would travel the last fifteen miles of her journey in an open cart during a torrential rainstorm. No earthly way.

Chapter 6

Water dripped from Florrie's sodden garments and pooled upon the flagged stones of the entry at Hartland Hall. Her new bonnet, bought what seemed years ago in London, was ruined. Her feet felt like solid, frozen lumps at the end of her legs, and she suspected it would be days before her fingers worked properly again. And if appearances were anything to judge, the woman who stood before her had just stepped straight from a child's nursery tale—the kind that kept one awake all night in fear. For she looked most suspiciously like a witch.

Dressed head-to-toe in some unidentifiable black fabric, the woman's iron-gray hair was pulled back from her face in such a tight bun that Florrie was certain the woman suffered constant pain. It certainly explained the pinched look on her face. In the dim light of the hall, her eyes looked large and luminescent. But it was her nose that added the final touch. It was long, sharply pointed, and had a wart perfectly placed upon its tip. She was such a personification of the dreaded Baba Yaga that Florrie would not have been in the least surprised to hear a stream of Russian issue from her lips.

Instead, it was pure Devonian. "No one said aught about a lady," she growled.

Florrie accepted this enthusiastic welcome. It was all a piece of this entirely dreadful experience. Of course, they would not be expecting her. How foolish of her to have thought otherwise.

"I am sorry that the communication did not arrive," Florrie said. "I am certain it is all the fault of the mail. But, as you see, I am here and I would like to be shown to my room. And to have a bath drawn immediately."

She drew in a hasty breath and continued before the witch

54

could speak. "My maid fell ill and she will not be arriving for some days yet, so I shall need someone to look after my things. Perhaps you can assist me today and tomorrow find some local girl who is willing to come in. And," Florrie added, as she stripped off her gloves and watched the water drip from the ruined leather, "I should very much like a cup of hot tea."

Old Mort dropped Florrie's trunk to the stone floor with a resounding thud that made her jump. Florrie whirled and glared at him. "Kindly treat the other one with a bit more care," she snapped. "There are breakable items inside."

Mort ducked his head and hastened out the door.

"Have someone bring the trunk upstairs immediately," Florrie said as she stepped toward the stairs. She turned again and stared at the housekeeper, who had not moved. "Are we waiting for something?"

"No one told us a lady was coming," the housekeeper repeated.

"So you said." It was the crowning touch to an unmitigated disaster. "I assume there must be at least one chamber that is fit for habitation?" Florrie doubted it. The house looked as if it had not been occupied since the Restoration. The sheets were probably still begrimed with the dirt from some Cavalier or Roundhead.

"There's the old mistress's chamber, but—"

"I am certain it will perfectly suit," Florrie said. "Now, Mrs. . . . ?"

"Burgess."

" . . . Burgess, if you could *please* take me there. If I do not get out of these wet clothes I fear I will contract an inflammation of the lungs, and I am certain you do not wish to have an invalid on your hands."

Still shaking her head, Mrs. Burgess led Florrie up the stairs.

Once Mrs. Burgess decided to do something, she was nothing less than determined, and Florrie was nearly forced to run to keep up with her. She caught only brief glimpses of the house as they raced up the stairs and down the corridor. Her dominant impression was of darkness; the house was heavily paneled with wood in the Elizabethan manner. Florrie prayed her room would be free of that, or at least painted.

And indeed, the chamber she entered was surprisingly light and airy. And bare. Curtains, bed hangings, and furniture were all missing. Only the massive poster bed in the center of the chamber remained.

"I shall have the bed prepared first," Mrs. Burgess said in an apologetic tone. "I always keep my linens fresh. It may take a day to restore the hangings and curtains. Mr. Burgess can move some furniture in."

Florrie nodded indifferently. She was so exhausted she could have sunk down upon the mattress and slept round the clock. Curtains and furniture were the least of her concerns. "If I could only have some tea. And the bath. And my trunks."

"I will hasten," Mrs. Burgess said, slipping out into the corridor.

Florrie walked over to the window and peered through the curtain of rain that enveloped the house. The room was at the back of the building, and the window looked out over the rear lawn. On a sunny day, Florrie surmised, she would be able to see the sea, but today all she could see was an unending wall of gray shadow. Wet, gray shadow.

She shivered, and it was not entirely from her wet clothing. Her paps could never have imagined what he was sending her into. That was the only possible explanation for this inhospitable welcome. One would not deliberately send their worst enemy to this place.

Once she had bathed and changed into dry clothing, she would find her paper and ink and quills, and pen a succinct letter to her father, telling him exactly what kind of situation he had cast his daughter into. He might even be moved to come to the rescue himself. Florrie fervently hoped so.

Alford shuffled the cards with the skill and precision of a seasoned cardsman. After laying them out upon the library table in an intricate pattern, he sat back in his chair and studied them, a slight frown marring his face. He reached for the brandy glass at his elbow, his frown deepening when he discovered it empty.

He knew good French brandy when he tasted it, and this had to be one of the best. Seb and Hervey had been right when they predicted he might be in for an adventure. Alford was very certain that no duty had been paid on this beverage. What a triumph it would be to return from his exile with a supply of prime brandy that would be the envy of every gentleman in London. In a few days, when he got to know the couple that cared for the place better, he would begin making inquiries. He could guarantee the suppliers of this stuff a long list of customers.

Alford leaned back in his chair and stretched, then rose. He sauntered lazily to the table sporting the brandy decanter and poured himself a generous serving.

This whole little visit might not turn out so badly after all, he mused. Which was good, since the very thought of making the return journey caused him to shudder. He would be very content to bide here awhile. The house was certainly old enough and full of interesting, if quaint, relics from the past. Exploring it might provide him with amusement for a day or two. After that, he could investigate the neighborhood—if the deuced rain ever stopped. It had started some time during the night, he had discovered to his great discomfort this morning when he awoke—in a bed that was sodden from the incessant drip coming down from the ceiling.

The housekeeper had been properly apologetic, explaining that each and every storm loosened tiles from the roof and it was not always possible to replace them before the next one hit. Alford did not much care how the leak occurred, but he was grateful when she assured him there were plenty of other chambers.

He had inspected his new room only long enough to ascertain that it looked out toward the sea—at least, the old man had assured him the sea was there. Alford could not see through the torrent more than ten feet from the house. It did not matter; he found he rather preferred the cozy warmth of the library, where the blazing fire and exquisite brandy enabled him to sneer at the elements. He could think of worse ways to spend an afternoon.

"My lord?"

Alford turned toward the ancient housekeeper, who had just entered the room. "Yes?"

"Will you be desiring your dinner downstairs again tonight?"

Alford nodded. Eating in the library was not at all that different than eating in his rooms in London. Eating in his bedchamber would only serve to remind him that he was at the other end of the world—alone.

"The bed's been made up in your new chamber. I hope you will find it to your liking."

"I thought it quite satisfactory when I inspected it this morning." Alford forced a smile. "I imagine the view is quite pleasant when it is not shrouded in clouds. That must occur what—once or twice a year?"

The housekeeper's dour expression told him his little jest was not appreciated—or understood. One was never quite certain with these country folk. He shrugged.

"Dinner in the library will be fine," he said with a curt nod of dismissal.

His earlier enthusiasm waned during the long afternoon, when interminable games of solitaire only made him more aware that he was, indeed, *solitaire*. What he would not give for a good hand of whist. Perhaps the butler or estate manager or steward or whatever fancy title he wanted to call himself played piquet, or ecarte. It was abundantly clear to Alford that one day of solitaire was about as much as he could endure.

He flung down the cards and rose from the table. If he was going to sit and be bored witless, at least he could do it closer to the fire. The wind had whipped up outside and the room had taken on a chill. Alford settled himself into the high, wing-backed armchair that faced the blazing warmth. Moodily, he stared into the flames.

"Your tea, ma'am."

Florrie started back from the window and whirled about. Mrs. Burgess had entered the room so stealthily that Florrie had not heard her. Or had she simply conjured herself and the steaming pot of water out of thin air? Florrie did not dismiss the thought out of hand. Baba Yaga's powers were extensive.

"Thank you," Florrie said.

"The bath water's heating," Mrs. Burgess said as she laid out the tea things on the small folding table she brought along. "I'll bring the tub."

"Very well," said Florrie. "And my trunks?"

"Ol' Mort's bringing them along any time now," she said and whisked out of the room as silently as she had come.

Florrie poured herself a cup of tea, uncaring that it had not had time to steep properly. It was hot, and that was all that counted. She clasped the cup with both hands, reveling in the warmth that spread through her fingers, then took a cautious sip.

Instantly, she spit the bitter liquid back into the cup. This was *not* tea. Florrie sniffed it carefully but did not recognize the odor. A herbal concoction, no doubt. But what herb?

A cold fear seized her and she set the cup down with a trembling hand. What if it was something not quite . . . safe? What if Baba Yaga had mixed up one of her magical potions and waited just outside in the hall for the mixture to do its work? She could wish Florrie dead or . . . worse. Florrie shuddered and stepped backward across the room, as far away from the poisonous brew as she could get. Only her father knew she was journeying here. Mrs. Burgess could do away with her with no one the wiser. No one would come looking for Florrie for a month, at least. By then, any evidence of her ever having been here would be long eliminated. It would be as if she had vanished into thin air.

Florrie jumped a foot when the door crashed open. Mrs. Burgess wrestled a large, tin bathing tub through the doorway.

"Water'll be along in a moment," she said in a matter-of-fact tone. She glanced at the full tea cup sitting on the table. "Too hot for ye?"

Florrie nodded.

"It should be cool enough soon," Mrs. Burgess said. "Be good for you to drink. Chamomile is most soothing for those who've just endured a long journey."

Florrie's knees grew weak with relief. Chamomile. Of course. A perfectly harmless herb.

Mrs. Burgess picked up the cup and brought it to Florrie. "I make up my own teas," she said proudly. "This one has just a touch of rosemary and lavender. Rosemary's good for warding off the chill and lavender is most calming."

"Th-thank you," Florrie stammered, taking the cup. She took another sip, feeling like a perfect fool.

It was this house, this journey, the whole dratted mess that had her so overwrought. After a nice, soaking bath, a warm meal, and a good night's sleep, Florrie knew she would be at peace with the world again. Tomorrow would be a much better day.

And indeed, she did feel much more in charity with the world after she bathed and changed into her warm, dry clothing, with the assistance of Mrs. Burgess. Florrie was grateful that she had spent so much time in Russia. Clothes designed for the Russian winter were marvelous for an English spring. She even hummed a little tune as she sat in front of the blazing hearth, drying her hair in the radiated heat.

She felt so good, in fact, that she determined to venture downstairs before dinner. Mrs. Burgess had given her directions to the library, which was, she promised, more of a drawing room than library, the enormous main hall in this Elizabethan house being more suitable for a banquet than a lone lady. Florrie carefully followed her directions and found herself standing before what she hoped was the library door. She pushed it open carefully and stepped into the room.

"Ah, there you are, Mrs. Burgess. Kindly set the tea tray on the table. I shall pour my own."

Florrie could just see the crown of the speaker's head over

the top of the winged-back chair in front of the fire grate. "Who are you?" she demanded.

The man eased himself from the chair and turned to face her. His mouth immediately fell agape.

"You!" he exclaimed.

Chapter 7

Florrie stared in stunned silence at Viscount Alford, whose face she was certain mirrored her own surprise.

"Is this your idea of a jest?" he demanded. "What are you doing here? I thought you had caused me enough trouble back in London. Have you followed me here to plague me further?"

"*I* plague *you*?" Florrie drew herself up indignantly. "Easy words from the man who caused the whole imbroglio to begin with."

"You have not answered my question," Alford said coldly. "What, precisely, are you doing here?"

"I should ask the same of you," Florrie retorted. "My father sent me here to stifle the gossip in London. The gossip caused by your unconscionable carelessness in signing those proxy papers."

"Impossible," said Alford.

"It was not impossible at all," Florrie said. "You signed them incorrectly."

"Impossible that your father sent you *here,*" he explained. "My father sent *me* here to still the gossip."

Florrie glared at him. "It looks as if you have botched this as well as Kit's marriage papers," she said. "Your father probably told you I was coming here to make certain you went somewhere else."

Alford shook his head. "He specifically said he was sending me here because it was so far from town. He should know what he is doing; after all, it is his house."

"This house belongs to your father?"

Alford nodded. "So, you see, it is quite impossible that I am here by mistake. Obviously, your father made the error."

"But he specifically said that I was to go to Devon because—oh!" Florrie stamped her foot. "They did this on purpose! Those conniving . . ."

"I cannot believe that my father would ever be part of such an underhanded scheme," Alford said.

"Oh, no?" Florrie's voice was scornful. "He probably suggested the whole thing. My father would never place me in such an untenable position."

"It does not matter whose ridiculous idea this was," he said. "If you leave now, you should be able to reach Bideford by dark."

"I leave? Why, pray tell, should I be the one to leave? You are the one who tossed us both into this bumble broth. It is up to you to resolve the situation. You can leave."

He looked at her coldly. "I hardly think you are in a position to order me off my own property, Miss Washburn."

"Lady Alford," she corrected with sweet sarcasm. "As your *wife*, my claim is as strong as yours."

He glared at her in exasperation. "Why on God's earth would you wish to stay here?"

"Because I refuse to undertake another torturous, unpleasant, and miserable journey until I have fully recovered from the first one," she said heatedly. "And the shock of discovering you here has probably added another week to the time needed for my recuperation."

"Fine, then," said Alford. "I'll leave."

"Have a pleasant journey," she said as he slammed out of the library.

Alford had a strong urge to cause physical harm to someone. Not someone, he corrected himself. Florence Washburn. He began to suspect she was some modern-day incarnation of a Greek fury, set on earth to torment him. He could not get away from her fast enough.

Making his way to the kitchen at the back of the house, Alford hastily calculated the time it would take him to return to London. Four, five days at the most with a decent coach and good changes of horses. He would be damned if he would stay away from town after this. Someone in London had a lot to answer for, and he was eager to discover just who was responsible for this latest situation. There was a devilish deep game being played here.

"Burgess," he thundered as he reached the kitchen.

"M'lord?" The wizened man looked up from his tea.

"There has been a royal botch-up in sending that stupid chit here," Alford said. "I am leaving. You and Mort can load up my tunks."

"Mort ain't here," Burgess replied.

"What, left already?" Alford sighed. "What kind of horseflesh do you have in the stable? I can pack a light bag and head back to Bideford on horseback; Mort can come back tomorow for my trunks."

"Ain't no horse in the stable."

"There should be several horses out there," Alford complained. "My father said there were horses here."

Burgess shrugged indifferently. "Gone for years. No one here to ride them. No use for them."

Alford scowled. "I guess I will have to wait until tomorrow for Mort, then," he said and turned to go. "What time does he usually arrive?"

"Mort ain't coming tomorrow."

"What?"

"Mort only comes once a week," Burgess replied.

"Once a week? He's been here for two days in a row."

"Bringing guests, he was."

"Certainly, there must be some way to get word to him to return early."

"Foot," replied Burgess.

"Foot?" Alford asked.

"Foot."

"Burgess, what do you mean by 'foot'?"

"Ye ken walk t'town."

"Walk? It is fifteen miles. Surely, some neighbor has a horse I can borrow. Where's the nearest farm?"

"Horses ain't much use round here. Might find one in Bude. But Bude's a few steps further than Bideford. Now a good pack pony might be had. Or one of the donkeys."

Alford could only picture himself on either animal, his legs dangling to the ground. "You mean the only way I am going to get out of here before Mort's next 'visit' is by walking to Bideford?''

Burgess nodded.

Alford flung up his hands. "This has to be the most ridiculous state of affairs."

Burgess stared at him blandly. "We ain't much used to comings and goings around here."

Alford turned on his heel and left the room. He would wait until tomorrow then, and walk the whole damn way to Bideford if he must. He did not want to spend more than one minute longer than necessary under the same roof as Miss Washburn. He might be tempted to punch *her* in the nose this time.

He turned his steps toward the library, then hesitated outside the door. He had no desire to say another word to that witch. And he did not want to see the satisfaction on her face when he announced his departure. He could easily spend the rest of his stay here ignoring her presence. Alford retraced his steps and headed up the stairs to his room.

"Ah, there you are, Burgess." Alford turned away from his contemplation of the ever-present mist that surrounded the house and gestured toward the fireplace. "It is beginning to be a bit cold in here. Could you light the fire?"

Burgess knelt to the task.

"How far can one see on a clear day?" Alford asked as he returned to the window.

"Beyond Lundy," the man replied laconically as the fire caught.

"Still pirates out there?" Alford asked.

"There's some that says there is and some that says there isn't," Burgess replied.

"Of course," Alford mumbled to himself and resumed his futile attempts to pick out any kind of shape in the swirling mist that lay about the house.

Until he realized that the swirling mist was inside. He whirled about. Choking, gray smoke spewed from the fireplace.

"Burgess!" Alford exclaimed. "What in God's name?"

He fumbled with the window latch, flinging the glass panes wide. The incoming draft swept through the chamber, mingled with the sooty smoke from the fire, and sent it whirling about the room, setting both men to coughing. Rain poured through the open window in wind-driven sheets.

"Put the damn fire out," Alford called as he pulled off his coat and ineffectively flapped it at the smoke.

Burgess poked and prodded at the glowing coals without much success. Alford grabbed the washbasin and heaved the cold water on the hearth. Sizzling steam mingled with the acrid smoke, but in a few minutes the air cleared.

"Chimney must be blocked," Burgess said matter-of-factly.

"Wonderful," said Alford. "Do you suppose it could be cleaned so I can have a proper fire?"

"You be leaving tomorrow," Burgess pointed out.

"I would like to be able to sleep in a room where the temperature is somewhat above freezing," Alford said between clenched teeth as he struggled to close the window. Already he was soaked to the skin from the driving rain.

Burgess shrugged. "The sweep comes out of Bideford. You could send him this way when you reach town."

Alford held on to the last remnants of his temper. Was it impossible to get anything done on the spot in this house? "I will do just that," he snapped. "Someday there may be some other misguided soul who has the misfortune to be stranded in this God-awful place. Perhaps they would enjoy the luxury of heated rooms."

"The fireplace in the library works," Burgess pointed out.

Alford sighed. It was probably the only working fireplace in the entire house. But unless he wished to freeze slowly in his room, he would have to return there. And rejoin Miss Washburn.

A slow smile of malicious pleasure crossed his face.

"Does the fireplace in Miss Washburn's room work?" Alford asked suddenly, a wicked gleam in his eye.

Burgess shrugged noncommittally.

"I would not be in any great hurry to clean it," Alford said with a sly smile.

"It's all the same to me," Burgess said. "I'll have the missus air out your room afor bed."

Alford nodded his ungrateful thanks and went in pursuit of warmth.

Florrie looked up from her book when Alford entered the library.

"Still here? I had hoped you were well on your way by now."

"Tomorrow," he growled as he sidled closer to the fire.

Florrie sniffed. "Have you perhaps been trying to burn the house down, Alford?"

"The damn chimney in my room is plugged," he said shortly. "I suggest you forgo the pleasure of a fire in your room until the sweep can be brought out from Bideford to clean it. Wouldn't want to risk a fire. This place could go up like a tinder box."

"How unfortunate for you," she said, with cloying sweetness. "I am grateful that my fireplace worked perfectly."

Alford flopped down in the chair nearest the fire. He could swear the damp mist outside was creeping into this very room. He fought down a shiver. He'd forgotten his wet shirt when he shrugged on his sooty coat, and even he had to admit that he smelled like a chimney sweep.

Florrie eyed him smugly. The poor man was obviously freezing and had come down in search of a heated room. Well, the fire may be warm, but he shouldn't expect any warmth from her. It served him right for having brought this mess down upon their heads.

"Mrs. Burgess says dinner will be served shortly," Florrie said. "I surmise you wish to eat in your chamber—assuming the smoke has been cleared out."

"Oh, no," Alford said. "I am certain I would be much more comfortable dining here." She was not going to drive him out again. Let her retreat this time.

Florrie frowned. She had no desire to dine tête-à-tête with Alford. But neither did she wish to retreat to her room. She would not allow Alford *that* satisfaction. If he wished to stay in this room, he could, but she would do her best to pretend

he did not exist. With that firmly resolved in her mind, she
turned her attention back to her book of Spanish grammar.

Dinner was eaten without more than a word or two shared
between them. Florrie watched with growing disdain as
Alford downed glass after glass of ruby-red claret. She sipped
her single glass of wine carefully. She remembered all too
well what had happened the last time Alford had been foxed
in her presence. He would not catch her by surprise again.

She picked experimentally at the overdone mutton. Mrs.
Burgess had apologized for the plain fare, explaining that
until Old Mort was back with supplies, she would not be
able to prepare more elaborate meals. Anything would be
an improvement over this.

Alford sat hunched over his plate, eating with a relish that
disgusted Florrie. She suspected he behaved in such a boorish
manner merely to annoy her, and she grew even more
annoyed at herself for allowing his ploy to succeed. It was
with great relief that she finished her meal and excused
herself for the night.

Florrie sat before the dressing table that had been moved
into her room during the day, brushing out her hair. The
fire burned merrily in the grate, she was wrapped in her
warmest nightrail and robe, and she felt quite smug at the
thought of Alford freezing away in his unheated chamber.
It served the lout right.

She had raised her hand to take another stroke, then her
arm froze in midair when the door on the opposite side of
the chamber slowly opened inward. Her breath caught in her
throat and she felt a scream building inside her.

"I wondered where this door led." Alford peered around
the edge of the door with a curious gaze.

"Get out of here!" Florrie shrieked.

Alford instinctively ducked. When no missile flew at his
head, he stepped into the room. "How convenient," he
drawled. "These must be the chambers of the master and
mistress of the house." He nodded back toward the open
door. "With a shared dressing room between. A cozy
arrangement for a married couple."

"We are not a married couple," she said.

He laughed. "If we were not, neither you nor I would be here. You'd be on your way to Kit and I would be enjoying myself in London." He took a step further into the room.

Forcing herself to remain calm, Florrie prepared herself for the worst. Was she going to have to fight off a drunken Alford again? She would be certain to leave him with more than a bruised nose this time. Her fingers tightened around the handle of her silver hair brush.

Alford made a quick survey of the room, even pulling the curtains aside to peer out into the darkness beyond the window. He stopped in front of the fire, holding out his hands to the warmth.

"So this is the famous working fireplace," he said. "How fortunate you are."

Florrie watched him intently while he prowled the room in curious inspection. He did not look nearly as foxed as she thought he must be, after watching him consume so many glasses of wine at dinner. But then, an experienced drinker could often disguise his condition well.

Alford stared at the flames, unsure of why he lingered in this chamber. If ever a position was compromising . . . . This was the exact thing that would bind him permanently to Florence Washburn, if word ever got out. He lowered his gaze and slanted a sidelong glance at her. She sat there tense and taut as if she expected him to attack her. The idea was laughable. Now that he knew who she was, no amount of persuasion on earth could induce him to lay a finger on her.

Still, she appeared a delectable bundle. Enveloped all in white and lace, with that honey-gold hair swirling about her shoulders, Florrie offered a tempting picture. He felt a slight pang of—regret?—at remembering how she was destined for Kit. For despite her shrewish tongue and ability to use her fists, Florence Washburn was a damnably attractive woman.

He laughed inwardly at his train of thought and glanced openly at her, his eyes sweeping her form from head to toe in an appreciative gaze.

"Are you quite finished?" she demanded acidly. "I should like to retire for the night."

"Oh, do not let me stop you," he said with a wicked grin.

She jumped to her feet and stepped toward him, a look of threatening menace on her face. "Get—out—of—my—room!"

Alford bowed. "As you wish, my dear." He turned back to the door and felt her gaze boring a hole in the spot between his shoulder blades. Turning his back on that bundle of fury was one of the hardest things he had ever done. But he dare not let her know just how much he respected her ability to cause him bodily harm. He slipped quickly into the passage and pulled the door shut behind him just in time to hear the dull thump of some weapon bouncing off the wood on the other side.

Florrie glared at the closed door. She wished she had tossed that brush a fraction of a second earlier, and caught Alford square on. The nerve of that man! There had been no mistaking that gleam in his eye—he had been ogling her as if she were Covent Garden ware. She crossed quickly to the door and examined it for some locking mechanism, groaning in frustration when she discovered no key in the lock. Turning back to her room, she went to the dressing table and half-pulled, half-pushed it across the room until it stood in front of the door. She would get the key from Mrs. Burgess in the morning; meanwhile, there would be no way Alford could make an uninvited excursion into her room during the night.

With a sigh of satisfaction, she turned down the covers and climbed into the high, wide, ancient bed, dousing the candle at her bedside. She could sleep safely now. And tomorrow, Alford would be gone.

Chapter 8

In the morning, Alford watched the incessant fall of rain with growing dismay. Except for a few short hours during the night, it had not stopped since his arrival. It grew quite apparent that he would not be able to make his way to Bideford today—at least, not without serious risk to his health. If there was any guarantee that one of the neighboring farms would have a suitable animal for him to ride, he would strike out on foot, but the thought of having to walk the entire fifteen miles to Bideford in this freezing spring rain was unpalatable. He was forced to admit that another day in Miss Washburn's company was more appealing. Barely.

His persistent nagging had goaded Burgess into unearthing what looked to be some form of medieval torture device to clean out the chimney in his room. Alford swore he would not spend another night freezing; he would sleep here in the library if necessary to keep warm. He had tossed and turned all night, restless from the cold, and every waking thought had centered on that invitingly heated chamber he knew was only a door away.

He cast a swift glance at Miss Washburn, who sat before the fire with apparent unconcern, reading her damned Spanish grammar. He did not for a moment believe she was gaining anything from her ardent perusal of the book. She flaunted the book out of spite, to remind him of where she was headed when this whole mess was resolved, and also to remind him that she would soon be his sister-in-law. He was glad he and Kit were not close; if he did not see Miss Washburn again for fifty years, it would not be long enough.

While Alford paced restlessly up and down the length of the library, Florrie watched him surreptitiously over the top of her book. The man was like one of the caged lions at the 'change. And his agitation was infectious. She had been looking at this same page for an interminable time.

"Sit down," she said irritably. "You are driving me mad."

Alford smiled. If only it were true. "Why, Miss Washburn, I had no idea you were so easily distracted from your *studies*. Perhaps you would be able to apply yourself better in the privacy of your own room."

"I find this room perfectly amenable to study," she retorted. "When I am alone."

"But as Burgess is cleaning out the chimney in my chamber, I am forced to remain here," he said.

"Then find something to do," she snapped. "Read a book. Or are you able to read anything more complex than the racing news and the betting book at White's?"

"My university tutors would be shocked to hear such aspersions cast upon my scholarship abilities," he said in a voice that was quietly mocking and yet as hard as steel.

"I had not thought your studies would have gone beyond the comparative merits of various forms of spirits and the mathematical odds at faro and hazard."

"Oh, I did much better than that," he said with a sneer. "I also mastered the art of fisticuffs, curricle racing, and pistol shooting."

"Such manly pursuits," Florrie drawled.

"Yes, indeed," he said. "But then, I do not suppose that a mere woman such as yourself can truly appreciate the skill involved. It is a slight more taxing than choosing a pair of gloves."

"Who do you prefer? Manton or Durs Egg?" Florrie's voice echoed her smug smile.

Clever chit, Alford thought. Thinking to impress him because she can rattle off the names of London gunsmiths. "It depends," he replied, "whether one is looking for accuracy at a distance, or reliability across the green."

"And, of course, the fit in one's hand and the relative ease of priming and loading," Florrie continued. "I myself feel that Manton's productions have been overrated."

"Oh, you do, do you? And you are such an expert at pistols?"

"I am reckoned a tolerable shot," she said.

Alford snorted. " 'Tis almost a pity I will be leaving so soon. For I would be tempted to challenge you to demonstrate your 'tolerable' prowess with a pistol."

It *was* a pity he was leaving, for she would dearly love to wipe that condescending smile off his face. No one who travelled the European continent in the last disruptive years dared to venture out unarmed—and mere possession of a firearm was not enough; one also needed to know how to use it. Her father had enlisted a number of willing assistants to tutor her into becoming a crack shot. She only wished she could display that skill to Alford.

Determined to ignore him, Florrie turned back to her grammar with a sigh. Learning a language from books was such a dreadful bore. It was so much easier and interesting to learn the language in conversation. But that would have to wait until she gained the Peninsula. That could not happen too soon for her.

Eager to be free from Miss Washburn's exasperating presence, Alford grabbed the brandy decanter and retreated to his room. Pouring himself a generous amount, he stared glumly into the flames of his newly cleaned fireplace, idly swirling the liquid in his glass. If it were not for that odious Washburn chit, he could almost enjoy his stay here. It was peaceful and quiet—something he realized he sorely missed in London. He half-believed he would prefer to stay and force Miss Washburn to leave instead.

He pondered the idea. She seemed adamant about staying. There must be something he could do to encourage her departure. Something so outrageous, so dreadful that she would not hesitate to set out for Bideford, even if it must be on foot.

He dismissed the idea of attempting to breach the fortress of her room. That could be too dangerous a course—for if she felt truly compromised, he would be stuck with her for the remainder of his life. That was a fate to be avoided at all costs. It must be something else.

Alford sat up straighter. If he did not directly compromise Miss Washburn herself, there was another way to evoke her disgust. What if he brought another woman into the house? The type of woman no respectable lady like Miss Washburn would dare to associate with. . . .

A capital idea! Although he had made no formal arrangement with that dancer before he left town, her professions of dismay at his departure had seemed genuine enough. He could offer her a more permanent liaison, based on her willingness to join him in Devon. He was willing to bet Miss Washburn would not remain under the same roof for more than five minutes.

A masterful plan. He would have a companion to make his stay much more pleasant, and be rid of Miss Washburn in the bargain. It was an idea that could not go wrong. With any luck, he would already have driven her away before Nanette even arrived, but if not . . . Alford set down his glass and went in search of pen and paper. He would be free of that irksome chit and have the lovely Nanette warming his bed in less than a fortnight.

Florrie carefully shook the beaded water from her cloak and hung it on the peg in the passageway between the kitchen and front hall. When the rain at last stopped earlier in the afternoon, she seized the opportunity to enjoy a walk in the fresh air. Although she was not certain whether it made much difference whether it actually was raining outside or not—it seemed to be just as wet. She frowned at her water-spotted half-boots. They would have to be dried carefully to prevent staining the soft leather.

Crossing the hall, she could not help but notice the letter laying on the table. Curious, she stepped closer in an attempt to read the addressee's name. Miss Nanette La Pierre. Florrie wrinkled her nose in disgust. That was a most unrespectable sounding name if she ever heard one. She noticed Alford had signed his father's name to the missive in order to gain free postage. Typical.

Curiosity warred within her and she reached out to grab
the letter, then she jerked her hand back. Alford's letters were
his own business. Weren't they? She turned to resume her
journey, then halted and whirled again. No telling what
interesting things she might learn. Snatching the letter,
Florrie slipped it into her pocket, and turned her steps to
the stairs.

In the privacy of her room, she heated her small penknife
before the fire until it was hot enough to slip easily under
the wax seal. Carefully unfolding the thick paper, she scanned
the contents. Color rose to her cheeks as she read the lines
penned by Alford.

This was outrageous! He was actually inviting his mistress
to stay at this house. Florrie was speechless at his audacity.
This surpassed anything she had thought him capable of.
Why, the veriest scandal would descend upon her head if
word of this ever reached the outside. If he thought she would
remain in this house for one minute while that—

Florrie sucked in her breath in a sharp "Oh!" That was
exactly what Alford intended—to drive her from this house.
He must have decided to remain himself, and wanted her
gone. And knew that no respectable lady would dare remain
after he had dragged his *cherie amie* here.

"The bloody nerve," she exclaimed.

Actually, Florrie did have to give the man credit for his
clever plot. It raised her opinion of Alford a notch or two.
He was not as indolent and obtuse as he liked to appear. In
fact, it was a rather crafty plan. If it had not been directed
at her, she would be tempted to congratulate him on it.

But she could plot just as easily. She sat down before the
dresser, tapping the letter against her chin as she thought.
Her first impulse was to toss the whole thing in the fire, but
Alford might notice if the letter disappeared from the table
before Old Mort stopped for the mail. But she doubted Alford
would examine a finished letter carefully.

Florrie set the letter aside and carefully refolded the cover
sheet. She once again heated her penknife and, after warming
the wax, carefully pressed the seal down until the letter was
fastened close. Examining her work carefully, she expressed

a satisfied sigh. All was neat and tidy, with no sign of her tampering. The pages of the letter she picked up and tossed into the fire. Let Miss La Pierre wonder at the strange missive she received. Peering around the corner of her door, Florrie made certain no one was in the corridor. She slunk down the back stairs, slipped into the hall, and deposited the empty letter in its original spot on the table.

Alford had made only one error—underestimating his enemy. Florrie chuckled as she headed for the library. Lord Alford was in for a long wait for his London lightskirt.

Cheered by his new plan to be rid of Miss Washburn, Alford was inclined to be in a generous mood that evening.

"Should you like to join me for a few hands of piquet?" he asked when the dinner dishes had been cleared away.

Florrie stared at him. Was this some devious new plot?

"You do play piquet?" he asked.

She nodded. "What stakes do you propose?"

"Stakes?" He looked surprised. "I thought this would be only a friendly game. Something to wile away the time."

"Unusual for a man with your reputation to be so unwilling to take up a challenge," she taunted. "Or do you fear that my skill will surpass yours?"

"Of course not," he said, fighting his irritation. He was only trying to be polite and here she was, snapping at him again. Lord, this chit would try the patience of a saint. "I did not know you were that interested in gambling, Miss Washburn."

"All diplomats are gamblers," she replied.

"Name your stakes, then."

"Shilling a point, ten pounds a game?"

Alford stared. She did not propose chicken stakes. "Are you prepared to lose such a sum of money?" he asked snidely.

"Are you?" she countered with a defiant stare.

Florrie had no clue as to Alford's skill at piquet; she could only assume it was tolerable, knowing his penchant for other games of chance. She was acknowledged to be a dab hand at piquet herself. It might prove an interesting match. And if not . . . well, she would make her father pay whatever she lost to Alford. He owed her that much after sending her to this abominable house. She took her seat across the table from Alford and watched while he shuffled the cards with precise skill.

The sight of his long, tapering fingers manipulating the cards was almost mesmerizing. He had very nice hands, she thought, remembering for an instant the feel of them against her body on that crazy wedding day in London. Then she hastily shook her head to dismiss the disturbing image.

Florrie picked up her cards and arranged them in suits. She glanced at Alford, who smiled at her smugly over the top of his own cards. After examining her own hand more carefully, she could see the reason for his smugness. Her cards were abominable. Two low quatorze's. If it weren't for that dratted queen and jack, she could have called carte blanche.

"Pondering your discard, Miss Washburn?"

Slapping her five worst cards on the table, she drew five more from the talon. They were equally bad. She noted with growing unease that Alford gave up nothing.

"Point?" he asked.

"Three," she said glumly.

"Five," he replied with a self-satisfied smile.

"I have a tierce," she said apprehensively.

"Two quarts and a quint," Alford said blandly. "Eighteen points."

Florrie knew now she would not even make her hand. "Quatorze."

"I have kings."

"Yours," she replied in disgust.

"That makes thirty-two," Alford replied. "Repique."

Florrie tossed down her cards. "I concede the game," she grumbled.

"You do not hesitate over things, do you Miss Washburn?" he asked, arching a supercilious brow. "Should you perhaps care to change our wager?"

"No," Florrie snapped, snatching the proffered cards from his hand. "One game does not make an evening."

"True, true," Alford said, nodding. He was quite willing to stop before further damage was done, but if Miss Washburn's stubborn pride goaded her into folly . . . well, she had only herself to blame.

Florrie was willing to concede, after several games, that she was in the presence of a master. Alford never bested her in such an insulting manner again, but he won steadily. She was forced into taking wild chances in hopes of a successful play, and her losses mounted steadily.

"You should make your living at cards," she said sarcastically, shuffling the deck.

"I do."

Florrie's eyes widened.

Alford poured himself some more brandy from the decanter at his elbow, ignoring her curious gaze. "Would you like some, Miss Washburn?"

Florrie hesitated, then nodded. "A small amount."

" 'Tis a shame to pour so little," he said, handing her the half-filled glass. "This is a fine vintage."

"I am not overly fond of brandy," Florrie said, taking a hesitant sip.

"Of what are you overly fond, then?" he asked.

"Champagne," Florrie replied.

"Of course," Alford said with a patronizing smile. "A lady's drink."

Florrie glared at him. "I will have you know many *gentlemen* prefer champagne over brandy or port," she retorted.

"Of course they do," he said sarcastically.

"Are you always so irritating, Alford, or are you making a special effort tonight?" Florrie demanded.

Alford placed a hand over his breast. "You wound me, Miss Washburn. Here I am, trying to be an amiable companion, and my efforts are flung in my face." He took a large swallow of brandy. "It is enough to drive a man to drink."

"T'would be a short drive in this instance," Florrie muttered under her breath.

"I did not ask to be sent to this God-forsaken corner of

the earth," he said with an angry scowl. "And I particularly did not ask for your 'soothing' presence, Miss Washburn. So do not expect me to act overjoyed at the situation."

"I have known cantankerous old men with better dispositions."

"They were not married to you," Alford pointed out.

"I await the news of the annulment with great eagerness," she snapped. "I would rather be wed to the Corsican himself than to you." She flung the cards onto the table. "What do I owe you?"

Alford reclined in his chair, swirling the brandy in his glass in an aimless manner that only increased Florrie's exasperation.

" 'Tis a sizeable amount," he said at last.

"I am not a pauper."

Glancing at the score paper, Alford mentally calculated her debt. "Forty-eight pounds, seven shillings," he announced. "That would buy you a few bonnets."

Florrie berated herself for having insisted on such high stakes. Her father would be most displeased.

"I might be amenable to making a few adjustments," Alford drawled, watching her closely.

"Such as?" she asked.

"I will wipe the whole debt free if you depart when Old Mort returns again," he said quickly.

Florrie drew herself up straighter in the chair. "I shall do no such thing," she stated haughtily. "It has already been decided that you shall be the one to leave."

Alford shook his head. "I begin to think I like it here."

Reaching for the paper, Florrie quickly scrawled her signature and the debt. "That should be satisfactory," she said, rising to her feet. "I bid you goodnight, Lord Alford."

He had not really thought she would rise to the bait, but Alford had to admit he admired her aplomb. She had a sense of honor worthy of a man. Too bad it meant he would have to think of some other method of driving her away.

After the thoroughly lowering evening, Florrie retired to her room. She made certain both doors to her chamber were securely locked before she stepped out of her clothing. Despite the way he had trounced her at piquet, Alford had been drinking steadily all evening, and she had thought he had begun to eye her with a bit of a leer by the end of the night. Stranded in this horrid house, she was truly at his mercy if he developed any improper ideas. And after reading that letter to his mistress, she knew he had several.

It would be useful to have her maid with her once again, she thought, as she struggled out of her gown. How long did the chicken pox last? She fully expected to have Sally arrive on the doorstep any day. But until she did, Florrie would continue to manage her own clothes. She did not feel comfortable with Mrs. Burgess.

Wrapped in her warm robe at last, Florrie crossed to the windows to draw the curtains. Across the rear lawn, the mist rose from the ground under the pale light of the half moon. It swirled about in wind-shaped wisps, growing ever thicker, almost looking like a living entity, growing, flowing, crawling across the lawn toward the house. She shuddered at the thought.

Grabbing the edge of the heavy velvet curtain, she started to pull it across the window, then stopped and peered out into the mist again. Hardly daring to believe what she saw, Florrie looked again, the curtain falling from her hand as she peered intently into the shrouded darkness.

There had been movement out there. She was certain of it. Not the mist; it was more definite and quick than that. It looked like a . . . a person, perhaps. With a trembling hand, Florrie reached up and unlatched the window.

An icy blast of air smote her as she opened it wide and leaned out. Everything grew dark as clouds scudded across the moon. There it was again! On the far side of the lawn. She stared in rapt fascination. As the figure drew closer, Florrie leaned further out the window to catch a better glimpse.

It was a woman, dressed in some flowing white garment. Her hair was long and the wind whipped it into wild disarray across her face and shoulders. Another drifting cloud momentarily blocked the light from the moon. Florrie's heart pounded; she held her breath while waiting to catch another glimpse of the mysterious figure.

As the pale moon's rays relit the lawn below, Florrie scanned it frantically for another glimpse of the white figure, but there was no sign. The woman had vanished. Completely. The moon had not been covered long enough for her to have crossed the lawn toward the house. Where had she gone?

As the cold seeped into her bones, Florrie reluctantly drew back and reached up to pull the window shut. Just as the window was within an inch of closing, an eerie wail rang out, rising and falling as if born by the wind. The hair on the back of her neck rose and Florrie stood motionless, frozen to the floor in fear. Then she tugged the window shut, fastened the latch, and jerked the curtains tight. In a quick dash, she reached the bed and crawled into it, night robe and all. Pulling the covers over her head, she huddled there until she stopped shivering from the cold—and trembling from fear.

The candle at her bedside burned brightly long after she was asleep.

Chapter 9

Florrie stretched lazily under the bedcovers, slowly allowing her body to drift into wakefulness. Through the heavy window curtains, only the faintest morning light trickled into her chamber. It was a most pleasant way to—

She sat bolt upright as she remembered the inexplicable events of the previous evening. Jumping from the bed, she ran to the window and peered out. It was a foolish action, she knew, for nothing would be there.

And indeed, the back lawn was one vast stretch of empty, verdant green, gently sloping down to the rock wall that marked the edge of the cultivated property. Beyond that, she had learned, was the rocky ledge leading to the cliffs and the sea below.

How different a sight it was this morning! The long-absent sun already had burned a hole through the early morning fog and the day promised to be pleasing. Florrie hoped she might even be able to catch her first glimpse of the sea. Even through the closed window she could hear the raucous cries of the seabirds who nested in the nooks and crannies on the cliff above the water.

Turning back toward her room, Florrie saw the burned-out stump of the candle beside her bed and grinned ruefully. She had been a royal pea-goose last evening. What she heard was the wind, nothing more. And that mysterious lady had probably been nothing more than a trick of the mist and moonlight.

Still . . . Florrie had sensed *something* odd in the air last night. Something dark and strange, and perplexing. The very thought sent a *frisson* of apprehension down her spine.

She was being silly, she chided herself while she dressed. It was like her first day, when she had half-believed Mrs.

Burgess to be a witch. Her imagination was far too active. No doubt caused by the untoward chain of events that had turned her life so topsy turvy in the last weeks. The sooner her life returned to normal, the better. And that meant getting Alford out of her life as quickly as possible.

Alford was already in the library when Florrie made her way there. He had polished off what looked to be an enormous breakfast, judging from the remnants littering his plate. She gave a disdainful sniff and rang for her own light breakfast of toast and tea.

Florrie settled herself in her chair before attempting conversation with Alford. Curiosity burned within her. How would he explain his new desire to remain at Hartland?

"It appears to be a promising day today," she said brightly. "The rain has stopped at last. No doubt you are pleased that you will finally be able to make your way to Bideford."

Alford shrugged carelessly. "I am not so certain that I will be leaving today. My father was right; the country does have a restorataive function. I have contemplated staying longer."

Florrie feigned curiosity. "Oh? Do you think that wise?"

"Whyever not?"

"We have no chaperon! Just think how it will appear to others. Why, if you continue to linger in my presence, it may be more difficult to obtain an annulment." She smiled sweetly. "You would not wish that, I am certain."

Alford laughed. "The only bar to our annulment, my dear, is for me to take you to my bed. And as pleasant as that event might prove"—he leered at her—"I am not in the slightest bit interested in leg-shackling myself to you. You need not fear for your annulment."

Florrie glared at him. How dare he even mention such a thing to her!

"Do not look at me like that," Alford protested. "You were the one to bring up the topic." He grinned wickedly. "Besides, you are soon to be a married lady. Surely you must have some knowledge of what transpires between a man and his wife."

"Of course I do," Florrie snapped. "That does not make it a proper topic for the breakfast table."

He shrugged. "If you find my conduct offensive, perhaps you should remove yourself. I am not going to put on airs in front of *you.*"

Florrie fumed in exasperation. She could not allow Alford to bait her so. He took great pleasure in disconcerting her and she only played into his hands by allowing her irritation to show. She was made of sterner stuff. Composing her features, she calmly poured herself another cup of the now-tepid tea.

"I trust your fireplace is now working to your satisfaction?" she asked. It was a pity Burgess had managed to clean it. Discomfort would have been a good ally in her struggle to be rid of Lord Alford.

"Quite well," Alford replied. "I was more than cozy last evening. Slept like a babe, in fact."

Florrie thought back to her own disturbing evening. "You did not hear or see anything . . . strange?"

Alford arched one brow. "Strange?"

Florrie flushed. "Unusual is perhaps a better word. I noticed an odd sound as I was preparing for bed. It was probably nothing more than the wind."

Her remark aroused Alford's curiosity. "Just what type of noise was it?"

Florrie waved a dismissive hand. "Oh, you know, the type of sound you get with wind swooping between the chimney pots, or along the eaves. A wailing noise."

"How did it sound? Was it long and low? Or short and high-pitched?"

"Long and—oh, what does it matter? I only wondered if you had heard it as well. I probably only noticed it last night with the rain gone. It was such a relief to hear something beyond that steady drip."

"Was the sound high-pitched or low?" he persisted.

"High," she replied. "Almost . . . almost as if it were a voice."

"A voice?" Alford sat up straighter in his chair. "You thought it sounded like a voice? How odd."

Florrie nervously twined her fingers together. Last night the figure she had glimpsed seemed so vivid. But today, in the light . . . Dare she mention it to Alford?

"Well, what did it sound like?" he prompted.

"A woman's voice," she said reluctantly.

"A scream?"

"No, it was a more mournful sound, full of despair rather than fear." She laughed uneasily. "If one can say such a thing about the wind."

Alford smothered his urge to laugh. In a minute, she would be claiming to have seen a ghostly figure in white hovering in the air. "You did not see or hear anything else while this was going on, did you?" he asked.

Florrie swallowed nervously. "Well, actually . . ."

"Go on," he prompted in an eager tone.

"I was looking out the window when this all happened. It was such a pleasant night with no rain at last, and the moonlight kept filtering through the clouds. I thought I saw . . . I thought I saw a woman running across the back lawn."

"No!" Alford exclaimed, fighting back his smile. The chit was full of the night terrors! And Alford knew just the thing to fan the flames—had not old Mort bent his ear with endless tales of local ghouls and phantoms? There must be a story to match Miss Washburn's fertile imagination. "What did she look like?"

"She was dressed in white, with long hair that whipped across her face," Florrie began, then halted. "I am not even certain I saw anything. The mist was so thick . . ."

"I think it is very possible you did see something." Alford struggled to keep the excitement out of his voice. He would lead her on a merry dance! Leaning forward in his chair, he whispered in a conspiratorial voice: "The Lonely Lady of Hartland Point."

"The who?" Florrie's hazel eyes widened.

"The Lady, as the locals call her." Alford sat back in his chair again, satisfied his words were having the desired effect. Florrie's face had paled by at least two shades and her eyes were round with nervousness.

"She's real?" Florrie asked.

Alford smirked. "As real as your imagination allows. The original lady's been dead for over a hundred years." He fought against his glee at the look on Florrie's face.

"You mean she is a *ghost*?"

He shrugged indifferently. "I am no student of necromancy. The locals say she is the spirit of some poor girl with a tragic tale—a husband lost at sea or in some battle—the usual thing."

"What else did you hear about her?" Florrie asked anxiously.

"On certain nights she walks about the neighborhood, looking for her long lost love." Alford struggled to keep a straight face at his embellishment.

"Does she . . . Has she ever been seen inside the house?"

Alford shook his head. "I do not recall. Had I known the tale would fascinate you so, I would have listened closer. Why not apply to Mrs. Burgess? She is likely to know all the ghostly details."

Conscious of his scrutinizing gaze, Florrie shook her head. She did not want Alford thinking she was a pea-goose. And truly, she was not absolutely certain she wanted to know more about the woman in white. "It is of little consequence," she said hastily.

Alford beamed with joy. He had planted the seed in that fertile mind, and all he needed now was to bring the plan to fruition. He thought he had just hit upon the perfect method of persuading Miss Washburn to cut short her sojourn at Hartland. And one that would afford him much amusement in the process.

Florrie prepared for bed that evening with deliberate haste. Tonight, when she pulled the curtains across her window, she did not so much as glance out onto the lawn. If there was some strange, other-worldly creature out there, she did not want to see it. Climbing into the high bed, she settled herself under the covers and blew out the bedside candle. Tonight she would sleep with a peaceful mind.

She was nearly asleep when a sudden, unfamiliar sound

caught her attention. Lying very still, hardly daring to breathe, Florrie strained to catch another hint of the sound. There!

It was certainly not the noise that had so disturbed her the previous night. This sounded more like a distant thud. A banging shutter, perhaps. Florrie wrinkled her brow as she tried to remember if any of the windows had shutters. She thought not.

The noise sounded again, slightly louder this time. And it had more of a metallic ring to it.

Florrie sat up, clutching the covers to her chest. Should she light her candle, and go out in the corridor to investigate? It would be so cold. . . . She sank back under the blankets. Better to remain in the snug warmth of her bed. It was probably just the ever-present wind—

A loud clang sent Florrie frantically scrambling for the light box on the table by the bed. Her hands shook so hard she could barely produce a flame, let alone light the candle. Somehow, she managed and the room was bathed in its yellowish glow.

That last sound had been much, much closer than the others. Whatever made it was moving. Which meant it had to be *alive*. She shivered, and not from the cold.

Straining her ears, Florrie thought she heard a faint scraping noise, very dim and muffled, but one which sounded continuously. It grew louder, she thought, almost as if . . . as if it were coming up the stairs at the end of the corridor.

Her heart racing, Florrie sat paralyzed upon her bed, hardly daring to breathe. There was no question that whatever was making that noise was coming closer. The sound was more distinct now, the metallic tone more pronounced with each . . . step. It had reached the top of the stairs, and was slowly making its way down the corridor toward her room. Closer, closer, it came, that strange metallic clank. Florrie clapped her hands over her ears to drown out the approaching sound but it did no good. Closer, closer . . .

Then nothing. Only pure, clear silence. She drew her hands from her ears and listened, but the only sound she heard was the thudding of her heart within her chest. Florrie stared at the door, as if trying to see through the heavy wooden panels. Then her eyes widened in fear.

Slowly, very slowly, the door knob began to turn.

Chapter 10

Florrie screamed and screamed and screamed. Not until she heard Alford shouting and banging on the door connecting their rooms did she stop.

"For God's sake, what is wrong?" Alford yelled. "Unlock the door!"

Grabbing the key from the bedside table, Florrie jumped to the floor. Her hand shaking, she barely managed to unlock the door for Alford.

It was a measure of her agitation, Alford thought, that she had given no heed to the fact that she greeted him clad only in her night gown. And that gauzy creation was as ineffective as any in hiding her pleasant curves. It took some effort to turn his concentration to her distraught face.

"Good God," he said, forming his expression into a mask of concern. "You are pale as a ghost. What happened?"

Florrie pointed to the door leading into the corridor. "Someone was out there, trying to get in my room."

Alford casually crossed the chamber and tried the latch. The door was locked, as he was certain it would be. He turned and flashed her a quizzical grin.

"You lock yourself in?"

"I do not desire any unexpected visitors in my room," she snapped.

"Good idea," he said, nodding his head. "Pass me the key."

She stared at him.

"Not that anyone would have lingered, after all the noise you made. But I should like to take a look in the corridor just in case."

Florrie handed him the key.

Alford made a great production of unlocking the door,

stepping into the corridor and looking this way and that. When he stepped back into the room, he shut the door firmly behind him, locked it and placed the key in Florrie's hand.

"Not a sign of anything amiss," he said. "What exactly happened?"

Florrie sagged against the bed post and for a moment Alford thought she really might faint. He leapt to her side and half-led, half-carried her to the bed. Placing his hands about her surprisingly tiny waist, he lifted her onto the high mattress.

"There is nothing there now," he said in the most reassuring tone he could manage. "You are perfectly safe."

Florrie looked into his pale blue eyes, and saw an assurance there that gave her comfort.

"I feel . . ." she began, hesitating, " . . . I feel like a total goose, Alford. Getting so hysterical, I mean. It is not like me at all. But someone was trying to enter my room."

"Did you hear anything before that?"

"There was the oddest noise," she explained. "I swear whoever it was came up the stairs and down the hall. There was a clanking sound, as if something was being dragged along the carpet. Then . . . then the knob . . ." She shuddered at the memory.

"There, there," said Alford soothingly, patting her gently on the back. "It was probably nothing more than a strange gust of wind. In these old houses, there are drafts everywhere."

"Drafts do not go about rattling door knobs," she said curtly.

"Maybe it was Burgess, seeking to ravish you," Alford said with a sly leer.

Florrie glared at him. "I thought you were *concerned,* Alford. Now you are treating this as if it was a joke. I was frightened half out of my mind."

He immediately sobered. "That was uncalled for," he admitted. "But there are only four of us in this house. And I cannot see why either Burgess would be wandering the upstairs corridor at this hour of the night."

"Somebody was out in the hall," Florrie insisted.

"Well, it was not I," Alford said dampeningly. He gestured at his bare feet and night clothes. "I was asleep in my bed."

It came as a sudden shock of realization to Florrie that she was sitting on her bed in her night gown, talking to a man clad only in his night dress. And he looked very much like a man who had just climbed from his bed, with his tousled hair and bared legs. Florrie quickly averted her gaze from his limbs, biting her lip to regain control. They were very nice legs.

"Florrie?"

She turned her head and saw Alford watching her with genuine concern.

"Are you going to be all right?"

She nodded. "I am fine now. I am certain you are right—it was just some trick of the wind."

Alford walked to the door again and demonstrated that it was still locked. "All safe and tight," he said, then turned his eyes on her. "Lock up after me when I leave and you will be as snug as ever." He stepped toward the connecting door and made to close it behind him.

"Alford?"

He paused. "Yes?"

"I am sorry to have disturbed your sleep," Florrie said, difficult as the words were.

"That is quite all right," Alford replied with a smile. "I always welcome the chance to come to the aid of a damsel in distress." He closed the door quietly as he left.

Florrie locked the door behind him, and personally double-checked the other one before she climbed back into bed. How odd that she found such reassurance from Alford's presence. He had been soothing and comforting in his attentions, easily quelling her fears. Of course, she thought with a self-deprecating smile, it was only because she had been so badly frightened that she welcomed it so. In the normal course of things, Alford would not have created such a favorable impression.

She doubted very much that she would sleep another wink this night. If only she had a book to read. But a trip to the library to locate one was completely out of the question. She would huddle here in her bed until daylight came again.

Twenty minutes later, she was asleep.

In the morning while he dressed, Alford could not help chuckling as he recalled the picture of the near-hysterical Miss Washburn gratefully accepting his assistance. He had discovered a hole in her self-assured manner wide enough to drive a coach and four through. It was going to be laughably easy to drive her from this house. One or two nights like the last one and she would run all the way to Bideford. He snickered at the thought.

Pulling his boots on, Alford stood and surveyed his appearance in the mirror. Not bad for a stay in the country. A casually knotted scarf replaced the usual starched cravat. No need for an elaborate neckcloth out here, he thought. And once Nanette arrived, there would be little need for clothes at all. That thought brought a wicked grin to his face.

Surveying his room before leaving, Alford noticed one item out of place. With a swift kick, he pushed the errant loop of chain further under his bed. Then whistling a bawdy tune, he went down to greet the morning.

He was surprised to find Miss Washburn in the library at such an early hour. He had thought she would have slept until noon after last night. But there she sat, freshly gowned. Only a very close perusal revealed the faint lines of strain around her brown eyes. She looked damn fine for a woman who had been scared witless eight hours before. He had to admit, the chit had spirit.

"Good morning, Miss Washburn," he greeted cheerily as he helped himself to some tea. "I trust you spent an uneventful night—after the initial disturbance?"

She nodded. "I looked the veriest fool, didn't I?" she asked ruefully.

"Oh, I would not say that," he said. "I thought you looked rather fine, actually, dressed only in your night gown with your hair down."

"Alford!"

He grinned. "You asked."

"I should have known better than to try to carry on a reasonable conversation with you," she snapped. "Remember, I am practically your sister."

"I'd say a wife is a sight closer than a sister," he replied dryly.

"Oh!" Florrie scowled.

"Of course, I am not certain I would like to be married to a lady who is in the habit of luring men into her bed chamber in the middle of the night," he continued with a smirk. Between fear of ghosts and fear for her virtue, he should be able to keep her so off-balance she would leap at the chance to be free of him.

Florrie resisted the urge to fling the pot of hot tea at him. Only the thought that he deliberately goaded her stilled her hand. She could not let him win this battle of wills. She would show him who was the stronger.

Alford saw the determination in her face and laughed inwardly. She was proving to be an admirable foe. Time to stage a strategic retreat, and allow her to drop her guard again.

"Should you like to take a stroll about the grounds this morning?" he asked. "It might be just the thing to clear your head from the confusion of the night."

Florrie regarded him suspiciously. Why was he suddenly being nice? She could not imagine that Alford truly desired her company. He had some nefarious plan in mind.

"Oh, do come, Miss Washburn. I will not bite." He flashed her his most engaging smile. "You know perfectly well you are safe with me. The fresh air will do you good."

He was a rather enigmatic man, Florrie thought later, when she found herself racing along at his side, forced nearly into a run to keep up with his long strides. One moment he was leering at her like a young buck in the pit at the opera, next he was all solicitous concern and anxious friendliness. She had not decided which attitude—if not both—was a studied pose. But after intercepting that letter, she was less inclined to underestimate Alford. She suspected a great deal more went on behind that bland countenance than he let on. Lord Alford was not entirely what he pretended to be. She almost wished he would be staying at Hartland, so she could catch further glimpses into his puzzling nature.

"Can you slow down?" she pleaded at last, gasping for breath.

Alford halted and grinned at her. "Too rough a pace, Miss Washburn? You only needed to say something." He waited patiently while she caught her breath, then struck out again at a much slower gait.

"It is easier to observe your surroundings when you are not galloping through them," she said acidly.

"I hardly thought the sight of the lawn warranted a close inspection," he retorted. "I am more interested in seeing what is on the other side of the wall."

"The sea."

He stopped and turned to her, a look of cross exasperation upon his face. "I am trying, Miss Washburn, to be amiable this morning. I realize you had a difficult night. But you must recall that my sleep was disturbed as well. The least you can do is be civil."

Florrie had the grace to look chagrined. "You are right, Alford. I am sorry." She took a few steps toward the high wall that protected the back lawn from the worst of the wind, then turned back toward Alford with a questioning look. "Are you coming?"

With a resigned shake of his head, Alford fell in behind her.

The tall, stone wall that enclosed the back lawn rose above even Alford's head. He examined the stonework carefully. Overall, it was in good repair. Moss clung to many of the rock surfaces and ivy and other twining vines roamed over its sides. In high summer, it would be a mass of greenery. Now, it merely hinted of what was to come with the first budding of the new leaves.

At the far west end, a gate was set in the wall. According to Burgess, there was a narrow path along the top of the cliff, outside the wall. Alford was curious whether there was a path down the cliff as well.

"You may wish to remain here," he said to Florrie as he

fumbled with the rusty gate latch. "I am not certain what the outer path is like."

"I am just as curious as you," she replied. She would not permit him to think her faint-hearted.

He shrugged. "Suit yourself."

Florrie followed him through the gate, then caught her breath at the scene that lay below them. The cliff top here was relatively wide—there was nearly ten feet of land between her feet and the edge. But to the north, she saw the path was no more than a few feet wide. And what fell off to the side fell quickly and sharply—350 feet to the ocean below.

She spotted the jumble of rocks that lay beyond the point. Watching the waves pound into them, the spray rising many feet into the air, Florrie took an involuntary step back. The area looked as dangerous and desolate as any she had ever seen. She watched nervously while Alford strode to the edge and peered eagerly down the slope.

"Is it steep?" she asked.

He laughed. "I do not think you would stop before you hit the water, if that is what you mean," he said. "If you'd put a castle on this place, you would never have worried about an attack from the sea."

Florrie stepped forward, but she could not quite force herself to get close enough to the edge to look over. Great heights made her nervous.

"I wish to walk toward the point," he said. "I shall be back in a few moments. Burgess said there was an old path down to the water and I aim to find it."

Florrie nodded. She had no desire to trace that narrow ledge, with only a few feet of dirt protecting her from the edge. "I will wait here," she agreed.

Alford set off toward the point, while Florrie more closely examined the gate set into the wall. It looked about as old as the house, its surface weathered and grayed from exposure to the harsh coastal winds. Yet incongruously, a tangle of rose vines trailed about the wall. She was surprised that something as delicate and beautiful as a rose could endure the punishment it must take. It would be a rare sight in a month's time with the wall all abloom. But she would be gone by then.

When she next glanced up the path, there was no sight of Alford. For a moment she was startled, then reasoned he must have already gone around the bend in the wall.

The wind whipping off the white-flecked sea chilled her, and it did not take long for Florrie to decide she had spent enough time outside the wall. Where was Alford? She really had no reason to wait for him—he would come back in his own time. But at the same moment, she did not want him to be out along these dangerous cliffs alone. If something happened . . .

Swallowing nervously, Florrie slowly turned her steps toward the north. She would go as far as the bend in the wall, she decided, looking ahead anxiously to judge the width of the path. It was not so dreadfully narrow. She would be fine as long as she did not look down to her left. Florrie picked her way through the scrubby plants that determinedly clung to the earth. This path was not much used, she thought, then laughed. It was hard to imagine either of the Burgesses rambling along the cliff tops. It might have been years since another person trod this walk.

She tried not to notice how the path was narrowing with each step. Where was that dratted man?

"Alford?" she called, but the wind whipped the name from her lips and carried it away. She doubted he would hear. Just to the bend, she promised herself. If he was not in sight then, she would return to the house and alert Burgess. He could go look for the foolish man.

Florrie touched the wall beside her, its solid bulk giving her a mote of comfort. She inched along more slowly now, carefully keeping her eyes averted from the cliff edge to her left. Only a few more steps and she would round the corner. Only a few more . . .

With a sigh of relief she saw how the path widened as it swept around the corner. And even better, there was Alford, heading toward her with his typical brisk stride. She took a few grateful steps toward him, still keeping her hand on the wall.

"Decided to go adventuring after all, Miss Washburn?" he greeted.

She nodded.

"Unfortunately, there is not much to see. There were a few points that look promising, but no clear path anywhere down the cliffs. They are just too steep."

"We can go back then," she said with obvious relief. She watched with indrawn breath while Alford casually brushed past her as if the path were as wide as Piccadilly. She carefully turned around and followed him.

The wind hit Alford like a slap to the face as he came around the corner of the wall. It was one thing to have it at one's back, but it was a daunting prospect when blowing in one's face. He ducked his head slightly and continued forward.

When the ground beneath his feet suddenly gave way, Alford reacted with a survivor's instincts. His feet scrabbled for purchase in the loose dirt as he flung his body forward. He landed on his chest with a thud that knocked the breath out of him.

Hearing Florrie scream, Alford staggered to his feet and whirled about, fearing she had lost her footing as well. But she stood on firm ground, her face white as talc and her hand clasped over her mouth, her eyes wide with horror.

He let out a deep breath and forced himself to smile. It had been a rather exciting moment. But he did not need a hysterical woman on his hands.

"I am all right," he said as he eyed the narrow but deep chasm that lay between them where the bank had given way. "I fear all the rain softened the earth." There was still a narrow ledge of dirt running along the base of the wall. "Give me your hand and I shall help you cross."

Florrie shook her head. "I can't."

"Of course you can," he said with encouragement.

She shook her head again, and took a step back. "I shall go around the other way."

"Do not be a fool," he said. "The path that way could be just as bad. The ledge widens out in a few more feet and we shall be perfectly safe. Give me your hand."

Florrie's arms stayed frozen at her side.

"Miss Washburn, every moment you and I stand here risks a further collapse of the bank." As if to punctuate his words, a small shower of dirt flowed down the side of the new hole. "Now, if you give me your hand, and place your foot along the wall, we can contrive to get you over the cut."

"But what—"

"Nothing is going to happen to you, Miss Washburn," he said reassuringly. "I promise."

Florrie looked at him doubtfully, but it was the second cascade of pebbles down the inside of the chasm that decided her. She inched forward toward the edge, her fingers trailing along the wall to her left.

Alford stepped as close as he dared to the chasm, afraid his greater weight would cause more earth to give way. He stretched out his arm, but it was not enough to reach her hand.

"You will have to come closer," he said. "Keep right up against the wall; the ground is safest there."

Florrie swallowed hard several times and pressed forward. She stretched out her arm as far as she could and Alford caught it in his grasp.

"Now, step to the wall with your left foot," he commanded. "Swing your right foot around and jump. I will pull you toward me and we shall have you on firm ground in a trice."

Florrie gingerly stepped forward, breathing a sigh of relief as she carefully transferred her weight to her left foot and the ground beneath it held. Closing her eyes tightly, she jumped toward Alford. Her feet landed on the edge of the bank.

Then, with a sickening lurch, she felt the ground vanish beneath her feet.

Chapter 11

Alford jerked her into his arms and staggered backward toward more solid footing. He did not stop until there was at least five feet of earth between them and the cliff edge. He leaned wearily against the wall, still clutching Miss Washburn to his chest. Relief washed over him. He had saved her, as he had promised. "Thank God," he whispered, hugging her close.

Having been exceedingly drunk the last time he had held Miss Washburn in such an intimate embrace, Alford was rather more conscious of the feel of her this time. He rather liked the way her arms were wrapped about him so tightly he could barely breathe. Her head lay against his chest and he was almost tempted to stroke the honey-gold hair that tumbled from its pins. Miss Washburn felt exceedingly nice. All those curves that had been hinted at in such a tantalizing manner last night when he viewed her in her night gown were pressed against him in a most pleasant manner. Most pleasant . . .

With a start he realized where his thoughts were drifting and he shook himself back into awareness. This would not do, he thought. It would not do at all. This was his brother's wife—or at least Kit's intended wife. The woman Alford wanted out of his life as quickly as possible. He pulled away as if he had been burned.

Florrie felt Alford stiffen and push her from him. She was suddenly conscious of how she still clung to him like a limpet to a rock—or as his precious trollop Nanette undoubtedly did. She disengaged her arms from around his waist.

"I trust we are recovered?" he said coolly.

Florrie heard the coldness in his voice and she was both angered and embarrassed. Angered, because he acted as if

she had been behaving foolishly. Embarrassed, because she
had. She looked down and twitched her skirts into some
semblance of order.

"Quite," she replied, not willing to meet his eyes.

"I should inform Burgess of the damage to the trail,"
Alford said, turning abruptly.

Once again, Florrie had to run to catch up to him. When
safely inside the gate, she gave up the effort.

"Thank you," she yelled at his retreating back, "for
saving me."

He turned and saluted her with that mocking grin of his.
"Think nothing of it, Miss Washburn. It was a lovely excuse
to hold you in my arms again."

Alford laughed at Florrie's scowl. She need not know just
how close to the truth it was.

After informing Burgess of the landslide, Alford made his
way to the library. Miss Washburn, he was certain, had
retired to her room to recover from the after-effects of that
rather exciting walk. He did not mind a few moments of
solitude to do the same himself.

He had to get her out of here. This awkward situation
simply would not do. Florence Washburn was attractive
enough, enticing enough that he no longer felt confident that
his aversion to her sharp tongue and her obvious dislike of
him would be enough to stay his hand in a moment of
weakness.

Like this morning. He had enjoyed holding her against
him, grasping her so tightly he could feel her soft breasts
pressed against his chest. He'd had to fight against the urge
to taste her lips, to see if they were as sweet as he
remembered.

It simply would not do. Florence Washburn was destined
for Kit. No matter that he and Kit were not close; he would
never stoop to stealing his brother's intended. And in any
event, Alford had no intention of becoming leg-shackled.
That was certainly the price that would be demanded before
any dalliance.

Yet Miss Washburn was quite correct when she had said
yesterday that their situation had great potential for creating

a scandal. And if he compromised the chit, he would be honor bound to continue this unintended marriage. That was something he had no desire to do. He would contrive to drive Miss Washburn from this house for her own good. And his.

Florrie took luncheon in her room. She had no desire to speak to Alford now.

That experience on the cliff had been shattering. She still recalled the sickening lurch in her stomach when she had watched the path crumble beneath Alford's feet, saw him fall. She had been frightened out of her wits. And then to be forced to cross that chasm . . . But Alford promised she would be all right and she had been. An inane sense of relief and security had washed over her when she clung to him, the thudding of his heart beneath her ear sounding a reassuring litany. For a moment she had forgotten all else and relaxed in his comforting arms.

Florrie tossed her head at the thought. It was ridiculous to think she was attracted to Alford. He was spoiled and arrogant, an idler and a wastrel. He had none of the ambitions she so admired in his brother. Alford would make an abominable husband. He would reel home at all hours from some gambling house or drunken party. Or his mistress's. It would not do. She may not be marrying Kit for love, but she did respect him. Alford had not done anything to earn her respect.

Even that dramatic rescue on the cliff had been turned into something else with his flippant response. How could she possibly have enjoyed being held in the arms of such a boor? She wished he would leave, and let her remain in peace. He owed her that much. This whole intolerable situation was his fault, after all.

Florrie remained in her room until dinner, when she finally joined Alford in the library. They ate without much conversation, only a few polite remarks on the flavor of the savory soup and the excellence of the wine. But she could not bring herself to retire upstairs when the meal was finished. Even Alford's annoying presence was better than solitude. She drew out her Spanish grammar and took a seat before the fire.

Alford leaned over her shoulder. "I thought you might be growing bored with your lessons," he said with a hint of a smile.

Florrie turned to him with a haughty gaze. "Oh, you did?"

"Yes," he said. "I took the opportunity of searching the library this afternoon for some more suitable reading. Not that there was much." He gestured at the shelves. "A more boring collection of tomes I have yet to see. But," he continued, bringing out the book he held from behind his back, "I discovered that Mrs. Burgess is an avid reader and has her own private collection."

Florrie smiled weakly. She could only imagine what Mrs. Burgess would read. Probably improving tales from Maria Edgeworth.

"Her tastes are rather dramatic, I fear," Alford continued, holding the slim volume in such a way as she could not see the title. "Popular novels and the like. I was not sure if you approved of novels."

"There is nothing wrong with novels," Florrie said with exasperation. "I find I quite enjoy a well-written one."

"Still, her likes may not be elevated enough for your tastes."

"Alford, quit dilly-dallying and tell me what you have."

He brandished the book before her. "*The Castle of Otranto,*" he said.

"I've read it," she replied casually.

Alford grinned. He had suspected Miss Washburn was fond of gothic novels. "But I have not. Perhaps you would consider reading it to me."

"Why should I read to you?"

"With your talent for the dramatic, Miss Washburn, I imagine you will be able to do it justice. Besides," he added impishly, "you recall I am not fond of reading anything more complex than the sporting results. I fear an entire book is beyond my capabilities."

Florrie considered. She enjoyed reading aloud—her father and she had done it often. And she was growing thoroughly sick of her Spanish grammar. At this point in time, anything looked more appealing.

"All right," she agreed. Alford was obviously in one of his good moods and she wished to take advantage of it. He could be pleasing company when he tried.

Alford smiled, handing her the book. If all went as planned, it would be more fuel for the fire. He settled in his chair, a look of expectant eagerness on his face.

" 'Manfred, Prince of Otranto, had one son and one daughter; the latter, a most beautiful virgin, aged eighteen, was called Matilda. Conrad, the son was three years younger—' " Florrie paused. "Are you really certain you wish to hear this, Alford?"

"Oh, certainly," he said from his chair opposite hers in front of the fire. "I love frightening tales. Someday you shall have to get Kit to tell you his. The lad has a fiendish bent for the occult."

Florrie stared at him. That was something she did not know about Kit. It struck her that Alford could tell her a great deal about his younger brother. But that was almost a form of spying, she told herself. She turned her attention back to the book.

" '—a homely youth, sickly, and of no promising disposition . . .' "

Alford sipped his brandy, watching her more intently than he pretended. He had to admit, she was easy on the eyes. The firelight glinting off her hair turned it the hue of burnished gold. And those lips . . . he watched their movement in rapt fascination.

After a few minutes, Alford uttered a deep sigh, and closed his eyes. There was no harm in looking; still . . . He leaned back and listened to her low, melodious voice. She read well, injecting a bit of the dramatic into the dry words on the page. He was of the opinion that gothic novels were so much claptrap, but there would not be such a hue and cry against them if women were not susceptible to their eerie tales. And he wanted Miss Washburn to be in the most susceptible of moods. She had already shown how impressionable she was. Mrs. Burgess had an immense stock of gothic novels. Horrifying novels by day, strange noises by night. He would have Miss Washburn fleeing the house in terror in no time.

And then he could have some peace—until Nanette arrived.

Florrie read on, through the horrors of the giant helmet crushing poor Conrad, Manfred's mad ravings, and the terrified Isabella's flight. Periodically she glanced over to Alford, who sat calmly sipping his brandy. He had hardly moved all evening, except to refill his glass, which she noticed he emptied at a steady rate.

She halted at the end of the first chapter.

"Finished already?" Alford inquired. "What a shocking tale. No wonder good fathers keep their daughters away from novels."

"There is nothing wrong with novels," she retorted. "For those with minds mature enough to appreciate them."

"You do not think that your education was ruined because of your novel reading?" he taunted gently.

"Of course not," she snapped, suspecting it was the brandy that made him so surly. "I have an excellent education. It is those poor women who have nothing beyond the smattering of knowledge that passes for a young lady's education these days who have problems. Ignorance is never a useful skill."

"But you precisely point out the dangers of too much education," he said. "If you were not educated, you would not know what had been kept from you. And you would be content."

"Why would I be content to live in ignorance?"

"You cannot be ignorant of what you do not know," he said.

"I would be ignorant compared to you, or Kit, or my father. Can you honestly say you would care to have a wife with whom you could not discuss the slightest issue?"

"Women are to be looked at and admired, not listened to."

Florrie snorted her derision. "Coming from you, that is not an unexpected attitude. Thank God, Kit is more sensible."

"Ah, but I wager one day he will regret that he has taken one such as you to wife," Alford said, the brandy making his tongue unguarded. "He will wish he had taken one who was more biddable, more conformable. A termagant like you will be a constant thorn in his side.''

''You call me a termagant? When you are the most arrogant, insufferable man I have ever known?'' Her eyes flashed dangerously.

''Is it arrogance to know that men are superior to women in every way? Look at that little incident this morning. You would still be standing on that crumbling path, paralyzed with fear, if I had not pulled you across.''

''I would not,'' Florrie retorted. ''I would have made my own way across. Or found another route. I did not need your help.''

''And you did not need me last night, when you were so frightened in your bed?''

''I do not recall calling for you by name,'' she said.

''I suppose you expected Burgess to come rushing up from the kitchen? Face it, Miss Washburn, despite your protestations, you are very dependent upon male protection.''

''I am not!''

''It is nothing to be embarrassed about,'' he continued. ''It is merely the way of the world.''

''I am perfectly capable of taking care of myself.''

''Then why is your father so eager to see you wed? I heard him say himself that he was relieved to have a husband's protection for you.''

''He meant that in the broadest sense,'' Florrie explained. ''The protection of a name, the status of a married woman. He did not mean a husband who would keep me under lock and key.''

''The world would be safer,'' Alford muttered. ''You could use a strong hand.''

''I would never marry a man who sought to dominate me,'' Florrie said. ''I wish for a man who will heed my opinion and be guided by my ideas.''

''You mean one who is content to be led around by the nose,'' he retorted. ''Do you think Kit is going to stand for that?''

"I do not want to lead anybody," she protested. "I only wish to have my views consulted and considered. In a marriage of equals, that would happen."

"If you are so equal to Kit, Miss Washburn, why are you not shouldering a gun on the Peninsula?"

"Kit is not over there to fight," she snapped. "He is a staff officer. He is there to think."

"And can you think as well as he when you are covered with mud, cold, wet, and starving?"

"I am used to hardship as well as the next person," she retorted. "Try spending a winter in St. Petersburg!"

"A frightening prospect, I am sure," he said with a mock shudder.

Florrie slapped the book shut. "This conversation is pointless, Alford. Your mind is as closed to new ideas as it is to literature."

"I never said I did not like literature," he protested. "Was I not a willing listener?"

"Your steady consumption of brandy did not imply an interested response," she said, standing. "But I suppose even a novel such as this is too taxing for your limited capacities."

He was on his feet in an instant and roughly grabbed her wrist. "I would not be so quick to pass judgment on others, Miss Washburn," he said in a voice that was as icy as it was rough. "You do not know a damn thing about me."

"I know quite enough to judge that you will never be half the man Kit is."

Florrie was appalled at her words before they were even out of her mouth. She watched icy rage flit over Alford's face, and she would have taken a step back if he had not held her wrist in his grasp.

"I . . . I should not have said that," she said quietly. "It was uncalled for."

Alford released her wrist. "Oh, no doubt you are quite correct, Miss Washburn." He grabbed the brandy glass from the table and tossed the remaining liquid down his throat. "After all, I would much rather drink, and game, and wench than involve myself in the affairs of state."

The bitterness in his voice puzzled Florrie. Was he not

happy with his life? She shook her head. The thought was absurd. She set the book down and grabbed her shawl off the chair back. "I shall see you on the morrow, Lord Alford," she said.

He nodded curtly and turned toward the fire, pointedly ignoring her departure.

He did not need some slip of a girl to tell him what a waste his life was. He knew it already. But what good was all his university scholarship, or his interest in architecture, or reform legislation when he could do nothing about any of them? He had an income that allowed him to live a life of relative ease when supplemented with his gaming-table winnings. He owned no property beyond his horses and carriage. His ideas for the improvement of the ancestral hall fell on his father's deaf ears. His avid desire to stand for parliament had been met with derision by those same paternal ears. There would be plenty of time for that when he took his seat in the House of Lords, Alford had been told. Leave the Commons to the professional men. The heir to an earldom would not want to sully his hands with a common political campaign. And with his father's hands on the purse-strings, he could do nothing on his own.

Alford scowled. His father denigrated his ambitions. Florence Washburn thought him a wastrel. And Kit . . . he did not know what Kit thought about him, if ever he thought of his brother at all. But he most likely would fall in at Miss Washburn's side. And Alford suddenly realized that he would like her to have a somewhat better opinion of him, although he was not certain why.

He reached for the brandy decanter and poured himself a generous glass.

Chapter 12

Alford stared bleary-eyed at the plate of cold toast on the library table. The lavish butter spread upon the pieces had congealeld into great globs of pale yellow grease and the resulting picture looked revolting. He turned away from the table with a shudder and focused his eyes on the brandy decanter instead. That looked much more the thing. He poured himself a glass and downed it in two swallows. Much more the thing.

"Rather early for brandy, is it not?" Florrie had slipped into the room while Alford was eagerly—a bit too eagerly in her eyes—downing his morning restorative.

"And what business is it of yours?" he responded sourly.

"Oh, dear, we are a bit grumpy this morning." She smiled sweetly and sat down at the table, where she eyed the cold toast with much the same lack of enthusiasm as Alford. "Did you ring for breakfast?"

He shook his head. Florrie frowned and walked over to the bell rope, which she pulled with clear enthusiasm. "I, for one, would like to have something a little more substantial for my morning meal." She returned to the table and sat down. Upon inspecting the teapot, she found the water tepid at best. She saw Alford pour himself another glass and wander to the windows.

"Do you always drink your breakfast?" she asked crisply.

"No," he said.

"My, we are touchy. I suggest a walk, Alford. Fresh air can work wonders with even the surliest disposition."

"There are times," he said, turning to face her, "when I find it impossible to believe that you have lived to such a ripe old age, Miss Washburn. Certainly, someone was tempted to strangle you long ago."

"Many times," she replied sweetly. "My father has proposed that remedy more than once."

"A pity he never followed through."

"He must have saved me for you," she said. She leaned back, baring her neck. "Here, Alford, my throat. Do your best."

He snorted derisively and turned again to the window. Florrie sat back in her chair, a smug smile on her face. If Alford was willing to enter into this war of nerves to see who would first leave the house, she would give him a spirited battle. She only wished she could reveal how she had already foiled his main plan. It was a pity that he could not expect any sort of reply for several days. She wanted to watch him wait, and squirm when he heard nothing from his precious Nanette.

"Likely to rain again today," Mrs. Burgess announced as she bustled in with breakfast.

"Nothing unusual," muttered Alford, still staring out the window.

Florrie eyed the slices of ham, hot buttered toast, and jam pots with enthusiasm. Let Alford drink his breakfast. She was hungry. She eagerly spread marmalade on her toast.

What did she care if it chose to rain again? It was not as if it would deprive her of any special outdoor activity. Walking across the lawn seemed to be the best this place had to offer in terms of outside recreation. It would not differ much from the long Russian winter. The warmth and sunlight of Portugal sounded more appealing than ever. She prayed the annulment would be procured soon.

"This has to be the wettest place on earth," Alford pronounced as he flopped into a chair by the table. He forked two gigantic slabs of ham onto his plate and dug into them with a relish that astounded Florrie.

"I imagine you must find it dreadfully dull," she said, smiling sweetly. "It must make you greatly miss all the diversions of London."

"That it does," he said rudely, with a mouth full of ham.

"Perhaps you should reconsider your return," Florrie said.

"You could be back there easily in four days. Think of what you must be missing!"

Alford eyed her warily. "So could you," he pointed out. "And since you have spent so little time in London of late, Miss Washburn, it would be boorish of me to deprive you of that pleasure. Please, consider yourself free to go. Anytime."

"Certainly, you cannot expect me to travel alone?" Florrie tried to look aghast. "Whatever would people say?"

"You arrived here alone," Alford pointed out.

"That was necessity," Florrie reminded him. "And 'twas only for a short time. My father would not be pleased if I arrived in London without a companion."

"You could always take Mrs. Burgess with you."

Florrie laughed without mirth. "I assure you, Alford, that will not be necessary. My maid will arrive eventually. Then perhaps this conversation will have some purpose."

Alford scowled. He had bungled things last evening, first arguing with the chit, then staying down here and drinking into the late hours, when he should have been upstairs carrying out his tactics of terror. He firmly pushed from his mind any memory of how delectable she had felt clasped in his arms on the cliff walk. His letter to Nanette should be reaching London soon; it was conceivable she could arrive by early the following week. He wanted to make quite certain Miss Washburn would be eager to leave by then—if she had not already departed.

He would have to swallow his irritation and ask her to read again tonight. And he must make very certain that she did not sleep well afterward. Perhaps the "Lady in White" should reappear, in a form a slight more substantial than wavering sea-mist. The thought cheered him. He would seek out an accomplice immediately.

"Why would I be wantin' to dress up in a bed sheet and go running about the back lawn?" Mrs. Burgess stared at Alford in puzzlement.

"Because I would like you to, Mrs. Burgess," he replied patiently. "It is merely a little joke I wish to play on Miss

Washburn. I would do it myself, but then I would not be there to judge her reaction.''

Mrs. Burgess shook her head. ''Can't see as there's any good reason.''

''Think of it as aristocratic eccentricity,'' Alford said. ''Ghosts and such are all the rage in London. Miss Washburn will be able to dine out for weeks on this tale. It will increase her popularity immensely.''

The housekeeper still looked doubtful. ''What if it rains?''

''Then we will have to contrive another such scenario in the house,'' Alford said. He thought for a moment. ''In fact, that may be a better idea altogether, Mrs. Burgess. It will pose less inconvenience for you. All you need to do is be seen for a brief moment at the end of the upstairs corridor, then you can return to your quarters.'' He smiled his most winsome smile. ''Please?''

Still shaking her head, Mrs. Burgess muttered her acquiescence.

''Capital!'' Alford exclaimed. ''I will come get you when Miss Washburn retires—I will do my best to encourage her in an early evening. Be waiting with your sheet and the whole matter will be over in a matter of minutes.'' He bowed low. ''I thank you from the bottom of my heart, Mrs. Burgess.''

Alford exited the kitchen, whistling a cheery martial air.

Now all he had to do was create the proper mood this evening. He would have to put on his most charming manner in order to get Miss Washburn to read again. But on a dark and stormy night, with only a few candles, and an eerie story . . . he thought she would be quite impressed by his little plan.

Florrie prepared for bed that night with little dallying. Why she felt more safe and secure when tucked under the covers, she did not know, but unquestionably she did.

It had nothing to do with that foolish book, of course. She had read it before and not found it particularly frightening. She had read much worse. But somehow tonight, a disquiet crept upon her. It seemed as if the whole house was creeping up around her, pressing inward.

It was only the rain raging outside, she reasoned. With

the curtains drawn and a fire blazing in the hearth, the library had been decidedly cozy. Alford had even listened attentively, sprawled in his chair with brandy in hand.

It was easier to be swept up into a story of that kind when one was reading, she thought. Her attention could not be diverted by a flickering flame, or a spot on the carpet. That was why Alford appeared so unaffected. Tomorrow, despite his protestations, she would insist he read. She would feign a sore and tired throat if he demurred.

Nestled under the covers, Florrie lay back against the pillows and pulled the blankets up to her chin. She heard the sheets of rain lashing against the windows, blown by the gusts of wind that danced and whistled under the eaves. On occasion, a particularly hard blast of wind hit the house, and she imagined that even its stone walls shook from the force. She could not imagine what winter would be like here.

She had almost drifted off to sleep when a particularly strong wind rattled the windows, shocking her into wakefulness. Florrie listened carefully, but discerned no other odd sound. She put her head back on her pillow, starting when she heard another noise. That had not sounded like the wind, it had sounded like—

An eerie wail scattered her thoughts. Florrie lay there in the dark, her heart pounding inside her chest. It was like the sound she had heard the night . . . the night she saw the lady on the lawn.

Swallowing hard, Florrie tried to calm her racing pulse. It was just the wind, she reminded herself. Lord knows, there was enough of it on a night such as this.

The noise sounded again, and she could have sworn it was closer. And inside.

She shivered, remembering the horrible noise in the hall the other night. Thank goodness, she always locked her door. She would be safe, no matter what lurked outside in the corridor.

As long as whatever made the noise was human. But Alford had labeled the lady a ghost. Did a locked door have any effect on a ghost?

Florrie clenched her fists until her nails dug into her palms.

There had to be a simple, rational explanation for all of this. There had to—

She sat upright as she heard the wailing voice again. There was no question it came from the corridor.

Florrie was too frightened to even light the candle at her bedside. Only the faintest of glows issued from the fireplace on the far wall, lighting her room just enough to make out the shadowy bulk of the furniture against the walls. Florrie was grateful she could not see the door. She did not want to know if anyone was trying the knob again. As long as it was locked, she was safe. As long as it . . .

A silent scream tore from her throat as the door slowly opened inward.

Chapter 13

In the shadowed light, Florrie saw a flash of white outside the door. A high pitched wail sent her diving under the covers, pulling them over her head to hide the hideous scene from her sight.

She lay there for what seemed an eternity, hardly daring to breathe, her heart beating as if it would leap from her chest. Stiffening in anticipation of what would come next, Florrie braced herself for some horrible fate.

When nothing occurred for several minutes, Florrie cautiously stuck her head out and glanced to the door. It was still open, the gap clearly illuminated by the dim light in the corridor. Slowly, cautiously, Florrie crept from her bed. She grabbed the silver candlestick from the table beside her, clutching it tightly in her fingers. It would make a tolerable weapon. With hesitant steps, she inched toward the open door.

Peering cautiously around the frame, Florrie saw nothing amiss at the north end of the hall. She looked the other way. For a moment, she thought she saw something white. Then an eerie wail echoed down the hall and the candle holder fell from her fingers with a resounding crash. Florrie tried to scream but no sound came from her throat.

"What the deuce?" Alford came barreling out of his chamber. Even in the dim light, he could see that Miss Washburn's face looked as white as her night gown. "What is going on here?"

Florrie tried to speak, but she could not find her voice. She shuddered instead.

Alford was all solicitous concern. He picked up the dropped candle holder and took her hand, drawing her back into the chamber.

"Your hands are like ice," he said, chafing them to bring back some vestige of warmth. "For God's sake, Miss Washburn, what happened? I heard the strangest noise."

"It was the Lady," she whispered in a harsh voice. "The one I saw on the lawn the other night. Except this time, she was in the house."

"You saw her?"

She nodded. "At the end of the hall." She flung herself into his arms and buried her face against his chest. "Oh Alford, it was awful. That same horrible wailing. And she actually started to come into my room!"

"My God!" He patted her in a comforting manner while a self-satisfied smile flitted over his face.

It was some minutes before Florrie regained her composure.

"How in the devil did your door come open?" he asked. "Did you forget to lock it?"

"No! I always check it the last thing before I get into bed."

"And this figure in white actually opened your door?"

Florrie nodded. "I heard a noise in the hall—that horrible wailing—so I was looking right at the door. When it opened I caught a glimpse of something white and . . ."

"Then what happened?"

"I pulled the covers over my head so I would not see any more."

"I see." He struggled to keep the grin from his face. "So you finally conquered your fear and went into the hall to investigate?"

She nodded. "I saw nothing and was ready to turn back into my room when I saw a flash of white at the far end of the hall. Then she wailed again and you came out."

"Most mysterious. I heard the noise myself, but I was too late to see anything."

"What does it mean, Alford?"

He shook his head. "I do not know. As a rational man, I cannot help but think there is some explanation for all this— some natural phenomenon, or some strange construction in this hosue that contrives these odd occurrences. But on the other hand . . . There are too many tales of the supernatural to make me a total disbeliever. Why, last year, Seb Cole swore he had seen a haunt at a country house.''

Florrie shuddered at the thought. "I heard many strange tales in Europe, of ghostly creatures and haunted castles. From perfectly sane people. It does make one wonder.''

"What wonderful luck, to find ourselves amidst such an experience.'' Alford smiled.

"I find nothing enjoyable about it," she said curtly.

"Oh, come now, Miss Washburn, do not say you are frightened of ghosts?"

"I am not afraid of ghosts," she snapped. "I merely resent these intrusions upon my sleep.''

"Understandable," he said, a slow smile spreading over his face. "Although I find I do not mind it at all, when it means I can be continually invited into your chamber." He reached out and straightened an edge of the lace at her throat. "Particularly when you are in such enticing disarray.''

Florrie's cheeks flamed. "You are appalling!''

He grinned. "Because I can appreciate the sight of an attractive woman? Come now, Miss Washburn, you are quite familiar with my reputation. How could you expect anything less from me?"

"I could hope that you would behave with decorum and respect toward your prospective sister-in-law!''

"Ah, but you are not yet my sister-in-law," he pointed out. "You are my wife." He took a step closer and delighted in her retreat. Ghosts and lechery. The two things most designed to send her fleeing from this house.

"Are you afraid of me as well?" he asked.

"No. I merely find you as bothersome as that misguided spirit who stalks the halls. Neither of you are welcome.''

"Old Mort is due back in a day," he said. "He would be most willing to transport you to Bideford, and set you on the stage for London.''

"You would like that, wouldn't you?" She faced him angrily, feet apart and hands on hips. "Well, I will not allow you to chase me off, Lord Alford. I am perfectly capable of defending myself against your lechery. And I find I am most intrigued by the thought of investigating these ghostly happenings. I will not leave.''

Alford swallowed hard. She could have no idea of how enticing she looked, standing so defiantly before him. Her night gown was pulled taut over her breasts and he could clearly see their hardened tips pressed against the fabric. He clenched his fists against the unbidden desire that rose within him. How could such an aggravating chit have such an enticing body? He needed Nanette here. Soon. Or he was likely to make the most horrible mistake of his life.

Florrie smiled inwardly when Alford refused to hold her gaze. She had shown him she was determined to remain here. She no longer felt threatened by his outrageous, suggestive remarks. One word from her, and he would find himself her husband for life. And she knew that he wished to avoid that fate at any cost. No, she had nothing to fear from him.

She was less certain about the ghost—if there was such a thing. Her rational mind told her it was impossible. Alford was probably right, it was some strange trick of the house that led to such eerie happenings. She could not allow herself to be upset over such a thing. It made her appear weak and silly. That she could not abide.

''Do you have anything more to say?'' she demanded. ''Otherwise, I think you could leave now.''

''Are you certain you shall feel safe, Miss Washburn? If a locked door can open by itself . . .''

''I am certain I must have failed to lock it properly. In these drafty corridors, it could easily blow open. I will be certain to lock it most carefully next time.''

He nodded. Now that her initial terror had subsided, she was back to being the acerbic, practical Miss Washburn again. He rather liked her better when she was scared witless. She was much more soft and vulnerable.

''Then I will say goodnight,'' he said, ostentatiously bowing his way out the door. She slammed it behind him, and he clearly heard the key turning in the lock.

Alford grinned. Oiling the lock to Miss Washburn's door this afternoon had been a masterstroke. It had been as easy as child's play to unlock it with the housekeeper's key. And Mrs. Burgess had played her part to perfection. Despite Miss Washburn's protestations to the contrary, he knew she had been badly frightened tonight. His plan was progressing with admirable success. He doubted the "Lady" would need many repeat performances before Miss Washburn was ready to decamp.

In the morning, Florrie refused to dwell upon the frightening events of the previous night. In the brilliant spring sunshine, the idea of ghosts and mysterious ladies in white seemed absurd. There had to be a logical explanation for all of this.

And to find it, Florrie determined to explore the house. She undoubtedly would discover some strange architectural oddity that created freak drafts of wind, which could easily produce the odd noises she had heard. And it *was* possible that she might have mis-locked the door. The wind could have pushed it open as well. She was less successful at coming up with a rational explanation for the white-clad form she thought she had glimpsed, but there was undoubtedly something that would account for that as well. A trick of the candlelight, perhaps.

Following breakfast, Florrie slipped out of the library without telling Alford her plan. He would probably insist on accompanying her, and she wanted to solve this mystery on her own.

Plus, she could not help but remember how she had cast herself so gratefully into his arms last night. Why did he always have to be present during her moments of weakness, when a sturdy male chest offered comfort and security? He would label her a vaporish female, when she was nothing of the sort. She was strong, confident, sure of herself. She did not need a male shoulder to lean on. She wanted to be a partner, not a dependent. And Alford had the horrible knack of always seeing her in the latter role.

She would show him. He would not be able to hide his admiration when she solved the mystery by herself.

Florrie began her exploration in the long gallery that lay

across the end of the house opposite her room. It was a dull and gloomy room. illuminated only from the windows at either end. Whatever paintings had once hung here were long gone, and the dark wood paneling only increased the darkness. The room was devoid of furniture, even curtains, and Florrie's steps echoed loudly as she walked across the inlaid wood floor.

She examined the windows at either end of the chamber. Both were latched securely and did not rattle in their frames. She doubted even the strongest storm would ring a sound from them. Frowning, she examined the walls more closely, but did not see any obvious cracks or holes that would allow air to enter from the outside. The doors hung securely on their hinges and the latch was not broken or bent. This room was not the source of her problem.

Florrie undertook a similar examination of all the other rooms on the first floor, but discovered nothing to support the theory that strange house-drafts were responsible for the odd occurrences. With a resigned sigh, she mounted the stairs to investigate the upper floor. Drafts could easily blow down the stairwells.

The upper floor showed ample signs of disuse. Dust lay thick upon the furniture covers in the first chamber she examined. It was obvious nothing had disturbed this room in years. She shut the door and went into the next chamber, which was in a similar condition.

This was getting her nowhere, she thought, as each and every room revealed the same undisturbed state. Any wind strong enough to blow open a door would have disturbed the dust. Some rooms looked to have been ignored since George III's accession.

Florrie pulled open the final door with a sense of frustration. But once she stepped through the door frame, a very different sight met her eyes.

The room was still dusty. and what little furniture it held was securely under cover. But a table and chair stood in the middle of the chamber. and they were both free of dust and dirt. Someone had been in this room recently.

She took a cautious step toward the table. A few crumbs

were scattered across the top. Florrie leaned over and inspected them closely. Bread and cheese. And decidedly fresh. She straightened and made to move, then froze at a sudden sound.

The faint noise of footsteps echoed in the corridor. And whoever they belonged to was taking great pains to walk quietly. Florrie looked around the room in panic for a place to hide, but there was nothing that offered much security. Only a large chest of drawers and a few chairs pushed against the wall.

She heard the faint sound of a door latch catching, and realized the person in the hall was looking into the other rooms on the floor. But it was done in such a stealthy manner that Florrie had no doubt of the person's aim. He was looking for her.

Her only hope was the element of surprise. If she stayed pressed against the wall alongside the door, she might pass unnoticed for the moment it would take her to dart into the hall when the intruder entered.

If only she had a weapon. But the room offered nothing more deadly than a chair cushion. Surprise was her main chance.

Florrie tip-toed across the room, the squeak of the floorboards beneath her feet sounding ominously loud in the silence. She paused halfway to the door, listening. No sound came from outside. Had the person heard her movement; was he waiting to hear another sound, just as she did?

Her heart thudded in her chest and she struggled for breath, not daring to draw too much air into her lungs. She took another cautious step forward and cringed at the unmistakable noise as she shifted her weight to that foot. Not wanting to prolong the agony, she quickly covered the last few feet to the doorway and pressed herself against the wall.

Biting her lip to keep from making any sound, Florrie strained her ears to listen for the sound of approaching footfalls. She heard them again, not loud, but clearly headed in this direction. Florrie raised her arms, in preparation to ward off a blow if necessary. She planned her escape carefully. She would run to the near stairs and hurtle down them, praying she did not trip and break her neck in the bargain. Once she reached the ground floor she could yell for help— surely one of the Burgesses would be in the kitchen at the rear. Alford, who was probably still in the library at the other end of the house, would be no help to her now.

With a pang of regret, she wished she had enlisted his help in her search. He would offer her a measure of protection against whoever sought her out.

The footfalls were closer now; Florrie heard the latch click on the room across the hall. It would only be seconds . . . She took a deep breath and tensed, prepared to move at the first opportunity, fighting against the overwhelming urge to shut her eyes. She listened in aching awareness as she heard each slow, deliberate step crossing the hall. First one, then another. Closer, closer, closer they came . . .

Chapter 14

Alford peered cautiously around the door frame and found himself staring into the wild-eyed gaze of Miss Washburn, who was backed up against the wall as if she wanted to become part of it.

"Playing hide-and-seek, are we? You might have clued me in earlier."

"Alford." Florrie nearly collapsed with relief at the sight of him, then her emotions quickly shifted to anger. "How dare you give me such a fright!"

"My apologies," he said with a mocking smirk.

"What are you doing up here?" she demanded.

"Looking for you."

"I don't see why you have to do it in such a skulking manner," Florrie snapped.

Alford placed a denying hand on his breast. "I? Skulking? I would rather say you are the one guilty of that action. You don't see me hiding in corners."

"I was hiding from you!"

"Oh." He grinned. "Thought the Lady was coming to carry you off, did you?"

"No," she said with irritation. "I thought that whoever had breakfasted in this room might be coming back."

He was instantly alert. "How do you know someone was eating here?"

"Look at the table." She waved her hand toward it.

Alford inspected the surface, picking up one of the crumbs and twirling it between his fingers, a calculating look upon his face. "You are right, this is fresh." He casually glanced about the chamber. "It certainly does not look as if the room has been used for anything else."

"What do you suppose it means?" Florrie asked.

He shrugged. "Perhaps this is Burgess's refuge from his wife. God knows, if I were he, I would not mind such a place."

"But why would he bother to come all the way up here?" Florrie asked. "There must be plenty of other rooms that are cleaner."

"And cleaner means that Mrs. Burgess visits them," Alford explained. "It is obvious she does not spend any time up here."

"But what if it isn't Burgess?" Florrie asked. "What if there is a . . . a stranger in the house?"

"Really, Miss Washburn, I think you have been reading too many novels. What possible reason would anyone have for being in this house?" Alford walked to the window and peered out. "Even if a burglar wished something, there would be no way to carry off any booty. And the house is so isolated that no casual wanderer is likely to happen by. It must be Burgess."

Florrie had her doubts, but she held her tongue. Let Alford think what he will. There was a mystery here and she was determined to learn more about it.

"Why were you looking for me?" she asked.

"Old Mort is here," he replied. "He is amenable to taking you to Bideford if you can ready your bags quickly."

"I have no intention of leaving," she said, glaring at him. "I thought it was you who planned to leave."

"Ah, but I have changed my mind, remember? I find the peace and isolation of the country far too soothing to exchange for the noise and disruption of London."

"Well, I am not leaving until my father sends for me," she said with determination.

"Suit yourself. But do not complain that you were not given the opportunity. Old Mort will be back again in a few days. Maybe you will change your mind by then." He turned to go.

Florrie hastily fell in behind him. She did not want to remain alone on this floor.

"What were you doing up here?" Alford asked.

"I was trying to determine how a draft could have blown my door open last night."

"Find anything?" he asked with an amused half-smile.

"No," she said slowly. "But that does not mean it could not have happened. I may have missed some architectural oddity that caused it."

"Undoubtedly."

"It makes much more sense than believing there really is a ghost walking the corridors," she argued as they started down the stairs.

"Ah, but think how much more romantic a thought that is." Alford turned to her. "You are a romantic, Miss Washburn, are you not?"

"I am a realist, Alford. And I find it hard to believe that there really is a ghost in this house."

But you did not think that last night, he thought. *Your current display of bravado is merely a product of the sunlight. Once it grows dark again* . . . He smiled in anticipation. He would plan something very special for tonight.

Alford had made light of the matter with Florrie, but the discovery that someone was making use of that isolated room upstairs did not sit well with him. Something mysterious was going on here at Hartland, and he was determined to come to the bottom of it. Starting with a thorough exploration of that room upstairs.

To avert suspicion, he slipped outside right after lunch. With a casual air, he made a circuit of the house, quickly noting the location of all the doors and any windows that might be used to gain entry. Fortunately, in a house this old there were few. No flimsy, glass-paned doors led out onto the terrace, no modern double-hung windows afforded an easy entrance. No, if one entered this house, it would be through the doors. He made a mental note to query Burgess about his locking habits.

Entering the house through the door at the gallery end, Alford crept quietly up the rear stairs. He hesitated at the first floor landing. Would it be of any use to examine this floor? He shook his head in decision. He knew very well who had caused all the disturbances on *this* floor. With determination, he gripped the banister and continued upwards.

Like Florrie, he had glanced into every room on this floor in his search for her this morning. Alford grinned again in remembrance of the look on her face when he had peered around the door at her. She looked like a cross between a frightened hare and Boadecia preparing to do battle. He was lucky she had not popped him on the nose again.

He did not exactly tip-toe down the corridor, but he found himself deliberately stepping lightly. Not that he expected to find some stranger lurking behind the door. It was half possible that his hastily concocted tale of Burgess seeking refuge from his wife was true.

The door was still ajar from their departure earlier. Cautiously pushing inward, Alford stepped into the room. Everything looked as it had in the morning, the dust covered cloths shrouding the furniture and the lone table and chair near the center of the room.

Why, or more important, who would choose to have their meal in this isolated roost? Alford pondered the question while he stared out the window. Like his and Florrie's rooms, this one overlooked the back lawn and the sea beyond. Was that in itself significant? Was the person who had been in the room waiting and watching for something?

With a sigh, he turned away from the view. There was little further to be learned here. Perhaps another visit, during the night, might prove more productive. With his hand on the door latch, Alford turned once more to see if he had missed anything.

By late afternoon, Florrie decided she had endured enough studying for one afternoon. She looked up from the grammar book she held in her lap for the hundredth time. Why was it so deucedly difficult to concentrate on these dratted Spanish verbs?

She was bored, of course. Despite the rather dramatic events that occurred after dark, the days here at Hartland were not filled with excitement. There was no lively conversation sprinkled with diplomatic gossip, no political intrigue, nothing, in fact, that so much as hinted of her usual pastimes. There were not even newspapers to keep her informed of the latest doings.

Her restlessness this afternoon certainly had nothing to do with Alford's absence. The man was free to come and go as he pleased. Although what he could have found to occupy himself with since luncheon, she could not guess. Perhaps he was making a lengthy inspection of the grounds, or had walked to the nearest farm. Or . . .

The thought froze her in the chair. He had been so interested in finding a path down the cliff face. Perhaps he had gone in search of it again, and attempted a descent on his own, and . . . The image of a broken and bleeding Alford lying crumpled at the bottom of the cliff brought the sting of tears to her eyes.

She shook her head. It was absurd of her to worry about Alford's whereabouts. He was a grown man, and he did not need her worrying like a nurserymaid. If he was foolish enough to attempt some treacherous seaside path, and injured himself in the process, well, he would only have himself to blame.

Florrie reminded herself how pleasant the afternoon had been without his irksome presence. Even when he was being his most amiable, she had the unnerving feeling that Alford was laughing at her—and why that was, she did not know. He seemed to take great enjoyment in baiting her; unfortunately, she only encouraged him by rising to the bait. She would have to be most careful in the future to avoid responding. Resolutely, she forced her mind back to her Spanish grammar.

Lost at last in her reading, Florrie did not look up again until the shadows of impending night were creeping up the library walls. She looked to the mantel clock and noted it was almost time for dinner. Alford had yet to make an appearance, and Florrie grew genuinely concerned.

Then she remembered what he had said this morning— Old Mort had come today. Had Alford, despite his protestations of enjoying the peace of the country, decided to take his leave after all? It would be just like him to do so without telling her. Florrie tossed down her book with a flare of anger and strode toward the door.

She raced up the stairs and came to a breathless halt in front of Alford's room. She tapped quietly, then more forcefully when no response came. When there was still no answer, she carefully tried the knob.

It was locked. What did that mean? Florrie chewed her lower lip while she thought.

If Alford had left without informing her, she had every right to be angry. And, logically, she had a right to know if he had left. This lengthy absence was quite unlike him; it justified her worries—and her plan of action.

With a nod of assent, she fished in her pocket for the key and unlocked her own room. Then she went to the connecting door that linked her chambers with Alford's and unlocked it as well.

Stepping through the doorway, she found herself in a smallish chamber, obviously intended as a dressing room. Had it been for the master or the mistress, she wondered? It was bare of furniture and gave no clue.

Another door led into what was Alford's chamber, and Florrie was grateful to find it unlocked.

A quick glance around the room told her that if Alford had traveled with Old Mort, he had not taken any possessions with him. A dressing gown was thrown over the foot of the bed; a traveling case sat neatly atop the chest of drawers. He had not left Hartland, then. But where was he?

She could not resist the opportunity to peer about. Of course, there would be little of his personality reflected in this guest chamber. How much more she could learn from his own rooms! But she could already tell that Alford was neat in his habits. It pleased her to find that he was not a slave to his valet.

Realizing she would learn nothing more of Alford's whereabouts looking around in his room, she made a move to the door, but halted as she caught a glimpse of what lay upon the bedside table. Scarcely believing what she saw, she stepped closer.

A partially burned candle stood in its silver candle holder. An undramatic sight; her bedside sported the same item. Next to it lay a book—so he did read on occasion! But what caught her attention were the spectacles that lay atop the book.

Alford? In spectacles?

Florrie walked around the bed to look more carefully. Gingerly she picked up the gold frames and peered through them. They made her vision blurry. But if Alford's eyes were bad . . . She bent over to see the title of the book Alford was reading with his spectacles in the secrecy of his room. *Improved Field Cultivation Techniques.* Florrie's jaw dropped in disbelief. Alford had an interest in agriculture?

Perhaps he only used it to lull himself into sleep. But the bookmark was placed nearly two-thirds of the way through the book. He must be reading it—for pleasure?

Florrie saw the corner of a paper peeking out from under the book, and temptation was too strong. Sliding the book to one side, she twisted her head to read what was written on it. "Swinton Hall—North Field—new rotation plan." What followed was a list of crops and dates.

She put things back as they had been, carefully restoring the spectacles to their previous position while she pondered this new information. Alford had definitely been keeping things from her. He did read items more weighty than the sporting news! And gave a thought to more than the odds at faro.

Florrie cringed, remembering the many times she had scornfully derided Alford for being a fribble, with no interests outside of the fanciful pursuits of a young lord. No wonder she had angered him so!

She felt a twinge of guilt at discovering the two things Alford had obviously been at great pains to conceal, and crept silently from the room. Could it be she would have to make amends? The thought of apologizing to Alford did not sit well. But if she had misjudged him . . . She carefully locked her two room doors and went down the stairs.

If Alford had not left with Old Mort, she was back to her original worry, only exacerbated now that she was looking upon Alford in a more charitable light. It would be dark within the half hour; if something had happened to him outside, there was no time to lose. She hastened to the kitchen.

"Have you seen Alford?" she asked Mrs. Burgess, who was busily stirring a pot on the stove.

"No."

"I am becoming concerned," Florrie said. "I have not seen him since luncheon. Did he by chance tell you his plans?"

"No."

The woman was a fountain of information. "Is Mr. Burgess about? Alford was looking for a path down the cliff the other day and I fear he may have continued his explorations today. Something may have happened."

Mrs. Burgess jerked her head toward the door. "In back."

Florrie smiled thinly and entered the back pantry. She never quite felt comfortable in Mrs. Burgess's presence.

Burgess was polishing the silver.

"Mr. Burgess, have you spoken with Lord Alford today?"

He shook his head.

Florrie frowned. "He has not been here since lunch," she explained. "I fear he may have gone out to explore the cliff path again. Did he mention any plan to you?"

Burgess again shook his head.

Florrie fought against her rising frustration. "It is very close to the dinner hour and Lord Alford has not been seen for some time. I am concerned he may have met with an accident."

"And what do you wish me to do?" Burgess asked blandly.

"I thought that it might be advantageous to make use of what little daylight is left to look for him," Florrie said with exasperation.

"He could be miles away if he took it in his mind to go walking."

"Well, since he has done nothing like that since he first arrived here, I doubt that was his intention today," she snapped. "It is more likely he went out to the cliff path. He said he was looking for some way down when we were there the other day."

Burguess turned toward her with a sigh of resignation. "I will go look," he said in a tone that indicated he wished to do no such thing.

"Thank you," Florrie said curtly.

Upon returning to the library, she watched out the windows in growing apprehension as the last rays of the sun swept across the lawn. Where had that dratted man gone?

A sudden idea leaped into her head. Alford had laughed at her fears that a stranger had slipped into the house and was using the second floor room as a haven. But what if her idea was true? The stranger could have crept up on Alford somewhere in the house and caused him harm. The man could be anywhere now, waiting for another victim to come his way.

She swallowed hard. These last nights had been bad enough, even with the strangely comforting presence of Alford. Without him . . .

Florrie shook herself. She was becoming as goosish as Alford had accused her of being. She *had* read too many novels. There was a rational explanation for the strange happenings near her room, just as there would be a perfectly reasonable explanation from Alford as to his whereabouts today.

But when Burgess returned from the cliffs, saying he had seen no sign of Alford, Florrie's fears grew. The sun sank below the horizon and Mrs. Burgess brought dinner. Florrie was so distracted she could barely eat. Something had happened to him, she knew it.

Well, even if the Burgesses thought nothing amiss at one of the guests disappearing, Florrie did. She was not prepared to go haring off outside into the dark night. But she felt quite capable of investigating within the house.

Arming herself with a heavy silver candle holder and her chamber candle, Florrie went first to the gallery. The door creaked ominously in a fashion she did not recall from her earlier visit. The dim light from one candle was not enough to illuminate such a large chamber, so she was forced to walk nearly the entire length of the room before satisfying herself that there was no sign of Alford here. Her steps echoed loudly in the empty room.

She looked into each of the other chambers on that floor without result, although she had not expected any. If someone was up to a nefarious plot, they would not risk discovery with the comings and goings of the household. No, they would be upstairs. . . .

Florrie's courage faltered and she could not bring herself to head up those dark stairs alone. Mr. Burgess would probably be as pleased about this as he had been about going outside, but Florrie was adamant. She wanted to satisfy herself that Alford was not in this house.

"Can't see why Lord Alford'd be bothering himself about what's up the stairs," Burgess grumbled as he climbed with what seemed excruciating slowness. "Nobody's been up here in years."

"Oh, but they have, Mr. Burgess. I myself was up here this morning."

He grunted.

"And there was evidence someone else had been there recently. One table was all cleaned of dust, and there were food crumbs left upon it."

If she had expected this revelation to elicit some response from Burgess, she was disappointed. He showed no outward reaction to the news.

"Here we be," he said when they reached the landing. "Now what's it you wish me to look for?"

"Alford," Florrie said curtly. She brushed past Burgess and went to the first door.

All the chambers looked as they had in the morning—empty and full of dust. Florrie thought she must be searching for a mare's nest after all when they reached the last room—the one where Alford had given her such a scare this morning. Florrie reached out to push the partially ajar door open, but it only moved a few inches before it hit something.

"How strange!" she exclaimed.

Curiosity getting the better of her caution, she wriggled

through the narrow gap between door and frame. Lifting her candle, she looked down with growing horror at the inert body laying upon the floor.

"Alford!"

Chapter 15

Florrie knelt beside Alford's crumpled form as Burgess struggled through the doorway.

"What's he doing sleeping up here?"

"He is not sleeping," Florrie snapped. She gingerly touched her fingers to the dark patch on Alford's head and her fingers came away red. "It appears he has hit his head. Run and get Mrs. Burgess. We shall need a basin of water, and some cloths to bind the wound. And scissors."

She glared at the man, who stood staring at her. "Go! Now!"

Not until she heard Burgess's footsteps grow fainter did she realize that she was now alone on the upper floor. Florrie swallowed hard and lifted her candle to glance apprehensively around the room. All looked as it had before. At least she knew that no one could be hiding anywhere in the chamber, having tried to do so herself. She turned her attention back to Alford.

He lay on his side, facing away from the door. Had he tripped and hit his head? She saw nothing on the floor that could have impeded his path. And he was too far from the table to have fallen and hit his head against it. Although, perhaps he had managed to move a few inches before succumbing to unconsciousness.

How long had he lain here, alone, hurt? Fighting the urge to cradle his head in her lap, she reached out and gingerly traced her fingers down his cheek. He looked so dreadfully pale. But his breathing was even, and Florrie prayed he was not seriously injured.

The Burgesses returned in what seemed an age to Florrie. She grabbed the cloths from Mrs. Burgess and directed her to hold the candle.

Gingerly drawing back Alford's hair, Florrie closely inspected the cut on his head. It was not deep, and for that she was thankful.

"Scissors?" she asked Mrs. Burgess. With them, Florrie clipped the matted hairs from around the wound.

As Florrie tore one cloth into a long strip, Alford began to stir. Florrie leaned down to hear what he mumbled. She was nearly nose to nose with Alford when his eyes flicked open and stared dazedly into hers.

"An angel," he whispered, his eyes fluttering shut again.

"Alford, you clunch, it is I. Florence. Miss Washburn." She resisted the urge to shake him into consciousness again.

He groaned and opened one eye. "You're not an angel?" he asked hopefully.

Florrie smiled in relief, and shook her head.

"That must be why my head hurts like the devil," he moaned. "If I were dead, I would feel better."

He raised his hand to his head, but Florrie batted it away.

"Let me get this bandage on first," she said. She pressed a neatly folded wad of cloth on the wound, then bound it tightly by wrapping the long strips around Alford's head.

Alford gingerly sat up. He took a few deep breaths to steady himself, keeping his eyes tightly closed until his dizziness passed.

"What happened?" Florrie asked, when he opened his eyes again.

He made a wry smile. "I suspect your mysterious diner coshed me over the head," he said.

Florrie's eyes widened. "Did you see anyone?"

Alford fractionally shook his head. "Caught me completely by surprise, from the back."

"How terrible!" Florrie whirled on the Burgesses. "What do you know of this?" She watched Burgess glance uneasily at his wife.

"Nothing."

"You mean there are strangers roaming through the house and you do not even know?" Florrie shivered. "We could be murdered in our beds."

"Might be Silly Willy," Mrs. Burgess said quickly.

"Silly Willy?"

"Willy. He don't have any other name. He's harmless enough. Lives out in the open mostly, 'cept when the weather's bad. He comes by for food sometimes. But he never hurt nobody afor."

"Have you seen this Willy recently?" Florrie asked.

Both Burgesses shook their heads.

"I think, for everyone's safety, that all the doors in this house should be locked." Florrie looked pointedly at Mrs. Burgess. "I think Willy has been hiding up here, for the table is cleared off and someone has eaten here recently. If all the chambers are locked, he will not have a refuge. And the doors and windows leading into the house should be locked, as well. Of course, this will be after you have thoroughly searched every inch of this house for an intruder."

Mrs. Burgess looked at her husbasnd, who nodded his assent.

Florrie kneeled again by Alford. "Do you think you can walk to your chamber if Burgess helps you?"

"Maybe," he said. "Let me try getting to my feet first."

With Burgess assisting, Alford struggled to his feet. He immediately reached for the table to keep from toppling over. His head ached abominably, and his eyes were not focusing well. And his stomach felt as if—

"Give me the basin," he gasped, sinking to his knees. Florrie snatched up the basin and placed it before him just in time.

Alford almost wished that Silly Willy or whoever his attacker was *had* hit him a trifle harder. Death sounded like an infinitely more pleasing prospect than what he was feeling right now. A new spasm shook him and he retched again.

Someone wiped his face with a cool, damp cloth while he knelt trembling over the basin. He heard footsteps scurrying about, but he dared not open his eyes. It was much better in the dark. He took several large breaths, shuddering with the effort.

"As soon as you feel ready, we should get you to your room," Florrie said quietly. "You will be much more comfortable there."

Alford nodded. Slowly, carefully, he sat back on his haunches. Nausea rose within him again, but he fought it back successfully this time. Still keeping his eyes screwed shut, he hung his head down. Somehow, it made the painful throbbing in his head less intense.

After several minutes, he finally dared to open his eyes. This time, the room did not dance about before him, but stood still and steady. One small improvement.

He carefully turned his head to the side and saw Florrie sitting beside him on the floor, concern etched in her face.

"I think I may live," he said with a shaky laugh. "You will not be a widow after all."

"You wouldn't dare die," she said, a smile flitting across her face. "Else I could not marry Kit."

Forgetting his condition, he attempted to grin but it turned into a wince as a shooting pain stabbed through his head.

Florrie rose and dragged the chair from the table. "Perhaps it will be better if you sat before trying to stand," she suggested. "I imagine it would be best if we could carry you downstairs, but I fear that is a task beyond the three of us."

"Why don't you just bring me a blanket and pillow and I can sleep here?" he asked wearily.

"Someone will have to sit with you through the night," Florrie said, "and you cannot sentence them to such discomfort. You will have to walk to your room."

Alford rested one elbow on the chair seat while Burgess grasped the other. Alford rose to his knees, then to one foot. With a final burst of effort, he shifted his weight and slid onto the chair.

The wave of dizziness was smaller this time, and he only needed to keep his eyes shut for a short while. Finally, he nodded to Burgess. Best to get it over with quickly. Grasping Burgess's arm, Alford cautiously stood up.

Leaning heavily against Burgess, with Florrie grasping his other arm, Alford slowly shuffled across the floor to the door and into the corridor.

"It looks a deucedly long way to the stairs," he sighed.

Florrie squeezed his arm in encouragement. "Take your

time," she said. "We have naught else to do this evening."

He shot her what he hoped was a lowering look, then concentrated on putting one foot before the other. Only once, on the stairs, did he stumble, and both Burgess and Florrie were quick to catch him.

"We shall need your key," Florrie said when they at last neared his room.

"Waistcoat." He grimaced at the effort needed to keep upright. Only a few more steps . . . He breathed in sharply as he felt Florrie's fingers fumbling in his pockets.

"Were you afraid of the Lady, too?" she asked him archly as she put the key in the lock. "Was that why you went back upstairs?"

"All ladies terrify me," he replied with a wan smile. Burgess and Florrie led him across the chamber and he sank down gratefully upon the bed.

"Do you think you could eat something?" Florrie asked as Burgess drew off Alford's boots.

Alford made a face. "Not immediately, if you please. My stomach is still none too steady."

Florrie nodded in agreement. "Weak tea may be best, then. I will have Mrs. Burgess see to it. Burgess can assist you into bed."

"You do not wish to help?" Alford raised a lop-sided brow.

His impertinence elated Florrie. It meant he was feeling more himself. "I shall return when you are comfortably settled, Alford."

By the time Florrie reached the confines of her own room, she was as weak-kneed as Alford had been.

Something was terribly, terribly wrong in this house. No ghost had struck Alford on the head. There was a stranger here, a stranger who meant them harm. She shivered. Once Alford was settled, and Mrs. Burgess brought tea, Florrie fully intended to lock herself and Alford into their rooms and bar both doors with furniture. She did not wish to take any chances tonight, when Alford would be of little assistance if something happened.

She heard Mrs. Burgess arrive with the tea, so Florrie unlocked the door to the connecting dressing room and knocked on the door at Alford's side.

"Come in," he said.

He looked better already, Florrie thought, eyeing him critically. He sat propped up against the pillows, sipping the steaming tea. His face had regained some color, and except for the stark white bandage wrapped about his head, he did not look as if he had undergone such a terrible ordeal.

"Feeling better?"

Alford nodded.

"I will sit with you for a while," Florrie announced. She looked at the Burgesses. "I suppose it is too much to hope that there is a doctor closer than Bideford?"

"I do not need a doctor," Alford protested.

"Clovelly," Burgess replied.

"Perhaps in the morning we should send for him. Is there some nearby farm lad who could take a message?"

Mrs. Burgess nodded. "Jemmy Swittle will be here in the morning with the eggs. I can send the lad off."

"I do not need a doctor," Alford reiterated.

"Yes, you do," Florrie retorted. "Injuries to the head are very peculiar things." She turned back to Burgess. "Who is the magistrate for this district?"

"What you be needing the magistrate for?"

"Someone attacked Lord Alford in this house," Florrie said evenly. "Had we not found him, he might have died. That is attempted murder. The authorities must be notified."

Burgess opened his mouth to speak, but his wife jabbed him sharply with her elbow. "The lad can see to that as well."

"Thank you," said Florrie. "You may go now. I believe Lord Alford will be all right. Thank you for your assistance tonight."

Burgess led his wife out of the chamber, muttering to her in a low undertone.

Florrie pulled a chair over to the side of Alford's bed. "You need not make yourself so comfortable," he protested. "As you said, I am all right. I do not need a nurse-maid."

Florrie ignored his comments. "What do you think happened?"

"Someone hit me over the head."

"And unfortunately, it did little to improve your faculties. Do you believe that story about Silly Willy?"

"It makes as much sense as any. The Burgesses have probably been slipping him food, and he's retreated upstairs to eat it. When he found me in his lair, he panicked."

"Do you think it has been he wandering the halls at night?"

"You would prefer it to be a human, rather than a ghost? I do not think it likely. It is understandable he wished to protect his hideaway. But what aim would he have in trying to frighten us?"

"I don't know," Florrie admitted.

"How did you happen to find me?" he asked, keeping his voice deliberately casual.

"You were gone for so long, I grew concerned. I even made Burgess go out and look along the cliff path." Florrie reddened. "I knew when you missed dinner that something was terribly wrong."

"Today it was your turn to play knight in shining armor," he said with a smile. "I . . . I am grateful, Miss Washburn."

"Call me Florrie," she said impulsively.

"You will not think me too forward?" he asked with a trace of a grin.

"As my future brother-in-law, I think I can allow such a lapse in formality."

His grin faded. "Is that what Kit calls you?"

"All my close friends do," she said quickly.

"Then I am honored, Florrie, that you count me among their number."

Both fell silent for a moment. Florrie did not wish to leave him alone—she knew that it was important to keep a close eye upon one suffering from a head wound—yet she knew Alford would not wish to be babied.

"Should you like me to read?" she asked, brightening.

"I am not certain I am up for the high drama of *Otranto*," he said.

She took a deep breath. "I could read from *Improved Field Cultivation.*"

He looked startled, then eyed her suspiciously. "What makes you think I should be interested in such a thing?"

She gestured to the table, where the book and the spectacles lay. "I was in here earlier," she confessed. "When I was searching for you. I thought that perhaps you had decided to go with Old Mort after all, and I was—"

"Snooping?"

"I merely wanted to see if you had left without telling me," she protested.

"Do you make it a habit of invading other people's rooms?" he asked coldly.

"You are known to have done so," she retorted.

He leaned his head back against the pillow and shut his eyes. "You are right, of course."

"Alford?"

"Yes?"

"Do you need your spectacles to read? Is that why you never read downstairs in the library?"

"Yes, Florrie, I need my spectacles to read."

"Then whyever do you not use them?" she asked, then realized the obvious answer. "You are embarrassed!"

His eyes flicked open. "I am never embarrassed," he said coldly.

"Yes, you are," she said, her voice triumphant. "You certainly did not want me to know about them, else you would have worn them long ago."

"I assure you, I am no more embarrassed about wearing spectacles than you are about wearing half-boots. There has not been any occasion to wear them since your arrival."

A monstrous thought dawned in Florrie's mind. "Is that why you missigned the marriage papers?" she asked suspiciously. "Because you were too vain to be seen with your glasses on?"

"I am not vain," Alford snapped.

"It is true!" she chortled with glee. "I can not believe you are such a clunch, Alford. You created this whole, horrible mess because you were too full of vanity to put on your spectacles and read what you were signing."

Alford sat up. "I think, *Miss Washburn,* that you have worn out your welcome. Feel free to leave at any time."

"Oh, I would not think of leaving an invalid alone. Tell me, what other dreadful mistakes have you made while refusing to wear your spectacles?"

Alford flung the covers back. "Leave. Now. Or I will personally escort you to the door."

Florrie stood up. She was not going to let him think he intimidated her.

"I will lock your door for the night," she said calmly. "In case your friend Silly Willy is lurking about in the halls tonight." She did as she said, then walked over and plopped the key into Alford's lap. "Sweet dreams." Back rigid, she walked to the connecting door and pulled it shut behind her.

Alford set the key on the bedside table and pulled the covers back up to his chin. It was cold. He lay his head back on the pillow and closed his eyes.

Damn that nosy girl. He could not deny her charge—of course he did not want to be seen wearing his spectacles. He'd be laughed out of every club in London. Why did she, of all people, have to discover his secret? She was liable to tell everyone she knew, particularly in light of the disaster with the marriage papers.

He felt as if he had been stripped bare in front of her, and he did not much like the sensation. First, she had been witness to that impressive performance over the wash-basin upstairs. Then he'd had to rely on her and Burgess to get back to his room, as though he were an invalid. He was only lucky she had not insisted on undressing him for bed! Thank God she had enough sensibility to spare him that indignity.

Yet Florrie's actions tonight surprised him. Despite her protestations, he had thought her an eminently silly widgeon. But in a crisis, she had ably taken charge. There was no sign of the trembling, terrified woman he held in his arms on the sea-cliff path, or frightened out of bed the previous evening. A rather complex bundle of contradictions, he thought, beginning to feel drowsy in spite of the throbbing pain in his head. Florrie was full of surprises. What else had he to learn about her?

Chapter 16

Florrie dressed for bed, but she was determined to stay awake through the night. Someone had to watch Alford until the doctor came on the morrow and declared him fit.

Florrie was not exactly certain why she needed to watch Alford; she only remembered that it was recommended practice for one with a head wound. But was she only to watch? Or was she to examine the patient for signs of—what? She desperately wished they were closer to town, and the doctor could be summoned at once. If Alford's condition worsened because of the delay . . .

He would resent her presence, she was certain. Alford was the type of man who hated to show any sign of weakness. And tonight he had demonstrated several. She had no doubt he would find some way to place the blame on her. It was her exploration that lured him upstairs, her discovery of the occupied room that led to his own investigation. And her visit to his room had revealed the truth about his eyesight.

Men were so vain. They constantly derided women for their interest in fashion and ornament, when they were all peacocks themselves. Why else would so many men stuff themselves into creaking corsets, use false calves under their stockings, and display the most colorful and elaborate waistcoats? Alford's refusal to be seen wearing his spectacles was a perfect example. Better to stumble around blindly than appear less than perfect. Men were such fools!

Florrie carefully traversed the empty dressing room and put her ear to Alford's door. Was he asleep yet? Or would he be able to sleep? His head must hurt dreadfully. But she did not hear any sounds that would indicate he was thrashing about in his bed. He was not moaning in pain. Perhaps all was well. She placed her hand on the latch and carefully opened the door.

The candle still burned on the dresser. Tip-toeing quietly, she crossed to the bed and peered down at Alford. He was sleeping like a babe, thank goodness. She reached out and briefly touched her hand to his forehead. He was cool; no signs of fever.

Florrie desperately wished she could remember what one was supposed to do for patients with head wounds. The memories hung tantalizingly on the edge of her mind. There had been a member of the embassy staff in St. Petersburg who had slipped on an icy step and taken a severe blow to the head. She remembered discussing the injury with the other ladies, but not what the doctors did about it. She bit her lip in frustration. If anything horrible happened to Alford, she would not forgive herself.

She was momentarily stung by the thought that she cared for Alford. Then reason regained the upper hand. Of course she cared what happened to him—he was family, after all. It had nothing to do with any personal feelings for Alford— which were quite sisterly, she hastened to reassure herself.

It was her fault, after all, that he had been hurt. If she hadn't been snooping around like a silly goose, looking for a ghost, she never would have found that room upstairs. And Alford would never have set off to search it himself. He could have spent his afternoon in the library, his spectacles perched upon his nose, reading away about modern agricultural techniques.

She sighed. There was little she could do about it now. For penance, she would keep herself awake all night, to watch over him. He would not need to know she was here. She wrapped her robe closer and curled up in the chair.

Alford awoke with an excruciating headache, which confused him for a moment. Too much brandy again? He didn't remember a lengthy conversation with the brandy decanter last night. And this pain felt different, more one-sided, more . . .

A confusion of images flooded his brain. His stealthy investigation upstairs, the sudden attack, the descending blackness. He remembered Florrie, and the Burgesses and . . .

Reluctantly, Alford opened his eyes, adjusting them to the dim morning light that crept around the curtains. He gingerly felt the bandage wrapped about his head, wincing when his fingers reached the padding over the wound. It had been no dream then, and this headache was not the product of over-consumption. Someone had deliberately hurt him.

It was a disturbing thought. He did not particularly want to have to walk around always keeping an eye on his back. The mystery would have to be solved quickly, before something worse occurred.

He recalled the Burgesses' talk of some local vagrant. Alford could not quite believe a total stranger had taken up residence inside the hall. Granted, the house was a rabbit warren, with its odd-sized rooms and ancient architecture, and it was certainly old enough to have something along the lines of a priest's hole or similar device that may have been used during Cromwellian times. But why would such a man wish to damage his position by hurting a benefactor? It did not make sense.

Of course, there was always the possibility that the Burgesses had more to do with this than they claimed. Alford thought he remembered seeing a wary glance pass between them. He had sensed last night that they were hiding something. A son on the run from the law or the military? A man like that might be desperate enough to kill whoever came into his path. If that were the case, Alford would have to be very, very careful.

Which meant what he needed was a weapon. He cursed himself for not having brought his pistols, but he had never considered that he would actually need them for protection in a house owned by his own family. And he could only imagine the age of whatever weapons were on hand in this house. Yet anything was better than his bare hands.

The first thing he wished to do was get Florrie out of the

house. A sharp pain stabbed at him at the mere thought of
her being in any real danger. Neither his father nor hers
would forgive him if anything happened to her. Nor would
Kit. He had caused his brother enough grief with the botched
proxy. How would he ever explain any injury to Florrie?
He would send her back to Bideford with the doctor.

Might it be better if he left today with Florrie as well—
and brought back the sheriff or magistrate to investigate? If
the Burgesses were involved in some manner, Alford did not
like the idea of being at their mercy. It would be far too easy
to arrange some sort of accident for him. They could put
some drug in the food, haul him out to the cliff and toss him
over, with no one the wiser. Florrie would testify to his
fascination with the cliff walk. It would all look like a tragic
accident. Alford shuddered at the thought.

Except for one thing. If the Burgesses had wanted to be
rid of either him or Florrie, they could have done it ages
ago. Why now? Because he and Florrie had discovered
someone was using the room upstairs?

It did not make sense. The use of the room meant nothing.
He would have been perfectly willing to accept his own
suggestion that Burgess hid out there from his wife. But after
being knocked over the head, Alford's suspicions were now
aroused. It was obvious he and Florrie had seen something
they were not meant to. But what?

The effort of concentrating only made his headache worse.
Alford closed his eyes and tried to let his mind drift. Perhaps
he could discuss matters with the doctor when he arrived.

He felt dreadfully thirsty and looked with longing at the
pitcher of water at the bedside. He had vague recollections
that he had been of little use last night, knew that it had taken
Burgess and Florrie to get him back to his room. Could he
handle something as simple as sitting up?

Gritting his teeth, Alford slowly raised his head from the
pillow. The pain did not become any worse, he noted with
relief. Moving cautiously, he managed to sit up without
mishap. Encouraged by his success, he swung his legs around
until he sat on the edge of the bed. From this position he
could not quite reach the water pitcher and glass. With

trembling resolve, using the edge of the bedside table to steady himself, Alford stood up.

And did not fall. Or even waver. He smiled at his success. If it weren't for the blasted headache . . . He poured himself a tall glass of water and drained it thirstily.

Alford turned his head to one side and his eyes widened in surprise as he saw a familiar form huddled and asleep in the chair across the room. Had she been here all night?

Sitting back on the edge of the bed again, Alford contemplated the sleeping girl. Florrie, he corrected himself. He remembered she had given him leave to call her that. But as he remembered more of what had transpired last night, a frown formed on his face. She had twitted him about his need for spectacles, and his vanity in refusing to wear them. She had not been gracious about it. In fact, she had been downright rude.

Should he wake her or let her continue to sleep in that contorted pose? She would probably awake with an unpleasant crick in her neck. He smiled at the thought. T'would serve her right for her verbal attack of last night. But as he watched her, seeing the steady rise and fall of her chest as she slumbered on, he took pity upon her.

He again rose to his feet, feeling much steadier this time, and slowly crossed the room.

"Florrie," he said, gently shaking her shoulder. "Time to wake up."

"Come back later," she mumbled and curled up into an even tighter ball.

Alford shook her harder this time. "Florrie. Wake up."

Her eyes fluttered open, then grew wider as she took in the sight of him. She sat up straighter, glancing about her as if uncertain where she was.

"I fear you fell asleep in the chair," Alford explained.

"What are you doing out of bed?" she demanded, fully awake now.

"Except for a raging headache, I feel perfectly fine," Alford said. He spun around. "See? Steady as a rock."

"I insist you remain in bed until the doctor arrives," said Florrie, scrambling to her feet. "Head wounds are very serious things, Alford. They are not to be trifled with."

"I do not need a doctor."

"Yes, you do," she insisted. "I am sure Burgess has already sent for the man and he will likely be here before noon. Climb back into bed like a good boy and wait to hear what he has to say."

"I won't," said Alford, more out of a desire to irritate Florrie than out of any strong conviction. He was not going to let this chit manage him any more than she already had. Last night, he needed her help. Today he did not.

Florrie put her hands on her hips and glared at Alford. "If you do not get back into that bed right now, I will march into my room and send letters off to everyone I know in London, telling them that you wear spectacles."

"That is blackmail," he protested.

"The doctor will be able to take the letters to the post," she said.

Alford scowled. He did not think she would really carry out her threat, but he did not want to call her bluff just yet. Then a wide grin of triumph spread over his face.

"I fear that under the circumstances, I would then be forced to write some letters of my own," he said. "Telling how a certain Florence Washburn spent the night in my room."

Florrie gasped aloud. "You would not dare!"

"I think we are both at point-non-plus," he said. "If you desist from brow-beating me, I will not say a word about where I found you this morning."

"You do not play fair, Alford," she charged.

He laughed. "A case of the pot calling the kettle black, I fear. Truce?"

"You really should rest," she said, deliberately ignoring the offer. "It would be the best thing for you."

"Only on the condition that you do the same," he countered. "I am certain you did not sleep well in that chair. Did you spend the entire night there?"

"No," she said. For she did not want him to know just how concerned she had been. Florrie was angry with herself

for having fallen asleep; much goold she would have been
to Alford if the need had arisen.

"Then," he said, taking her by the shoulders and steering
her toward the connecting door, "you go back to your own
room and try to get some sleep. I promise I will hop back
into bed the moment you are gone."

"All right," she agreed reluctantly.

The doctor, when he arrived, made Alford think twice
about divulging confidences. He barely looked capable of
practicing medicine. One button hung by a string from the
man's waistcoat, while another had totally disappeared. His
linen was none too clean, and there were suspicious stains
on his breeches.

"So, bumped our head on something did we?" An overpowering odor of garlic emanated from the doctor as he
began to unwrap the bandages around Alford's head.

"Something like that," Alford replied.

"And probably hurts like the devil today."

Alford nodded, then winced as the doctor pulled the
bandage away from the wound.

"Well?" Alford asked when the doctor said nothing.

"Looks fine to me," the doctor replied. "Not worth
stitching. A little sticking plaster ought to do the trick. Any
dizziness today? Blurred vision? Vomiting?"

"I was sicker than a dog yesterday, but I feel fine today,"
Alford replied.

"No signs of fever?"

"None."

"Stand up," the doctor commanded. "Now, walk across
the room. Turn around, and walk back toward me. Slowly."

Alford did as the doctor commanded.

"Now," the doctor continued. "Close your eyes and stand
on one leg."

Feeling exceedingly foolish, Alford did as he was directed.

"What's your mother's maiden name?"

"Brooke."

"What year did Nelson die?"

"1805."

"How old are you? What year were you born?"

"Twenty-seven. 1784."

"Brains don't seem addled to me," the doctor said, reaching into his bag. "I'll leave some powders for the headache. If it isn't better within the week, send for me again."

He put the powders on the dresser. "Mix one of these in a glass of water. No more than three a day." He turned and looked at Alford. "Don't suppose you want to settle your bill today?"

"Talk to Burgess," Alford said. "He can take it out of the household account."

"Good man, Burgess. He keeps a good eye on things here."

Alford was tempted to add "not good enough," but he did not. Until he was certain about the Burgesses's involvement—or lack thereof—he did not wish to raise any suspicions.

"Remember, send for me if there are any changes. You've got a hard head there." The doctor waved vaguely as he left the room.

Had Alford been better convinced of the doctor's competence, he would have been well-pleased with his pronouncement of good health. But at least he had something for the headache. Alford grabbed a packet off the dresser, catching a glimpse of himself in the mirror. He drew back with a start. What in God's name had been done to him?

The blob of sticking plaster looked more amusing than frightening. But his hair! It looked as if it had been lopped off with a mowing scythe.

Florrie! He remembered the cool touch of her hands as she had bandaged his head. She had done this to him—on purpose, no doubt. He stormed through the connecting door.

"What did you mean by butchering my hair in such a man—Good God!"

Florrie was clad only in a thin lawn chemise—much sheerer than her night wear—and in the few seconds before she reacted to the intrusion, Alford had the opportunity to see a great deal more than she would have wished. An appreciative smile lit his face.

"Get out of here!" she screeched, diving for the bed and her robe.

Alford could not tear his eyes away. Every curvaceous line of her body showed under the diaphanous fabric and he felt an unexpected heat rise within him. He watched in stunned dismay as she threw on her robe and hastily pulled it closed.

"How dare you burst in here unannounced," she yelled. "You have no right. Get out! Now!"

"I had not intended . . ." he stammered. His fingers ached to reach out and wrap themselves in the honey-gold hair that spilled over her shoulders. He wanted to pull the robe from her shoulders so he could feast his eyes again on what lay beneath.

"I do not care what you intended, Alford." Florrie glared at him. "Please get out of my room."

He suddenly recalled his purpose. He gestured to his head. "I suppose you did this as a joke," he said.

"Did what?"

"Hacked off my hair with whatever blunt instrument you managed to put your hands on," he snapped.

"It was Mrs. Burgess's shears and, no, I did not do it as a joke. I did it so I could bandage your head properly."

"I look like some freak at the country fair."

"No, you don't. What you do look like is an arrogant aristocrat who does not have any sense of propriety or gratitude."

"I am supposed to be grateful because I will be forced to shave my head in order to have some semblance of symmetry there?"

"Stop being such a dandy, Alford. No one is going to see you out here except me. And I could not possibly think worse of you than I already do."

Alford continued to glare at her, but without any real vehemence. She was right, of course. It was ridiculous of him to complain about such a paltry matter. He was suddenly aware that she had twisted him around in circles. She had an uncanny knack for doing that.

"I am sorry," he said stiffly. "I know you were trying to help. I am rather grumpy today because my head hurts."

"As it well should," she said, the anger leaving her voice. "That was a nasty cut and a heavy blow to have knocked you unconscious, Alford. Do not treat it lightly."

"The doctor pronounced me healthy enough."

"The doctor was here? Whyever did you not tell me?"

"I did not think he needed to see you." Alford grinned. "I am the one with the injury."

"I wanted to speak to him about your care," Florrie said. "I am certain he would wish you in bed right now."

"He said nothing of the sort," Alford said. "Gave me powders for the ache and said I was fine."

Florrie sniffed. "I would not place too much trust in the pronouncements of a country doctor."

"Quite true," Alford said. "While you, on the other hand, are more than qualified to pass judgment on all manner of medical conditions."

"I never said that," Florrie retorted.

"Then stop ordering me about. I am not a child. I am perfectly capable of taking care of myself."

Florrie frowned but held her tongue.

"I am being a rotten patient, aren't I?" He smiled wryly.

"Yes, you are," she said, with an answering smile. "But I find men usually are. Papa is a veritable dragon when he becomes ill. It is just a weakness in the male character, I think."

"Florrie . . ." Alford's voice held a hint of warning.

"Back to bed," she said, waving her hands at him. "Shoo. Scat."

He retreated before her onslaught, backing through the doorway while he tried to keep from laughing. Florrie grabbed the door and prepared to close it behind him.

"Florrie," he said, before he ducked into his own room.

''What?''

''I envy Kit,'' he said, recalling what he had seen earlier. ''He will have a lovely wife.''

Florrie slammed the door shut with a resounding thud.

Chapter 17

Florrie assumed Alford would remain in bed for the remainder of the day, and was therefore surprised when he entered the library shortly before dinner.

"Should you be up?" she asked.

"I feel quite fit, *Doctor* Washburn. And famished."

Florrie's cheeks reddened. Let him ignore her advice. She would wash her hands of the matter.

Alford settled himself into the other chair before the fire while Florrie poured him a cup of tea. "I suppose it is too much to hope that Burgess found some sign of the intruder?"

"I did not ask him," Florrie said, handing him his tea. "But certainly, whoever it was must surely be gone by now."

Alford shrugged. "One would hope so."

"You are feeling better?" Florrie asked with an uneasy look.

"My head still hurts. But not as badly as before."

"I do wish you had called me when the doctor arrived." She studied him carefully. "You are certain he said you were fine?"

"There is probably little he could have done if I wasn't," Alford observed. He smiled. "Relax, Florrie. I promise not to die until the annulment is obtained."

She gave him an exasperated stare. "Really, Alford. My major concern is for you."

He patted the ragged ends of his hair. "That *must* have been the reason for your excellent job of barbering."

Florrie grinned. He must be feeling better if he was still harping about the way she had trimmed his hair. "It gives you a more countrified look, Alford. Somewhat bucolic, in fact."

"Exactly what I was looking for," he said glumly.

"Alford?"

"What?"

"Do you think there is any connection between this attack on you and the person who tried to get in my room?"

A sudden coughing fit overtook Alford.

"Do not drink your tea so fast," Florrie admonished him. She looked at him expectantly. "Well? Do you?"

Alford carefully schooled his features into an expression of innocence. "I had not thought about it," he said, quite truthfully. "But none of the stories I have heard about the Lady indicated she brought harm to anyone. And it was no ghost that banged me over the head."

"We still do not know if what I saw was a ghost," Florrie said, then laughed at the thought. "Alford, the idea is absurd. This is the nineteenth century. We are long past the age of primitive superstition."

A mischievous gleam crept into his eye. "You firmly disbelieve in the idea of ghosts, then?" He could not resist the impulse to twit her. "You certainly gave some very convincing demonstrations that you thought otherwise."

Florrie glared at him indignantly. "One is scarcely a rational creature when one's sleep is disrupted in the most alarming manner," she protested. "Now that we know there is—or was—some stranger in the house, it makes much more sense that he was the cause of it all."

"That does not explain the woman you saw on the lawn. Or the one you said you saw in the hall."

"I do not know what I saw," Florrie admitted. "The first could easily have been the sea-mist. The second might have been a trick of my imagination, or the shadows."

Alford sat back in his chair, as if considering the matter. He felt rather foolish about his attempts to frighten Florrie, now that real danger lurked within the house. He only wished he had succeeded in driving her away for her own safety.

"You are probably right," he said, and laughed. "It is absurd to think we even considered the idea of a ghost. We can only blame the influence of that dreadful novel."

Florrie's eyes narrowed. "You were the one who first mentioned this wandering lady."

"I was only repeating the tale I had heard," Alford said. "I never once, if you will recall, made any claim to the truth of the story."

"Oh, it does not matter." Florrie shook her head. "Now that you have been injured, we have a much more exciting mystery to solve."

He shrugged with calculated indifference. He did not want Florrie aware of his concerns. She would probably insist upon launching a new exploration of the house. He must keep her out of harm's way. "I think there is little mystery. Silly Willy is probably the culprit and I doubt he will make another appearance for a while."

"But what if the tale is truly exciting?" Florrie asked, her eyes aglow with excitement. "What if it is an escaped French prisoner, making his way to the coast where he will be picked up by a French vessel?"

"I highly doubt it," Alford said dryly.

Florrie pouted. "Dartmoor is not so dreadfully far from here."

"Any Frenchman in his right mind would go south, rather than north," Alford pointed out. "We are in the opposite direction from France, Florrie."

"But that is precisely why he would come north," Florrie said with mounting excitement. "No one would think to look for him here. Why, this could be the major escape route for every prisoner in England."

"And exactly how many French prisoners have escaped in the last year?" Alford asked.

Florrie's face fell. "I do not know."

"I am certain the number is tiny," Alford said. "Else a hue and cry would have been raised."

"What makes you think you would have noticed?" she asked sarcastically. "I doubt it was included in the racing news."

"I read the papers, Florrie," he said with exasperation. "The *Times*, the *Post* and the *Chronicle*. So I can vouch for the matter."

"Whyever do you read all three?"

"Each paper takes a slightly different view of the political situation. The truth is usually somewhere in between."

"You read the parliamentary news?" Florrie stared at him in amazement.

"Yes, I read the parliamentary news," Alford said crossly. "Little use that it is."

"You are interested in politics?" Florrie asked in surprise. He gave her a suspicious look, then relaxed. "Yes, I am."

"Tory or Whig?"

He smiled. "Whig. of course. My father's a Tory."

"Alford, I can truly say that you have amazed me," Florrie said.

"But not to the point of speechlessness," he teased.

"That," she announced archly, "takes a great deal. If you are so interested in politics, why are you not more involved?"

"How can I be?" he asked bitterly. "I cannot take a seat in the Lords until I inherit the title."

"There is always the Commons."

"Do you have any idea of the cost of an election campaign?" he asked. "Not to mention the difficulty of finding an available seat. Without help, it is impossible."

"Have you asked your father?"

"Many times. He refuses."

"There might be others who would be willing to promote your candidacy," Florrie suggested. Her brain whirled with these new revelations. Alford had built up a completely false facade—for what reason? Why would a man who was possessed of a great deal of intelligence, an interest in politics and agricultural matters, hide behind the image of an indolent rakehell?

Alford sighed. "There are few who would support a Whig candidate," he said sadly. "Far too many seats are held by landowners who want no part of change. It is precisely why the election system needs to be reformed—but it cannot be done from the outside. And there are many who are determined to keep the reformers out."

"But with the Prince now Regent. will that not help your cause?"

Alford's face grew bitter. "The Tories are as deeply entrenched as ever. The Regent turned his back on the Whig cause the moment the Regency was proclaimed."

"It must be dreadfully frustrating for you," Florrie said in sympathy, suddenly realizing just how much impact that frustration had on his life. It explained so much about him—his determined pursuit of excess was an escape, not a vocation.

"It is," he acknowledged, with the sudden realization that he had never discussed this with anyone—outside of the ongoing arguments with his father. Why was he baring his soul to Florrie, of all people? He regretted his candor. It would matter little to her. "But certainly no more frustrating than waiting for dinner to arrive. Are you sure Mrs. Burgess is cooking tonight?"

Florrie was taken aback by the abrupt switch in the conversation, but shrewdly guessed that Alford had regretted his uncharacteristic loquaciousness. She smiled sweetly. "Have another cup of tea. I am sure dinner will be here momentarily."

The prompt arrival of dinner stilled Alford's tongue, and Florrie was unable to get more than the most innocuous remarks from him for the remainder of the evening. It was not long before he pleaded tiredness, and a headache, and her offer to read more about the mysterious castle of Otranto did not elicit a favorable response.

Although Florrie insisted she was far too awake to take to her own bed, Alford insisted she could not remain in the library alone. Florrie had to agree the prospect did not much appeal to her. Not that she feared any attack. It was, actually, that without Alford it would be deucedly boring to remain downstairs. Alford escorted her upstairs, and Florrie smiled at his insistence upon locking her door himself.

She had not realized until the past two days just how much she enjoyed his company. His wit could be acidic at times, but never dull. Life was decidedly flat without the opportunity to trade barbs with him. And she was eager to pry more secrets from him.

Alford's professed interest in politics had come as a great

surprise. So few members of the Lords actually enjoyed the work. It was a pity someone like Alford, who welcomed the challenge, could not be allowed to take his seat now, supplanting his father, who sounded as if he had far too many old and fusty ideas.

Florrie began to wonder, for the first time, whether Alford and Kit were really so dissimilar. She had always assumed so. But as she thought about it, she realized that impression had been fostered more by the earl, and his tales of Alford's behavior, than any observations on her part. She and Kit had never really talked about his brother. Was Kit as unaware of Alford's interests as his father?

It was a sudden shock to realize she had sadly misjudged Alford. She had relied entirely on hearsay for her opinions. Granted, Alford had done little to dispel the image, but since it was an image he had carefully cultivated, that could be expected. Florrie was chagrined to find she had not the perception to see beyond that image to the real man underneath. It bespoke a sad want of understanding on her part.

For the first time she considered the plight of an elder son. They rarely entered the army, for the succession must not be endangered. They did not work with the foreign office, for what was the point of training them for a diplomatic career they would abandon when they took on the title? Politics was closed, for it was highly unusual for a future lord to take a seat in the Commons. They really were not allowed any useful pursuits. All they could do was wait and watch.

Certainly, that was the case with Alford. He could only sit back and watch other men—men like Kit—pursue their own dreams and ambitions, while his remained stillborn. Yet, she argued with herself, Alford could have rebelled against his father, if he had wanted something badly enough. It was a pity he had not set his heart on the military, for he could have snapped his fingers at the earl and purchased a commission. But the political arena was a different animal. One did not enter it without backing, and a man at odds with his father would have a difficult time. A pity Alford had not cultivated Tory leanings. . . .

Florrie realized she had been thinking on Alford's situation for far too long. When all was said and done, it was of little concern to her. After all, once this farcical marriage was annulled, they would have little contact. Alford's future did not affect her.

She was still not of a mind to retire, so she walked to the window. Below, the lawn looked to be almost in daylight from the light of the full moon. But the wall along the cliff loomed like a dark, shadowy form, and beyond it lay the blackness of the sea.

Suddenly a light punctuated that inky blackness. It winked out as quickly as it had appeared, and for a moment Florrie thought she had imagined it. But as she peered harder, it appeared again, for only a moment.

It must be a boat rounding the point nad and heading up the channel, she thought. A common enough occurrence. She was almost ready to draw the curtains and prepare for bed when she saw another light flare briefly. This one looked as if it was on top of the cliff wall.

Florrie stared intently at the spot where the light had first appeared, but it did not reappear. Had it only been some trick of the moonlight? Was there something atop the cliff wall that would reflect light? What reason would anyone have for shining a light on the cliff wall?

Then she remembered her conversation with Alford before dinner, and her theory that his mysterious attacker had been an escaped French prisoner. He could be out there now, signaling his compatriots in the boat—which would account for the light she had seen on the sea! Florrie tensed with excitement. There *was* something going on here at Hartland.

Florrie hastily pulled the heavy draperies closed to block out the light from her window, then crawled under them so she could watch the drama being played out below. She frowned when there was no further sign of any lights, either on the sea or the wall. Disappointment grew within her. Was nothing else going to happen?

Then, as she watched with growing horror, a thin, white-robed figure drifted across the lawn.

The Lady!

In sick fascination, Florrie watched the mysterious figure

progress as it drew closer and closer to the wall. She was heading directly for the spot where Florrie had seen the light! Then, in the blink of an eye, she simply vanished.

"Oh!" Florrie exclaimed in both frustration and fear. The figure had disappeared into thin air. It was not possible.

Florrie's eyes remained glued to the scene outside for many long minutes, but there was no further sign of any activity on land or sea. Puzzled, she at last climbed from beneath the curtain and sat down before the dressing table.

It was all so confusing. Escaped prisoners were flesh and blood and very real. But the white-robed figure? Ghosts could not possibly exist. There had to be some other explanation. But the more Florrie thought on it, the more logical became a ghostly solution. Each time Florrie had seen the Lady, she had vanished as quickly as she had come, in a very unhuman manner. Yet someone had attempted to enter Florrie's room two times. Someone had taken a meal in the room upstairs. And someone had hit Alford over the head in that same room. How did it all fit together? Or did it?

She shivered. There was something very strange and mysterious going on in this house, and she was not certain she really wanted to know what it was. Perhaps it was a good idea to leave, after all. There might be danger here for everyone.

But she did not like the idea of leaving before the mystery was laid to rest. And despite Alford's current amiability, she did not want him to think she had been driven away by fear, of all things. She would remain as long as he did. Perhaps they could solve the mystery in the meantime.

Chapter 18

In the morning, Florrie hesitated upon telling Alford what she had seen the previous evening, fearing he would belittle her experience. Why was it that she was the only one to see these baffling occurrences? Alford would be less sanguine if the mysterious lady in white were traipsing through *his* bedchamber. But at last Florrie decided to speak with him. Perhaps he could come up with a logical explanation.

"I saw a rather strange sight from my window last night," she said casually while she buttered her breakfast toast.

"Oh?" Alford raised a curious brow.

"I saw lights. Both on the water and on the cliff wall."

"Lights?" Alford regarded her quizzically.

"Like a lantern, or some such thing. I know you thought it silly yesterday, but do you think there is some truth to my theory that your attacker was an escaped Frenchman? He could have been signaling his countrymen to pick him up."

Alford kept his face carefully neutral, but inside he fought down his excitement. Florrie may just have stumbled across something very close to the truth.

"Did you see anything more than the lights?" he asked casually.

Florrie studied the table cover. "I thought I saw a white figure again," she said at last.

"The Lady?"

"I don't know. I saw someone—or thing—dressed in white, crossing the lawn. When it reached the wall, it disappeared."

"Interesting." A hint of a grin touched his face.

"Alford, what is going on? Do you think there are French prisoners escaping?" Florrie paused. "Or are we really being haunted by the ghost of a woman who's been dead for ages?''

He smiled. "I am sure there is some rational explanation."

Florrie eyed him with skepticism.

"Would you feel better if we went outside and looked around?" Alford asked genially. "Perhaps your French spies will have dropped a tricolor in their haste."

Florrie wished they had. It would explain much. "I would love to go outside," she said with feigned sweetness. She would dearly love to prove to Alford that what she had seen last night was not all in her imagination.

Once free of the house, Florrie tried to hasten Alford across the lawn, but he would have none of it.

"I sustained a serious injury two days ago," he protested mockingly. "I am nearly an invalid. Have some consideration."

"If you were wounded so severely, you should be in bed," Florrie countered. "Besides, I saw how much you ate for breakfast. No invalid would dare put away that much food. It won't wash, Alford."

He put up his hands defensively. "Caught out again," he said, laughing. "I should have known I could not pull the wool over your eyes, Florrie."

Florrie colored slightly at hearing her name from him, still unaccustomed to his use of it. Yet she felt strangely elated by it as well. Somehow, it sounded oddly different on his lips, formed in his lazy drawl. More personal. More intimate.

She hastily turned away.

Alford saw the momentary confusion in her face, and it engendered the same emotion in him as well. Confusion over exactly what he felt for this snippy, outspoken miss who was never loath to point out his numerous faults—yet he could recall the tender touch of her hands as she carefully ministered to him after his injury, and her concern as she had watched over him during the night. He wanted to see more of that gentle, caring side of her, the side she would show to her friends—or those she held in affection.

"I think this is where I saw the light," Florrie called.

Alford looked up, startled. While he stood lost in thought, Florrie had reached the garden wall. He hastened to her side.

"You said the light was on top?" he asked as he casually surveyed the ground for any suspicious signs.

"It would have to be, wouldn't it, in order to be seen from the sea?" Florrie answered sarcastically.

"If they were signaling to the sea."

"I told you there was a boat on the water. It had a light as well."

Alford looked at the wall, and then examined the ground at his feet more carefully.

"Well," he said at last, "if there was a light atop the wall, there is little we can do to check. Unless you have a ladder handy."

Florrie peered intently at the irregular stone surface. "I think I can get a toe-hold here if you can lift me up," she said.

"I don't think that at all wise," Alford said. "Perhaps Burgess has a ladder."

"It will only take a moment this way," Florrie pleaded.

"All right," said Alford reluctantly. He had seen all he needed to, and doubted Florrie would discover any new evidence on top of the wall. But if she was so determined . . . He locked his fingers together and held them out for her foot.

Florrie stepped into his outstretched hands. Placing one hand on his shoulder, to steady herself, she grabbed for a handhold on the irregular wall surface as Alford boosted her up. She was able to get one booted toe into a crevice, but her position was precarious.

"See anything?" Alford asked.

"I need to go higher," Florrie replied. "Can you boost me up more?"

Alford obligingly lifted her higher. Florrie found another toe-hold and pulled herself up until she could peer over the top of the wall. To her disappointment, she saw nothing out of the ordinary. No candle stubs, or spills, or any sign that anything had been atop the wall. She glanced out to the sea, knowing no boat would be there, but feeling compelled to look anyway.

"I hate to be rude, but this is becoming a trifle difficult," Alford warned.

Florrie glanced over her shoulder at Alford, who did indeed look awkward holding up her foot at near shoulder level.

"Oh," she said, startled, and immediately moved to step down. She stuck the tip of her boot in what seemed to be a safe recess in the rock wall, but the instant she put her weight on it, the stone crumbled. Her fingers slipped from their tenuous grip and she fell backward . . . into Alford's arms.

"Oof!" he cried as they tumbled to the ground.

"Oh, Alford, your head!" Florrie twisted in his grasp until she faced him. "Are you all right?"

His eyes fluttered open. "An angel," he murmured.

"Alford!" Florrie did not know whether to be relieved or angry at his teasing.

He opened one eye. "Most women I know would find it a compliment to be compared to an angel," he complained.

Florrie grinned, then her face grew serious. "Are you really all right? I didn't mean to fall on you. You did not hit your head again, did you?"

"How could I possibly complain about a minor tumble that ended with you laying on top of me, clasped in my arms?" He grinned wickedly, tightening his grip about her waist. "I would say it was a fortuitous event."

She should be struggling to free herself, but Florrie suddenly wondered what Alford would do next. He had leered, intimidated, and threatened her with his attentions ever since she arrived. But he had never actually attempted anything. Would he now? Florrie raised up on her forearms and looked down into his face.

"You would?" she inquired, trying to read the thoughts in his clear blue eyes.

It would be so easy, Alford thought, to bridge those few inches that separated them. To place his lips on her own full, slightly pouting ones. To see if she had passions equal to the ones of anger and fear he had already seen. So easy . . .

He watched her watching him, saw the varied emotions that played across her face and shone in those soft hazel eyes. Amusement, curiosity, apprehension, and . . . invitation?

He mentally shook his head. Not Florrie. Not Kit's intended.

"I think," Florrie said at last, surprised at the disappointment she felt at his inaction, "that you are a fraud, Alford."

He grinned, relieved she had granted him an easy escape. "Caught me out at last. My reputation will be in tatters now." He relaxed his hold on her and she rolled off him.

"Oh, your secret will be safe with me," she said, with a faint smile. "Just think how lowering it would be to confess that I could not inspire you to new levels of lasciviousness."

But you shall not know to what degree I was tempted. Alford laughed lightly. "Kit will thank me, I am certain."

Florrie scrambled to her feet, disconcerted by his mention of Kit. Of course he would think of that. A true gentleman would. And Alford, she was discovering, was much more a gentleman than he pretended.

"You never did say whether you saw anything atop the wall," he said casually, falling in step beside her as they returned to the house.

She shook her head. "No sign of anything. Perhaps I did imagine it after all. Some strange trick of the moonlight, I suppose."

Alford nodded in feigned agreement. He had his own ideas about what was going on, but he did not wish to enumerate them to Florrie. She was safer in her ignorance. If what he suspected was true, they would not be bothered for a while. Plenty of time to get her out of the house and back to London, where she would be safe.

Florrie found Alford strangely subdued for the rest of the day, which she credited to the lingering effects of his sore head and that unexpected tumble. She was relieved when he chose to retire early.

The more time she spent in his company, the more confused she grew. It had been much neater, and simpler, when she had thought him a shallow pleasure-seeker. It was easy to dismiss him then.

But the new Alford, the *real* Alford, was not so easily dismissed. He was intelligent, witty, and informed. With no outlet for any of those talents. Florrie could understand his frustration. Was it not akin to what she often felt, as a woman? Her aspirations would all be tied to her husband's; her diplomatic successes would be in the drawing room and not the halls of power. Despite her grasp of European politics and personalities, she would only be a consultant, never a player.

She had placed all her hopes and plans on this marriage with Kit. He was being groomed for a diplomatic career; their marriage would put her in the only position of power she could hold. It had seemed the best opportunity for her. But was it really? Dare she wish for more? Like a husband who sent the blood singing in her veins with a look, or whose slow, widening smile sent shivers up her spine?

Sighing quietly, Florrie began her preparations for bed. Right now, she felt so confused that she no longer knew what she wanted. Except a good night's sleep. In the morning, things might be clearer. Perhaps.

She had been asleep for some length of time when her eyes blinked open at the sound of a strange noise. Florrie shut them again and rolled over, seeking sleep, then froze at a new noise.

Someone was in her room.

Hardly daring to breath, she lay there listening. She heard nothing but sensed a foreign presence. Dare she roll over again and try to look through half-closed eyes? Or should she yell for Alford now? Even if he awoke immediately, he might arrive too late. Better to feign sleep, and pray that whoever it was would go away.

With her ears straining to catch the faintest sound, Florrie lay there, trying to remember to breathe normally so the intruder would not know she was awake. She almost began to think she had imagined everything, when she heard a faint sound that could only be a cautious footstep on the ancient floorboards. Florrie peered through her barely opened lids and caught the clear outline of a person standing between her and the fire.

Caution be damned. Florrie leaped from her bed with a

shriek and raced to the connecting door, not daring to look
behind her. "Alford! Alford!" she cried as she raced through
the dressing chamber.

Alford was in the midst of a very pleasant dream that
involved himself, an intimately lit setting, and a woman who
bore a remarkable resemblance to Florrie. "Go away," he
mumbled sleepily.

"Alford, wake up," Florrie said, tugging at his arm.
"Someone is in my room."

He sat up instantly, shaking the cobwebs from his brain.
Damn. He had thought there would be no further problems.
Quickly he looked around his dimly lit chamber for some
sort of weapon.

"You stay here," he said to Florrie as he climbed out of
bed. Pouring the contents of the water pitcher into the basin,
he hefted the pitcher and headed toward the dressing room.

"Be careful," Florrie pleaded.

Alford stepped cautiously through the doorway and toward
the half-opened door to Florrie's room. He wished he had
more light. But he could not carry this damned pitcher and
a candle and expect to protect himself. Slowly, carefully,
he pushed the door into Florrie's room open inch by inch.

The glowing coals in the fireplace gave off enough light
for Alford to see that no one was in the room. Unless he
or she was hiding. Raising the pitcher in preparation, Alford
slipped into the room and peered behind the door. No one.
He walked around the end of the bed, finding no one
crouched on the other side. The room was unoccupied.

"Florrie," he called. "Bring a candle."

She must have been standing in the dressing chamber, for
she was at his side in an instant.

"No one is here," he said.

"But someone was, I swear it, Alford. He must have
slipped out the door."

Alford walked to the door and turned the knob. It was
securely locked. "What exactly did you *think* you saw?"
he asked her.

"I saw a *person,* standing between the bed and the

fireplace, so there was a clear outline,'' she said with a trace of anger. He did not believe her.

"Are you certain you were not dreaming?" he asked, remembering his own lost dream with regret.

"I was not." Florrie stamped her foot with irritation. "Someone was in this room." She glared at Alford. "Did you look under the bed?"

He quickly did so, but no one was there.

"I think you must have had a very vivid dream," he said soothingly. Nearly as vivid as his own. He eyed Florrie with an approving gaze. The woman in his dreams had worn her hair down around her shoulders in just such a manner.

Florrie whirled about, looking all around her room for a sign of something amiss. There had been someone here, she was certain of it. But where had he gone?

"Look, over on that wall!" She pointed to the paneling near her dressing table. "There is something odd about the wall."

Taking the candle from her, Alford crossed the room. Setting the light on the table, he knelt and examined the wall.

Florrie was right; something was strange. This section of panel was out of line with the others. Almost as if . . .

Alford sucked in his breath with a rapid "oh." After all his poking and probing, the panel was no longer flush with the wall. There was a definite gap. A movable panel. Was it a door? He carefully felt all around the edge with his fingers. If he could only get a grip on the side and pull, he could . . .

Alford sat back on his haunches in amazement as the panel in his hands slowly swung inward. The faint odor of musty damp wafted into the chamber.

"A secret passage!" breathed Florrie as she peered over his shoulder. "I wonder where it leads?"

Chapter 19

"I don't know, but I mean to find out," said Alford, rising to his feet. He started back to his room.

"Where are you going?" Florrie asked anxiously.

"I plan to explore that passage," Alford said over his shoulder.

"But what if there is danger?" Florrie asked, scurrying behind him. She drew up short in the doorway to his room when he waved his breeches to her.

"I am going to get dressed," he said. "You can stay if you wish," he flashed her his best leer, "or you can quietly return to your room."

"I'm going with you," Florrie said.

"No, you are not," Alford replied as he sat down on the edge of the bed to pull on his socks. That task complete, he stood again. "If you are going to linger about while I dress, the least you could do is get me my boots."

"Oh," said Florrie with an exasperated sigh, and she returned to her room.

She had absolutely no desire to head down that dark passageway with Alford. Or with anyone. But she did not want to remain here alone, either. And she did not want Alford off exploring on his own. His head was by no means healed and he should not venture anywhere unaccompanied. What was she to do?

Steeling herself for the ordeal, Florrie rummaged under the bed for her slippers. She would go with him, whether he wished her to or not.

She was still deciding which dress would be best to wear when Alford came striding through the room, pulling on his coat.

"Wait," she said, "I am going with you."

"I told you before, you are not." He glared at her. "Look at you. You cannot go traipsing around in the middle of the night in some dark and dank tunnel in your night clothes. What would your father say?"

"I can be dressed in a few minutes."

"Florrie, stay here. I will be back soon." Alford knelt before the opening in the wall and placed his candle inside.

Florrie frantically tied up her slippers and threw on her warm robe. "I am ready," she announced.

"No."

"Yes. It is my passageway," she insisted. "It leads to my room. I was the one who was frightened out of my wits by whoever used it. I have a right to know what is going on."

Alford shook his head. Impetuous female. Yet he admired her willfulness. "Come along if you wish," he said. "But I will not be responsible if anything happens to you."

Florrie snatched up her candle and crouched beside Alford, peering into the dark cavity. At its opening, the passageway was little more than three feet high. But after a yard, the ceiling rose to a man's height, and the floor dropped down into a series of spiraling stairs. She watched anxiously while Alford crawled to look down the stairs. Then he straightened and held his candle high, watching the flame carefully.

"I do not see any signs of a draft," he told Florrie. "I think we will be safe with these open candles. Bring your lightbox just in case."

Florrie grabbed it and some spills and followed Alford into the passageway.

"The drop is steep and these steps are narrow, so be careful," he warned when she was at his side. "If you trip, I do not want you taking me down as well."

"Perhaps you should follow me," she said sarcastically.

They carefully followed the narrow, wooden steps, which circled downward for a fair distance. Alford judged they must be at the depth of the cellars, at least, when the steps stopped and the floor leveled out. The tunnel was not cut to a great height here, and it was all Alford could do to refrain from ducking his head as they slowly followed the passageway.

"Are we under the house?" Florrie whispered.

"I judge we are at the right depth," said Alford, "but I cannot see the use of a passage under the house. More likely we are moving away from it."

"Why is this here?"

"I don't know," Alford snapped. "Perhaps it is a remnant from the Tudor religious squabbles. Or Cromwell's time."

"Has this house really been here that long?"

"Florrie, I am not an expert on the history of Hartland. I never even knew it belonged to the family until my father mentioned it. But yes, I think it is old enough to have been here for Cromwell, at least."

"Perhaps it was used to hide Royalists," Florrie suggested eagerly. "Maybe even Charles himself!"

"If it had, this house would be in every guide book in the country," Alford replied dryly. "I suspect the purpose was more private."

"Like smuggling French prisoners out of the country?"

Alford turned to her in exasperation. "I do not for one minute believe that is what is going on here, Florrie. I hate to discount your theory, but it simply won't wash."

"Then what is *your* theory?"

"Time will tell," he said enigmatically.

Florrie scowled. He probably had no idea at all of what was occurring.

After a short distance, the passageway began to narrow. Florrie, trailing Alford, grabbed hold of his coat tail. It gave her a small mote of comfort. She wished she had not been so insistent on coming along. It was altogether too dark and dirty down here. There were probably spiders. Or worse. She glanced apprehensively over her shoulder. What had become of the peson in her room, who had certainly escaped down this way? What if they ran into him?

"Alford?" she asked weakly.

"What?"

"Are we going to follow this passage to its end?"

He stopped and turned toward her, his face shadowy in faint candlelight. "Regretting your impulsiveness, Florrie? Wishing you were back in your snug, warm bed?"

"Yes," she retorted. "I am."

He laughed. "This does go on much farther than I thought it would." He glanced at the candle in his hand. "And we will not have light for that much longer. It would not be a bad idea to turn back. I can wait until morning and explore it more properly. I own I would feel more comfortable carrying a lantern. A freak blast of air could throw us into total darkness."

"It could?" Florrie moved one hand protectively around the flame of her candle and stepped a pace closer to Alford.

"Yes, it is best that we turn around." He looked at her expectantly. "Lead on, Miss Washburn."

Florrie was not at all certain that she wished to lead, but it was comforting to know that Alford was directly behind her. Now no one would be able to creep up on her in the dark. She walked with an increasingly fast pace until they reached the bottom of the stairs.

Alford gestured to the steps. "Ladies first."

Florrie awkwardly gathered up her skirts in one hand and started up the narrow steps, holding her candle high before her. It had been so much easier going down!

Alford waited until she was nearly out of sight around the curve until he started after her. This managed to put him at eye level with her ankles, which were quite enticingly revealed beneath her raised skirts. Her hips swayed in a most alluring manner as she trod up the stairs. Alford sighed, knowing the futility of his thoughts.

As Florrie neared the top of the stairs, she grew puzzled. Had they not left the secret door open? No light from the room shone through the opening. Had the candle burned out? Or . . .

"Alford," she said in a quavery voice. "I think someone has shut the opening."

He stepped up behind her. "Are you sure?"

"No." She flattened herself against the wall to let him pass. "But I cannot see any light from my room."

Alford squeezed past her, dropping to a squat as he reached the low-ceilinged entry. The panel was definitely closed against them. Holding his candle closer, he peered at the inside wall, looking for some sign of a latch or lever that would open the section of panel. Seeing none, he set the candle down and began tapping along what he thought was the outline of the door. Nothing happened.

"Why don't you just pull on it?" Florrie suggested. "Perhaps a draft blew it shut."

"There are mighty powerful 'drafts' in this house," Alford muttered under his breath. "They can open and shut doors with regular frequency. And there is no handle of any sort on this side." He rose to a half-squat and examined the top of the panel.

"There must be some way to open it," Florrie said, fighting down her rising panic. "What is the point of having a secret passageway that you cannot get out of?"

"Would you like to try?" Alford asked curtly.

"Yes," she snapped. Alford moved aside for her.

Florrie examined the wall as carefully as he had, but she saw no sign of any opening device.

"Perhaps it takes a magic password," Alford quipped.

Florrie shot him a withering stare. "Open Sesame?"

Alford sat down on the top step. "I think we have two options," he said quietly. He saw the growing nervousness in Florrie's eyes, and wished suddenly that he had not tormented her so in past nights. She was already on edge and he did not want a hysterical woman on his hands just now. "We can stay here and wait for someone to come into the room, then call for help."

"Mrs. Burgess rarely comes to my room," Florrie pointed out. "And in any event, my door is locked. As is yours."

"Surely Mrs. Burgess has a key?"

"What is our other option?" Florrie asked, even though she knew what it would be.

"We go back down the passage and find out where it leads," he explained. "It is bound to exit somewhere, probably on the estate grounds."

"Will our candles last long enough for that?"

He shook his head. "I do not know, Florrie. All we can do is try. If we douse yours, that will give us all that more light."

Florrie shivered. Neither course was very appealing. "What do you suggest?"

Alford debated. If it was only he, alone, he would take the second course and discover where this passageway led. But with Florrie . . . Which course made rescue, or escape, more likely? He must make certain Florrie was safe.

There was the mysterious intruder to consider. Had he hidden in some unseen alcove while he and Florrie explored the passageway, then escaped through her room, shutting the exit behind him? Or was he still below, waiting for them in the darkness? Where would Florrie be safest?

"I think we should try to find the way out," he said at last. "There will be an end to this somewhere. We shall have to go along until we find it."

Florrie swallowed hard. Standing here, they were only inches away from the secure comfort of her bedroom. But what now appeared to be a solid wall lay between them and sanctuary. The ceiling over her head and the walls seemed to close in on her, shrinking as she cowered beneath them. Why, oh why, had she insisted on accompanying Alford? She clenched her fists until her nails dug into her palms, willing herself to calm.

"I will go along with whatever you suggest," she said, with a show of false bravado.

Alford smiled with an encouragement he did not completely feel. "Brave girl. Let us keep both candles while we negotiate these stairs. You go first this time."

Florrie nodded and headed back down the stairs again.

"Alford?"

"Yes, Florrie?"

"How many miles have we walked?"

"Five or six at least," he joked. "Are you growing tired?"

She nodded, then realized how foolish a gesture it was in the inky blackness that surrounded her. "I am."

Alford looked at the candle he held. It was their last one, and it would not last much longer. How far could this blasted tunnel continue? The floor had been tilted at a downward incline for some time now. His head began to throb from the effort of concentrating, and the lack of sleep. He was not certain what time Florrie had dashed into his room, but it must have been past midnight. What time was it now? Two? Three? It was easy to lose all track of time, and distance, in this dark hole.

"I would let you rest," he said gently, "but we need to keep going, Florrie. The candle . . ."

Peering around his shoulder, Florrie saw how little wax remained. She looked to Alford for some comfort.

"We will find a way out, won't we?" Her wide eyes implored him.

"Of course we will," he reassured her. "And the quicker we walk, the quicker it will be." He hated to drive either of them so hard, but he did not relish the idea of being in here in the pitch black darkness any more than he suspected Florrie would.

They proceeded onward, walking as fast as they dared over the increasingly rough floor. Alford stumbled more than once over some rock in his path, passing a warning on to Florrie.

The candle was beginning to sputter when Alford called a halt.

"I am afraid we are out of light, Florrie," he said. "Hang tightly onto my coat and I will lead on." He felt her take hold of him with what was close to a death grip.

He continued to walk as quickly as he could, ducking now and again to miss some dangling spider web or low spot in the ceiling. Then the flame flickered, and sputtered, and winked out. They were left in the darkness.

"Florrie?"

"Yes?"

"I am going to have to walk much slower now," he said, praying that she would remain calm. "Shuffle along behind me. I will tell you if there are any rocks underfoot so you will not stumble."

"Thank you," she said in a voice so quiet he could bearly hear.

It was a totally new experience, he discovered, to walk surrounded by total darkness. Discarding the useless candle holder, he kept one hand along the wall, and the other stretched out before him. That would work adequately enough as a warning unless he stumbled over something underfoot. And at the pace he was going, even stumbling would not be much of a danger.

"Alford?" Florrie asked after they had walked along in the darkness for a while. "Can we stop and rest?"

There was little reason not to, now. "That sounds like a good idea." He stopped and turned toward her in the dark. Taking her hand, he gently guided her to the ground. The tunnel, while dark and dusty, was not damp or intolerably cold. He sat beside her, their backs against the rock wall.

"Not exactly the adventure you expected, I wager."

Florrie made a wry face in the dark. "Not quite." She shivered.

"Cold?"

"A little," she confessed. "More nervous than anything. I do not like the dark."

"Pretend you are in your bedroom, with the drapes drawn and the candles out," he suggested. "Very little difference."

"Ah!" she shrieked.

"What?"

"Something brushed my cheek! It was a spider, I know it was." She buried her face in Alford's shoulder.

"Don't like spiders, do you?"

"I hate them," she said, her voice muffled. "As you should well know."

"Why should I—good Lord!" He had completely forgotten that long-ago incident from childhood. How monstrous he had been!

Memory flooded through him. He must have been—what—ten, eleven? It was the first time Florrie had spent any time at Swinton Hall and she had insisted on accompanying Kit and him *everywhere*. She had been, in fact, a regular pest. Determined to be rid of her presence, Alford had lured her into the wine cellar and locked the door, then spent the afternoon fishing with his brother. Florrie spent hours in her dark prison before Alford was forced to confess his crime.

His punishment had been severe, and well-deserved. He tightened his arms protectively around her.

"It was an abominable thing to have done," he said at last. He looked at the darkness surrounding them. "I suppose you can call this poetic justice. 'Tis only a pity you are here as well."

"It is not so bad this time," she said in a quiet voice. "I am not alone."

She was silent for a moment. "Alford?"

"Hmm?"

"We will get out of here, won't we?"

"Of course we will," he said with more conviction than he felt at the moment. "I will personally see to it."

"Promise?"

"Promise."

"Thank you," she said, snuggling closer against him.

He heard the trust in her voice and winced. Much good he would do her. He berated himself for not insisting that she remain in her room. Neither of them would be in this fix now if she had. Then a thought chilled him. Had that panel really shut on its own accord? Or had someone deliberately closed it behind them? If so, and Florrie had remained behind . . . Perhaps it was better she was with him. This way, he was in a position to protect her from any danger.

Not that he would be able to do much, with no weapon beyond his fists. He had no way of knowing what lay ahead and they could be walking into a highly dangerous situation. He had no fears for himself, but Florrie . . . He dared not allow anything to happen to her. She had been placed in his care, and he was obligated to keep her safe. For Kit.

For Kit. The very words cut deeply through Alford. He did not want to keep Florrie safe for his brother. With sudden realization, Alford acknowledged he wanted her for . . . for himself.

What a damnable coil! The situation would be laughable if it were not so complicated. It would make a glorious farce. Here he was, married by accident to his brother's betrothed. Alford was bound by honor to free her from the bonds, but now he was not so certain he wanted to. And Florrie . . .

Florrie probably still wished him to the devil, if all was told. He had brought her nothing but trouble, locking her in cellars when she was a child, ruining her wedding, then tormenting her nights with his staged hauntings. She had every reason in the world to look upon him with disfavor.

Sadly, he knew he could not offer her half of what Kit could. There was no glorious diplomatic career in Alford's future. Only a life of idleness and dissipation. Even if he managed to convince his father to allow him free rein at Swinton Hall, what would that mean to Florrie? Diplomatic hostesses did not practice their trade in Sussex. The very least she would settle for was London. And there was nothing for him there. She would grow as bored as he with a life of endless waiting.

As he listened to Florrie's slow, even breathing, he realized she had fallen asleep. Alford smiled. He liked the feeling of her asleep in his arms, huddled against him for protection and security. It was a pity he could not offer her either.

For a lady he was supposed to keep his hands off, Florrie was too damn attractive. It was not fair. It would try the patience of a saint to be in such close proximity to her and not be tempted—and he was by no means a saint. If she was anyone else . . .

But she was not.

With a sigh, Alford planted a gentle kiss atop her head. Now, in the darkness, he could at least pretend she was his. For a short while.

Chapter 20

Alford must have drifted off to sleep, for he awoke with a start. The total darkness disoriented him and it took a moment to remember where he was. Trapped in the tunnel. With Florrie.

He could not see her in the total darkness that surrounded them, but he did not need to. She was still snuggled up against him, her breathing slow and even. Alford realized with a pang how much trust the simple act of sleeping implied. She had total reliance on his ability to keep her safe.

Yet what was he doing now to achieve that aim? Sitting on his backside in a narrow tunnel? They had to continue onward if they were ever to find the way out. But he had not the heart to wake her. Her sleep had been interrupted once tonight. That was enough.

But he was awake and impatient to get them away from this dark cavern. They had to be close to the exit. The passage had already gone on much longer than he would have guessed; they were probably only a few twists and turns from the end. He could quickly investigate on his own, and with any luck be back before Florrie awoke. He could greet her with the good news. Alford found he liked the idea of appearing a hero in her eyes.

Carefully, so as not to disturb her, he sidled away. Cradling her head on his leg, he shrugged out of his coat. Alford folded it neatly and slipped it under her, pillowing her head. Then he rose to his feet and stretched his cramped muscles. Thank God his head felt better.

He would have to hurry. If Florrie awoke while he was gone, she would be frightened. He must not go too far; he had to be able to hear her if she called. With one hand at the wall at his side, Alford slowly moved down the tunnel.

He had only gone what he judged to be twenty or thirty paces when he saw a faint gleam up ahead. The end? He quickened his pace eagerly.

The tunnel branched, he discovered, as the wall beneath his hand abruptly vanished. Peering down that path, he saw a definite glimmer of hope—light. He hastened forward. The light grew stronger, increasing in brightness until Alford was certain it was an opening of some sort.

He reached it at last, the prickly brambles that had overgrown—or deliberately covered—the opening allowing in only filtered slivers of daylight. But there was no doubt he had found the exit. He turned to hasten back to Florrie, then halted. What lay outside the exit? Visions of the sheer cliffs that fell from the point danced through his brain. Would this be a cruel joke—an opening half way up the cliff side, an exit but not an escape?

Grimacing, Alford tore at the brambles with his bare hands, trying to create an opening big enough to allow a glimpse of what lay outside. His hands were scratched and bleeding when he was finished, but it had been worth the effort. The tunnel opened out onto a sloping, grass-covered hill. Nary a cliff in sight.

Alford sped as fast as he dared back through the tunnel. He would have Florrie out of here in a trice. A thrill of relief raced through him. He had lived up to her expectations; he had saved her.

In his excitement, Alford neglected to keep his hand before him, and he walked straight into the far wall of the tunnel when he reached the fork. "Oof!" he groaned.

Florrie opened her eyes to utter blackness and she was not certain whether she was really awake or not. But when she felt the hard stone floor beneath her, the memories of the past evening flooded over her.

"Alford?" she whispered. "Alford?"

But no reply came. Crawling on her hands and knees, Florrie blindly reached out, groping for his form. The first beginnings of panic rose within her. She was alone.

All those long-buried memories of that horrible day at

Swinton Hall came tumbling through her head and she was
reduced once again to a tearful five-year-old, whimpering
in the corner. Gulping in air, Florrie clenched her fists,
gritting her teeth with the effort. *I will not behave foolishly,*
she chided herself.

She carefully felt about the floor again, locating Alford's
coat at once. She hugged it tightly to her chest, seeking
security from it.

He must have gone on, looking for a way out. He would
not have left her here alone, on purpose. Not again. She
brushed away a trickling tear with the back of her hand.

Should she stay and wait? Or follow after him? The latter
would get her out of this nasty tunnel sooner. With determination Florrie rose to her feet and took a few halting steps.

Until she realized she had no idea which way to go. In
her mad scramblings, she had become all twisted about.
When they had stopped, the tunnel continued to her left, but
was it now her left, or her right? With a low moan of
frustration, Florrie sank down to the floor again. She had
been foolish, and stupid, and now could not do anything until
Alford came back for her.

If he ever did.

No, no, he would come back, he would. He had promised
to get her out of here, hadn't he? A gentleman's promise
was like an oath, it could not be broken. He would come
back.

Florrie jumped at the faint sound that reached her ears.
She listened carefully, but heard nothing else.

"Alford?" she asked doubtfully. She raised her voice.
"Alford?"

"I am coming," he called back, hearing the panic in her
voice. He raced up the tunnel toward her.

"Alford? Where are you?"

"I am here, I am here," he said, reaching out with both
arms. "Reach out your hand."

Florrie did as he said and he caught it in his. She latched
on with a grip of iron and he pulled her into his arms.

"Where were you?" she demanded. "I woke up and you
were gone and I was so frightened!"

"It is all right, I am here," he said, crushing her against his chest, stroking her back as he sought to calm her. "I found the way out."

"What?"

He released her from his arms, keeping hold of her hand. "We were laughably close," he explained as he led her along the passage to where the first faint glimmers of light could be seen. They quickly reached the exit and Florrie blinked in the unaccustomed brightness.

"Damn!" Alford exclaimed. "We left my coat. It would have been good protection against those thorns."

"Don't go back for it," Florrie said quickly. She did not wish to be left alone again, even in the light.

"I will go first," Alford offered. "I can make a bigger hole for you to follow."

Florrie winced as Alford, on his hands and knees, began tearing his way through the tangled vines. In one moment his sleeve would get caught, in another, the back of his shirt. The vicious brambles seemed to have a mind of their own, reaching out and grabbing him as if they wished to keep them imprisoned in this dark cavern forever.

"I've cleared a path," he called at last, from outside. "Keep low and you should be all right."

Hunching over, Florrie carefully kneeled in the opening Alford had forged. But the hem of her robe caught almost immediately, and as she turned to free herself her hair snagged on another branch.

"Damnation!" She jerked at her robe and ripped it free. Wrapping her skirts around her legs as closely as she could, Florrie inched forward. Her knee caught on the bunched fabric and she heard another loud tearing noise. Tears of frustration welled in her eyes. She pulled her skirts loose, one knee at a time, moving forward as far as she could, then repeated the procedure. Every other shift forward managed to tangle her hair in another branch.

She glanced up, seeing Alford peering in at her.

"It's these skirts," she gasped. "I swear, the next time I go crawling through bramble bushes I am wearing breeches!"

Alford grinned and moved back from the opening. Florrie finally managed to crawl the last foot and collapsed in a heap on the grass.

"Are you all right?" Alford asked, leaning over her.

Florrie looked up and thought she had never seen a more pleasant sight than his face silhouetted against the brilliant blue sky above. She nodded, tears of relief streaming down her face.

"Don't cry," Alford said soothingly, wiping away a trickling tear with a finger. He lowered himself to lay beside her, propped up on one elbow. "You are a very brave lady."

She daubed at her eyes with the sleeve of her gown. "No, I am not," she protested. "I was horribly frightened."

"But you did not show it," he said, staring at her lips in rapt fascination. They looked fuller, redder than he remembered. Lips that begged to be kissed.

Florrie managed a wan smile. "I had to put up a brave front for you, Alford."

"Thomas," he whispered as he inched closer until his mouth hovered above hers. "My name is Thomas." He saw her wide-eyed, startled, gaze, saw the curiosity in it as well. She knew what he was going to do next—and wondered about it. This time, they would both find out.

"A very brave lady," he repeated, then lowered his mouth onto hers.

Those lips were as soft and warm as he imagined, pliant, and to his delighted surprise, not at all resistant. Alford wrapped one hand in her honey-colored locks, cradling the back of her head as his lips explored hers with soft, gentle kisses.

He felt her fingers lightly caress his cheek and he groaned with delight at her touch. He pulled her to him, molding her body against his, allowing his kisses to grow more demanding. He felt the heat rising in him and groaned again, this time in frustration.

He could not, he dared not. Florrie was not his. With a sigh of dismay he wrenched his mouth from hers and rolled to one side.

Florrie struggled to catch her breath while she struggled against her . . . disappointment? Those kisses had shaken her beyond belief, as had her response to them. And there was no mistaking the keen regret she felt when Alford withdrew. It was over so quickly, she had not even had time to . . .

"Florrie?"

She kept her gaze directed at the sky overhead.

"Florrie, look at me."

Reluctantly, she turned her head. Alford was gazing at her, his pale blue eyes reflecting mingled guilt and—what? Desire? Longing? And sadness, as well.

"I should not have done that," he said quickly.

She laughed shakily. "Neither should I. But I daresay we have both done a lot of things we should not have."

"It was only . . ." His voice dropped. "I was only so pleased we were safe. At last."

Florrie shut her eyes, surprised at the tears that stung her lids. What had she expected him to say? That he had been consumed by overwhelming passion? More likely he had been motivated by curiosity. It had been part of her motivation. The other part she was not certain she wanted to think about right now.

She had never kissed Kit, so there was no way to compare the two brothers. But she had kissed and been kissed enough times to know that it had never been like this before. Exciting, exhilarating, and oh-so-tempting. She found that frightening. It made her feel so dangerously out of control.

"We had best return to the house," Alford said at last.

"You are right." Florrie sat up, ruefully examining her torn clothing. She tried to run a hand through her tangled hair, and finally dared a glance at Alford. "I must look a fright," she said, then quickly looked away as she saw the answer in his eyes.

Alford scrambled self-consciously to his feet, reaching down a hand to help Florrie up. The sooner they returned to normality, the better.

"Where exactly are we?" she asked as she looked about the hillside.

"I think we are northeast of the house," he replied. "The land flattens out at the top of this slope and the house should be there, just beyond those trees."

"Oh." There was nothing else to say. Alford kept her hand in his and they slowly trudged up the slope.

"What do you suppose the Burgesses will say to all of this?" Florrie asked as they reached the crest and the house came into view. "Do you think they were the ones who shut the panel?"

Alford shook his head. "I cannot be certain, but I do not think so. I think they know some of what is going on here, but are not actively involved themselves."

"What is going on?" Florrie asked.

"I want to explore that tunnel more thoroughly before I answer that," he said. "I think it will answer all our questions."

"You are going to go back down?" Florrie stopped and stared at him, aghast.

"Better prepared, this time," he said with a laugh. "I shall take a dozen candles."

They had reached the front lawn, and Florrie thought suddenly of the image they presented, if anyone was watching. She, in her torn and dirty robe and gown, Alford in his equally disheveled shirtsleeves. Hand-in-hand, like two grubby children. The very picture made her laugh.

"And what do you find so amusing?" he asked, relieved she could find something to laugh at.

"Our appearance," she said.

"Ah, well, it was a more enthusiastic morning stroll than we had anticipated," he said. "But quite in keeping with our country setting, don't you think?"

"Undoubtedly."

Mrs. Burgess greeted them with a look of surprise, but did not inquire into the cause of their uncommon appearance. Florrie acted as though it was an everyday occurrence for her to appear at the front door in her torn and dirty night clothing. Even Florrie's request for the key to her room raised not an eyebow from the dour housekeeper.

Alford followed Florrie into her chamber, firmly shutting

and locking the door behind him. "I want to examine the panel more closely," he said. "If there is no latch on the inside, the opening mechanism must be in this room."

The panel was so firmly shut that it took him a moment to find its exact location. He carefully examined the surrounding wood, tapping and pressing it with his fingers.

The latch was hidden simply in a strip of molding. When Alford pressed against the exact spot, the panel popped open.

"Laughably simple," he said as he examined the mechanism on the panel.

"But why would they have a panel that only opened from this room?" Florrie asked.

"It would be easy enough to make one's escape down the tunnel," Alford replied. "And this way you do not risk strange intruders coming into the house."

"But that means . . ." Florrie's voice trailed off.

"That whoever left the panel ajar *was* in your room last night," Alford finished for her. And if that person had not come through the passage, he had come through her locked door. And that was all his fault. If he had not oiled the lock so well, no one could have made such a silent entrance.

Alford hastily closed the panel. "Once the door is shut, we know no one can come through that way. If you shove the chair against your door, you would have plenty of warning if someone tried to enter from the corridor."

"Alford, what is going on?"

He avoided her troubled gaze. "I expect we will find some answers today," he said, wearily rubbing the back of his neck. "But if I don't get some sleep right now, I fear I will not be able to do anything later."

"Promise me you will not go anywhere on your own?"

Alford grinned. "Unless you think I can make it through your room and into the passage while you sleep, I think you have nothing to fear."

Florrie nodded and walked with Alford to the dressing room door.

"Thank you," she said. "For keeping your promise."

He looked at her with a puzzled expression.

"You found a way out."

"I had a personal interest in the outcome," he joked, uncomfortable with her gratitude. After that improper kiss, she had every right to be angry with him. That she was not, he reckoned a miracle. "Sleep well now."

"I shall."

Florrie insisted upon bathing before she attempted sleep. Refreshed from her bath, she sat in front of the fire, drying her hair in the reflected heat. Now, she had time to sit and think. But she was not at all certain she wished to.

What had happened this morning with Alford had been quite an accident, she was confident. And it most surely meant very little. It had been sheer relief that had prompted Alford's kiss. He had admitted that himself. There was nothing more to it than that.

Which was just as well. Alford was not a part of her plan. She would marry Kit, cultivate useful acquaintances on the Peninsula, and be prepared to go with him to wherever he was sent once he undertook his diplomatic career. That was what she had always planned for herself. It was what she wanted—wasn't it?

Once, the friendship she had shared with Kit would have been enough. Now, she was no longer certain. And that made it difficult to ignore her confusing reactions to Alford. If she had only kissed Kit, been held in his arms . . . then she would know how to deal with these conflicting emotions. She would be able to prove that it was just opportunity, not desire, that made Alford so captivating.

Because he was certainly not at all the kind of man she wished for herself. Granted, he was not the brainless gamester she had initially labeled him, but that did not make him any more respectable or responsible. He still had done nothing with himself. Surely, if he really wanted to, he could have overcome his father's oppositions and done *something*. Just because he had held her close when she was frightened, and kissed her when they were safe, did not mean he would be a suitable partner.

But a tiny voice inside her head told her she was lying to herself. Told her that she would experience more passion in a week with Alford than she would in a lifetime with the amiable Kit. But passion did not a marriage make, she argued back. She wanted dependability, security, and success. When had Alford ever demonstrated any of those qualities?

When had he ever been given a chance, that persistent voice asked. He'd been hemmed in by his father, society's conventions, and limited opportunities. No one expected him to do anything with himself. Why criticize him then, for behaving as he did?

Florrie stopped her brushing and stared into the flames. She did not like the way all her neat, orderly plans were coming apart. She should be in Spain with Kit right now, not in Devon with his brother.

Alford—Thomas—upset all her plans, set her senses whirling, and made her wonder exactly what it was she wanted from life. He was dangerous. Uncontrolled. Disconcerting.

A part of her wanted to leave Hartland today, now, before it was too late. Another part wished to stay, to play out these strange circumstances to the end, to discover what would happen. And it was that part she wished to listen to.

She yawned. Maybe it would all make more sense after she slept. But she doubted it. Nothing had made very good sense ever since Alford had mistakenly scrawled his signature on the wrong line of the proxy papers. And she was dreadfully afraid that it would take more than a simple annulment to chase him from her thoughts.

Chapter 21

Alford lay upon his bed, desperate for sleep, but unable to free his brain of its swirling thoughts. What he had done was unbelievable. Unconscionable. It was far, far worse than that simple kiss. He had fallen in love with his brother's wife-to-be.

It was a contemptible action. One that even he, with his rather misspent life, could not tolerate. He had already created enough grief for those two. Had it not been for his lamentable, drunken mistake, Florrie would be with Kit now, married and forever beyond his reach.

Alford knew it was foolish to even think that his feelings would matter to her. He had no illusions about how she viewed him. There was nothing in his past that would win the smallest crumb of approbation from her. He had wasted his time and his life quite effectively up to this point. Even if Kit was not involved, the outcome would be no different. Alford had nothing to offer Florrie.

He thought briefly that if given the opportunity, he might be able to win her respect and admiration. Lord knows, he would try. To gain Florrie's approval, he would tackle anything, take any risks to prove himself. He smiled sadly. How awkward to be finally fired with ambition, only to no purpose. A perverse twist of fate had placed the one woman he wanted totally out of his reach.

There was only one solution. He had to leave Hartland, as quickly as possible. Once he had explored that bothersome tunnel, and made certain Florrie would be safe from any intruders, he would pack his bags and leave. It was the best thing for both of them. He would not succumb to temptation if he removed himself from it. And if she ever suspected his depth of feeling . . . well, he did not wish to become a source of future amusement for Kit and Florrie. It would only create awkwardness at family gatherings.

If only he had not kissed her! That had been an act beyond foolishness. For it had been a shattering experience, for him at least. He only hoped his glib apology had sufficed to stifle her curiosity, praying she would quickly forget the incident.

Alford struggled with mixed guilt and longing as exhaustion crept up on him. Later, when he was rested . . .

He sat up suddenly with a groan of dismay. Nanette. He had forgotten about her completely. She could arrive at any moment! He could only imagine Florrie's reaction. Jumping from bed, Alford frantically searched for pen and paper. If he was lucky, she had not left London. And in the event she had, he would pen a note to Old Mort, telling him under no circumstances to bring any lady to Hartland. Nanette's arrival would only put a seal on Florrie's contempt for him. He had to spare her the humiliation of that situation. God, what a coil he had wound about himself.

Alford felt less than rested when he awoke in late afternoon. His sleep had been a twisted jumble of images: Nanette creating havoc, Florrie, pliant in his arms, kissing him with wild abandon, juxtaposed against the harsh and condemning face of his brother as he jerked her from Alford's clasp. He winced at the image.

Pacing his room, Alford thought he would drive himself mad with his regrets and longings. He needed something—anything—to take his mind off Florrie. Descending into the tunnel again would be exactly the thing. He ignored his promise to her. It was his responsibility to keep her safe—for Kit. And the sooner he could resolve the mystery, the sooner he could flee from temptation.

Alford walked boldly into the kitchen, unafraid of a confrontation with the Burgesses. Whatever their involvement, he suspected they were only passive players. He thought he had little to fear from them.

"I need a lantern," he said to Burgess. "Two, in fact, if you have them."

"What you be wanting a lantern for?" Burgess asked.

"Scientific experiment," Alford replied blandly. "Open flame is too dangerous—might set the house on fire."

Burgess eyed him dubiously. "Mightn't you be better doing such a thing outside the house?"

Alford shook his head. "Too much wind. Don't worry, it's safe enough if arranged properly." He looked at Burgess expectantly. "The lanterns?"

Shaking his head, Burgess went in search of the desired objects.

Armed with his lanterns, an ample supply of candles and lighters, and a stout kitchen knife he had purloined from beneath the unobservant eyes of Mrs. Burgess, Alford hesitated in the dressing room, outside Florrie's door. He pressed his ear to the wood, wondering if she was still asleep. No sound issued from the other room.

She would be angry with him when she discovered what he had done, but he did not care. She would be far safer in her room. And Florrie's safety was his major concern. Hopefully, after today he could guarantee it. Then he could leave her, knowing he had done all he could.

He cautiously tried the knob, which to his relief was unlocked. Now, if he could only slip through her room, open the panel, pass his supplies through and close it again without waking her. A not inconsiderable task . . .

Slowly he eased the door open. Peering cautiously around the door frame, he saw Florrie's sleeping form upon the bed. So far, so good. Carrying a lantern in each hand, he tip-toed as silently as he could manage across the floor. One or two boards squeaked ominously underfoot as he passed, but the figure on the bed did not stir.

The panel opened with laughable ease this time. Alford set both lanterns inside. He started to climb into the opening, then hesitated. It was foolish, but there was no way to be certain of what lay ahead of him. He wanted one last look at Florrie—just in case. Carefully retracing his steps, he stood beside the bed. Her soft hair lay gently tumbled on the pillow, her face formed in a peaceful expression. It hurt just to look at her, when he knew how ridiculous his longings were. He bent down, intending to plant a whisper of a kiss on her brow.

Instead, he found himself staring into her suddenly opened eyes.

"Alford?" she asked sleepily.

Damnation! He stepped back.

Florrie struggled to sit up, her gaze taking in the opening in the wall, instantly wide awake. "You were going down the tunnel without me!" she said accusingly.

Alford nodded.

"Well, I won't have it," she said.

"But if you remain here, you can let me back in," he countered. "I don't want to crawl through those brambles again."

"We could just as easily prop the door open with a chair," she said, grabbing her robe from the foot of the bed. She hastily pulled it on and clambered from the bed. "Now, if you don't mind, I should like to dress."

Alford's fingers clenched at the thought. He recalled the day he surprised Florrie in her chemise and a stab of physical longing pulsed through him. How he wished to assist her.

Noting Florrie's look of exasperation, a wide grin spread over his face. He could not resist the urge to tease her once again. And perhaps he could yet dissuade her from accompanying him. "Do not let me stop you," he said, arms folded across his chest as he leaned in a negligent pose against the bedpost.

That cheeky grin sent shivers of remembrance down Florrie's spine. That kiss—those kisses—this morning. What had they meant? Had they been just another part of his incessant teasing? Or had they meant more? She had almost begun to take Alford's brazen remarks in stride—until today. Now . . . how serious was he? Did he truly desire her?

Alford saw the confusion on her face and his grin faded. He did not want to increase her disquiet. He had caused her enough trouble already.

"Call me when you are ready," he said, and escaped to

the dressing room, pulling the door shut behind him with more violence than he planned.

Florrie sat down on the edge of the bed with a sigh. What was Alford doing to her? Her thoughts were all in a jumble. This was so unlike her! She was always in control of herself, her thoughts, her emotions. But with Alford . . . He created the most chaotic sensations.

Mechanically, she drew out her serviceable traveling dress from the wardrobe and fastened herself into it. She laced up her sturdy half-boots, and laid out her heavy cloak. If she had to scramble through the brambles again, she wanted some protection against their grasping branches.

Florrie jerked open the door to the dressing room, stepping back in surprise as she came face-to-face with Alford.

"You're ready?"

"Yes," she said, turning quickly before he could study her carefully. She schooled her features into a semblance of normality.

"If we move the chair," Alford pointed, "we can prop the panel open. That way, we can have at least two exits."

Alford dragged the piece of furniture across the room while Florrie retrieved the lanterns and lit the candles in each.

"Ready?" Alford asked.

She nodded.

It was not so bad this time, Florrie thought, as she followed him down those narrow, twisting steps. "Do you think these stairs were originally built into the house?" she asked Alford when they reached the bottom.

"Highly likely," he said, peering around the small chamber. He had not bothered to explore last night, but he wished to be more thorough this time. Under the curve of the stairs, he discovered the faint outline of another doorway, set into the wall.

"Where do you suppose it leads?" Florrie asked.

"Probably to the cellars," Alford replied. He wished he had thought to explore that part of the house earlier. It might have saved both of them endless trouble.

"Do you think these are the only set of hidden stairs in the house?"

He shrugged. "It is difficult to tell. The house could be riddled with them. Perhaps they all lead to the cellars, and then join up to the main tunnel here."

Florrie wondered at the type of person who would build such things into his house—or the times that would make such building a necessity.

The brighter light from the lantern only served to illuminate the spider-webs that hung at crazy angles from the sides of the tunnel. Florrie grimaced at the sight. It had been better in the dark, when she could not see them. She was glad Alford was in the lead.

Florrie's arm ached from the weight of the lantern when they arrived at the side passage that had been their escape. Alford peered ahead into the darkness, then turned to Florrie.

"I would feel better if you would remain here."

"Alone?" she squeaked. "No!"

"I am not certain what we shall find at the end of the main tunnel," he said quietly.

"You must suspect, if you are worried," she said. "Tell me."

Alford scowled, but knew she would not agree to remain unless he told her his guess. "I could not put my finger on it until the night you saw the lights."

Florrie's face brightened. "You mean someone *is* helping French prisoners escape?"

"Rather the oppsite, I suspect."

She stared at him in alarm. "French spies are coming to England?"

"More likely French contraband," he said with a wry smile. "Like the fine brandy in the library."

"Smugglers?" she asked incredulously.

He nodded. "It makes sense. It was full moon the night you saw the lights. An isolated area of the coast . . . a nearly abandoned house. I would not be surprised to find they have been using Hartland as their headquarters."

"Why did you not tell me you suspected smugglers?" she demanded. "I have been terrified."

Alford smirked. "Thought it really was ghosts, did you?"

"No!" she retorted. "But I certainly would have been

more comfortable knowing what specific threat we faced."

"My pardon," Alford said, sketching a bow. "Next time, I assure you, I shall share my suspicions with you."

"Do you think it was one of them who was using that room, and who knocked you on the head?"

"Probably. And that is why I wish you to stay here," Alford insisted. "If they are using this tunnel, they might not appreciate our explorations."

"I feel safer with you than I would alone," she said.

There it was. Her blind trust in him to keep her safe. And right now he wanted her admiration and approval more than anything in this world. Alford considered. It had been two nights since the cargo was unloaded; it may have already been dispersed around the neighborhood. It was unlikely any of the smugglers would still be around; they would not try to move any remaining goods until after dark. And he did feel better having Florrie in sight.

"All right," he agreed. "Follow me."

The tunnel bore straight for a short while, then turned abruptly and descended down steep stairs hewn in the rock. Alford was grateful they had not come this far in the dark earlier. He most likely would have gone hurtling down them.

The stairs continued for a considerable distance. Alford began to hope there was an exit here; he did not relish the thought of climbing back up again. But he should have expected it—they would end up at the bottom of the cliff. He could already smell the sea in the air, and thought he felt a slight breeze.

Indeed, in only a few more steps, the ceiling opened up over their heads and they looked into a goodly-sized cave. The floor was covered with sand and barrels and chunks of wood.

"You were right," Florrie breathed.

Motioning for her to remain on the steps, Alford dropped to the cave floor. He lifted the lid from one of the whole barrels, but it was empty. The last shipment must have been moved already. Crossing the sandy floor, he walked to the narrow cave entrance. It opened out onto a small strip of sand between two towering rock formations.

They must row the cache in from the boats, he mused, store it in the cave, then row it back out to transport it along the coast. He could not imagine any number of men lugging the heavy casks of brandy up those stairs. It was a clever setup. The cave was nearly inaccessible from the sea. And no one would ever find the tunnel entry within the house. In an emergency, the smugglers could move the cache out through the house or the tunnel.

The house was the key, of course. The smugglers used it as their headquarters to signal the incoming boat that it was safe—the lights Florrie had seen the other night. Alford was now certain it had been one of the smugglers who knocked him over the head. Surely, the Burgesses were involved in some manner. He breathed a sigh of relief. At least the mystery was now solved, and once the smugglers were convinced he and Florrie posed no danger ot their little enterprise, they would likely be left in peace.

"What do you find?" Florrie asked impatiently from her vantage point on the stairs.

"Nothing, I am afraid," Alford replied. "They probably moved all the cargo out the last few nights."

"Do you think . . . was it one of them who entered my room last night?"

"I suspect so."

Florrie shivered. "How can I ever sleep again? What if they try to murder us in our beds?"

"I do not think they will bother," Alford said. "I think a word or two dropped to the Burgesses will end any danger."

"You think the Burgesses are involved?"

"Think about it, Florrie. A house with a secret passage-way leading to the beach, a house that has been unoccupied for years? It is the ideal location for a group of smugglers." He grinned. "The Burgesses must have been aghast when we showed up."

"Will talking to them keep us safe?" Florrie asked doubtfully.

"Smugglers, on the whole, are not a bad lot," Alford said.

"Oh?" Florrie eyed him reproachfully. "You are intimately acquainted with them, I suppose?"

Alford laughed. "Not quite. But if they know they have nothing to fear from us, I doubt they will pay us any more heed. I'll request a sizeable order of brandy from the next shipment. That should lay their fears at rest."

"But if all that was caused by the smugglers . . . what about the Lady?" Florrie asked.

Alford cringed. If Florrie ever found out about his attempts to frighten her away . . . "That was probably them as well," he said hastily. "Not nearly so romantic as a ghost, but more believable."

Florrie felt oddly disappointed to have such a prosaic explanation for matters. Not that smugglers were exactly ordinary, but they were not as exciting as a ghost. Despite her denials, she had been half-disposed to believe they existed.

"It is a long climb back," she said, casting a rueful glance up the stairs.

"And an even longer swim," Alford pointed out. "I think there is little choice. Upwards it is."

Florrie gathered up her skirts and trailed Alford up the stairs. She said little during the return to the house. Not because she wished to conserve her breath, but because she needed time to absorb all the new discoveries she had made today. Finding the smugglers cave was the least of them.

She tried to objectively assess her deepening feelings for Alford, but had little success. There was no logical reason for them. He was not at all the kind of man she wished for a husband. He had no standing in diplomatic circles or the political arena. He was intelligent but lazy, bored but indifferent to any cure. Florrie still believed that had he really wished to, he could have found something useful to do with himself.

Yet, how would she have reacted to a similar situation? Her father had encouraged and nurtured her interests, not stifled them. Would she have fought against him if he had? Alford had not totally accepted defeat—he had his new plan for agricultural improvements. All he really needed was a chance to prove to his father—and to himself—that he *could* do something.

Florrie brightened at the thought. Surely, with her father's contacts, she could find someone willing to lend Alford assistance. If Barstow vetoed the agricultural improvements at Swinton, there were many more landowners who would welcome them. There were men in the Foreign Office who owed their position only to connections, and not skill. They needed bright, decisive assistants. There even might be the possibility of a seat in the Commons, Florrie mused. How much could one election cost? She had a good deal of money of her own. Enough to finance a campaign for Alford?

She would have to sound him out very carefully, to ascertain which prospect held the most appeal. But she thought with some judicious prodding, he might be persuaded to take something on. And any of those prospects would make a good start. In short time, Alford could be well-established. It was a promising solution.

Except, of course, she had no idea of Alford's feelings for her. She placed far too much importance on that kiss. Had he himself not apologized for his actions? She always suspected Alford saw her in a slightly contemptuous light, and a few innocent embraces did not mean he thought differently.

Even worse, there was the matter of Kit. Florrie was betrothed to him. They both knew it was not a grand passion, but that did not obviate her obligation to take his feelings into consideration. She knew that Kit would not hold her to her promise. He was too much her friend. But could she toss Kit over on the mere hope that Alford's feelings for her had warmed?

Chapter 22

After helping Florrie from the tunnel, and settling her in the library, Alford went in search of Burgess. If they could not reach some accommodation with the smugglers, Alford was determined to get Florrie out of the house today, if he had to carry her all the way to Clovelly himself.

"So, Burgess," Alford began, when he had run the man to ground in the pantry, "do you get paid for your role in this smuggling operation, or do you take your cut in goods?"

The man cast a hesitant look at Alford. "I beg your pardon, sir?"

"The smuggling ring that operates out of the cave below the cliff—are you the ringleader, or only the watchman?" Alford saw the fear in the man's eyes, and laughed. "Good Lord, Burgess, I do not want to turn you over to the magistrate. I only wanted to order some brandy. If it's the same thing you've been serving in the library, I'll take a cask or two."

Burgess visibly relaxed. "I think that could be arranged, sir."

"I trust there will be no more incidents like the other day?" Alford touched the healing wound on his head. "I do not give a damn what sort of illicit activities are going on in the neighborhood. But I do take exception to physical attacks."

"T'were an accident," Burgess said. "No one meant you any harm."

"Good, good," said Alford, turning to go. He paused, and looked back. "And Burgess, I think that it might be a nice gesture if some lace or silks were presented to Miss Washburn. She has had an unpleasant time of it, what with people wandering through her room and being shut up half the night in a dark and dusty tunnel. It would make amends."

Burgess nodded.

Alford felt a thrill of satisfaction. There was nothing to fear from that quarter anymore. They could smuggle in the entire brandy production of France, for all he cared. Just so Florrie was safe.

His steps slowed as he neared the library. He had done what he set out to accomplish, which was to assure her safety. That had been easy. But now there was no longer any reason for him to stay. Remaining in her presence would only serve to remind him of what he could not have. Yet a perverse desire to torture himself further led him to the door.

Florrie looked up with apprehension as Alford entered the room. "You were gone for so long, I began to be frightened," she said quickly. "Did you talk with the Burgesses?"

"Everything is taken care of," he said. "I think we have nothing more to fear from the smugglers."

"The Burgesses were working with them?"

Alford nodded. "But I convinced Burgess my only interest in his activities was in ensuring myself a steady supply of brandy. He assured me we can expect no more trouble."

Florrie smiled with relief. At least she could feel safe in her bed once more.

Alford prowled the room nervously, hesitating before the brandy decanter, then continuing his circuit. He had to leave, he knew that. But he would like to leave knowing Florrie thought more highly of him than she had when this all started. How, precisely, could he convince her that he now wanted to make something of his life? He finally sank down in one of the chairs flanking the fireplace and stared glumly into the flames.

"How does your head feel?" Florrie asked. An inane question, but one could not exactly ask what he had meant by that kiss this morning. Even though it was the thing she most wished to know.

"It feels fine," Alford replied.

"Did you—?"

"Are you—?"

Alford laughed. "Ladies first."

Florrie took a deep breath. "I was curious about the book you are reading. The one about agriculture."

"Oh." Alford smiled sheepishly. "Agriculture is one thing my father is not interested in. I thought I might convince him to allow me to make a few changes at Swinton."

"Is Swinton the only property with a farm?" Florrie asked.

Alford nodded. "There are a few other houses, here and there, but none have enough land to make a farm worth bothering with."

Despite her literary proclivities, Florrie had difficulty conjuring up the picture of Alford as a contented country landowner. "You would prefer the country to London?"

Alford paused. "They both have their attractions," he said evasively.

He had talked about his interest in politics, but Florrie was now uncertain how serious he was. Would he rather grow corn or formulate policy? "I imagine it is easier to keep track of politics in the city," Florrie said, hoping to draw him out.

"That's true," Alford agreed. "But what of you? I imagine this sojourn in Devon has given you your fill of country life."

"I would hardly call this isolated outpost an example of country life," she said with an ironic smile. "One usually is not beset with ghosts and smugglers in the country."

"Well, take Swinton then. Would a fortnight there bore you to tears?"

"I always enjoyed my visits there," she said carefully. Did he intend to tender her an invitation? The prospect of visiting Swinton in Alford's company was appealing. Particularly if they could be alone again.

"I don't think I have spent a full month at Swinton since I was fifteen," he said, half to himself.

"You will probably need to if you plan to make improvements," she pointed out.

"I know," he said, flashing her a rueful smile. He abruptly changed topics. "How do you think your father will get along without you in Sweden?"

"Tolerably, I hope," she said. "I own I have some reservations about how well he will manage by himself."

"It must have been an interesting life for you, moving from

one capital to another," he mused. "Did you ever miss not having a permanent house?"

Florrie smiled sadly. "Swinton was probably the closest thing to a home I ever had." She glanced at him shyly. "Did you hate it there so very much when you were younger? Is that why you were always away?"

"My father and I—" Alford broke off. There was little point in going over that again. Florrie would not care about his struggles to live up to impossible expectations. "Our interests diverged."

Florrie felt an onrush of compassion. It was difficult for her to imagine anything but a close relationship with her father. She pitied Alford for not having a more understanding sire. She could only guess at the pressures Barstow had applied to his eldest son. Alford had rebelled in the only way he could.

"I know my father was disappointed not to have had a son," Florrie said quickly. "I struggled against that for the longest time. I tried to do as much for him as I could."

"I am certain he is very proud of you," Alford said softly, envying her that close relationship. If he ever had sons . . ." He smiled sadly. "Tell me, how did your parents come to name you Florence? Is it a family name?"

Florrie laughed. "I was born there—quite by accident, I understand. I was to have been named after my grandmother. But Mama insisted on a permanent reminder of the event."

"And you, of course, are thankful they were not in Rome or Naples when the happy event occurred." Alford grinned.

"Or St. Petersburg." Florrie giggled.

An awkward silence descended. Florrie struggled for a topic that would lead him to some revelation. She desperately wished to know exactly how Alford viewed her. "Do you plan to go to Swinton when you leave here?"

"Perhaps," he said, dismayed by the question, for it only reminded him of what he ought to do: leave. Immediately. Each minute he lingered only made the pain of his eventual loss worse. He smothered a bitter laugh. One could not lose what one never had. He envied Kit with all his soul.

"I always liked Swinton in the spring," Florrie said,

recalling past visits there. "The gardens are at their best then."

"My mother always said that," he blurted out, shocking himself with his candor.

"I do not remember her very well, I am afraid," Florrie admitted, wondering if Alford and his father would have dealt together better if Lady Barstow had lived longer. Perhaps she could have softened her husband's criticisms, or stiffened her son's resolve.

"Neither do I," he said softly.

Florrie glanced at him, surprised by the mingled sadness and regret in his eyes. A tremor ran down her spine and she hastily looked away.

Alford stared at the floor. He did not wish to dwell on those who were dead—his mother and hers. Yet the future looked equally bleak, knowing he could not have Florrie. He lapsed into silence.

"The Derby and the Oaks will take place soon," Florrie observed. Would the lure of the gambling draw Alford away? "I imagine you will not wish to miss them."

Her remark startled him. Lord, he had not even thought about either race since his arrival at Hartland. And he usually had considerable sums of money riding on both. All his thoughts had been concentrated on ridding himself of her presence—or contriving a way to keep her at his side forever.

"Have you ever attended?" he asked.

Florrie shook her head. "Would I enjoy it?"

"Very much so, I think," he said, with a smile. "It is a quite suitable race meeting for ladies."

"Perhaps I shall go, one day."

Alford had an overwhelming urge to catch her up in his arms, shower her face with kisses, and blurt out his declaration of love and desire until she agreed to remain with him forever. "Shall we try a hand or two of piquet before dinner?" he asked instead. "Perhaps you can win back some of your money."

Raw panic attacked Alford following dinner. What were

they to do in the hours until bed? Another halting conversation like the one earlier would be too much for him. He racked his brain for some reason to keep her contentedly in the library. After last night's ordeal she would desire to retire early. He must contrive a plan.

He sat in his chair, nursing the glass of brandy in his hand, watching her while she repaired the rents in her night robe with neat, even stitches. It was a surprise to see her occupied with something other than her Spanish grammar.

"No stomach for verbs tonight?" he asked lightly.

Florrie glanced up in surprise. Somehow, in light of her changing attitude toward Kit, learning Spanish no longer seemed important. "I am not certain it is such a useful task," she said.

"Would you like me to read?" he asked.

Florrie looked at him with an amused smile. "More of *Otranto*?"

He laughed. "I would have thought you have had your fill of mysterious happenings."

"I have no objections to them, as long as they are happening to someone else," she replied. "I would very much like to have you read, Alford."

"You only wish to see me wearing my spectacles," he retorted, pleased he had found some way of keeping her attention.

"Quite right," she replied. "I am certain you will look like a university don with them."

Alford guffawed. "Watch your tongue, young lady, or I will enthrall you with the latest crop rotation techniques instead."

"A fascinating subject," Florrie murmured, delighted that they had been able to recapture their light-hearted teasing. "I am breathless with anticipation."

Alford wished she was breathless with some other emotion, but quickly retrieved his spectacles and the book, and launched into the further travails of the inhabitants of Otranto.

Florrie relaxed against the back of the chair, closing her eyes, listening with real pleasure to Alford's voice. He read well. She would like to spend many more such evenings in front of the fire, listening to him read. But she found it increasingly difficult to concentrate on his words.

What a topsy-turvy day! She had gone from the terror of the tunnel into Alford's arms, from vague misgivings about her future to a growing conviction that the orderly life she had planned with Kit was no longer meant for her. But how could she know if her future lay with Alford?

She examined him carefully from beneath lowered lids. He looked so very different in his spectacles. More mature. Responsible. He *had* undergone a masterful turnaround in these last days—from indolence to commanding authority. He had led their foolish first expedition into the tunnel with aristocratic aplomb, soothing her fears and finding an escape. That valiant second foray into the smuggler's den demonstrated his bravery and determination. But would the Alford who had emerged in a crisis remain when life returned to normal, or would he settle back into his old patterns?

She wished she were a gypsy fortune-teller, so that she could predict the future. Would she be happy with Alford? Kit would be the safer choice, the logical choice. And Florrie had always prided herself on her logic. She had carefully planned the course her life would take, and now one perplexing, infuriating man was turning all her plans upside down.

With a sudden pang, Florrie realized that whatever happened, she could not go through with the marriage to Kit. It would be too much a matter of second best. She had not wanted this to happen, but it had. For now that she knew Alford—yes, loved him—she would always measure Kit against him. And Kit would always suffer in comparison. It would be grossly unfair. Better he found a lady who thought the world of him than one who longed for another.

She knew Alford would never be as manageable as Kit. He would always do precisely as he pleased. It would be her task to channel his inclinations into productive paths, but she knew she could never push him into something he did not wish to do. And if he reverted to his old ways . . . there was little need for her. It might be better if she walked away now, while it was still possible.

But the very thought of walking away from Hartland, and Alford, tore at her heart. She feared it was already far too late for that. She loved him. Best to remain, and wait, and hope that her confidence in Alford was not misplaced. And pray that she could somehow capture his interest.

She had felt so secure in Alford's arms. In that nasty, dark tunnel, he had held her, comforted her, taken care of her. And she realized with a sudden shock that she *wanted* a man who made her feel that way, wanted a man she could turn to for solace and strength. A man she *needed*. She had never considered such a thing before, but now she knew how important it was. Her father, and their travels, had taught her to be self-reliant, but there were times when it was a joy to lay the burdens on the shoulders of another. Especially when they were such broad, attractive shoulders.

Florrie's cheeks flamed, and she ducked her head, praying Alford would not notice. She could not deny that physical attraction played a large part in her longings for Alford. When he had kissed her, she wished he would never stop. Tonight, sitting across from him in the library, was an exquisite torture. Every glance at his lips brought memories of their touch flooding back, along with the feel of his body pressed against hers as they clung together on the grass. She wanted him, ached for him. . . .

Perhaps it was her innocence that caused her feelings to rage in such an out of control manner. Alford had ample dealings with lust and desire—his reputation did not derive from his monkish habits. When he thought of her, was it different from the way he thought of any woman? He had accosted her that day so long ago in London without any knowledge of her identity; was one woman as good as another for him? She had seen much in her travels, but her experience with men, and the passions they engendered, was highly limited. Was she confusing love with desire?

She suddenly wished her father was here now, instead of on his way to Sweden. She could talk with him with a frankness few daughters could; he would help her make sense of all this. But he was not here, and she would have to make some sense of this on her own.

Florrie's thoughts tumbled through her brain. Alford and love. Alford and marriage. Alford and . . . Her body gradually slumped against the side of the chair as sleep overcame her.

Alford smiled fondly at the picture of her asleep in the chair. He welcomed the opportunity to study her without the need to disguise his longing. Those oh-so-kissable lips were turning upward in a faint smile. How he wished it was with thoughts of him. Poor Florrie. It had been an exhausting day. For both of them.

With a yawn, he closed the book, stretching out his booted feet toward the fire. He sat for a long time watching Florrie, noting the slow rise and fall of her chest beneath the soft fabric of her gown. It was a bittersweet moment, duty and honor warring with his personal desires. If only he could talk to Kit. Perhaps his brother was not so firmly committed to Florrie. But Alford knew that was only wishful thinking on his part.

With a sad smile, Alford rose unsteadily to his feet. Florrie would be far more comfortable in her bed. Sighing, he knelt beside her, gently shaking her shoulder. Like the gentleman he was, he would escort her to her room, bid her a fond goodnight, and retire reluctantly to his lonely chamber.

Hours later, a sudden noise intruded into Florrie's subconscious. She blinked sleepily into her pillow. It had been such a marvelous dream; what had awakened her? The darkness told her it was still night. She lay quietly, trying to recapture the threads of her dream that lay tantalizingly out of reach. Only a few more moments . . .

An icy chill swept the room and Florrie pulled the blankets closer. The fire must be out. She smelled the unmistakable odor of sea air. Odd—she thought she had closed the window. Florrie groggily rolled over, peering into the darkness.

And froze. There, silhouetted against the open window, was a Lady. Her white garments billowed about her, blown by the chill breeze flooding the room, her face obscured by the long, flowing shawl wrapped about her head. Florrie stared in wide-eyed horror as the Lady took a step toward the bed and stretched out her hand toward her.

"Alford!" Florrie screamed. "Alllllllfoooord!"

Chapter 23

Startled from his sleep by Florrie's cries, Alford burst through the door, prepared to do battle with whatever demon threatened her. He barely had time to scan the room for an intruder before Florrie hurtled herself at him, clinging to his neck as if she would never let go. He rather liked the feeling of it.

"She was here," Florrie wailed in a terror-stricken voice. "I saw her clearly. Oh, Alford, I was so frightened."

"There, there," he said soothingly, patting her back and trying to ignore the feel of her thinly-clad body pressed tightly against his. "Who was here? What did you see?"

Florrie took a deep breath to quell her quaking. "The window was open," she began haltingly. "And standing in front of it was . . . was the Lady. She was all dressed in white—just as when I saw her on the lawn. Then she began walking toward the bed." Florrie buried her face in Alford's shoulder again.

A bad dream, no doubt. Alford felt a twinge of guilt. He should not have been reading *Otranto* after all else that had happened. It was enough to give anyone nightmares. And it was all his fault, for having scared her so in the preceding days. Once again, guilt assailed him.

"Florrie, Florrie," he whispered, holding her trembling body close. "It is all right, I promise you. Whatever was here is gone now."

Alford held her tightly, gently stroking along the length of her back. Gradually, he felt her trembling ease, and the tension fled her body. She was soon still, and soft, and warm. He looked down and pressed a gentle kiss atop her head.

Florrie lifted her head from his chest and looked at him. "Thomas, I—"

"Hush," he whispered, placing a finger to her lips.

She looked at him with such trust and confidence that he nearly flinched from her gaze. *Don't look at me like that,* he pleaded silently, but by the time he thought, it was already too late. He took his finger from her lips and cupped her cheek in his hand. He gently tilted her face, and lowered his, until their lips met.

It started slowly, that kiss, building from a soft brushing of skin on skin to something more powerful, more painful in its pleasure. His lips grew demanding, hungry, as the passion he had held in check for so long bubbled to the top, seeking an outlet. Slowly, carefully, he eased both of them down onto the bed.

Florrie felt wrapped in some strange otherworld, her senses honed to a super-sensitivity that had every nerve in her body screaming with tension. Dimly, she sensed Thomas pushing her gown from her shoulders, felt his lips trail along her neck and shoulder.

"Thomas," she breathed, wrapping her hands in his thick hair, reeling with shock and excitement at the sensations he aroused in her. She wanted him, yearned for him, ached for—

A chill blast of air swept over her as he abruptly pulled away.

"Thomas?"

Alford took a deep, shuddering breath. "Florrie, I am so sorry," he said, averting his eyes from the tempting sight of her. "I swear, not a word of this will ever pass my lips. He will never know."

"Who will never know?" Florrie sat up and looked at him in puzzlement.

"Kit."

"Oh." Kit. Of course the thought of him would give Alford pause. Honor demanded it. Damn honor! Florrie took a deep breath. "I think that . . . that Kit and I will not suit after all." The dawning hope she saw rising in Alford's face caused her own hopes to soar. Was it possible that he did care for her?

Alford could hardly draw breath, so stunned was he by

her words. If Florrie was no longer tied to Kit, there was
nothing to bar his pursuit of her.

Except his own failings. His lamentable past hovered over
his head like a dark, threatening cloud. He had so little to
offer her, compared to Kit. He was a fool to think otherwise.

"What do you mean, you won't suit?" he asked, a rough
edge to his voice. "Kit is everything you want. Talented,
ambitious. He'll probably end up as Foreign Minister one
day."

"I do not think that is as important to me as it once was,"
she said quietly.

"Oh? And what is?"

Florrie looked down at her hands, although she knew
Alford could not see her eyes clearly in the shadowed room.
"I do want a man with talent, and ambition, who has a sense
of purpose. But I also want someone who wants to protect
me, care for me."

"Kit would do that," he said.

She shook her head. "No, he wouldn't. Not in the way
I would wish. Kit and I . . . well, he looks upon me in far
too brotherly a fashion."

"And how would you like a man to look upon you?"

Florrie lifted her head and dared a glance at him. "Like
a lover would."

"Oh, Florrie," he whispered, his hand reaching out to
stroke her cheek.

Florrie watched the swift play of emotions that crossed
his face. Did that darkening expression mean he was not
pleased, realizing the implications of their very compromising position? She pulled her gown closer, desperately needing
some reassurance from him. Was she merely a convenient
female?

Alford was beset with impatience. He knew it would take
weeks, if not months, to win her approval, her admiration.
Yet she sat there in such an enticing display, her eyes
beseeching him for he knew not what. And he could not wait
another minute. He had to know. Now.

He shifted to draw his face closer to hers, so he could see

clearly the look in her eyes, know her first reaction to what he asked.

"Florrie, I . . . I do not wish our marriage to be annulled," he said hoarsely. "I want you to remain . . . my wife."

"Your wife?"

"I love you, Florrie," he said simply. There, it was out. He could only wait, and hope.

"You do?" she squeaked.

He nodded, searching her eyes for some indication of what she felt. "I promise I shall do my best to earn your admiration, to be a man you can be proud of," he said hastily. "I will defy my father and take up politics, or run the farm at Swinton; whatever you wish me to do. Anything. Everything."

Florrie continued to stare at him in bemusement. What had he said? He loved her? A slow smile of realization spread over her face. She reached out and drew him to her again. "I would be honored to be your wife, Thomas," she said with a wide smile.

"You would?" he asked, delight dawning on his face. He did not even allow her a reply but took her up in his arms again, kissing her in such a way as to make certain she was firmly convinced of his intent.

"I shall take you back to London," he promised, when he could speak again. "We shall have a proper wedding this time." And time to change her mind, if she so wished.

"We are already married," she whispered, running a finger along his jaw line, stopping at the faint cleft in his chin.

He wanted her so badly his body ached from the effort to control his desire. But what had begun quite by accident must be finished with cold deliberation.

"Are you certain?" he asked, searching her face. "You can think on it, Florrie. If we . . . if I . . . we will not be able to go back. You must be certain."

"Make me your wife, Thomas," she pleaded as she pulled his head to hers for a kiss. "Tonight. Now."

"Oh, God," he groaned. He captured her lips again in a searing kiss, while his hands sought to free her from the

confinement of her gown. He trailed kisses across her face
and neck, dipping his head lower until he captured the tip
of one breast in his mouth, tasting her heated skin, reveling
in her smooth flesh.

He felt Florrie's fingers teasing under the neck of his shirt,
skimming across his shoulders, feeling soft and smooth
against his skin. He groaned in need and want. Slowly his
hand slipped down her side, feeling her ribs, the curve of
her hip, the silky skin of her thigh.

The first rush of panic welled within him. He wanted
Florrie so badly he was ready to explode, yet in the very
act of making her his forever, he would cause her pain. The
thought nearly unmanned him. He ran a tentative hand over
the soft curve of her belly, stroking lightly while he lifted
his head to capture her mouth again. While his tongue danced
along her lips, he inched his hand lower and lower, toward
the apex of her passions.

Florrie gasped at his shocking touch, overwhelmed by the
strange and surging sensations coursing through her. She felt
hot and flushed, with something building inside her.

"Thomas, Thomas," she murmured, half in wanting, half
in apprehension.

"It is all right, love," he whispered, coaxing her legs
apart, seeking her warmth with his fingers. He groaned at
the wetness of her, knowing he must be patient, must prolong
his pleasure to bring her hers. If he did not die first. His
fingers stroked her in a rhythmical motion that sent his lower
body into flames.

Florrie arched her body against his caressing hand, her
mind devoid of any thought beyond the mad pleasure he
brought her. His mouth and tongue burned a path of liquid
fire over her breasts while that wicked hand teased and
stroked her into ever higher spirals of pleasure. A white-hot
heat flooded her body as she arched and twisted with shuddering tremors. "Thomas," she gasped.

Alford could hold back no longer. Slipping a hand under
her hip, he drew her to him as he slowly eased his way into
her softness.

"Ah, Florrie," he groaned as her heat enveloped him. He

kissed her nose, her cheeks, her lips as he fought against his desire. "I swear it will hurt only this one time," he whispered, as he cautiously began his gentle thrusts. He felt himself press against her barrier, then steeled himself for what he must do. With one hard jab he made her his, his lips covering Florrie's as her gasp broke out. He did not dare move for fear of hurting her more.

"Thomas," she whispered.

"I am sorry," he groaned.

"It is quite fine," she said, with a comforting smile. She tenderly kissed his cheek.

"Oh love, I do not deserve you," he whispered, then his body took over, his motions quickening while he held her to him. He could not tear his eyes away from her face, afraid to close them for fear she would somehow disappear from his vision. Then he felt that convulsive tightening in his loins, the flash of heat through his body, and his release.

Alford lay wrapped in her arms for several minutes, still stunned at the enormity of the love and protectiveness he felt for her, and the exquisite pleasure she had brought him. Florrie. His wife.

"Thomas?" His long silence disturbed her.

He reluctantly raised himself, resting on his forearms, while smiling down at her. "Yes, love?"

His words brought a smile to her lips. "I love you," she whispered.

Alford leaned down for a long, languorous kiss with his lady wife.

Mrs. Burgess gave no sign of surprise at finding Alford in Florrie's chamber when she brought the tray of tea and chocolate in the morning. Alford retrieved his robe and insisted upon serving Florrie himself. It was a difficult task, for he could barely keep his eyes off her as she sat propped against the pillows, her honey-gold hair splayed across her shoulders. She looked so deliciously wanton. And she was his.

He handed her the cup and turned back for his own, glancing at the window as he did so. "Look, Florrie, here is the cause of all the problem last night," Alford announced in a triumphant voice as he handed her a white, filmy shawl. "This was caught in the window latch; the breeze must have made it look like a figure."

Florrie ran her fingers over the soft, white folds. "It is lovely," she whispered, then looked up at Alford with widening eyes. "But it is not mine."

He stared at her in consternation. "Then who . . . ?"

A faint, musical laugh emanating from the empty air floated across the chamber.

Chapter 24

"My lord?" Burgess stood at the library door. "Visitors have arrived."

Alford looked up from his book, reaching automatically to remove his spectacles. "Visitors?"

"A Mr. Cole, and party."

"Seb!" Alford jumped to his feet. "See them in, Burgess. And bring some brandy and glasses."

He turned to Florrie. "You remember Seb Cole, don't you, love? He was at the wedding."

Florrie wrinkled her nose as she tried to put a face to the man. "Tall and blond?"

Alford shook his head. " 'Fraid not. I wonder who is with him?"

"Alford, Alford," Seb greeted heartily from the door. "Your salvation has arrived at last. And we brought you an added present in the bargain." He waved his arm with a flourish.

Lewiston Hervey walked into the room, a lady on his arm. He handed Alford a packet of papers. "The annulment papers. All they need is your signatures and—" he nodded to Florrie—"the lady and you are free." He patted the woman's hand. "And a special present to celebrate your freedom."

Alford hoped his face did not look as sick as he felt. He glanced quickly at Florrie, then looked at the lady simpering on Hervey's arm. Nanette. Oh God.

From Alford's reaction, Florrie had a very good idea just who this unknown woman was. His London trollop.

"I—uh—I," Alford babbled. "What are you doing here?"

"I was concerned about you, Thomas," Nanette said with an artful pout. "When I received that mysterious letter . . ."

217

"So we asked her to come with us on the trip," Hervey interjected. He smiled at the lady at his side. "Right nice traveling companion, too."

Alford thought he blanched an even paler shade, if there was such a one.

Seb laughed. "Buck up, old boy," he said, clapping Alford on the back. He turned to Florrie, bowing low. "You probably do not remember me, Miss Washburn. Sebastian Cole." He jerked a thumb at his companion. "Lewiston Hervey. And Miss Nanette La Pierre."

Every ounce of diplomatic skill that Florrie had acquired over the years came to the fore. "How do you do," she said, a false smile pasted on her face. "Would you like to sit down? I know you have had an arduous journey." She stared pointedly at Alford. "Perhaps you would care to ring for refreshments for *our* guests, my lord?"

Alford still stared dumbfounded at the new arrivals, his hands convulsively clutching the papers he held. How in the deuce was he ever going to explain this to Florrie? Someday he would kill Seb and Hervey.

"Alford," Florrie said sharply.

"Refreshments. Yes," he stammered and raced from the room.

"Rustication can do that to a man," Seb said, taking a chair near Florrie. "I trust he has not been too much of a trial, ma'am?"

"We managed to reach an accommodation of sorts," she said with a wry smile. "How is it that you have the annulment papers?"

"We ran into Barstow at the club and he told us they'd been finished. Then explained about the—uh—error in the housing arrangements."

"Could have knocked me over with a feather when he told us you and Alford ended up at the same house," Hervey said as he seated Nanette. "Figured he'd be dead by now. Seeing what you did to his nose that one time."

"Do not think I haven't been tempted," Florrie said from between gritted teeth.

Alford reappeared at the door. "Uh—Florrie, could I speak with you for a moment?"

Florrie smiled graciously. "You will excuse me?" She followed Alford into the hall, closing the door behind her.

Alford felt sheer, utter terror sweeping through him. There had been so little time—only a few days. Would Florrie believe him, would she trust him? How could he convince her that Nanette was the very last person in the world he ever wanted to see?

"Interesting friends," Florrie said, enjoying his obvious discomfort. "Miss La Pierre seems particularly . . . intriguing. I wonder I have not met her before."

"Of course you haven't, she's—"

"Your mistress?" Florrie finished.

"No! Yes! I mean, she was, in a way, but not for a long time."

Florrie stifled her urge to giggle. Alford's discomfort was amusing. But not quite amusing enough to gloss over the real worry she felt. She knew many unmarried men kept mistresses. But so did many married ones. Would Alford do the same? Old habits could be difficult to break. "Do go on," she urged.

"It was long before I—I mean—I wrote for her to come when I wanted you gone," he explained jerkily. "I thought her presence would encourage you to leave."

"Astute observation," Florrie said dryly.

"But I do not want her here now!"

"Are you certain? There are men I know who would love to have both their wife and mistress in residence. So convenient."

"She is not my mistress!" Alford reiterated. "It was never that formal an arrangement."

"She must have been somewhat convinced of your interest if she traveled all the way to Devon," Florrie said sharply.

Alford hung his head. "I may have made a few wild promises . . ." he mumbled.

Florrie took pity on him. "I know. You really should be more careful about what you put to paper, Alford."

His eyes narrowed. "How do you know?"

"I read your letter," she replied simply.

"You what?"

"And it is really very awful of you to use your father's frank for your private letters, Alford," she chastened him. "It only increases postal costs for the rest of us."

"You opened my letter and read it?" Alford stared at her, mouth agape.

"It was a trifle shocking, I will own," Florrie said with an impish smile. "That is why I thought it had best be put on the fire."

"You burnt it?"

"Only the letter. I sent the franked envelope on."

"Florrie!" Alford stared at her in amazement at her audacity, then burst out laughing. "You wretch," he cried, gathering her up in his arms. "You adorable wretch."

"Am I really?"

"What?"

"Adorable?"

He squeezed her hard. "Yes, you are," he said.

"More adorable than Nanette?"

Alford sighed. He placed his hands on Florrie's shoulders and held her away from him. "I do not wish any lady in my life but you," he said. "Forever."

"That is a mighty grand promise, Alford," she said, her expression growing serious. "I would rather you not promise anything you will be hard pressed to follow."

He grabbed her up in his arms again. "I think, Lady Alford," he said, as his head bent toward hers, "that you will be all the female I can handle."

Florrie stood on tip-toe to meet his kiss.

"What do you suppose happened to Alford?" Seb asked idly while he refilled their glasses. "And Miss Washburn?"

Hervey shrugged. "Who cares?" He cast an admiring glance at the glass in his hand. "This is damned fine brandy."

Burgess entered the library, carrying a tray, with a packet of papers under his arm.

"Lord Alford extends his apologies," Burgess said. "He is occupied with a rather pressing matter at the moment." He set the tray down and handed the papers to Seb. "He requested that you burn these for him."

Seb stared at the papers. "These are the annulment forms!" he exclaimed. "Are you sure Alford said to burn them?"

"Those were his exact words," Burgess said.

Cole and Hervey exchanged incredulous glances.

"Lord Alford also wished me to point out that there is a tolerably fine inn in Clovelly. He says you will have plenty of time to reach it before darkness." Burgess took a deep breath as he rattled off the rest of his speech. "He regrets that he and Lady Alford will not be able to see your departure."

"Lady Alford? Who's Lady Alford?" Hervey asked in confusion.

Seb tossed back his head and roared with laughter. "That rogue!"

"Departure! I am sick to death of traveling," Nanette pouted. "It is far too cold and damp in Devon."

Seb and Hervey exchanged glances.

"I think we can find a way to keep you warm, Miss La Pierre," Seb said smoothly, offering her his arm. "Perhaps we can discuss it on the way to Clovelly?"

"We were intolerably rude, not saying goodbye to your friends," Florrie whispered in Alford's ear as she snuggled closer against him.

"Ah, but think what trouble it would have been to dress again." He grinned and kissed her brow. "They will understand."

"Poor Nanette," Florrie said. "She came all this way for nothing."

"I am certain that Seb and Hervey will see that she is amply rewarded for her touble," said Alford.

"Do you suppose they will tell all London what happened?" she asked, tracing swirling designs across his bared chest with her finger.

"Undoubtedly," he replied.

"People will say shocking things," she said.

"Then we will simply avoid London until the talk dies down," he said, taking her hand and drawing it to his lips. "It should not take more than four . . . perhaps five months."

Florrie giggled, her lips hovering a scant distance from his cheek. "And shall we spend the entire time like this?"

"Most certainly," he said, turning suddenly to pin her beneath him on the bed. "In fact, four or five months may not be nearly enough time." He trailed kisses from her brow to her chin. "Oh, Florrie, how I adore you."

"Mm," she replied, her eyes fluttering shut and a contented smile upon her face. Four or five months would be perfect. Just in time for the fall opening of Parliament—and all manner of intriguing political opportunities.